Independent Bones

ALSO BY CAROLYN HAINES

SARAH BOOTH DELANEY MYSTERIES

NOVELS

NONFICTION

Independent Bones

CAROLYN HAINES

MINOTAUR BOOKS
NEW YORK

First published in the United States by Minotaur Books,
an imprint of St. Martin's Publishing Group

INDEPENDENT BONES. Copyright © 2021 by Carolyn Haines. All rights reserved. Printed in the United States of America. For information, address St. Martin's Publishing Group, 120 Broadway, New York, NY 10271.

www.minotaurbooks.com

Library of Congress Cataloging-in-Publication Data

Names: Haines, Carolyn, author.
Title: Independent bones / Carolyn Haines.
Description: First edition. | New York : Minotaur Books, 2021. |
    Series: Sarah Booth Delaney mysteries ; [23]
Identifiers: LCCN 2020056324 | ISBN 9781250257871 (hardcover) |
    ISBN 9781250257895 (ebook)
Subjects: GSAFD: Mystery fiction.
Classification: LCC PS3558.A329 I53 2021 | DDC 813/.54—dc23
LC record available at https://lccn.loc.gov/2020056324

Our books may be purchased in bulk for promotional, educational, or business use. Please contact your local bookseller or the Macmillan Corporate and Premium Sales Department at 1-800-221-7945, extension 5442, or by email at MacmillanSpecialMarkets@macmillan.com.

First Edition: 2021

10 9 8 7 6 5 4 3 2 1

For the women who came before,
those who cleared the way for us to fight for equality.

Independent Bones

1

The first scattering of sycamore leaves tumble across the grass in front of me as I walk with my PI partner and friend, Tinkie Richmond. We cross the newly christened "Erkwell Park" in the heart of Zinnia, Mississippi. Tinkie and I are at the grand opening of the park, a space donated and supported by our good friend, Harold Erkwell. A playground and entertainment center are much needed in our county, and Harold took it on as a personal mission. While parks have not been a high priority in a poor state, Harold donated all the funding to create this little bit of heaven on the outskirts of our bustling Delta town.

"Harold worked on this all summer," Tinkie says as we admire the landscaping of native trees and a host of flowering shrubs that will be Nirvana for butterflies and bees next spring and summer. She points as she talks. "Swing sets, slides, a splash pad, tennis courts, that adorable putt-putt course with boll weevils." She sighs. "My baby is going to love coming here."

I hold my peace. Tinkie, who is pregnant, and as big around as she is tall, looks like she might pop out a two-year-old ready to lift weights and pole-vault.

"I know you're thinking it, so you might as well say it," she says.

"That baby is going to be born with teeth." I grin to take the sting out. This baby is the thing Tinkie wants most in life and all of her friends are anxiously awaiting the birth of the next generation's Queen Bee of the Delta. Even Tinkie's parents, who have been touring Europe for what seems like an eternity, are coming home for the big event, which should happen in two weeks. Tinkie is going to produce a little Scorpio—watch out, world!

The sunny breeze is soft and teases Tinkie's sun-glitzed curls as we watch children and adults play in this wonderful green space. Some forty yards away is a dais with a speaker system. A striking woman with abundant black curls, dark eyes, and red lipstick takes the stage. I didn't realize Harold had planned speeches.

"Who is that?" I ask Tinkie. She knows every woman in the Delta, their pedigree, their political persuasion, and their moral character.

"I've never seen her," Tinkie admits. "But I can take a guess. She must be that professor of Greek literature who's writing a book. She rented the old Compton house not far from Cece. Her name is Alala Diakos."

"She's intriguing." With her perfect posture and toned body, she projects power.

"I've read some of her articles. She's a force to be reck-oned with, but I'm not sure Zinnia will be receptive to her . . . philosophy."

"Which is what?" I've never heard of the woman.

"Men who abuse women should be exterminated with the utmost efficiency. Hopefully, by a mob of angry women."

I glance at my friend. "And you disagree with that?"

She laughs. "Nope. But, I just wouldn't say it out loud. She's been giving speeches around the Delta and she's stirred up some hot protest from the Neanderthal con-tingency." Tinkie glances around the park, where folks have begun to gather at the dais. "Looks like she could start some trouble here."

"In Zinnia? You think there are people who support men who abuse women?"

Tinkie stops and frowns. "Of course there are. We just aren't friends with them. Look under any rock, though, and you'll find a man who thinks males should be able to control women. You know Mississippi didn't vote to ratify the Nineteenth Amendment until 1984."

That tidbit stops me in my tracks. "Are you serious?"

"Deadly serious. Harold and Oscar were approving home loans for women back in the 1990s when other banks wouldn't. If a woman didn't have a husband or a daddy to cosign, a lot of banks wouldn't loan her money. Financially, even today, women are second-class citizens."

I didn't have to respond. The Greek professor with the flashing eyes begins to talk. She introduces herself and explains her presence in Zinnia. She's rented a house where she can write in peace and draft her nonfiction book, *The Moon Rises*, the story of the fight for women's equality.

Dr. Diakos says, "Until we have equal pay and equal say, we are not equal citizens." The statement draws applause from the crowd gathered around the dais to hear her talk, mostly younger women and a few men. Dr. Diakos obviously has a local following.

The professor continues. "Basic fact: retired women are twice as likely to live in poverty as retired men."

"Because they aren't smart enough to manage money!" a man in camo shouts. He stands defiantly at the back of the crowd. "Women need a man to manage their business. That's the fact *you* need to grasp."

I didn't have to ask Tinkie who the man was. We both recognized Curtis Miller, a well-known domestic abuser who Coleman had arrested at least five times. Unfortunately, Miller's wife, Tansy, had refused repeatedly to take legal action. Even now she shifted to take a protective stance in front of her husband, who outweighed her by at least sixty pounds.

"That Tansy doesn't have sense enough to pour piss out of a boot," Tinkie said. "Look at her. Like she's going to go all Rambo on anyone who comes at Curtis."

I shook my head in disbelief and disgust. Curtis had broken her arms at least twice, fractured her eye socket, bitten off part of her ear, and broken her fingers. In a town like Zinnia, everyone knew the dirty details of their marriage and the pattern of violence. But not even Coleman could persuade Tansy Miller to press charges or leave Curtis.

Dr. Diakos ignored the heckling. "Women still shoulder most of the household chores, even if the woman also holds a job."

"That's because cooking and cleaning are women's work," Miller yelled out. "Get over it and get in the kitchen where you belong. If you had a man to keep you satisfied, you wouldn't be yowling in the public park like a cat in heat."

I quietly dialed Coleman. When he answered, I just said, "Better get over to the park. It's going to get bloody. Bring the deputies."

"On the way."

I set my phone to video so I could document what was likely to be a physical encounter as the female supporters of Dr. Diakos began to move toward Miller.

"Y'all better leave my husband alone." Tansy stepped out in front of her husband. "Go on, shoo!"

I thought of a mouse defending a lion. And she was sporting a black eye to boot. Some unfortunate women had no concept of how a real relationship worked, where partners were equal. Too often women caught in the web of men who were bullies had grown up in families where the pattern played out again and again. No matter how smart or talented, they'd find themselves trapped. Tansy's situation was tragic.

As the crowd quickly began to turn into a mob, I saw a flash of wiry gray and white hair on four legs. Oh, how well I knew that devious little fiend. As if things weren't hectic enough, Roscoe Erkwell, Harold's no good, troublemaking, bruise-mashing canine was right in the middle of everything. And Harold was nowhere to be seen. The dog ran to a parked truck with giant mud tires. Someone had left the door open and he hopped up in the seat. When he jumped out, he had a lacy red thong in his mouth flapping in the breeze.

"Roscoe!" Tinkie and I called simultaneously. "Come here!"

Per usual, Roscoe completely ignored us. He ran up

to Tansy Miller and dropped the panties at her feet. Her eyes went big and round and her mouth followed. She picked up the thong with fingertips and held it up, then turned to look at her husband. "Those are Moody Moody's panties. I recognize her getup from the Silver Stallion men's club. How did they get in your truck, Curtis?"

His response was a backhand.

And that's when the fight started. Whether he was bright enough to realize it or not, Curtis Miller had stepped into a fire ant mound. The women, as if reacting to a command, advanced on him all at once, kicking, spitting, and screaming. All hell broke loose. I glanced up at the dais, where the good professor stood with a satisfied look on her face. This was exactly what she'd hoped for, or so it seemed.

Coleman and both deputies, who'd arrived in the nick of time, waded into the group and started sorting it out. Curtis was on the ground and the women had done a number on him. He held a tooth in his hand and looked like he was about to cry. Typical bully. I waved DeWayne over. He held two struggling and cursing women, one under each arm.

"Curtis started it," I told DeWayne.

"I'll get some cuffs on him when I can turn these two brawlers loose. Put a foot on his back until I get back."

I was happy to oblige.

Tinkie started into the fray, but I snatched her wrist and drew her out of danger. "You cannot mix it up with those people," I warned her. "Now stay here with Curtis. I have to find Roscoe. Someone is going to kill that dog because he has his snout in everyone's personal business."

"Can I sit on Curtis?" Tinkie asked. The red spots in her cheeks told me she was stoked and ready for combat.

"Whatever floats your boat," I told her, straining on my tiptoes to keep Roscoe in sight.

"I want to break his face," Tinkie said.

I sighed. "Wanting something never killed anyone, but if you get hurt, *I* will kill you. Oscar won't have to worry about you. Now stay put!"

DeWayne, who'd come up for the end of the conversation to claim his prisoner, laughed at me when I gave him the stink eye as I ran toward the dais, in the direction Roscoe had gone.

Dr. Diakos stepped down to say something to me, but I brushed past her. I was more than a little annoyed that she'd started a riot on such a lovely fall day. "Roscoe! Roscoe! Where are you?" I stepped into an area thickly planted with beautiful shrubs. Up ahead I heard Roscoe's evil growl. Whether he was angry or pleased, hungry or sated, happy or sad, he generally sounded like a possessed person. It was part of his charm.

"I'm going to bake you in the oven," I said sweetly to Roscoe. "With a meat thermometer stuck right up—"

I stopped in midsentence. Poking out of the bushes was the barrel of a rifle. The sniper's gun, like something from World War II, was propped up on a stand, but the shooter was nowhere in sight. I dropped to the ground to see where the gun had been sighted. No surprise, it was right at the dais where Dr. Diakos had been standing. Someone had planned to shoot her. I backed away from the rifle, feeling for my phone in my jeans pocket. I had to let Coleman know.

"Never touch a man's gun."

The voice came from behind me and I whipped around

to confront a young man—or upon closer inspection, a young woman. She carried a rifle and wore dungarees held up with braces, a long-sleeve white shirt, and a man's fedora. Her hair was cut short, and she stared down into my eyes with a steely gaze.

"Who are you?"

"Pearl Hart, at your service." She grinned. "I'm a lot more like you than you think." She cocked her hat to one side and waited.

"Should I know you?"

"If you had a better grasp of history, you might. I'm an adventurer, a highly educated person, and . . ." Her eyes were alive with merriment. "An outlaw. I'm the second woman to rob a stagecoach and the first one not to die while doing it. I did a stretch in prison. Eighteen months. I was famous in Arizona for my fearlessness and wit. When I was brought before the bench, I told the judge, 'I shall not consent to be tried under a law in which my sex had no voice in making.' He convicted me anyway."

"Jitty! What are you doing here in the middle of a riot!"

"Looking out for you and that baby incubator you hang around with."

Jitty seldom traveled to town to seek me out, but she always had something on her mind when she did put in an appearance. In her latest disguise as an outlaw, bank robber, and feminist, I didn't have to look far to see what her message might be.

"What's up?" I asked, even though I knew she'd never give me a direct answer.

"Equality has always been a dream for women. Too many have settled for second best. Not your mama, though. She demanded equality, and most often she got it. But your daddy had her back, every single hour of every single day."

"You don't normally stroll down memory lane without a reason. Why are you here?" I was eager to notify Coleman about the gun, but I also wanted to give Jitty every chance I could if she had wisdom to relay.

"I'm here to give you a caution. A lot of men don't like smart or uppity women."

"And?"

"Be careful. You think you can't get hurt but you can, and Tinkie's gonna need your skills with that new baby."

I had zero experience with babies. They scared me more than criminals, because babies were so fragile. "I'll always be there for Tinkie, but she can hire a nanny to do the hard stuff."

Jitty patted her rifle. "For friendship, you do whatever must be done." She pulled a bandana up over her nose and gave me a wicked wink before she took off. "Happy trails to you," she sang as she disappeared, accompanied by the sound of clip-clopping horse hooves.

I looked back at the area near the dais. Coleman had cuffed Curtis Miller and had him standing with Tansy, also cuffed, along with several prominent Zinnia women, not cuffed but certainly chastised for bad behavior. Roscoe was hard at work as well. He went right past the women and Tansy, stopping in front of Curtis Miller, where he hiked his leg and peed, the waterfall of urine splashing all over Miller's pants and shoes. Miller struck out with a kick, which Roscoe dodged easily, then doubled back and knocked Miller's support leg out from under him. The man went down hard, face-first.

"Get that dog," Coleman said to Tinkie, who waddled

forward, slow as molasses. She could move quicker; she just didn't want to. She was waiting to see what Roscoe would do next. I knew my partner backward and forward.

Miller was rolling around on the ground, grunting and threatening, moaning about his nose. Budgie, Coleman's second deputy, grabbed Miller by the handcuffs and pulled him to his feet. "I'll put him in the patrol car," he said, pushing Miller in front of him.

"You can't take my husband in!" Tansy hurled herself at Budgie. Tinkie's little foot stuck out and tripped Tansy, sending her stumbling into DeWayne's arms.

"I'll cut your throat. I'll poke your eyes out." Tansy caught her balance and turned on Tinkie.

"You keep defending that man and you won't live long enough to do anything," Tinkie warned her. "Wake up and smell the coffee. Don't you realize he could permanently harm you?"

"You don't know a damn thing about me and my husband," Tansy said.

"I know that love can't fix him or protect you," Tinkie responded.

Tansy made a run at Tinkie, but Coleman stepped between them.

"Break it up. Tansy Miller, you're in enough trouble. Calm down." He faced the crowd of spectators that had swelled to over a hundred. "There's nothing going on here!" Coleman dispersed the crowd while Budgie put Miller in one patrol car and Tansy in the backseat of another. "Budgie, could you and DeWayne take the Millers down to the jail? I think they need some time to think about things."

"Sure thing, Sheriff," Budgie said. "What about the women who attacked Miller?"

"I'll handle that," Coleman said. "Now ladies, line up. If you don't cooperate, I have another patrol car to fill or I can call the Baptist church and borrow their van." He rounded up the Zinnia women and took their names and gave each one a stern warning about the consequences of mob behavior before he cut them loose.

When almost everyone was gone, I led Coleman toward the dais. To my surprise, Dr. Diakos had also vanished. She'd packed it in while I was distracted. But the gun was still there—and Coleman gave me a look that telegraphed his suspicions were the same as mine. Someone had planned on shooting the professor.

He called out to DeWayne, "Let's bag this and anything else you find near here. Sarah Booth found it, so we can rule her out."

"What the hell?" DeWayne said. "Were they going to kill that professor?"

"Looks like that might have been the plan," Coleman said. "Until Sarah Booth thwarted them."

"No," I said. "Not me. Roscoe. I know he's frustrating, wicked, and possessed by the very devil, but he's smart. He brought me over here and showed me."

"That damn dog," Coleman said, shaking his head. "About the time I'm ready to send him to the electric chair, he does something wonderful." He nudged me on the arm. "Kind of like you, Sarah Booth."

2

Tinkie and I headed over to Millie's Café when Coleman was finished with us. Tinkie needed sustenance to keep her blood sugar from falling and to keep "the little parasite," as I'd taken to calling the baby, happy. Cece Dee Falcon, the society, entertainment, and now with her new title of hard news editor for the paper, joined us. Cece had recently been given a big raise based on the success of a column she and Millie Roberts, the café owner, had cooked up. "The Truth is Out There" was a wild combination of tabloid news, celebrity gossip, local legend, society news, and investigative journalism. It had become enormously popular and Cece and Millie were now "must have" guests at every party or event from the Delta all the way to the Outer Banks. On top of that,

Millie's Café had the best home cooking anywhere in the world.

While we waited for our orders, I gave Cece the footage I'd taken at the park fiasco.

"Who is that woman?" she asked of Dr. Diakos, and Tinkie and I went through the whole thing.

"Is she really writing a book?" Cece asked.

"She says she is." I wasn't heavily invested in the book one way or the other. "She's smart, informed, and makes a lot of excellent points. She also likes to stir people up."

"I'll track her down and interview her," Cece said. "That'll be fun. So spill about the gun you found in the park."

I gave her the details but asked her not to put them in the paper until she talked to Coleman. Cece was a go-getter for news, but she was also our friend and she walked that fine line between reporting all the facts and trying not to interfere in an investigation.

"I'll give Coleman a call," she promised. The bell over the door jangled and she smiled and nodded. "Or I can ask him right here."

I was a little surprised when Coleman showed up at the café, hungry as a bear out of hibernation. I'd expected him to be busy for at least another hour or so dealing with the Millers.

When we'd finished our lunch, Coleman signaled me to step outside with him. Aside from answering Cece's questions, he'd been quiet since he arrived.

"What's wrong?" I asked him when we were standing by the trunk of his patrol car.

"That Diakos woman, the professor?"

I nodded.

"She taught last year at Ole Miss and this year she

has a sabbatical to finish her book. She said she came here because it's an easy drive to Ole Miss if she gets called in."

"Okay." I didn't know where this was going.

"Before she moved here, she was a suspect in the murder of a professor at Ole Miss."

Now this was news, and no wonder Coleman looked so glum. It bothered him to have suspects in a murder running around town, even if they seemed at first glance to be relatively harmless.

"Was she charged?"

"No. There wasn't enough evidence. But it's one reason she was awarded two semesters off to write a book this year. The administration at Ole Miss pulled some strings to get her that sabbatical."

"Keep her off the campus," I said. "That's one way of handling a murderer—if she's guilty. What about the rifle set up to shoot her? You think that plays into the Oxford murder?"

"I don't think so. Curtis says the rifle belongs to him, but he denies knowing how it got in the park. It's an expensive gun. A collectible."

"Do you believe him?"

"Not at all." Coleman gave a crooked smile. "That man flaps his gums and nothing comes out but lies. His wife is . . . sad. I think he's beaten her so many times she has brain damage. Curtis wouldn't know a collectible from his elbow. That make of gun is deadly accurate, though. Highly prized for that. It was the preferred gun for snipers in World War II."

"Can you track it?"

"Maybe. If it isn't stolen. Anyway, I'm hoping Tansy will take action to save her own life and tell me what she knows about Curtis and his plans to shoot Diakos. That way I could charge and convict him so Tansy won't end up being his punching bag every weekend."

"Once you're convinced that's what you deserve, it's hard to think your way out of it." I felt a pang of compassion for her. "She's not going to turn on Curtis."

"Very true, but the law can't help her until she helps herself."

That was also very true. "Is she still in jail?"

"I told DeWayne to cut her loose, but we're holding on to Miller. He'll be there for as long as I can keep him."

"For the gun?"

"And starting a riot. And assault. And anything else I can throw at him. I've asked Penny Cox from Selena's House to try talking to Tansy about making a break for freedom while I have Miller locked up. I hope she does."

Selena's House offered shelter to battered women, children, and pets. Penny, who ran it, was handy with support and facts when trying to convince women to make safe choices for themselves and their children—and she was also quite handy with a firearm. I'd seen her shoot in a couple of local competitions. She was hell on clay pigeons and paper targets. The women under her care would be safe.

"Maybe Penny can reach Tansy. She's good at her job."

"Penny has a real passion for helping women, even when they don't want to help themselves."

"You've done everything you can. So have about forty other people who've tried to intervene. Penny will talk to her and Tinkie will, too. Tinkie can be very persuasive."

"It's worth a try."

"I'll take care of that," I promised.

"Thanks. Now I have to get back to work. I put in a lunch order for Budgie and DeWayne." He nodded to the cash register where Millie was waving him over. Lunch hour was always busy and Millie had been run off her feet the whole time we were there, but she took care of Coleman.

"Let me know if you get anything specific off that rifle."

"Will do." Coleman said his goodbyes to my friends and was gone.

"Coleman has lost weight," Tinkie said, her blue eyes twinkling. "I think Sarah Booth chains him in the bedroom and won't feed him."

"I think she works it off him," Cece said.

"I think you two don't want me to turn this around on you!"

We were all laughing as we paid the tab and walked out into the sunshine that hit me with a favorite memory of my childhood. October had always been one of my favorite months, and there were times when the light was like a touchstone to travel back in time. The memory of picking black-eyed Susans along the roadside with my mother to make a huge bouquet for a prop for the local theater returned with an ache that made me catch my breath. As a child, I'd been cocooned in happiness that I thought would last forever. A lie that still sliced my heart.

"You okay?" Tinkie asked. She put her arm around my waist. "You look pensive."

"The light brings back memories." I saw her brow furrow in concern. "Good ones. Just things that are gone and can never come back."

"You should have a baby, Sarah Booth."

"I'm going to wait and see how you do with child-rearing, Tink. You're the test subject."

"Chicken," she said, punching me lightly.

"Damn straight. I'm very much a chicken. My life is pretty fantastic and I mean to just enjoy being with Coleman and my friends as much as I can. I'm not ready for more responsibility."

"Nothing wrong with that. I need a nap," Tinkie said.

"Then a nap you shall have." She did look tired. She was carrying around at least forty pounds of baby weight, all right in her stomach. "Does the idea of giving birth scare you?"

"Yep. A lot. But the idea of continuing to feel like I've been stuffed with two hundred servings of pasta is tiring. I just want it behind me. I'll be glad to hold this little one in my arms."

I put an arm around her shoulders. "None of us can wait for that. This poor baby is going to be rotten with love and attention."

"I like hearing that," she said. "I know I had every privilege money could buy, but I never felt that . . . arbor of love."

"Your baby will bask in love." I walked her to her car and closed the door once she was behind the wheel. "I'm going back to the park to find Roscoe. I'll drive him to Harold's house and put him inside. That dog is truly going to get killed, or get someone else killed."

"That thong!" Tinkie started laughing. "Roscoe caught Curtis Miller red-handed boinking that stripper in that horrible truck. I'll bet they made it rock."

"We've been lucky in our families and the men we've been involved with. Of course they aren't perfect, and we've both had heartaches, but I can't imagine any man raising a hand to either one of us. And if one did, he would certainly regret it."

"He wouldn't live to tell about it," Tinkie agreed.

"We were raised to understand we couldn't and shouldn't tolerate such things. Think of the dive bars we've gone in on cases. We never expect anyone to even try to harm us."

"We have been lucky. It's a form of entitlement, isn't it?" Tinkie asked.

I'd never thought of it that way, but she was right. "Yes. We believe we're entitled to decent treatment."

"Can that be taught, do you think?"

"Penny Cox is trying to teach it. If our public schools weren't so backward about sex education and family dynamics, we might be able to reach young girls and start that foundation of self-confidence."

"That's kind of what Professor Diakos is doing, isn't it?"

"In a way, I guess. It's just her tactics . . ." Again Tinkie had connected dots that I'd missed. "I completely agree with what she says, but she's sure stirring up a lot of ill will and anger." The direct, face-to-face confrontation was like stomping an ant bed.

"Sometimes it takes a good hard wind to clear out the cobwebs of the past." Tinkie turned the motor on. "While you were mooning over Coleman, Cece said Dr. Diakos is going to give a lecture tonight I'd like to attend. Will you come with me?"

"Sure." I might not want to hear a lecture but I wanted to watch the crowd and be sure a sniper didn't pick off Dr. Diakos. She might infuriate people, but she had a right to say what she wanted. Especially when I knew some people really needed to hear it.

"Then we have a date."

"Let's just hope you don't deliver that baby in the audience."

3

Erkwell Park had emptied considerably by the time I got back there. Most of the adults were gone, leaving half a dozen children playing on the slides, swings, and jungle gym. Mothers, talking and laughing among themselves, sat on benches watching the youngsters. Several had infants in strollers that they rocked back and forth. It was a scene of peace and happiness, and it made me smile. These women, the young mothers, were the lifeblood of Sunflower County. They were bringing up families, contributing to the community, building the citizens of the future. Soon Tinkie would be one of them.

"Sarah Booth?"

I turned, expecting Jitty had reappeared at the park but found my good friend Madame Tomeeka, aka Tammy

Odom. Tammy had gone to high school with Tinkie and me. Now she was Zinnia's resident psychic. She had prophetic dreams, could glimpse the future, and often gave me a warning when dangerous things were ahead for me or those I loved.

"Are you going to hang your psychic reading shingle in the park?" I nodded at a beautiful table and chairs under a cypress tree. "The weather is perfect." Tammy had a very long list of clients—Zinnia's most prominent ladies often sought her counsel. But an outdoor reading would just add another element of joy to the mix.

"I'd like to, but I have things to do. I'm here looking for you. Tinkie said you were here."

"And I'm looking for Roscoe. Have you seen the evil little brat? He contributed to a riot earlier today."

Tammy's expressive face was touched with the ghost of a smile. She was always deviled by melancholy, but she never let it stop her. My life had been hard, but so had Tammy's. Her greatest joys were her daughter, Claire, and Claire's daughter, Dahlia, named for my family farm. Claire had recently married a musician and was touring around the blues clubs in the Deep South with little Dahlia in tow. It was hard on Tammy for them to be away from Zinnia, but she was not a woman to clip the wings of her only fledgling, no matter how much she missed her daughter. Knowing things about the future was not necessarily the gift a sane person would ask for, either. Tammy didn't have the power to stop anything from happening. All she could do was analyze her dreams and visions and do the best she could to alert us. Looking at her face, I expected that she'd tracked me down to give me one such warning.

"Roscoe's hiding behind the dais," Tammy said without batting an eye. "He's the reason I'm here, Sarah Booth. Well, part of the reason."

"What has Roscoe done now?" I wasn't going to defend the mutt, but since I was the one who gave him to Harold, I would try to make right whatever sin he'd committed.

"I had a dream that he was digging something up. Something important."

"What was it?" I believed Tammy when she said it was important.

"I couldn't see, but there was a red aura around Roscoe. That's always danger."

"You know how bad Roscoe is—breaking into people's trash, digging holes in their yards, enticing their dogs to escape fences and go for a romp, stealing shoes and everything else he can pick up."

She laughed softly. "I know his reputation well. He is definitely a very bad dog. But it isn't dog behavior that he's engaged in."

"Can you give me any details?"

"Not yet. I just know Roscoe is going to be part of something dangerous, and very soon. Unless Harold can keep him shut up in the house."

"I'll tell Harold. For sure. Am I in danger?"

"Not you, but there's a woman. Dark hair, dark eyes. She's not from Zinnia, but she's here somewhere."

She was describing Alala Diakos. "What danger is she in?"

"She stirs up people's emotions. There are people who intend to stop her. They feel threatened by her."

I told Tammy about the melee with Curtis Miller that had occurred earlier.

"That's exactly the kind of thing I saw. It all makes sense now. Was this Dr. Diakos in danger?"

"Maybe." I told her about the gun Roscoe had led me to and about Curtis Miller's denial that he had intended to shoot the speaker.

"Sarah Booth, this woman has kicked over a hornet's nest. Someone is going to get stung."

"And that someone is likely to be her," I agreed. "I'll try to keep an eye on her and I'll be careful. Hey!" Roscoe came bounding out of the shrubbery. With his wiry little beard and squinty eyes, he was the embodiment of naughtiness. His evil little growl indicated he was happy. He jumped into my arms, licking my face and grumbling.

"Glad you have him safe in your arms," Tammy said.

"For the moment. If you get any more visions, would you call?"

"You know I will. I'll focus on what's going on. This professor. What's she doing here?"

"She's a professor of Greek literature. She was teaching at Ole Miss, but she's here in Zinnia for a year writing a book on the battle for women's rights in America." I almost told her about the murdered professor at Ole Miss, but I stopped short. Tammy wasn't a gossip by any means, but Dr. Diakos had never been charged with anything. I didn't want to hook a rumor to her leg that she had to drag all over town.

"Thanks. See you soon."

Tammy was more concerned now than when she'd first arrived. And that worried me. I turned to walk back to my car—Roscoe was heavy in my arms—when the dog started growling and struggling to get down. The bushes beside the dais moved, yet there was no wind. Had someone been there, spying on me and Madame Tomeeka?

Roscoe really wanted to get away from me and I held on tighter. If he escaped, it might take me hours to corral him again.

"Not today, Roscoe," I told him as I hurried toward my car. "Not today."

It was probably a kid playing hide-and-seek. I wasn't working on a case. No one had any reason to be spying on me at all.

Evening had fallen when Tinkie and I set out for The Club, Zinnia's prestigious private meeting place, restaurant, and golf course, where Dr. Diakos was set to speak. The lecture was sponsored by a university grant, and I was surprised by the venue and the crowd. The Delta's elite had turned out in force. I was also impressed with the décor. Someone—the Mississippi League of Women Voters, to be exact—had really pulled out the stops. They had mannequins dressed in the garb of the suffragettes around the room, and plaques highlighting various women who had worked for the right for women to vote. It was a mini-history lesson in the sacrifices the women who'd come before me had made so that I could live in a more equal world.

"This is remarkable," Tinkie said. "So much hard work. And these women were beaten and imprisoned, just for demanding the right to vote."

"Women today can't afford to forget this. Alala is right. It's our job to teach the younger generations coming up behind us." I thought of the things that Jitty, as a person without any rights for most of her life, and Grandma Alice, who could not have survived without her friendship with Jitty, had endured. Even decades later my mother had struggled against gender stereotyping. Our generation couldn't give up the fight for equality for all.

Coleman had been finishing up paperwork and Oscar had a meeting in Memphis, so Tinkie and I were stag. When we arrived at the gathering, I watched Diakos work the room. She was a smooth operator. I had a glass of wine and Tinkie opted for water as we spoke to local residents, but we mostly hung back to watch. At last it was time for the lecture. We took our seats in the front of the room with great anticipation.

Whatever else one could say about Alala Diakos, she was a spectacular speaker. With her vivid descriptions and enthusiastic presentation, we were able to follow the fight of American suffragettes as they battled seemingly insurmountable odds for the right to vote. And it was not a pretty history. I'd known the broad strokes, but none of the details. Alala, as she asked everyone to call her, had strong views on many things, and she didn't back off or back down.

"America was based on stealing land from the original owners—the Natives—who were slaughtered by the thousands. Black people were brought here in chains and sold into slavery where they had no say over what happened to their physical bodies or their families. White women, of course, had a somewhat easier road to walk. But oppression takes many forms. For centuries, women around the world have suffered under the rule of men. Some men may have been benevolent, but few saw the need for women to have independence and equality and *to codify that into law.* Keeping us 'barefoot and pregnant,' after all, benefited the men."

A murmur ran through the audience, but no one spoke and Alala kept talking.

"Many Native tribes subscribed to equality between the sexes, but the *Mayflower* brought more than just human bodies across the ocean. The ship brought European mores and laws that infected this country from the very beginning. The rigid view of the Puritans was just the beginning, regulating what women wore and said in public. Where they could be seen. What they could do. How they had to walk and talk and comport themselves. But the true control was financial. Mississippi was the first state, in 1839, to allow white women to own property in their own name. This is one of the reasons I'm in Zinnia, Mississippi."

She continued with a long list of dates and times showing how women had slowly worked their way toward financial equality. "It was 1881 in France where we were allowed to open bank accounts. The United States didn't follow suit until the 1960s."

The lecture was lively and informative, and the Q and A session went smoothly. This was an audience of people who were interested in the topic, unlike what had occurred earlier at the park. Still, I was relieved when it was over without incident.

I helped Tinkie to her feet and we headed for the door, but not before Alala spotted us. "Ladies, I want to thank you for your help earlier."

"No problem," I said. "Have you spoken with Sheriff Peters?"

"I have. He told me about the gun." She shrugged. "Some men will kill to remain in power. But as women awaken to the necessity of fighting for equality, the balance will change."

"Curtis Miller isn't anyone to mess with," Tinkie said with a pinch of annoyance in her voice. "He regularly beats his wife and he wouldn't think twice about hurting you. Steer clear of him."

"Good advice," she said. "I have to point out, though, that men who threaten violence often end up dying a violent death. Haven't you noticed that?"

Neither Tinkie nor I answered her question. "Just be aware that you're stirring passions, and people who are enraged seldom stop to think." I tried not to sound like an old schoolmarm delivering warnings for misbehavior.

"I can take care of myself," Alala said. "In fact, my name is the war cry of my female ancestors." She made the famous "alala" call to battle. "I'm named for the daughter of Polemos, the personification of war. In Greek mythology, my uncle is Ares, who viewed warfare as sport. I am bred to fight."

"Love the ancient creds," Tinkie said sarcastically, "but they won't stop a bullet. Just be careful. That's all we're asking."

"Alala, don't do anything stupid," I said.

"I never do. Understand I won't be cowed or controlled by fear."

Based on that, she could be in for some real difficulties during her stay in Zinnia.

Snuggled up against Coleman, I watched the fire crackle in the bedroom. One great thing about my old house was the abundance of fireplaces. We were pleasantly tired and sated, but worries haunted the shadows of my brain. Alala Diakos was playing with a loaded gun. Men like Curtis Miller would hurt her. They might not mean to kill her, but a bullet to the spine would cause irreparable damage.

"What's bothering you?" Coleman asked.

One of the best things about our relationship was how much I could share with him. How much he understood about my worries and my joys. "I wish that professor hadn't come to town."

"She spoiled the grand opening of the park, that's for sure."

"Well, technically, it was Curtis Miller who spoiled it."

"True enough." He repositioned his arm so he could draw me against the solid warmth of his body. I snuggled into the safety net he offered, aware of what a rich treasure he gave me. "Don't be thinking bloody thoughts, Sarah Booth."

My man knew me too well. "I would never do such a thing."

"Right." He kissed the top of my head.

His cell phone rang and we both groaned. Coleman had quite a large physical area to cover, and while crime was low in Sunflower County, there were still criminals to chase.

He had a brief conversation and then got up. "We released Curtis Miller at just after six o'clock this evening. He was shot dead about an hour ago."

"What?" This was startling. "Did Tansy finally decide to stand up for herself? You know it's self-defense, Coleman. He was going to kill her eventually."

"Tansy didn't kill him. She claims she was in the ER being treated for a sprained wrist."

"The bastard twisted her wrist? Again? Dang. Who did kill him?"

"Someone with a .38. Shot right to the heart."

Tansy might have beaten a drunken Curtis Miller to death with a frozen chicken, but she didn't strike me as the kind of woman who would pull the trigger of a gun aimed at a man's heart. But then again, it was possible that Tansy had finally, simply had enough. The questions were how bad was her injury and could she still shoot accurately.

"I'm going to the crime scene," Coleman said as he picked up his pants and slid into them.

I grabbed my jeans and dressed. There were worse ways to spend an October evening.

"Do you really want to go?" Coleman asked. He looked longingly at the fire and the bed, where Sweetie Pie, my fabulous red tick hound, and Pluto the black cat, had sprawled.

"I do. I'm going to bring Sweetie Pie and Pluto, so I'll take my car. Where's the body?"

"Behind Playin' the Bones, out in a cotton field."

"Damn." My friend Scott Hampton owned the blues club and Cece's significant other, Jaytee, played harmonica in the band there. It was a favorite gathering place for me and my buddies. Surely none of my friends were involved in this mess, but it would probably be a headache for Scott and the band. Then again, it might draw more tourists. That was one thing I'd learned about murder—it could break either way.

4

Driving through the lush cotton fields of the Delta with the top down, I reveled in the cold night air, the black sky filled with winking stars, and the silvery rows of cotton revealed when the moon came out from behind a stray cloud. Sweetie Pie, ears flapping in the wind, rode in the passenger seat. Pluto had the backseat to himself.

This land was part of my soul. I'd never been a farmer, not like prior generations of Delaneys. I leased most of my land to Billy, a farmer friend, and together we'd begun working toward a more organic approach to planting and harvesting. We had a long way to go, but we were slowly moving forward.

The vast acreage of the Delta had once been farmed

by enslaved people, a stain on the history of the state and my family that no amount of washing could remove. Facts were facts. Now the pesticides, chemicals, and GMO crops that had been pressed on too many farmers were going to be a kind of economic slavery if they weren't able to break free and treat the land and crops with respect.

"American consumers are waking up, Sweetie Pie." I often talked to my dog and found her to be a fabulous conversationalist. She almost always agreed with me, too. Another benefit of canine company. "Folks don't want bedsheets or clothes made from cotton grown in poison. Things are slowly changing for the better."

She gave a soft yodel of agreement.

"Tinkie should have her baby soon," I went on. I liked to keep Sweetie Pie up on all significant events.

"Ow-owowowow." Sweetie Pie sympathized with the coming birth. She was one compassionate hound, and she knew about such things. When I'd first gotten her and had her spayed, a stump of an ovary had grown back and for a while she'd been one wild pup! She had dogs from all over the county at Dahlia House paying court—until a second surgery took care of the matter.

"Who do you think killed Curtis Miller?" I asked her. Sweetie Pie sometimes displayed a bit of psychic ability, but she had no answer for me on this question.

I pulled into the parking lot of Playin' the Bones and got out of the car with Sweetie Pie at my heels. The red and blue lights of emergency vehicles came from the very back of the large parking lot behind the club. I walked over, making sure to steer clear of the crime scene tape that had been strung around an area about as big as a baseball diamond. In the center was a man lying in the dirt. Doc Sawyer, the Zinnia sawbones who'd delivered me and who kept me and my friends patched up from our various adventures, knelt beside the body. Doc not only ran the ER, he was also the county coroner. Sunflower County was lucky to have a medical doctor who could perform autopsies, though I didn't think cause of death would be hard to establish in this instance.

I ducked under the crime scene tape and went to stand behind Doc. It was pretty clear Curtis Miller had died from a gunshot wound to the heart. Coleman handed me a cup of hot coffee that someone from the blues club had brought down for us. It was welcome on the cold night.

"Do you think Tansy did it?" I asked Coleman.

"No. Her right arm is in a brace. She's right-handed."

"Any suspects?"

He nodded slowly. "Yeah. Dr. Diakos."

"The Greek professor? Is there evidence?"

"She and Curtis got into it at a roughneck bar earlier this evening."

"She must have gone there after her talk at the Club. What happened?"

"According to two witnesses, Miller and Daikos got into a heated argument at the Red Top Bar. Miller pushed her. She kicked him in the . . . privates. He told her he would kill her. She told him to come on and try, that she'd shoot him dead."

"And did she shoot him?"

"No, they both left the bar."

"Why is his body here, at Playin' the Bones, if he was drinking at the Red Top?"

"I don't have that answer right now. This isn't the site

of the murder. We're still looking for that. This body was dumped here."

"But you still suspect Diakos? She's not strong enough to load up a dead Curtis and then dump him here."

"She may have had help. We just don't know, and I do suspect her. But I'm considering other possibilities, too." Coleman was never one to accuse a suspect without evidence, and for now he didn't seem to have a whole lot to go off of. I didn't know about Dr. Diakos, but Curtis Miller had a reputation for drinking too much, getting too loud, and starting trouble. Scott, the owner of Playin' the Bones, had mentioned several times that he'd had to toss Curtis out of the blues club. Miller's behavior at the Red Top was a matter of public record—he was drunk, loud, and aggressive on a regular basis.

"Any physical evidence to connect Diakos?"

Coleman gave me a look. "Not yet."

It was clear, for whatever reasons he wasn't sharing with me, that Coleman really suspected the slender college professor of murder.

"Was Tansy in the bar tonight?"

"No. Doc said he gave her something to knock her out. Her wrist was really painful. She was home alone when Curtis went there, but later the assumption is that she was asleep at Selena's House. In fact, she likely doesn't know Curtis is dead. I've got to tell her."

I could have offered to go with him, but I wasn't going to. I had a few questions for Doc. "Tansy's going to fly all over you like a wet hen. Take some pepper spray."

"Sarah Booth is right about that," DeWayne said as he came up. "In fact, why don't I call her and ask her to meet us at the sheriff's office. That's the best place. You can never tell; she might have a gun. Best to be on territory, you know."

"Smart," Coleman said. "Give her a call. I'm heading to the courthouse. Sarah Booth, you coming?"

"I want to talk to Doc for a minute. Then I'm going back to Dahlia House. I promised Pluto a special treat if he waited in the car."

"Meow!"

I whipped around to find my black cat sitting docilely on the ground beside Sweetie Pie. He'd failed to stay in the car. Typical Pluto.

"Better get him out of here," Coleman said. "If he disturbs evidence, I'll have to put him in jail."

"Very funny." A jail cell would never contain Pluto. The cat had an uncanny ability to escape.

"Then I'll have to put you in jail."

I couldn't be certain he was teasing me. Coleman was deadly serious about the integrity of his crime scenes. I scooped the cat up in my arms. "Doc, when you have a minute would you speak with me?"

"Will do. Where's Tinkie? No, don't answer, I'm just glad she's not here. I expect to get the labor and delivery call any minute. Looking at her, I would have guessed she was due two weeks ago. That is going to be one big, healthy baby."

"Yeah, she's definitely ready." There was only one holdback. "Once the baby is out in the world, Tinkie won't be able to protect it as easily. I think that's why she's not going into labor."

"Very true, Sarah Booth. And that's when I expect you and all of her friends to step in and keep that young'un safe." He patted my arm. "Let's get out of here. I'll meet you at your car."

I'd just gotten settled with the cat in my arms and the dog in the front seat when Doc opened the door and slid into the passenger seat. Sweetie Pie jumped to the back and hung her head over Doc's shoulder so he could scratch her ears.

"What's the story on Curtis?" I asked.

"Shot at pretty close range. Maybe ten feet. He wasn't shot here. The body was dumped. I'll know more after the autopsy, but it looks like Curtis was on his knees when he was killed."

If Doc was correct, that would rule out a claim of self-defense. A man on his knees wasn't a likely threat—unless he, too, had been armed. I was as bad as a TV detective, jumping to conclusions when I had no facts.

"Can you tell what happened?"

Doc, who was an old hand at crime scenes and autopsies, just sighed. "He's got cuts and bruises on his face, maybe consistent with being pistol-whipped. I can't say for certain."

"Curtis did fall on his face today when his hands were cuffed behind him. Roscoe tripped him."

"That could explain it."

"Or not." I could read Doc fairly well. "So you think someone had Curtis on his knees and beat him up a little. You sure Tansy couldn't do it?"

"I'm sure. She was in a lot of pain. I gave her an injection that would have sedated a horse, so I know she was completely knocked out."

"Does she have family? A father, brother, someone who might defend her?"

"No. Not as far as I know. Why are you so involved in this? Are you on a case?"

He had an excellent question. I wasn't on a case, and I didn't want to be. "No case. We're taking a break from detecting. Tinkie is about to pop. I don't want her to get overwrought working."

"Good idea. Oscar would approve. Now I need to get back to the hospital. I'll have more information when the autopsy is complete."

I looked over to see Coleman collecting evidence. "I guess I'm going home. Curtis was just such an ass today in the park. And he had a rifle there, like he was going to shoot Dr. Diakos."

"I hear she's a real pot stirrer." Doc chuckled. He liked feisty women.

"She is. And until Tinkie has that baby, we don't need any pots in Zinnia stirred."

Doc patted my arm. "I hear what you're saying and I see your lips moving, but I don't believe a word of it!" He got out of the car. "Call me tomorrow if you want more details once I'm done."

"Thanks, Doc." It was time to head home to my warm bed and hope that Coleman made it back before the sun came up.

I was sipping my first cup of coffee when Coleman showed up, chilled to the bone and grim. He took any murder in Sunflower County personally, even the death of a man like Curtis Miller.

"Anything new?" I loved discussing cases with him. It was one of the many things that enriched our relationship.

"Tansy Miller is suing the sheriff's office and me personally."

"Good luck with that, Tansy." People were always talking about lawsuits.

"She feels we should have done more to protect Curtis. According to her, he's in no way responsible for his early demise."

"Will she wise up and change her life or just marry another abuser?" Tansy was a pretty woman. She struck me as someone who needed a man in her life, but there were decent men to pick from.

"Maybe she'll move to another county." He slumped at the kitchen table and I poured him a cup of coffee. "I don't want to be the one who works her murder."

"Did she have any idea who might have shot Curtis?"

"Tansy was still at the home for battered women, and she insists it was the Greek professor."

"I'm more inclined to believe it was one of Tansy's male relatives."

"Her dad and brother were both out of town." Coleman rubbed his temples.

"Any idea where the .38 came from?"

Coleman didn't respond because his cell phone rang. He groaned and answered it.

When he stood up and paced the kitchen as he listened, I knew something was really up. I topped off our coffees and waited.

After he hung up, he sat back at the table and reached for my hand. "That professor. What do you know about her?"

"Not much. I haven't really poked around trying to find anything. Why?"

"I told you about the male professor at Ole Miss who was shot and killed shortly before Diakos left the campus and moved here. She was the prime suspect."

"That's a big school with a lot of professors, students, and potentially angry parents. What connects Dr. Diakos with the murder?"

"The dead man, Alex Loxley, was a known abuser of women. Complaints by students and faculty were never officially filed and therefore no charges were ever brought against him. But, apparently, he was viewed as a sexual predator and an abuser by some of the faculty and student body."

This did sound more than a little suspicious. "Was he shot with a .38?"

Coleman nodded. "Straight in the heart. Just like Curtis Miller. Same angle, as if he were on his knees, based on what we could get from the Lafayette coroner's autopsy."

"And you really suspect Dr. Diakos of two murders?" I found myself wanting to defend a woman I didn't know.

"She's a person of interest, but there's a lot more investigating to do. Curtis Miller had a long list of enemies. I'll check in with the law enforcement around Ole Miss to see what they've uncovered in the Loxley murder."

"You'd better catch some shut-eye first," I said. Coleman looked exhausted.

"I should go back to the office, but you're right, maybe a couple of hours."

I eased the coffee cup away from him. "We can make a fresh pot when you get up."

"What's going on with your day?" he asked.

"I'm going to work in the flower beds this morning, then go with Tinkie to her doctor's appointment."

Coleman kissed me on the cheek, yawned, and headed for the stairs.

I cleaned up the kitchen and found my work gloves,

trowel, and snippers. The horses had been fed, and while I longed for a ride, I decided to garden. It was another gorgeous day, and if I hustled, I could finish up the work before it was time to meet Tinkie. I had just stepped out the front door when my cell phone rang. I didn't recognize the number.

"Delaney Detective Agency," I said.

"This is Dr. Diakos. I'd like to hire your agency."

For a split second I thought it was a prank. "Why?"

"To prove I'm not a murderer."

This was no joke. I had to wonder if Coleman had already sent one of the deputies to arrest the professor. "Are you being charged?"

"Any minute now," she said.

She was very positive that the law would soon be on her doorstep, and I happened to know that she was right. I remembered what my friend Tammy had said—that Alala stirred people up and that some folks wanted to stop her. "Why don't you wait to see if you're actually charged?" I asked.

"Because I will be, and I'd like for you and your partner to get off the starting block ahead of the game. Can you both come over? I have some information I'd like to give you in person."

"Let me call Tinkie. I'll pick her up and meet you in an hour. At the old Compton house?"

"That's correct. I'll be waiting for you."

5

I swung by Hilltop, Tinkie's home, and picked her up, along with her little pup, Chablis. Tinkie was fashion perfection—accessorized, coordinated, and well-groomed even in her late-term pregnancy. And so was Chablis, her little Yorkie. Chablis had her own stylist, and at times her outfits were coordinated with Tinkie's. Today, Tinkie wore black leggings, a red, black, and white sweater, black boots, and a black beret. Chablis's little hat was set at a rakish angle, and her sweater was the same colors as Tinkie's.

"Don't you say a word," Tinkie said as she got into my car. She put Chablis in the backseat with Sweetie Pie and Pluto. "The baby will be here soon and I want Chablis to realize that she can *never* be replaced, not even by a child."

"When you cram Chablis into human clothes, the dog probably thinks you're punishing her," I said. Yeah, I enjoyed giving Tinkie the dickens when I could, which wasn't very often.

"Fiddledeedee. And just so you know, I canceled my doctor's appointment. I won't be badgered today." Tinkie brushed aside my teasing. "Fill me in on the Ole Miss murder. I knew Curtis Miller and I fully understand why he's dead. Someone should have killed him long before now. But I'm dying to hear the scoop on the other killing."

I told her what I knew as we drove toward the Compton house, which was in the same neighborhood where Cece lived. Until I found out the parameters of the case Dr. Diakos was offering, I had to use extra caution. The old Compton house had at least an acre yard, lots of shrubbery, and a driveway that wound to the back of the house. I was careful to pull all the way into the driveway where my antique Mercedes Roadster was hidden from view. Cece was a newshound and if she saw my car, she'd know something was up. We couldn't hide the fact that Alala Diakos was a murder suspect forever, but we could release the information when it was most advantageous to us.

We hustled up onto the porch and found Alala waiting at the door. She ushered us inside.

"Thank you for coming."

She wore a red silk blouse and blue jeans, but she carried herself as if she were visiting the Queen of England. She had a real presence. Once we were seated in a lovely sunny parlor with a view of the most magnificent syca-more tree, I sipped a cup of coffee that she had offered and waited.

"I didn't kill that Miller man," she said. Her own coffee was untouched.

"You said you were going to be charged. Why would that happen?"

"After the lecture last night, I . . . ran into Miller."

This was news I already knew, but it was good she was bringing it forward on her own. I put my cup down and played dumb. "Where? I didn't see Curtis Miller at your talk. It's unlikely he was hobnobbing with the Mississippi League of Women Voters or the country club crowd."

"I got into it with him at a bar."

"A bar?" I asked.

"Yeah. At the Red Top Bar."

I certainly didn't see Alala Diakos as the kind of woman who would seek company in the Red Top, a drinking establishment on the outskirts of town that catered to mostly young, testosterone-amped men. Heavy metal music, lukewarm beer, and fistfights were the normal or-der of the evening there.

"What on earth were you doing at the Red Top?" Tin-kie said. "Not even Sarah Booth will go in there, and she'll go almost anywhere."

"I went looking for Curtis Miller." She tilted her chin up in defiance. "The more I thought about the event in the park, his gun there, the way he intended to intimi-date me—I had a thing or two to tell him."

"You're aware that his wife went to a safe house for battered women, right? Curtis nearly broke her wrist."

I watched her closely, but she seemed to be playing it straight with me.

"Yes. He beat her sometime before I showed up at the Red Top. He was bragging about it when I walked in. He was crowing about how he'd showed her the way a wife should act. He was very aggressive toward me."

"Maybe you should have figured he wouldn't want to see you."

"I didn't care what he wanted."

Tinkie waved a hand. "Forget all of that. What happened at the Red Top?"

"He attempted to backhand me and I threw him to the ground and beat his butt." She cleared her throat. "I also kicked him in the testicles. Hard. He was rolling on the floor and crying. Like a baby."

That kind of humiliation—to be bested by a woman who couldn't weigh more than a hundred and twenty pounds—would have been hard for Miller to swallow. It was a good thing he was dead or her life would likely be in danger from a sniper's bullet.

"Did you do this in front of his friends?" Tinkie asked.

"I did."

"Not smart." I shook my head. "And you left him alive?"

"Very much so, and roaring mad. He threatened to kill me and I told him to bring it on but that he would get hurt. I told him I'd shoot him dead."

"You threatened him only hours before he was killed." Coleman had told me this. "That's a pretty good reason for you to be the prime suspect in a murder."

"Which is why you're sitting in my parlor," she said. "Other than his wife, who else would want him dead?

I need to provide other viable candidates for who killed him."

"That's exactly what Tinkie and I will need to find out."

"And I want you to get started on that today."

"Are there any *other* reasons you might be under suspicion?" I wondered how truthful Alala would be with us.

She looked down only for a fraction of a second. "There was a problem at the University of Mississippi. An English professor was shot and killed. I was questioned but never charged."

"Did you beat him up, too?" Tinkie asked.

"Hardly, he was a wimp." She tapped her forehead. "And not the brightest lamp on the street. Physically, he was a slug."

Alala had no prohibitions about speaking ill of the dead, and I had to admit that I liked that. She called it as she saw it and offered no apologies. That might also get her slammed into a jail cell.

"What happened?"

"And what was his name?" Tinkie asked.

"Professor Alex Loxley was his name. Full professor of literature. And a known victimizer of young women in his classes."

"Isn't that a fireable offense?"

"It is if someone actually files a complaint."

"None of the students wanted to come forward?" Tinkie asked.

"That's correct. He was known to be a vindictive man and, with his power as a professor, he intimidated students into silence. Those young girls." She sighed. "They said his class was behind them. It had been an unpleasant experience, but it was over and done. They didn't want to bring it up. They thought, rightly, that it would haunt them the whole time they were going to school. Loxley was also part of the cool university scene. He was invited to a lot of student parties. The male students thought he was wonderful. So the girls simply didn't want to pay the price of kicking up a fuss. They were also afraid if they brought charges that it would fly back on them."

"How so?" Tinkie asked.

"Very few relationships are a hundred percent pristine. For instance, a girl might have gone to his office hoping for a flirtation and a negotiation for a better grade. Young women just becoming aware of their sexual power are often naïve. Sometimes they see a situation as a lark—until it spins out of control. Young college-age women are not always the most mature. I'm sure you remember those years."

Boy, did I. "So what happened to him?"

"I honestly don't know. He was found in his home on the floor before a roaring fire. He'd been shot in the heart."

"And you were the main suspect because . . . ?"

"I'd confronted him publicly a few days prior, demanding that he resign."

"I'll bet the school loved that." I could see the panic this scenario likely brought about in the administration. It was a public relations nightmare.

"They weren't thrilled, and were less so when I was picked up for questioning by the Oxford police during the middle of one of my classes." She refilled my coffee cup. "The administration's solution was to give me the next year off to write a book. Get me off the campus.

My contract at Ole Miss was only for two years, so I'm already looking for my next visiting professor gig. Just in case I don't finish the book or I can't sell it."

It wasn't a bad solution from the university's perspective. It removed the source of controversy without the messiness of firing her. "And here you are in Zinnia, with another dead man in your sphere of influence."

"There's something else you should know. The night Loxley died, I had a public confrontation with him. I warned him that there would be a price for his behavior. I told him he'd wake up dead."

A direct parallel to what she'd told Curtis Miller—and what had happened to him. I could see why she was a "person of interest."

"Do you have an alibi for either murder?" Tinkie asked, getting down to brass tacks.

"I was home, researching and writing when Loxley was killed. When Curtis Miller was killed, I was reading."

"Was anyone with you to confirm your alibi?" Tinkie followed up.

"I'm an adult. I don't need supervision."

"So you were alone?" This was what I'd feared. "No alibi, no matter how mature you are."

"Sue me for not needing a man to watch over me."

She was mighty touchy on that subject. "Who do you think killed Dr. Loxley?" A change of subject was in order.

"It could have been one of any number of people."

"You have to be more specific if you want us to help," I pointed out.

"There was a graduate student, actually his assistant, he abused with regularity. Margaret McNeese. Smart woman, but no boundaries. There was also a faculty member in the English department, Dr. Becky Brown. I heard he was very abusive with her, too."

"Did she file a complaint?"

"Not to my knowledge. I don't know if anyone ever filed a formal complaint. I had some discussions about Loxley with the chair of the department, but I couldn't complain because he hadn't hit me. I hadn't witnessed any such event—I'd only heard talk about his abuse." She shook her head slowly. "No one else was willing to come forward."

"Do you think either Ms. McNeese or Dr. Brown were capable of killing him?"

She shrugged. "I haven't put a lot of thought into it. I don't consider his death a loss or even a crime, so it's hard for me to judge."

"Don't say things like that." Tinkie was serious. "That will get you convicted faster than solid evidence if this goes before a jury."

"She's right." I backed up my partner.

"It's time for women to speak out. They don't have to take this abuse anymore." Alala thrust her chin forward.

"We agree with you, but now's the time for self-protection, not giving speeches." I now had a list of potential suspects for the Oxford, Mississippi, murder of Dr. Loxley, which gave me some direction. I could put together another list of people who might want Curtis Miller dead, including his wife. Often, private-eye work was a process of elimination. Tinkie and I stood up. It was time to go, once we had our retainer in hand.

Alana wrote the check and handed it to Tinkie. "When can I expect some results?"

"As soon as we have some," Tinkie said airily. "Focus

on writing your book and let us do our jobs. Just keep your lips zipped and stay home. The more you talk, the more suspicion you throw on yourself. And no more public speeches."

She blanched. "That's impossible. I have a talk in Memphis soon."

Memphis was a world away from Sunflower County. "Okay, but take someone with you the entire time and please don't make rash statements about killing people or who deserves to die."

She nodded, but only time would tell if she'd truly heed our advice.

6

The October sun warmed the day to the perfect temperature. When I parked at Selena's House, the haven for abused women and children, I discovered the house was one of the larger in town on a lot that included several acres. Sweetie Pie and Chablis were asleep on the backseat. Pluto had moved up to sit on the console of the car.

"Stay put," I warned him as Tinkie and I got out to confront Tansy Miller.

Penny welcomed us in and sent word upstairs for Tansy to join us.

The head of the home had a nurturing vibe that even I could recognize. She tut-tutted over Tinkie, putting a hassock under her feet, showering my partner with excitement and attention on her impending motherhood. Tinkie ate it with a spoon.

Penny's nut-brown hair swung free around her face, and she constantly cleaned her glasses on the front of her shirt. She had the unique ability to make people feel wanted and safe.

When we were settled, she served us coffee and cake as we sat in a small private office waiting for Tansy. Tinkie and I had decided to work the Zinnia case first. The most immediate threat to Alala's freedom was the murder of Curtis Miller, and though Oxford wasn't that far away, I also didn't want to leave town with Tinkie ready to pop.

Penny bit her bottom lip. "Poor Tansy. Before she gets here, I want to tell you a few things. She's been crying all morning." She sighed. "Don't badmouth Curtis. It won't help her heal. Don't try to force her to talk bad about him; she won't. Years of dealing with these women have taught me that you have to let them come to you. It isn't just the physical punches and broken bones, it's what Curtis did to her sense of self. If you push her too hard, I'll ask you to leave. She's only just now beginning to pull herself together."

I wanted to snap back with something sharp about how a woman crying for an abuser was wasted emotion, but I knew better than that. We all had our weaknesses, and loving the wrong person was not something I could throw stones at. I'd been guilty of worse and was well aware that mocking someone else's pain was a fast ticket to my own torment. Life had taught me that I suffered from boomerang karma. The minute I called someone out on something, I found myself in exactly that same spot within a week.

Penny filled our coffee cups. "Can you vouch for Tansy last night?" I asked her. I didn't expect Penny to keep tabs on Tansy through the night, but some of the women, like Tansy, might be in danger from an abuser. At times of danger, a few of the area volunteer firemen and EMTs took turns watching over the place if a high-risk woman was in residence. Sunflower County had a pretty tight system of men and women who fought against domestic abuse, when a victim allowed them to help. It was possible someone had been on watch last night and could definitively say that Tansy had remained in Selena's House.

"The house is almost empty now," she said. "These abuse cases seem to come in waves. Like it's contagious. Paulette is in the aqua room, but she'll be leaving in the morning to go to San Francisco to live with her sister. Her room is on the other side of the house from Tansy. I can only say for certain that Tansy went up to her room not long after Doc released her from the hospital." Penny hesitated as she tidied the stack of paper napkins on the tray. Clearly she had something more to say but was debating about whether she should speak or not.

"And she was there all night?" Tinkie asked.

Penny met my gaze. "No. She wasn't. I went in to check on her about eleven and she was gone. The residents aren't supposed to leave the premises after ten. My first thought was that she'd gone back to Curtis. A lot of women have to leave an abuser more than once, but she was in bed this morning."

"Do you know where she went?"

"I don't. She didn't say anything about it. I was just relieved she hadn't gone home to Curtis. Based on Tansy's hospital records of broken bones, bruised internal organs, and near choking, I was afraid he'd kill her this time. Now I hear someone killed him. Violence begets violence." She sighed. "The human animal is brutish."

"Do you know how long Tansy was absent from Selena's House?" I asked.

"I don't. We provide a safe place for abused women and children, but I learned years back that if I want to live and run this place, I can't coerce a woman to be safe. My room is on the other side of the house. I locked my door and went to bed. I honestly thought I'd get a call saying she was dead. I didn't wait up for that."

Living with women who chose constant turmoil and drama would wreck a person unless she knew how to step back. I understood Penny's decision to lock the door and turn off the drama.

Our conversation was interrupted when Tansy stopped in the doorway in torn jeans, a halter top, and sandals. Her eyes were red and swollen and she bristled when she saw us. "Penny said someone was here to see me. She didn't say it was you. I don't have to talk to you."

"No, you don't," Tinkie said, "but it might be smart if you did."

"You can't do anything worse to me. Curtis is dead. No one can bring him back." Her eyes filled with tears but she fought them back.

"We might be able to keep you from being accused of his murder if you'll let us," Tinkie said softly. "We're trying to help you." The high spots of color on her cheeks told me her emotions were on the rise. Tinkie felt sorry for Tansy. She was just made that way.

"I wouldn't kill Curtis. I loved him. Everyone knew that. I did everything for him. Nobody would believe I killed him. Ever. That's a load of cow manure. You're just trying to upset me."

"I promise we're only trying to figure out what happened last night. Just tell us where you were and we'll be on our way," I said.

"I don't have to tell you squat." She sauntered into the room, leading with her hips. "Tell them, Ms. Cox. Tell them to get out of here."

Penny shook her head. "Tansy, they're trying to help you."

"That one"—she pointed at Tinkie—"thinks her poop don't stink. And that one"—she pointed at me—"runs around town like she's James Bond nosing in everybody's business. Maybe they killed my husband."

"We had no reason to kill Curtis," I said. "He wasn't beating the living daylights out of us."

"Or cheating on us," Tinkie pointed out. That sent a flush up Tansy's face.

"None of that would have happened if it wasn't for that mutt. That damn dog needs to die. Curtis and I were doing great until that dog dropped Moody's underwear at my feet."

That was some logic—blaming the dog for her husband cheating. "Tansy, where were you last night?"

"I went for a walk. So sue me."

"Did anyone see you along the path you walked?" The halfway house was about a mile from the Red Top, but on a cool October night it would be only a brisk walk. Tansy could easily have legged it down there.

"No one was out and about, except for some young woman who jogged by me, twice. Crazy health nuts," she said, but a funny look crossed her face. "I could have sworn she came out of that big shrub in the backyard. Anyway, I looped through town, went over to the courthouse and through some neighborhoods. I like to look at the houses with the lights on and imagine what the people inside are doing. Watching television or playing a game of cards or just talking." Her lips turned down. "Most of the houses were dark. Folks had gone to bed."

The streets of Zinnia did roll up at five o'clock. Millie's stayed open for supper, but after it closed, there was only the Sweetheart Drive-thru. Of course there were teenagers out and about, and those over twenty-one could sometimes be found in the local bars outside the city limits. "No one saw you?"

"I don't think I saw a single car. This town is deader than roadkill after dark." She held up one finger. "Wait, I did see one car."

"Tell us about it," Tinkie said. "If we can find that car, we can prove your alibi."

"It was a sports car. Red. Going about a hundred miles an hour and it was coming from the direction of the Red Top."

"What time was this?" I asked, not because I believed Tansy actually saw a car but because it was part of the routine.

"Whoever was driving was flying."

"Did they see you?" Something about this was cock-eyed.

"Doubtful, but I know who it was. That college teacher zoomed by but I saw she was looking straight ahead. She didn't see me on the side of the road." Tansy's smirk was masterful.

"You saw Dr. Diakos speeding at midnight?"

"You bet I did. Coming from the direction of the Red Top. I think she killed my husband and she's going to try to blame me."

I had one more tactic. "Tansy, why did Curtis take a hunting rifle to the park and set it up in the bushes?"

"He likes to kill squirrels. Says they're varmints. Says he's doing a public service."

"Was he planning on killing Dr. Diakos?" Tinkie asked.

She shrugged. "Wasn't any of my concern. Curtis said she was a foreigner and she was going to stir up trouble in town. He said he was going to have some fun with her."

"Fun in what way? Shooting her?"

"No!" She waved her hand. "He wouldn't shoot her in plain sight. Get real. He was just going to liven things up."

"How did he know she was going to give a talk? Her remarks weren't part of any planned event. There wasn't any announcement or anything."

"Dr. Feminazi has a big mouth, that's how. She was in the Red Top the night before, too, spouting off about the park and how she was going to take over the opening and give the men in town something to think about."

Tinkie and I sighed. Her statement did sound exactly like Alala Diakos. She would want to rub the men's noses in it.

"Have you found an alibi for Dr. Diakos?" Tansy asked. "She's the one that killed my man. She's the one you should be talking to."

"Trust me, we will have a long conversation with her," Tinkie said. "Now we have to go."

Penny walked us to the door. "Tansy won't stay here long," she said. "Miller was the biggest part of her world. He was her anchor. I'm worried that she'll up and take off, and she doesn't have anywhere else to go. She can't afford the rent on their place, and I don't think she'd consider going home to her parents. Not a good situation there from what I understand."

I nodded. "Hopefully we'll have this cleared up before long, and maybe some time living in a place where she's treated well will give her a new perspective."

"Have you talked to Moody Moody? I heard she's involved in this." Penny was up-to-date on the gossip.

"Do you know Moody?" Tinkie asked.

"She lived here for a while, back when she left a bad relationship. I did my best to keep her from dancing, but it was quick and easy money and the men made her feel beautiful." She shook her head. "She has a steady boyfriend but I heard she really had a thing for Curtis. She comes from the same kind of background as Tansy. Abusive."

"We'll head there now. Thanks for the tip."

Tinkie and I were almost to the car when my partner stopped to look at me. "I like men. I like Oscar in particular, but even before Oscar, I liked being on the arm of a man. But Curtis? What does he have that makes Tansy and Moody go for him?"

Any answer I might come up with defied logic, so I kept walking to the car where the heads of two dogs and one cat suddenly popped up.

Moody Moody, her stage name, lived in a trailer in a nice mobile home park on the south side of town. It was an old, established facility with ten units, most of them in good repair. An old Toyota Corolla was parked near the front of the home. Since it was afternoon and we figured Moody would be up, Tinkie and I knocked on the door.

Tinkie's stomach gave a growl that sounded downright deadly.

"If Moody is home and she heard that noise, she'll think you've come to cook her and eat her," I said.

"If I don't get some lunch, I may." Tinkie took her food seriously these days.

The door opened and Moody, eye makeup on and hair teased in a bouffant, looked at us. "What do you want? I don't get the feeling that you're witnessing for a religious group."

"Delaney Detective Agency," I said. Moody was all of twenty-one. Maybe younger. She was a pretty girl with blue eyes and full lips.

"Private dicks. Just perfect! Beat it. I just woke up. I have errands to run before work tonight."

"Curtis Miller was killed last night. Do you know anything about that?" She wasn't going to let us in and Tinkie's stomach cut another low, angry complaint.

"Curtis?" She frowned. "What are you talking about? You say he's dead?"

"Shot to death." Tinkie reached into her pocket for a mint.

"He's really dead?" She shook her head. "No. That can't be right. Who would do that?" The shock on her face looked real to me.

"That's what we'd like to know. How about your boyfriend? Is he around?"

She came out of the trailer and closed the door. The three of us stood on the tiny wooden porch, which allowed no room for anyone to move. "You clear out of here. Right now. Todd's in there asleep and I don't need him hearing anything about Curtis Miller."

I went in hard. "You saw Curtis yesterday. Or perhaps

it was the night before last. After you finished dancing. You had a little love session. In his truck." I was making a wild guess, but the panties in the truck were a solid bit of evidence.

"Hush your mouth!" She glanced back at the door as if she feared it would fly open and Todd would rush out. "Who told you that?"

"Tansy Miller." That was the truth. Tansy had blurted it out when Roscoe dropped the panties at her feet.

"How would she know? Curtis could tell her he was going to have a chat with St. Peter at the Pearly Gates and she'd buy it hook, line, and sinker. Not the brightest bulb in the house, if you get my drift." She kept glancing back at the door. "You have to go. If Todd hears this, he'll kill me."

"Maybe Todd already knows," I said softly. "Maybe Todd decided he didn't like you two-timing him with Curtis and he decided to put an end to it."

"You think Todd killed Curtis?" Moody was appalled at the suggestion. "Heck, no, he wouldn't. Todd and Curtis are friends."

"Such good friends Todd wouldn't care if Curtis was enjoying the pleasures of your body?"

Moody leaned against the trailer door. "Todd doesn't have a say over what I do or who I do it with. I've made that perfectly clear. I just don't like rubbing his nose in it."

"Where was Todd last night?" I asked.

"Right here. With me. Once I got off dancing, he picked me up and we came here to have a few drinks."

"Did anyone see you?" I asked.

"Old Miss Maloney. She sees everything that goes on here. Ask her." She pointed to the next trailer and, sure enough, an older woman was sitting in a bay window watching every move we made. "She doesn't miss a thing. Now beat it out of here. Todd's easygoing, but everybody has a limit, you know." She slipped inside her trailer and closed the door with a firm click.

Tinkie and I walked over to the next trailer and a woman who looked to be in her eighties opened the door. When Tinkie's stomach lodged a complaint, Miss Maloney didn't bother asking. She just got a sleeve of soda crackers from her kitchen and handed them to Tinkie, who tore into them with a grateful thank-you.

It didn't take two minutes to steer the conversation exactly where we needed it to go. Miss Maloney had sharp eyes and a bone to pick with Moody and Todd.

"Yeah, Moody and that man of hers showed up drunk as lords about midnight. I thought that girl would break her neck getting up the stairs. How she dances on a stage without injuring herself is anybody's guess. But she got in the door and I heard them laughing for about half an hour. I guess when you're skunk drunk everything is funny." She rolled her eyes. "Living in sin. Folks got no shame anymore."

Moody might not have shame, but she and Todd had airtight alibis for the murder of Curtis Miller.

"Miss Maloney, do you know this man?" I showed her a photo of Curtis Miller on my phone.

"Sure. He's a big blowhard. He was over here beating on Moody's door yesterday, bellowing about a dog and some underwear. She was working, so I yelled at him to leave. He shook his fist at me and said he'd just as soon hit an old woman as a young one."

"Was he drunk?" Tinkie asked.

"Hard to tell with a man like him. But he had someone with him in his truck."

This was a new angle. "Could you identify the person?"

"No, I didn't get a good look. The truck windows are blacked out, like the thugs do these days. I just caught movement. Looked to be someone slender. They were looking over at me so I closed my curtains, but the window was still open."

"Man or woman?" Tinkie asked.

"I didn't see enough to tell. They skedaddled. I heard him say to the passenger in his truck, 'She's not home and that old bat will call the police.' Of course I had the phone in my hand and was just about to dial."

"Was there a response?"

"I couldn't hear it if there was, but then Curtis said he had an important meeting and once it was done, he'd be sitting in the catbird seat."

"Did he say who he was meeting?" I asked.

"No, he didn't. At least not loud enough for me to hear. He was always kind of a mumbler. Like he had a mouthful of marbles coated in shi—well, you know. Now would you ladies like some tea? I have some wonderful oolong and some delicious cookies." She patted Tinkie's knee. "This baby doll needs some nourishment. Lord, her stomach sounds like the Creature from the Black Lagoon."

7

An hour after we left Miss Maloney's trailer, Tinkie and I headed back to downtown Zinnia. There was no help for it. It was either feed Tinkie or listen to her stomach complain. The tea and cookies had tamped down the tummy talk for about ten minutes. Now Tinkie was complaining again about being hungry.

Going to Millie's Café was the perfect solution. Tinkie could get grub and I needed to talk to Millie and possibly Cece. If Madame Tomeeka showed up, that would be an additional bonus. Millie would let us put the dogs and cat in her office so they could also have a fine meal while we talked. After lunch, Tinkie would likely want a nap and it was my intention to take Sweetie Pie, Pluto, and Chablis to the brand-new nature trail that started in the new park, wound around the city of Zinnia, and twisted and turned through some wild places just outside the city limits. The dogs loved the exercise of a brisk walk and Pluto, who was looking a little too rotund, needed to stretch his legs. Besides, I wanted a little time to figure out who might have been in Curtis's truck. Someone had moved Curtis's body to the field behind Playin' the Bones. Someone strong. Curtis wasn't fat but he was tall. A woman like Tansy would never be able to put him in a trunk and get him out. And where had he originally been killed?

I was deep in thought while Tinkie went over her menu options as we drove to Millie's. I slipped the critters into the office while Tinkie found a table. In a moment, we were seated with Millie hovering over us.

"Tinkie, girl, you look tired. You can't carry that baby and run around like Sarah Booth." Millie was only a few years older than us, but she'd taken on the role of mother hen. She cooked for us and pecked at us when she thought we weren't taking care of ourselves.

Tinkie did look tired, and I noticed her hand was soothing her stomach. It had become a habit in the past few days. I worried that she would pop like a tick she was so large, but she was just too hardheaded to stay home.

I put in orders for the critters, and Tinkie and I sipped icy sweet tea and relaxed. "This is wonderful," Tinkie said when Millie put an order of fried dill pickles on the table. "Exactly what the doctor ordered." She dug in while still looking at the menu, which we had memorized. Pregnancy had made her indecisive, and as she said, it was always good to explore every option.

We decided on our food and Millie sent the order back,

then joined us. The worst of the lunch rush was over, and she was ready to sit a spell.

"Any luck on finding Curtis's killer?" Millie asked. "Cece was in here about forty minutes ago and she said he was shot point-blank in the heart. Like the killer walked right up to him and just pulled the trigger. No fight and no defensive wounds. Nothing unusual except for dumping the body in the cotton field in back of Playin' the Bones." She thought a minute. "Curtis was a big old boy. Not fat but healthy, you know. You would think he would have fought back."

"You would think," I agreed. Millie had more information on the murder than I did. Working with Cece had given her an even better main line into town happenings than running the café. "Any idea where he was killed?"

"Cece didn't say. Do you think that feminist professor killed him? Maybe it happened at her house." Millie used the word *feminist* with reverence, not disdain. "The only thing is, if she did, she had to have help to move the body."

Millie was right about that. "Alala doesn't have an alibi, but neither does Tansy. Those two women together could have done it. And Moody Moody's boyfriend, Todd, has an alibi." Tinkie brought Millie up-to-date with everything we knew.

Millie frowned. "Todd Renfield? What's he got to do with any of this?"

"Moody is living with Todd and was sleeping with Curtis," Tinkie supplied. "We thought maybe Todd killed Curtis out of jealousy, but Todd and Moody have an alibi. Each other."

"Why do people call her Moody Moody?" Millie asked. "That drives me nuts."

"I would think that you, as the coauthor of 'The Truth Is Out There,' the most investigative newspaper column covering real events and those spawned by creative genius, would know the reason for the name of Sunflower County's most talented exotic dancer," I said.

"I know her real name is Cynthia Moody. I know Moody Moody is her dancing name, but why?"

I couldn't help chuckling a little. "Here's the story I heard. When Cynthia started dancing at the gentleman's club, she thought Cynthia was a boring name. She worked up her dance routine to 'Tuesday Afternoon' by the Moody Blues."

"Amazing song," Cece said as she slipped into the fourth seat at the table.

"Anyway, Cynthia was a huge fan of the Moody Blues so she picked the name Moody Tuesday to dance under. You know, like a stormy Tuesday. A moody Tuesday."

Cece and Tinkie were grinning. "A little artistic for a stripper," Cece said.

"Folks could never make the connection, though, and the Tuesday part got lost and she just became Moody Moody."

"I'm sorry I asked," Millie said with a grin. "Benign neglect. That's how she got that name."

"I can tell you how Pig Lips Hanson got his name," Cece said.

"Stop it." Millie shook her head.

"No, don't stop! I want to hear that," I said. I'd known Pig Lips, a local contractor, for ten years and never heard the story of his name.

"Stop it this instant." Millie was laughing. "You are

three terrible people. Now I see Tinkie's order is up. Cece, what will it be?"

"Only coffee. Thanks."

Millie went back to work and I turned to Cece, waiting expectantly. "Well?"

Cece sighed. "He kissed a pig on a dare and one of his real good buddies photographed it. In the photo, he has this really blissful look on his face. He could never live it down."

"Thanks." I grinned. "What have you found out about Curtis Miller and Tansy?"

"I found out you and Tinkie need to be very careful. As you've determined, Curtis went to the park to deliberately provoke Diakos." Cece pushed her hair out of her face. "There's an undercurrent of real meanness afoot in part of the county. Two women have qualified to run for county supervisor and one had her car beaten with a crowbar and the other's house was spray-painted with the words 'Women Don't Belong in Office.'"

"This happened in Sunflower County?" I asked.

"Just last month."

"You never mentioned it," I said accusingly to Cece.

"Because I didn't know. It was hushed up. I just found out when I started checking around about Curtis. There's a group of men who are raising hell about women getting elected. They don't like it."

"Because these men feel an elected office belongs only to a man. And to be more specific, a white man," I said. In the old days the supervisor's job in a rural farming county dealt with a lot of heavy equipment, road building, bridge repairs, so-called manly things. Now, though, the work was primarily financial and clerical. But it was still considered a man's job.

"I've heard some rumblings about women taking over," Cece said. "And Claire Matturro is running for county prosecutor. That's really creating a stir."

The election was still over a year away, but there was going to be hot competition for many offices. "As women demand equality and win public office, there's a type of man who feels very threatened. Curtis is one of those men. He had to beat up on Tansy to feel powerful and masculine."

"Women have had the right to hold office for a long time. This isn't really new," Tinkie pointed out.

"No, but it's only recently that women are becoming seen as capable, maybe more capable than men. Perhaps the letter of the law is the same, but community standards, in some places, are shifting because women are speaking out." I'd given this a lot of thought as I watched the backlash nationally against women running for political office. "For the men who believe it's a husband's right to control his wife, a woman like Alala Diakos is dangerous. She threatens that privilege. That's scary to some people, and not just men. When you upend the way things are, a lot of people have to scramble to find their place again. It makes them mad."

"Unbelievable," Tinkie said. "The best, most qualified person should be the boss or hold the office or whatever. Gender or race shouldn't matter."

"You're correct, and I only wish that was the way the world worked, but it isn't," Cece said. "When I decided to give up being seen as male, I understood much of what I was letting go of in the way of privilege. But not all of it. Men have a birthright they aren't even aware of, until it's not there. I don't regret it, of course, but I am keenly informed of the disparities now." She sighed. "But back to the case. I haven't been able to get any names, but I've heard rumors that there's a group of men gathering at regular intervals to rebel against these changes in society. They want to keep the power and force women 'back to their place.' They're against people of color also. It's a serious movement fueled by a lot of fear and anger."

"This could get really ugly," Tinkie said. Her hand went protectively to her belly again.

"It could," I said. And it was up to me to make sure my partner wasn't in the way of danger. She'd be in the hospital soon, giving birth. I just had to keep her out of trouble until then.

"These men . . . any idea who they are?" I wondered if Cece was holding out on me.

"You and I both could probably list some people who might be involved, the local cretin contingent with a few nabobs thrown in, but I won't say names until I have some evidence. Trust me, I'm looking to pin them down."

That wasn't comforting. "Do you think Curtis was attending any of those meetings?"

"It's his kind of crowd, for sure, but I can't say. I've had some feelers out for more information, but so far nothing. This is a secretive bunch. And well-armed, from what I hear. That survivalist assault-weapon mentality. Plenty of bullets, soap, and toilet tissue stockpiled." Cece checked her watch. "I have an interview. Time for me to go." She finished her coffee and stood up. "Tinkie, are you okay?"

Tinkie quickly removed her hand from her stomach. "I am. My belly just feels tight."

"You're packing a lot of baby in there," Cece said, bending down to kiss her cheek. "It won't be long now and I can't wait!"

Tinkie's face paled.

"You okay?" I asked.

She glanced around and leaned closer to us. "Don't tell anyone, but I'm scared."

Neither Cece nor I was going to be the friend who passed her concerns off with a lie. We were both on edge, too. "I don't blame you," I said, "but Doc says you're completely healthy and the baby is, too. If there was a reason to worry, Doc would have told you."

"Now that the time is almost here, I'm not certain I can do this."

Cece laughed softly. "You don't have a choice, baby girl. My adopted niece or nephew is coming whether you want her or him to or not."

"That's what's scary," Tinkie said. "I can't imagine my mother ever giving birth. I mean, how did she do it? She's not one to exercise or sweat or be anything except perfectly turned out. This baby birthing is going to be . . . ugly!"

"But oh so beautiful, in the long run." I patted her shoulder. "I promise not to take any photos and post them on social media."

Cece snort-laughed and Tinkie stood up. "If you do, I will kill you, Sarah Booth. I will."

"I'll keep Sarah Booth in check," Cece promised. "She's just messing with you."

"I am," I agreed. "But look, now you aren't scared. You're mad. Isn't that better?"

Tinkie shook her head. "Thank goodness you never thought to be a psychologist."

I picked up the check and went to pay, knowing Cece would console Tinkie far better than I could. When I was done at the counter, I waved them out the front door and gathered the animals. It was time to put on our private-dick hats and get back to work, once I delivered Tinkie and Chablis to Hilltop for a nap.

The idea of a horseback ride was tempting, but instead I set up my computer on a table on the front porch and prepared to work. It was a perfect fall day, no humidity. Sweetie Pie was at my feet and Pluto had installed himself on a cushion on one of the rocking chairs. I typed in *Dr. Alala Diakos* in the search line.

Out in the pasture, Miss Scrapiron whinnied and Reveler ran toward her, reared up, pawed the air, and then bolted. The crisp air had even the horses geared up for a frolic. Suddenly, the horses whirled and faced the driveway, focused on something. A woman stepped out of the shadow of a sycamore and walked toward me. I knew this woman, wearing a shirtwaist dress that swept to her calves and completely impractical high heels, was not real. She'd stepped right out of the pages of some old 1930s magazines my mama had stored up in the attic, and her hair, bobbed to her shoulders and curled around her face, completed the dated look. As she slowly approached, I knew she was Jitty, but in a guise I didn't recognize. Whoever Jitty was pretending to be, she was well dressed, if a little dated.

"Can I help you?" I asked when she arrived at the steps.

"Just stopped by to see if you needed any professional help decorating your home." She spoke in a soft accent that was a blend of Midwestern and Southern.

"You *walked* here?" It wasn't the most intelligent question, but I was floored.

"Oh, in my day, I've walked, ridden horses, robbed

trains . . . it was a fine and exciting life. Now all of that is behind me and I'm just hoofing it."

This was Jitty without a doubt. But Jitty doing what? "Who are you?"

"My friends call me Della Rose or sometimes Rose of the Wild Bunch, but I was born Laura Bullion. I've had a lot of different names. What does a name matter?"

"The Wild Bunch? Like the outlaws Butch Cassidy and the Sundance Kid?" I was a huge fan of the movie, and while this woman looked to be in step with the thirties, there was something about the way she held her shoulders and defied me with a brazen stare that told me she was no one to tamper with.

"They would be my friends. A couple of them were my lovers. You have no idea what it was like to be free in a time when women were chattel. The world of the outlaw was one of the few places a white woman could live fully. If she was smart enough, bold enough, fearless enough—she was accepted as an equal. And I have to say, the men were handsome and often with the finest manners."

"Which couple of men were your lovers?" I had to know. Paul Newman and Robert Redford, Butch and Sundance in the iconic movie, were heartthrobs of another generation, but they would forever be the blue-eyed and the golden-haired outlaws of celluloid—and in my dreams. If Jitty/Della Rose had slept with the real deal, I wanted her to dish some dirt.

"Not the ones you're thinkin'," Jitty said. "I took up with News Carver after my aunt died. She was his wife and she died of fever. He took me with him into the outlaw trade. And then, I met the Tall Texan. That's when I rode with the Wild Bunch. Did three years in prison for a train robbery. The Great Northern train robbery, if you know your history." She pushed her dark hair off her face and I saw pride and longing in her features. Even though she was a ghost impersonating a dead outlaw, I could feel the power of her memories. "Outlawing wasn't all glamorous. It was hard work. But I didn't stand in anybody's shadow. I was my own man."

"Man?" I couldn't help that I was swept up in Jitty's charade.

"Only a man could have a shadow back then. Women were only pale shades, too insubstantial to even cast a shadow. They couldn't own land or inherit or vote and many were enslaved with no rights at all. If a woman had children and wanted to leave a marriage, the man almost always got custody, if a judge would even consider granting a divorce. There was only one path forward for most women. They married, they bred, they produced children, and they worked until they died. I escaped that. I lived my life on my own terms."

"And you became an interior decorator?" I was going back to her original statement about helping me decorate Dahlia House.

"Finally gave up robbing trains and banks, changed my name, moved to Memphis, and became a seamstress for the posh set. Moved on to interior decorating. I had a flair for making things look better than they were. Died there in 1961 at the age of eighty-five, or thereabouts. Stop by Memorial Park in Memphis and see my marker. Got a bronze plaque with a rose on it. I was the last of the Wild Bunch to die."

"Care for a drink?" I asked. I had a lot of work to do, but first things first—I had living history standing in front of me. Jitty might play me false in a lot of things, but in her incarnations as historical people, she was accurate.

"Whiskey?"

Oh, she was a girl after my own heart. "I'll fix us up."

"Neat," she said. "Just remember one thing, Sarah Booth, standing up to be counted makes you some enemies, even among women who should know better. But staying in the shadows of men can't be tolerated."

I hurried to the parlor to make us drinks, and when I walked back outside, the porch was empty. She was gone. I held my Jack on the rocks and her neat drink and stared down the empty driveway. Sweetie Pie lifted her hound dog head and gave me a half-hearted yodel, as if to say, "She had places to be."

"Right." I took a sip of my drink and sat down at the computer. Laura Bullion, aka Della Rose, aka Rose of the Wild Bunch had left me with more questions than answers. But Jitty would never tell me the truth. She couldn't. She also wouldn't give away anything, and, ultimately, the reason didn't matter. It was up to me to figure out why she'd presented herself in the past few days as female outlaws. One partial answer was pretty clear: both Pearl Hart and Della Rose were feminists. They were women who'd claimed their place beside men as equals. Now that was something to chew on.

But first, my goal was background on Alala Diakos. I put my fingers to the keyboard and began tapping away.

8

Alala Diakos had her own Wikipedia page, which listed her impressive academic credentials and the previous institutions where she'd worked. She was a native of Athens, Greece, and after reading a brief bio, I better understood the origins of her name and her pride in her heritage. She was born to be fierce.

As Alala had indicated earlier, in Greek mythology, Alala was the daughter of Polemos, the personification of war. Her aunt was the war goddess Enyo, and her uncle was Ares. Alala attended the war god Ares on the battlefield and was known for her bravery and valor.

I could see that Dr. Diakos had certainly lived up to the warlike attributes of her name and taken them to heart.

She enjoyed doing battle, and that was what concerned me. For all of her scholarly pursuits and accomplishments, she was a street brawler. And at about five-four, and maybe a hundred and ten pounds, she wasn't exactly a glamorous lady of wrestling.

I read on and learned that she'd written a series of poems in her twenties that won literary awards, and she was a recognized authority on Greek and American literature. She'd taught classes in Athens, London, Paris, Nashville, and most recently in Oxford, Mississippi.

Feminist literature was her specialty, and I found myself nodding along as I read about her. Alala had been born with a silver spoon in her mouth, and she'd spat it out and begun to preach the power of the feminine. Her real parents had been Greek diplomats who hobnobbed with presidents from around the world—and had publicly disapproved of her political agenda.

Alala didn't need a paid sabbatical to write her book. She had a family who could fund her literary pursuits any time she chose to ask. And yet she was living in small-town Mississippi in an extremely nice but modest rental home.

She'd won a number of academic awards and her poems had been published in several prestigious magazines. The book contract she'd inked with one of the biggest New York publishers was said to be in the high six figures. I supposed that with the #MeToo movement and the mobilization of women in politics, the publishers were expecting the book to be a hot seller. And even if it wasn't part of the book, the lingering scandal of dead male abusers linked to her name couldn't hurt publicity.

On top of that, Alala had her own YouTube channel and podcast, and she had countless followers on Twitter and Instagram. She was a social media maven, and despite myself, I was impressed.

I checked out some clips of her talking to a group of young women at the University of Mississippi. They were enthralled by her statistics on how women had been consistently disenfranchised and impoverished since the country began. She sparked the fire of rebellion in them. As the camera panned over the young faces, I saw the idealism. Alala was a powerful motivator. And she'd parlayed that into her platform. When I checked online I realized she was already stacking up pre-orders on her book, and lots of critical and academic attention. There was plenty for her peers to be jealous over.

Alala had taken what the modern world offered—a social media platform that reached millions—and begun to wage a war against patriarchal society. After listening to a few of her podcasts, I could see exactly why Curtis Miller had decided to terrorize her. To men like Curtis, Alala was dangerous to the extreme. An excellent public speaker, she was also charismatic and believed so deeply in her cause that she clearly had a talent for drawing out an audience through the depth of her feelings. She'd built a following. Possibly a cult.

I found myself swayed toward her passion—getting angry at the way women had been cheated economically, socially, politically, and career-wise. As Alala pointed out, that extended even to the spiritual realm where women seldom had a place as preachers or leaders. When Alala listed all of the injustices—and then toted up the cost—it was staggering.

Why had women tolerated this system for so long? That was the most dangerous question she asked and the one that had my brain spinning. I started thinking about where I and my friends fit into this picture. I wasn't a traditional woman by any standard, and particularly that of the Southern woman. Tinkie, who was as strong and independent as I'd ever been, had accepted the disguise of belle and learned to bend men and the world at large to her will with charm, guile, and sweetness.

My "bull in the China shop" approach seldom netted the positive results that Tinkie could get with a sweet smile, a helpless laugh, and a simple request. Growing up, before I'd learned the ways of the world, I'd thought Tinkie was a bit of a sellout to women because she didn't do battle. Time had taught me very differently. Tinkie was more powerful than any other woman I knew in many, many ways.

Cece had also charted her own path, making her passion to be who she truly was a crusade for justice and acceptance that I admired.

Millie, with her ability to mother us and everyone else in town, had her own set of strengths. She worked hard and expected the same of others. Nurturing was her strength, but it never included excusing or pandering to the egos of men or anyone else. She'd taught me pride in having a dream and fighting for it.

Madame Tomeeka, too, had defied all feminine expectations. Despite objections from some religious communities and condemnation from a lot of other sources, she'd crafted a life and career with her unique talent of psychic abilities at the heart of her day-to-day existence. She'd saved lives with her prophetic dreams—mine included. She'd never married, though she'd had a baby, and she'd never looked back at the choices she'd made.

While I was evaluating the strong women in my life today, I had to include Jitty. She'd been raised in slavery, but she'd created a bond with my great-great-great-grandma Alice that had sustained both of them through a war I couldn't even imagine. Ignoring social structure, class, and even the laws at the time, Jitty and Alice had united as equal friends to find a strength that still astounded me. They didn't care what the law or society said. They were a team, and they had lived through the worst of times because of it.

I had a lot of tremendous role models when I looked around, and plenty like my mother, who were on the other side. I came from a long line of strong women who defied convention. So what was going on with women who clung to the more traditional roles society had herded them into? Were they happy? It was hard for me to believe, but evidence indicated that a lot of them were. Either that or they were too afraid to claim true independence.

My cell phone rang and I picked it up without looking. Sometimes, I liked to surprise myself.

"Sarah Booth," Coleman said, "where is your client? Cece told me that you'd been hired by Alala."

"She was home a few hours ago." His question sent off a dozen alarms. "Why?"

"I just got a report from the Nashville police department. Alala Diakos was a suspect in the murder of a man there. A woman beater who was found shot through the heart last spring."

"What?" This was news to me. I'd been busy checking out Alala's story for her time in Zinnia. The murder of Dr. Loxley in Oxford was up next on my agenda. Now I had another murder in Nashville—also linked to Alala by time, place, and victim profile. Opportunity was one of the three prime components of any crime. Motive was another, and Alala had that in spades. Means, the third component, would be harder to put together, but it could be done. As soon as Coleman got the specifics on the Loxley and Nashville murders, I'd know if the same type of gun had been used in all three killings.

"You need to bring Alala in, or at least get her to turn herself in," Coleman said. "I need to question her."

"I'll call her. Or better yet, I'll go by and pick her up myself."

"Thanks, Sarah Booth. If she can clear some of this up, it'll go a long way toward mitigating the suspicions she's aroused."

"I hope she'll cooperate."

"If she doesn't, I'll pay her a visit. It would just look better for her if she came in voluntarily."

I considered picking up Tinkie on my way, but the largeness of her pregnancy worried me. Since she hadn't called me, I was going to assume she was napping—as she should be. Instead, I let Sweetie Pie and Pluto into the front seat of the Roadster.

For the past few months I'd been on Pluto's bad list because I'd been gone a lot, working cases. The dog and cat were often a great help in my detective work, but sometimes they simply couldn't tag along. While Sweetie Pie enjoyed being attended by Deputy DeWayne Dattilo, who adored all of my critters, Pluto was a one-woman kind of cat. And, he was miffed. I could tell by the way he rode with his front paws on the dashboard, ignoring me as much as possible.

"I took you to Millie's for that grilled redfish she made for you," I reminded him. To no avail. Sweetie Pie licked my hand, but Pluto pretended I was not there. I was dead to him—at least until suppertime.

There was no avoiding the prying eyes of neighbors when I pulled into Alala's driveway. Jaytee, Cece's live-in boyfriend, was raking leaves on their front lawn. He was the finest harmonica player I'd ever heard, and he loved my friend. For that I would always love him. But he was as much of a gossip as Cece, and even as I waved brightly to him, I cursed the fact he'd seen me. Trying to hide would be even more impossible.

I knocked on the front door, and was surprised when it pushed open under my knuckles. I didn't even turn the knob. "Alala," I called into the interior of the house. "Are you home?"

There was no answer.

Sweetie Pie brushed past my leg and took off down the hallway of the house, followed by Pluto. The cat flicked his tail at me just once before he made a right into what was likely a bedroom.

"Hey, you two!" I shouted, trying to get them to come back. I wasn't often shy about poking around someone's house without permission, but Alala didn't strike me as the kind of client who would appreciate a trespasser. When the critters didn't return, there was no other option but for me to go after them.

I slipped inside and legged it down the hallway. "Alala!" I called loudly. "Alala, it's Sarah Booth and I'm in your house."

Still only silence. But movement outside one of the windows told me someone was outside. I hurried to the glass and looked out. I caught what might be the movement of a slender person in the wooded yard, but it could also have been only the wind blowing the branches. I stared for a moment, but whatever or whoever I'd glimpsed was gone.

"Damn." I followed the dog and cat into a room so dark that it was like falling into a well. There had to be blackout curtains on the window. I fumbled for a light switch and when the room flooded with light, I took a step back from the mayhem. The room had been tossed. Makeup and jewelry had been knocked from a small vanity onto the floor. One high-heeled shoe, with the heel broken off, was in a corner. The mattress had been pulled from the bed and an armchair had been flipped over and the bottom gutted. Worse yet, there was no sign of Dr. Diakos.

Sweetie Pie sniffed the room, then headed down the hall and into the kitchen where the back door was wide open. She barked twice, looked over her shoulder, and took off. Clearly, I was to follow. Pluto, who could run really fast for a fat cat, shot out after Sweetie Pie, and I was sucking hind tit and running hard to catch up with my animals.

I wasn't sure what had happened at Alala's, but I was positive it wasn't good. Her disappearance alarmed me, and I pulled out my cell phone to call Coleman.

"There's been a break-in at Alala's house. The front and back door are open. She's gone. I don't know if she was taken or if she left on her own." I was panting as I ran and talked.

"You okay?" Coleman's voice held tension.

"I'm following Sweetie Pie and Pluto. We're cutting through the yard and headed east. I don't know if they're on Alala's trail or the trail of an intruder."

"Check in every five minutes."

"Okay." I had to get off the phone and concentrate on

breathing and climbing a fence. Sweetie Pie sailed over it like it was tiny. Pluto leaped to the top and bounded over. I was going to have to climb the vine-covered sucker.

I hauled myself up the fence and finally over, but by the time I hit the ground on the other side, I knew I was too slow. Sweetie Pie was baying like she'd hit a hot trail. I followed her voice through another yard, this one far more manicured and easier going, until I came out on the street half a block from where my dog stood on the sidewalk barking at a fast-disappearing black pickup truck. Pluto was sitting on the sidewalk, grooming his paws.

Once I had Sweetie Pie out of the street and sitting obediently at my side, I called Coleman.

"Sweetie Pie chased someone out into the street. I think they got away in a black pickup."

"Did you get the plates?"

"I wasn't close enough," I said. "I couldn't even tell the model." The black truck against the dark asphalt of the road at such a distance had made that impossible. "I'm not even really sure it's involved in any of this."

"Any sign of Alala?"

"No." I thought for a moment. "But I don't think whoever I was chasing had her. They moved too fast, unencumbered."

"I'm here at her house. Yeah, looks like someone tossed her bedroom looking for something. I'll gather some evidence. We need to alert Alala."

"I don't have a clue where to look for Alala. Not if she's traveling under her own steam and certainly not if she's been . . . abducted. Cece said there was a group like the White Citizens Council rising up to keep women down. She said they were here in Sunflower County. Curtis Miller was a member. They could have taken Alala."

"Mississippi has a long history of dancing with those types of groups," Coleman said. His voice was cold. "They won't last long here in Sunflower County. I won't have that hate here."

Coleman meant what he said, but he was one man in a county of twenty-five thousand. He had two deputies and a lot of willing volunteers if he needed them, but that was hardly enough manpower to keep a determined hate group at bay. Especially if the group had outside funding.

Alala had awakened a very dangerous snake, or at least she'd made me aware of it. Perhaps it had been awake all along and I'd just failed to realize it. The changes sweeping over America and even Mississippi had generated anger and fear, and those emotions always produced a dangerous backlash.

9

I joined Coleman at Alala's house, but there were no new leads as to where she might be. I should have asked her about any friends she'd made in Zinnia, but I hadn't. Now, I didn't even know where to begin looking.

Because I'd been guilty in the past of trying to protect Tinkie by not telling her everything, I called and filled her in. "Do you have any idea where Alala might be?"

"Check the park. The day she hired us, I think she mentioned that she goes for a walk every day. Since you're in town anyway, it shouldn't take long."

It was a great idea. I loaded the dogs and cat into the Roadster and we took off for Zinnia's new park.

I was happy to see the swings and playground equipment alive with laughing children. Mothers or nannies watched over their charges as a breeze sent multicolored leaves tumbling across the grass. A group of toddlers chased the leaves, and I remembered the great pleasure of playing in the grass and dirt as a child. This park would give a lot of children the opportunity to experience the outdoors. Again, I was awed by what Harold had done.

A ball of energy with wiry hair burst out of some shrubs, circled the playing toddlers, and took off down the nature trail. Roscoe! The evil little dog was in play. Obviously, he'd figured a sneaky way out of Harold's house while his master was at work. Now he was on the loose and trouble was sure to follow.

Time for a red alert to Harold. I dialed him at the bank. "Roscoe is in the park. So far, he's just running wild and the children seem to love him. But he could break bad any minute."

"Can you catch him?"

"I'll let Sweetie Pie round him up. He took off down the nature trail. When I get my hands on him, I'll give a call."

I slipped my phone in my pocket and let Sweetie Pie and Pluto out of the car. We took off at a slow jog. Once upon a time I'd run track—in high school—but that was long ago. Now I was a plodder and would soon be a walker. I could rely on Sweetie Pie to lure Roscoe back to me. My sweet hound had a whole lot of sex appeal to one particular demon dog.

The nature trail circled the part of the park that contained the playground, tennis courts, basketball courts, and the dais. It then cut through undeveloped property that wound around some natural lakes, a sweet little stream, and then circled back to the park proper, creating a one-mile loop.

I hadn't had a chance to walk the trail, so I eagerly followed Sweetie Pie, and Pluto followed me. It was a lovely day for a walk, and had I not been concerned for Alala and Roscoe—both of whom seemed far too capable of getting into trouble—it would have been perfect.

I'd only gone a short distance when I heard a dog barking. Roscoe! I recognized his voice. And then there was the bay and yodel of my hound. Beside me, Pluto started to sprint. When Pluto ran, I knew something was afoot. Though I was already winded, I picked up my pace and tried to keep up with my cat. If anyone saw me falling behind Pluto, I would be shamed.

Running deeper into the woods, I heard the dog's barking grow more frantic. Then there was the sound of cursing. I rounded a blind curve and stopped in the path. About two hundred yards in front of me a figure lay on the ground, unmoving. A person wearing a dark hoodie stood over the prone person, holding a bat.

The hooded person drew back to strike the person on the ground, but a brown and white furball flew from the side of the trail and grabbed the person's arm. While I couldn't see the features of either human, I clearly knew Roscoe. I put everything I had into a sprint forward. Roscoe must have gotten a good grip because the attacker screamed and dropped the club. They shook free of Roscoe and took off down the secluded path. Roscoe and Sweetie Pie were hot on the criminal's heels.

I rushed forward to find the professor unconscious on the ground. She was bleeding from a blunt force wound on the side of her head, but she was breathing. I had a decision: pursue the attacker or attend to Alala.

I called 911 for an ambulance as I knelt beside her. I couldn't tell how serious her injuries were and I was afraid to try to move her in case her spine had been damaged. She moaned softly and sat up on her own. When she looked at me she frowned. "Did you hit me?"

"No. Do you know what happened?"

She thought a minute. "Yeah, I remember. It was such a beautiful day, I went for a walk to get my thoughts in order. I find I can think better if I'm moving, and I'd finally decided where to start my book. The perfect opening." She grew more animated as she talked. When she started to her feet, I stopped her.

"An ambulance is on the way. You need to be checked out."

"Absolutely not!" She found her cell phone in her pocket and called 911 to cancel the ambulance.

"That's not a great idea," I said. "You could have a concussion or some kind of neurological damage."

"I'm fine." She held out her hand for me to pull her to her feet and I obliged.

"Did you see the person who struck you?"

She shook her head. "I honestly don't remember what happened. I saw that adorable little dog—the one that was at the park yesterday. Roscoe. He was having a blast and creating all kinds of mayhem."

I'd never heard Roscoe referred to as adorable. Normally he elicited a whole 'nother vocabulary filled with what my aunt Loulane would call "blue" words. "You saw Roscoe? What was he doing?"

"First he was digging all of the dirt out of the sandbox. The children were screaming and crying." She bit her lip to keep from laughing. "It was awful, but it was also funny. It was as if the dog knew what he was doing and he was getting a good laugh out of it." She held up a hand. "I know that sounds like I've slipped a cog, but

I swear. His little face, with that goatee, I saw glee in his eyes."

I didn't think she was bonkers. I knew Roscoe. I'd be willing to put money on the fact that he did that just to hear the children scream.

"Then what happened?"

"He ran away from there and hit the tennis courts. I was afraid he was going to get injured, but he seems impervious to pain. He caught one tennis ball on the fly and took off running. The two players were chasing him and cursing. Then he made it to the splash pad where he put his paw on one of the squirter things and spewed water on two women sitting on a bench. They sounded like they were dying."

Oh, Roscoe had been on a tear. Any minute now Coleman or a dogcatcher would show up to nab him. "It sounds like Roscoe's had a very full day."

"He knew he was in trouble, so he headed for the woods, and I followed. That's when someone came after me, I guess. I didn't see them. I didn't see anything. I just felt a blow, and that was the last thing I remember."

It was rotten luck Alala hadn't caught a glimpse of her assailant, but the good news was that she didn't appear to be seriously hurt. "You're really lucky you didn't scape up your hands or knees or face."

"I must have dropped like a sack of flour. The path is soft dirt, thank goodness. Had it been pavement . . ." She didn't finish the thought.

In the distance I heard the sound of barking and a child screaming. "Roscoe!" I yelled. The little devil had disappeared again. "Alala, why would someone attack you in broad daylight?"

"I don't know."

But she looked away when she answered. I had a strong suspicion she wasn't telling me the truth. "You need to go straight to the courthouse and talk to Sheriff Peters. If you have something others want, you should tell him."

"Now talking to that sheriff, that's a chore I won't mind doing." She smiled. "I heard you two were an item. He's a good-looking man. While I think the male of the species is responsible for a lot of woe and suffering, I can still appreciate a handsome man."

"He is that, and he's a good man."

"So why do I need to talk to the sheriff?" she asked.

"First, someone broke into your house."

"What?" She seemed really surprised. "When? Did they rob me?"

"Your bedroom was tossed. Any idea where that came from?"

Alala shook her head. "No. I don't have a clue. Everything was fine when I decided to come for a walk."

It was only a little too convenient that Alala went for a walk, leaving her house to be rifled. And that she'd been assaulted in the park. There was definitely something she wasn't telling me.

"Why were you at my house?" Alala asked.

"I stopped by to pick you up to take you to the courthouse. The sheriff is aware of the murder of Dr. Loxley in Oxford, and also the man who was killed in Nashville. You were living and working at both places at the time of the murders. All three men were shot in the heart with the same caliber weapon. They were all known abusers."

Alala blew out her breath, but she remained unrattled. "I didn't kill anyone. I shouldn't have to say it, but I didn't. Just because I speak out against men who violate women doesn't mean I would kill them."

I was glad to hear that. "You do more than speak out. You say things like abusers should be killed."

"It's true, but I'm not telling anyone to do it. And I certainly wouldn't go on a streak of vengeance. Let me make it clear. If I saw a man hitting or intimidating someone and had a chance, I would stop them. With whatever it took. But I wouldn't plot to murder someone."

"Alala, don't say that. You really are a suspect. There's no point digging yourself into a deeper hole."

"Historically, women have been beaten and murdered by the very men who are supposed to love them. They've been sexually assaulted by men who hold the power of a job over them. When a woman fears for her life, she has a right to defend herself."

"I don't want to argue with you, especially about this, because I agree with you. But I also don't want to see you cooling your heels in a jail cell because you couldn't keep your piehole shut. When you talk to Coleman, tell him whatever it is you're not telling me about these personal attacks. I'd call him myself, but whoever hit you is long gone."

"Did you get a good look?"

I shook my head. "I was too far away. Just a medium-sized person in a hoodie. They could run fast."

Her shoulders drooped a little. "Look, I'm not really hurt. Whoever attacked me, it could have been random. I'll tell the sheriff the truth. I promise."

Frankly, I was shocked. I couldn't believe she was going to listen to me. "We'll stop by your house on the way to the sheriff's office. I also need to catch Roscoe and take him home. His little crime spree is going to get him put in the pound . . . again."

"He's a great little dog," Alala said. "He has such a . . . sense of humor."

"True. But not everyone finds him amusing."

"Perhaps he can come stay with me during the day while his owner is at work. I'd like that, and I could keep an eye on him. I really mean it. I'd love to babysit."

It sounded like a pretty good solution to me. I managed to get my pets and Roscoe into the backseat, and Alala in the front. We had places to go and people to see.

10

On the way to Alala's, I called Tinkie. Though she fussed at me for not calling her sooner, she sounded a little relieved. She agreed to meet me at the courthouse. I told her to take her time because I had to stop by Alala's house. In the background, I could hear hammering and the plaintive cries of Gumbo, the cat she'd adopted from Columbus, Mississippi, on our last case. Gumbo had belonged to a woman currently caught in the judicial system. Though I'd volunteered to give the kitty a good home, Tinkie had fallen in love with the little calico. Now she was Tinkie and Oscar's feline, a companion for Chablis.

Roscoe, thirty pounds of sheer determination to get what he wanted, balanced on the console between the front seats. Occasionally he would lean toward me and give that strange little *huuh, huuh, huuh* wheezy bark that sounded way too much like the laughter of a cartoon dog named Mutley. Roscoe was too smart for his own good, and I sincerely believed he enjoyed the mayhem he created.

I decided to take Roscoe home first, since I didn't trust him to remain in the car with Sweetie Pie and Pluto. Roscoe did whatever he wanted whenever he wanted to. He could be a bad influence on Sweetie Pie. Pluto was already just like Roscoe, so no danger of contamination there.

I pulled in down the long drive bordered by live oaks that were laced with twinkling lights. On the evenings when Harold was hosting a party, which happened fairly often, this driveway was a magical alleyway to elegant entertainment. Harold was the best party host in the Delta, and now he often hired Millie and her crew from the café to cater his events. A win-win for all the attendees.

Sure enough, when I arrived at Harold's place I saw that the screened door had been mostly destroyed. Roscoe's escape from house arrest had done little other damage that I could see, and the screen was an easy enough fix. I'd had visions of the little demon chewing through a wall or something. He was capable of it.

I picked him up and carried him into the house, wondering where I could put him that would be safe and secure. My problem was solved when I saw a big, roomy kennel complete with a cushy bed, toys, water, and dry food.

"Bad dogs go to Heaven," I told him as I put him inside and quickly latched the door. "They also go to jail. Roscoe, someone is going to shoot you or poison you."

He gave me a series of wheezing grunts, as if he were explaining his conduct. I could imagine what he was saying, "Piss off, Sarah Booth. I was having a blast and here you come along, the fun police."

"Roscoe, it would kill Harold if you were injured."

"Me, injured? You're deluding yourself. I can take care of myself."

"Roscoe, do you have demon blood? Because you sure act like Hell just spat you out."

"I'm just a dog, Sarah Booth. And dogs just wanna have fun."

"Sarah Booth." Alala touched my shoulder. She'd quietly come inside. "Are you okay?"

No, I was mortified that she'd overheard my fantasy dialogue with Roscoe. I felt like a silly child caught in a stupor, and I rubbed at my mouth to be sure I wasn't drooling. "I'm fine. I was just thinking. Let's get over to your house and try to catch Coleman there." Perhaps if we showed up at the scene of the break-in, he wouldn't have to take Alala down to the sheriff's office.

Ten minutes later, I parked in front of Alala's house, glad to see Coleman and his crew were still there. We went inside and Alala assessed the damage to her bedroom. She seemed to take it mostly in stride, though I could see she was angered by the destruction of her room. "My jewelry wasn't expensive, but some of it came from family members and was of sentimental value to me." She picked up a bracelet from the floor and put it on top of the vanity. "Who would do this?"

"Do you have any idea what the intruder was looking for?" Coleman asked her.

"No, as I said, I don't have any true valuables. Some things of sentimental value, but not monetary."

"And the man who attacked you on the nature trail?"

"I'm not even certain it was a man," she said. "I didn't see them at all. Sarah Booth saw someone in a hoodie. I was taken completely by surprise."

I'd already reported the incident, so I kept silent.

"Dr. Diakos, you appear to be in the center of a lot of death and mayhem."

"Are you accusing me of—"

"I'm not accusing you of anything. But in the last three places you've lived, men you knew have been murdered. That's a lot of coincidence."

"Perhaps someone is trying to frame me." Alala held her shoulders back and her head high.

"Perhaps they are," Coleman said. "But you need to give us some help. Who would want to frame you? Why? What ties a dead man in Nashville, who also happens to be a university professor, to a dead professor in Oxford, and now a dead man in Zinnia? So far, you're the only link I have."

"I'm innocent of all wrongdoing."

"Then help me. Who would want to harm you? Who would break into your house?"

"I'm the only person who lives here and I have little of value. As you can see, I was away from the house and was even injured." Alala rubbed her scalp gently. "I don't have a clue who's out to get me, but someone is."

Sweetie Pie had disobeyed my order and trotted into the bedroom, snooping and sniffing. She edged over to Alala and nudged her.

"What is she doing?" Alala asked.

I didn't really know. Sweetie Pie always had an opinion, but I couldn't tell what she was expressing—or wanting Alala to do. Sweetie Pie used her snout to nudge

Alala in the thigh. Then she went to the doorway and howled again before she disappeared down the hall.

"She wants you to follow her," I said. I'd seen this behavior before, but never with a stranger.

Alala walked out the doorway and down the hall, following where Sweetie Pie led. I was hot on their heels and Coleman was right behind me. He had a healthy respect for Sweetie Pie's talents.

My pup went out the back door, where Pluto, who'd also disobeyed and left the car, was waiting for us. Sweetie Pie sat beside Pluto, barked, and looked up at us.

"What's wrong?" Alala asked. "Timmy in the well?"

"I wouldn't mock Sweetie Pie Delaney. That dog has a lot of common sense." Tinkie had arrived on the scene—Budgie had told her where I was—and she was all about defending my hound.

"Apologies to the dog," Alala said. "I wasn't mocking her. Not really."

Coleman went to the dog and cat and then stopped. "Sarah Booth, would you get the evidence kit from the bedroom? This looks like a footprint. I need to make a cast."

I stepped closer. It was a footprint. With a rather small, distinct tread. "Alala, do you have shoes that would leave this kind of pattern in the dirt?"

She took a look and shook her head. "I don't wear sneakers. Too tacky for words."

"The kit," Coleman reminded me.

He normally didn't ask me to run errands if he had DeWayne or Budgie, but I knew he wanted to protect the print. He didn't trust Alala. I quickly retrieved his gear and watched as he made a mold. "This could help us find the person who broke into your house."

"Is it a woman?" Alala asked. "That's a pretty small print for a man."

"Size eight, double AA," Tinkie said. "I'm an expert on shoes. I'd say they are possibly Merrells or a shoe like that with a good arch support." She shrugged. "I've had to research arch supports since I weigh as much as Jumbo the baby elephant now. My arches are falling."

"A high instep isn't everything. You still have your brain. And everyone said the baby would hinder your investigative abilities," I teased her. "They were wrong."

While the mold was setting, Coleman stood and faced Alala. "Do you know any women who would break in and go through your things?"

To my surprise, Alala avoided the question by turning away. A few possibilities raced through my mind—a lover, the wife of a lover, a best friend betrayed, another academic who had a score to settle. Even as I came up with a host of ideas, she said nothing.

"Dr. Diakos, you need to answer," Coleman said with just enough force to make it clear he expected a response. "I'll find the truth eventually."

"It could be Margaret McNeese."

"And who is this McNeese person?" Coleman asked patiently, but I heard the edge of annoyance in his voice.

"She's a graduate student at Ole Miss. The dead professor there, Loxley, she was his grad assistant. He abused her." I supplied the details because Alala was getting a stubborn look on her face.

"And why would she be interested in wrecking your bedroom?" Coleman continued. It was fun to let him do all the heavy lifting, while Tinkie and I could just reap the benefits.

Finally, Alala looked up and met Coleman's direct gaze. "I wrote an article for the campus newspaper about professorial abuse of students. The woman I portrayed in the article was an amalgamation of many campus incidents—and I said that clearly. But a lot of folks instantly assumed it was Margaret." She shrugged one shoulder. "I told her it wasn't personal or intentional, but she was really mad. Margaret is a health nut. She's always running around in yoga pants and sneakers. She might have come here for some revenge."

I thought of the jogger Tansy had claimed to see the night Curtis was killed—and the movement outside Alala's window earlier.

"You mentioned someone else who was also harassed," Tinkie prompted.

"It couldn't be her," Alala said. "Becky Brown is big. She wears an eleven shoe, if not bigger. I doubt she'd be running all over Zinnia, breaking into my house."

"And I presume Margaret McNeese would wear something like a size eight shoe?" Coleman said with a tone that told me he wasn't buying any of this shoe size business.

"Correct. She's more my size," Alala said. "And as I mentioned, she's into fitness. Runs around in those awful lace-up exercise shoes all the time. I'm not a fashionista, but that kind of shoe is just ugly."

"I thought you didn't pander to patriarchal expectations!" Tinkie was all over it. She loathed a hypocrite.

"That's not pandering. That's just stating a fact. Right, Sheriff?"

Coleman was too smart to be dragged into this conversation. "When you wrote the article for the campus publication, did you call out Dr. Loxley?"

"No, but I made it pointedly clear that was who I was talking about."

"And what was your relationship with Loxley?" Coleman asked.

"We all knew one another. The humanities are like the stepchild of any university. We're not practical like business or engineering. We don't attract big grants or have rich and famous alumni. The only thing we do is teach students to think, to feel, to use their brains and emotions to draw conclusions. We often socialized together. All of the Humanities faculty knew each other."

I saw where Coleman was going, and I was curious. If this Margaret was here, spying on Alala, there could be two interpretations: either Margaret wanted to prove Alala was guilty of killing Loxley, for whatever reason, and therefore Curtis Miller, or Margaret was the killer and had possibly come to find or possibly plant evidence to use to frame Alala.

"This person who hit you on the head. Could Margaret have done that?" Coleman asked Alala.

"She's tall and strong enough. But why? And how would she know I'd decided to go to the park for a walk?"

"Good questions," Coleman said. "When I have the answers, I'll be able to see how your intruder, if it is Margaret McNeese, fits into the picture."

"I would say it's more likely to be Tansy Miller," Alala said. "She was really angry even though ultimately I'm trying to help women like her who are in bad situations."

"Unappreciative," I agreed. Tansy was ready to beat up everyone who tried to interfere in her life, even if they were trying to help. "But she's not the person I saw in the park. Your attacker was bigger than Tansy."

"You'd think a victim of domestic violence would revel

in her freedom from that abusive man," Alala said. "I mean, no messy divorce. No airing dirty laundry. No threats and intimidation. No splitting the assets. Just bam, she's free."

I signaled to her to shut up. She was talking to the sheriff, not a faculty gathering.

She ignored me completely and kept talking. "You would think she might offer a reward for getting that lout out of her life."

Tinkie finally grabbed Alala's arm and twisted it. "Shut up," she whispered fiercely.

"Oh, let her talk," Coleman said. "In fact, Dr. Diakos, I need you to come with me to the courthouse. I want to take a statement from you."

"Can't we do it here?" she asked.

"No, I'm afraid not."

"I'm on a schedule for writing my book. It's my writing time. I really can't go anywhere."

"I'm sorry."

Coleman could say he was sorry all day long but the glint in his blue eyes told me otherwise. "Alala, it would be best to go with Coleman and get this behind you," I said.

"I didn't kill Curtis Miller. That's all I can tell you about what happened to that . . . man. I have bigger fish to fry—like writing my book. Which this is completely interrupting. My muse is here and I need to listen to her."

"It won't take long," Coleman said. He packed up his evidence kit, got his mold, and started to escort Alala to his patrol car, but she balked and pulled free of his hand. He gave me a meaningful look. "Maybe you should talk to your client," he said.

"Bay-ou-ou." Sweetie Pie let out a yowl I'd never heard

in the past. Everyone turned to look at her. Pluto brushed up against the dog and then came to rub against my legs. The critters were acting weird.

"Alala, it would be best if you went with Coleman."

"Best would be if I went to my desk and started on my book."

"Bay-ou-ou," Sweetie Pie trumpeted again, only this time she gently took my hand in her mouth and tugged.

"What's going on?" Tinkie asked. She held Chablis in her arms, but the little Yorkie jumped to the ground, took off, and disappeared under a huge, leafy shrub. Sweetie Pie was right behind her, and Pluto flanked them on the left.

Out of curiosity, I eased to my knees and crawled under the bush just as Chablis threw dirt in my face. By the time I brushed it out of my eyes, she was barking excitedly.

"What's down there?" Tinkie asked.

I drew in a deep breath. "It's a gun—a .38. Chablis has dug up a gun."

"Don't touch it," Coleman said. "In fact, it would be best if you and the pets cleared out of there."

I did as he requested and Coleman stooped down and reached under the shrub. In a moment he stood up, the gun held with an evidence glove. "You're right, it's a .38," he said. "The type of gun that's killed three people."

"That's not my gun," Alala said. She looked from Coleman to me to Tinkie. "You believe me, don't you?"

"You have to come with me." Coleman gripped her arm. "I can put handcuffs on if necessary, but I hope I don't have to do that."

"No, I'll go with you." For the first time Alala looked

worried. Really worried. "I don't know who put that gun there, but it isn't mine."

"We'll check on you," Tinkie said to Alala as Coleman led her away. "And we'll lock up," she called to their retreating backs. "Do you think he's going to arrest her?" Tinkie asked.

"No. Not that she doesn't deserve it. There's evidence someone else has been on her property. The wrecked house, the shoe print. I don't think he'll charge her. Not yet. If she keeps blathering about how Curtis needed to die, she's going to end up on death row in the Central Mississippi Correctional Facility, but Coleman isn't going to arrest her today."

Tinkie and I whistled up the dogs—Chablis had joined Sweetie Pie outside—and we found Pluto nodding off under a beautiful Chinese fringe bush. It was time to go.

"Should we go back to Dahlia House to work on those women Alala mentioned?" Tinkie asked.

"You have dinner with Oscar. I'm going to start dinner for Coleman." I held up a hand to stop her gleeful cackle. "I'm cooking chicken and dumplings and I can cook that. Absolutely. So no wise comments about my food. While I'm cooking, I'll check around a little on Alala Diakos. There is something off about our client."

"I second that," Tinkie said, rubbing her lower back. "Call me if you find anything."

11

With Sweetie Pie and Pluto on my heels, I rushed up the steps to Dahlia House.

I'd barely cleared the threshold before stopping dead in my tracks. Someone had changed the front parlor into a saloon and gambling den. A beautiful woman in a green antebellum gown sat at the front table, shuffling a deck of cards.

"Take your chances on a game of twenty-one?" she asked.

She was very pretty, with the accent of a Southern belle.

"Who are you?" I knew it was Jitty, but aside from that.

"Some call me Madam Vestal," she said, leaning forward to lay out the cards and reveal her décolletage.

"This is my gambling house and I can promise you a fair game of chance."

My ambition was a bathroom and a cup of coffee, in that order, but I paused. Jitty was great with veiled messages and I'd learned it was worth my time and effort to pay attention. Was I gambling with my future? What was she trying to convey? Jitty did love her puzzles. "Do you have a given name?"

"I was once known as Belle Siddons, back in the day when my rich daddy tried to protect me by marrying me off to a nearby plantation owner. I should say Daddy had a fervid wish to control me. We had our own plantation, plenty of land. I was provided with a very nice dowry." She cut me a sly look. "Too bad I had a taste for adventure. That wasn't allowed for a woman. No"— she shook her head—"a woman was supposed to stay at home, raise the children, keep the old mansion filled with graciousness and charm. A rather tedious life, if you see my point. Though, trust me, that was a gilded cage compared to those forced to work the fields. Tedium wasn't a luxury they were allowed to experience."

Now, I was interested. Belle had rejected the traditional female role, and at a time when such behavior wasn't allowed, particularly in the South. "What happened, Belle?"

"I found a cause. The Confederacy. I thought Daddy would approve, but he didn't. I was caught as a spy and did time in prison. That was the end of Big Daddy's protection. I was wayward, disobedient. No good."

I'd read about the conditions of the prisons during the Civil War. Hellholes. I'd honestly not been aware that the Confederacy had used female spies, but there was a hint of real beauty in Belle Siddons, and dressed up in that gown, with her laced-in waist and pushed-up breasts, I could see that she was a fetching illusion. Many a Union soldier would have given away state secrets if he could whisper them in her ear. "What happened after you got out of prison?"

"I followed the gold rush and created"—she waved a hand around the saloon that had suddenly appeared in my parlor—"my own gaming establishment. I have a talent for twenty-one and a way with entertaining men."

"The house always wins." I wasn't much of a gambler but I knew a few witty sayings. "You must have cleaned up."

"Times were hard, but if someone panned some gold nuggets, the cash did flow at the gaming table. The money, the laughs, the whiskey." She chuckled softly, but there was a sad note in it. "I had a good life, until Cupid's arrow struck hard and true. Met me a man named Archie McLaughlin. He was something else. I fell in love with a stagecoach robber." She slipped beneath the tide of her memories for a moment. "I discovered my spying abilities were useful in that business, too. I was skilled at gathering information from the stagecoach drivers to tell my man, Archie, so he could time his robberies." True sadness moved across her face and she began to age. The hard lines and deep sorrow came over her so swiftly it looked as if her features were crumbling.

"What happened?"

"I made a mistake. I mentioned a robbery was going to happen to the wrong person, a man who betrayed me. He told the law about the robbery. Archie was caught and hanged."

The demons she carried were worse than any punishment the law could ever inflict on her. "I'm so sorry." And I was.

"Guilt will do terrible things to you." She looked away and swallowed.

Okay, she was an accessory to robbery, a woman who used her wiles to weasel information out of men. She'd used her beauty and charm for nefarious purposes. But she'd suffered. It was plain to read upon her face. And I liked her. "Everyone makes mistakes." There wasn't much else I could say.

"For a time I had the best life could offer. Archie and I lived high on the hog. When we were flush . . . I loved that man. And then one night, I drank too much and talked too much. I ended up in Hell."

She turned and headed for the door. Music from a player piano rolled over the room in a tinkling of the ivories and then Jitty/Belle was gone. The saloon vanished and the old parlor was back with the horsehair sofa, the bar on the sideboard, the fireplace, and a window that overlooked the pasture where my horses grazed.

I hurried upstairs to my bathroom while I considered my next move. Belle Siddon's visit had left me unsettled, anxious. I didn't want to do it, but I had to call Tinkie. She would be rightfully furious if I didn't tell her I was headed to Ole Miss. I knew she was tired, and I wanted to spare her. I punched in her number. To my relief, Oscar answered.

"Sarah Booth, Tinkie is asleep. I'm not going to wake her. She's exhausted."

"Good." I could be honest with Oscar. "I'm going to Ole Miss to look up a potential suspect or two, a teacher and a grad student. Would you let Tinkie know when she wakes up?"

"Sure."

"Do tell her I called. I don't want her to think I'm pampering her because she's pregnant, but she does need to rest."

"So you want her to be angry with me instead of you?" He was only halfway kidding.

"I'm sure you can distract her enough to keep her from being too angry." Oscar and Tinkie loved each other. She was a little fractious about her independence. She'd had to fight hard against the social mores of her world because of the way she'd been raised. She didn't want any man telling her what she could and couldn't do, and Oscar was pretty good at playing those cards to win. "Rub her feet when you tell her. She loves that. But be sure and tell her they look smaller."

He laughed. "I found her in the closet the other day sitting on the floor and just staring at all the boxes of shoes she said she can't wear anymore."

"Once she has the baby, her feet will go back to normal." I had no idea what I was talking about, but it sounded like something Tinkie would want to hear. When a woman was less than two weeks from delivery, little white lies were balm for the soul.

Sweetie Pie and Pluto, sensing I was headed out, were on the front porch waiting. The minute I closed the front door, they tore across the porch and jumped into the Roadster. If I ever had to trade that car for one that wasn't a convertible, it was really going to cramp their style.

It was a bit of a drive to Ole Miss, but I could make

it before five o'clock, when offices officially closed. And I didn't want to wait another day. If Margaret McNeese was the person who'd broken into Alala's house and then attacked her, I wanted to catch up with her while the deed was still fresh in her mind. And I wanted to find out who'd planted a .38 on my client—if indeed that was the case.

I churned along Highway 8 to Oxford, Mississippi, with mixed feelings. I missed my college days, when life was just one endless possibility—ahead of me—not behind me. I was at an age now where every decision I made permanently closed a door. Tinkie's impending motherhood put that question squarely in front of me. We were both thirty-four. Even though I'd never give Jitty the satisfaction of admitting it, my biological clock was definitely ticking. For one brief moment I allowed myself to think of the miscarriage I'd had when I'd first come home. I hadn't known I was pregnant until I wasn't.

I loved Coleman, and he would make an exceptional father. It didn't take much imagination to slide into a daydream where Coleman and I sat on the front porch watching two children, a boy and a girl, playing badminton in the front yard. The little girl looked just like my mother. The boy was the spitting image of Coleman.

I shook off the fantasy as I hit the city limits of Oxford. The problem with my little daydream was that I wasn't sure I wanted that life. I wasn't sure I could live through it if I had a child and something tragic happened. I wasn't sure I would want to. I wasn't sure I could devote myself completely to the needs of a baby. And I wasn't certain, with the chemicals polluting the planet, that it was fair to bring a child into such a mess of a world. I wasn't sure how Coleman felt about the idea of reproducing. The bottom line—I wasn't sure.

The only thing I was sure of was that Jitty would skin me alive if I didn't hatch out a little Delaney. But I'd cross that bridge when I had to.

12

I pulled into town. Oxford and the university had spread and grown since my college days, but it was easy enough to find the humanities building on campus where I hoped Margaret McNeese still worked as a graduate assistant. I also wanted to look up Dr. Brown. It wouldn't hurt to put a few questions to her, maybe gig her into saying or doing something that would indicate her guilt. I felt the attack on Alala was more likely to have been committed by a woman. Alala wasn't struck hard enough to hurt her badly, and the way her house had been wrecked seemed more petty than intent on real destruction. Plus, the footprint outside Alala's back door seemed to be a woman's. I was hedging a bet that I would find the culprit in the Ole Miss English department.

I hated to leave Sweetie Pie and Pluto in the car, but
the day was cool and crisp, weather-wise. They wouldn't
get overheated, and I doubted they'd be welcome in the
university building. I pulled a dog bone and a catnip
mouse from the glove box and told them to entertain
themselves. I figured this shouldn't take me more than
half an hour. It was getting close to five o'clock and soon
the offices would be empty. Sweetie Pie, Pluto, and I
could take a stroll around the campus once I was done
with my work.

The secretary directed me to Dr. Brown's office. It
seemed that since Dr. Loxley's death, graduate assistant
McNeese had been assigned to Becky Brown. Interesting. Two women who might have a reason to have it in
for Alala. And possibly for Dr. Loxley.

Brown's office was down a warren of hallways built
for efficiency, not aesthetics. It was rather like entering a
poor tenement building. I found the room and knocked
on the door. There was the clatter of furniture and the
door pulled open on the force of a hurricane.

I stepped back before I could stop myself. Becky Brown
was at least five feet ten inches tall and looked like a
cornstalk. Or a number 2 pencil with a greasy fringe of
bleached blond hair. I couldn't stop myself from looking
down at her feet, which were indeed clodhoppers.

"What?" she demanded.

She had an accent, but I couldn't place it. Not yet.

"May I have a word?" I held out a business card.

She took it and read it. "Private investigator?" She was
intrigued. "What are you investigating?"

"The murder of Dr. Loxley."

"The cops never charged anyone. They let the murderer leave town. What do you think you can do?"

"Find the truth. That's what I'm paid to do." I had her accent now. Well-bred Memphis. Someone in her family tree had taught her to speak like a lady.

"Oh, yeah?"

Footsteps headed toward us down the side hallways and she grabbed my shoulder and jerked me inside. "You have to be quiet." She closed the door and locked it. When the footsteps stopped outside and a fist knocked at the door, she put her finger to her lips. "Don't say a word."

"Who are you hiding from?" I asked.

"These students. They'll suck you dry. Just because you get a crap salary to teach them, they think you owe them every second of every day." She checked her watch. "I'm out of here in five minutes and I don't want to listen to some student whine about a grade for the next half hour. Just be quiet."

While she'd been taught gracious phrasing, she'd missed the rest of the doctrine on being a gracious person.

Someone banged on the door. "Dr. Brown, I know you're in there. The secretary said you were. You weren't in class today and I need to talk to you now." The student, an irate young woman, pounded on the door. "Open up. I'm going to write a letter to the dean about you."

"I'd be worried if she were literate enough to write a letter," Becky Brown said, rolling her eyes. "Not much of a threat coming from someone who can't string together a complete sentence. Her letter would make my case for flunking her."

This was not the relationship I'd had with my college professors. I'd really liked and respected my teachers. Had times changed that much? I felt suddenly very old. "Hiding from her isn't going to solve the problem."

Brown flung herself into her chair. "No, but it'll delay it for a while. I just need ten more minutes and a clear path from here to my truck. Then I'm gone. Disaster prevented for another day."

"You give the grade. You have all the power. Just tell her. What's the worst that can happen?"

"Oh, car tires slashed, house spray-painted, being accosted in the parking lot by an irate boyfriend. A lot could happen."

Times really had changed. If students had attempted physical assault on professors back when I was in college, they would have been immediately expelled, if not arrested and jailed. "Have those things happened to you?" I asked.

"The car tires, yes. But the ante has been upped. As you know, one of my colleagues was murdered last year. Shot through the heart. If it wasn't Alala who did it, then I'm guessing it was a student enraged over a grade."

I couldn't have asked for a better segue. "How well did you know Dr. Loxley?" I wasn't sure if she was friend or foe of the dead professor.

"He was a brilliant man. Absolutely brilliant. His interpretation of *Beowulf*." She closed her eyes. "Oh, it just sends chills all over me. Masterful."

"Dr. Brown!" I called her out of her literary fantasy before she embarrassed herself. "Who killed Dr. Loxley? You said the killer had left town."

She opened her eyes and frowned. "The police never arrested anyone, but they couldn't investigate their way out of a paper bag. Everyone on the faculty knew that crazy Greek bit—woman did it. She hated Loxley and everything he stood for. She tried to get him fired for diddling some of the students, but what she couldn't grasp was that the students enjoyed their relationship with Loxley."

"I don't think it was the diddling. I think it was the slapping, punching, et cetera, that she objected to."

"And she never proved a single charge against him. Sour grapes. Professional jealousy. If she had proof, she would have shown it."

"The students wouldn't come forward and confirm Dr. Diakos's accusations about Loxley. Do you believe he was physically assaulting them?"

"In a nutshell," Brown said, "Diakos accused Loxley of predatory and violent behavior toward a graduate student, but when Loxley was brought up before the dean, the student refused to say he'd done anything wrong. That really pissed Alala off. She looked like a fool and everyone on the faculty knew it. Her days were already numbered here, so they figured a way to let her work out her contract. The dean and administration, because she was a visiting professor with all of her fine credentials, just swept the whole thing under the rug. Loxley got shot and she got a year off with pay to write a book. It's just not fair."

Oh, I could see that Becky Brown would never think life was fair, no matter what happened to her. "Do you really think petite Dr. Diakos killed another professor?"

"Petite doesn't have anything to do with it. She had a gun. That kind of equalizes the size issue, don't you think?"

She had a good point, but I wasn't done. "The police investigated but they never charged Alala with anything." I saw the mistake I'd made the moment the words were out

of my mouth. I'd referred to Alala by her given name—
and that implied a relationship. Becky Brown was not
dumb. She caught it also.

"Are you friends with Alala Diakos? You're on a first-
name basis?"

"She's my client." Lying now wouldn't be helpful at all,
especially since I'd given her a business card for Delaney
Detective Agency, had she bothered to look at it.

"And she hired an investigator why? She got away with
Loxley's murder here. Why are you poking into the past
and stirring things up?"

"There's been another murder in Zinnia. A man, a
known abuser, was shot in the heart." I watched her
closely.

It was like sunshine spreading over her face. "Well, I'll
be damned. She got away with it once and decided to try
it again. I thought she was smarter than that."

"You really believe she killed Loxley and now another
man?"

"Here's what's really tragic about all of this," Brown
said. "Loxley, as brilliant as he was, was not a nice man.
He was a serial cheater. But what Alala failed to understand was that some women like to be manhandled. It's
a turn-on for them. She could never grasp that."

Nor could I, but Tansy Miller was evidence of that
mind-set. Defending or excoriating Loxley was of no importance to me. "When was the last time you were in
Zinnia, Mississippi?"

"Why would I go to Zinnia?"

"Maybe to see Dr. Diakos." Maybe to plant a gun on
her property. I didn't say it but I was sure thinking it.

Dr. Brown shook her head in disdain. "I was in Sunflower County yesterday. I own some property there.

Outside of town. And you have no right to question my comings and goings."

I ignored her complaint. "You own a house?"

"No, not a house. Rural property. I drove over to see if the road needed any attention before cold weather sets in."

"Did you stop by Dr. Diakos's house?"

"Why would I do that?"

"Did you?" I was tired of her dodging.

"Alala Diakos wouldn't invite me in if I did stop, and I had other fish to fry. I have no idea where she lives."

She wasn't going to give me a straight answer and I couldn't compel her. Perhaps Coleman would have to haul her in. I changed directions. "I'm looking for Margaret McNeese."

"Join the club. I don't know where that little twit went. I've been looking for her for the past four hours."

"Why are you looking for her?"

"She's *my* GA now. You know, graduate assistant. When Loxley died, I inherited her. A shame, really. I don't like her. She doesn't like me. We have, at best, an armed détente. But I do expect her to show up for work, which she hasn't today."

"Has the secretary checked on her?"

She shrugged. "How should I know? It's not my place to track down employees who don't show up when they're supposed to. I'll just let payroll know to dock her."

Great. "Dr. Brown, where do you think McNeese could be?"

She turned her head and gave me a slanted look that could liquefy nails. "If she's not here at work, she should be at home." She pulled out her phone and called. In a moment, when a machine answered, she said, "Margaret, this is your boss. Call me the instant you get this. No excuses. A man is dead."

Well, that ought to do it. Or make her run for a country without extradition.

"How long has Ms. McNeese not been at work?" I asked.

"Oh"—she waved a hand—"two days? I'm not certain."

"She works for you, right?"

"Have you ever had to work with a GA? No, obviously. She's *paid* to work, but that guarantees nothing. And she's so unpleasant, it just wasn't worth the effort to look for her."

"Tell me about this GA. What does she do? What's her literary interest?"

Brown frowned. "She's smart enough. Not brilliant, but smart enough. If she applied herself she could do well in the field of literature. Her area of interest is contemporary fiction. Faulkner, Hemingway—the testosterone writers." She made a face.

"Those men gained fame in the 1940s and '50s. I thought you said contemporary?"

"Literature is always behind the times. Deal with it."

I wasn't really after academic reading recommendations, so I moved on. "What about her personal life?"

"Is that a joke? GAs don't get to have a personal life. They need to devote their time to research, writing, helping the professors they're assigned to. These students today think there should be time for cooking and dancing and dating. No. That's not what graduate school is all about. It's about nose to the grindstone until graduation. There's no room for messing about if you want to get into a good doctoral program."

Good thing I'd never had a yen to go for an advanced degree. "But didn't she date Dr. Loxley?"

Brown's face froze, and I thought of one of the Furies, the dangerous entities that haunted and hounded mankind in ancient Greek mythology. Alala Diakos and her warlike name had me in a mythological frame of mind. "She *wanted* to date Alex, but he wasn't interested." It was clear Brown still had an emotional attachment to Loxley, even though he was dead.

"That's not the story I heard. In fact, I heard he had a sexual relationship with her and physically assaulted her."

"She made that story up and, like I said when she had a chance to tell the dean her complaint, she denied anything untoward had ever happened."

"And you're sure of that?" I asked.

"Alex could be . . . forceful, but he didn't . . ." She faded to a stop. "You need to get out of my office. I don't have to talk to you." That was, unfortunately, a true fact.

"Can you give me McNeese's contact information?"

"No. It's against the university rules to give out personal information on a student."

"Okay, would you call her and leave my phone number so she can call me back?"

"Why do you want to talk to her?"

"Someone shot Loxley. Someone shot Curtis Miller in Zinnia." I watched her closely for a reaction, but failed to see one. "I think the same someone killed both men." I saw no reason to tell her about the Nashville murder.

"Well, that has nothing to do with me."

I didn't believe her for an instant. About anything. Everyone in Zinnia knew where Alala lived. That was just part of small-town life. Brown could have been the person who wrecked Alala's bedroom, except her boda-cious feet didn't match the print at the back door. And there were no other prints around the planted gun—which only meant that someone had been careful. Brown could also have been the person who attacked Alala in the park. But why?

"I've asked you to leave. So vamoose." She waved her fingers at me like I was a pesky fly.

"Thanks." I stood up and went to the door, then turned. "Someone broke into Alala's house and attacked her. That someone was looking for something. I won-der what it might be. What could Dr. Diakos have that would incite someone to break and enter and attack her?" I grinned. "I don't know today, but I'll find out. Oh, and Dr. Brown, don't be surprised if Sheriff Coleman Peters shows up one day this week to talk to you. He has a lot of questions."

"Get out!" She was furious now.

I wasn't done with Becky Brown. Not by a long shot, but for now, it was time to leave. Besides, I'd heard faint footsteps outside the door. I opened it wide and stepped into the narrow hallway where a glowering student leaned against the wall.

"She in there?" She jerked a thumb at the office.

"Yes, she is." I smiled and left the door open as I made my exit.

13

Sweetie Pie and Pluto were huge hits at the beautiful fountain that provided a perfect fall gathering place for Ole Miss students. My college friends and I had made wishes and tossed coins into this fountain when we believed our potential was endless. When I walked over and looked down, coins winked back at me in the sunlight. Wishing rituals spanned generations.

I'd promised my pets a walk around campus, and this was a great place to begin—right after I watched for Dr. Brown to exit the English department and go to her vehicle. She'd said she drove a truck. I gave it eighty/twenty odds that the truck would be black.

I'd barely planted my butt on the side of the fountain when I saw Dr. Brown coming out of the English department. She made a beeline for the faculty parking lot, and I shifted my location so I could watch her closely. She went straight to a black truck, got in, and drove away. Now I had no doubt that Dr. Brown had broken into Alala's house. She could have planted the gun, or she could have driven an accomplice to do so. A smaller person who would have left a smaller footprint. As I watched her leave the lot in her truck, I knew it was the vehicle I'd seen racing down the street away from the Greek professor's home. What had she been looking for? Was it merely to plant evidence against Alala? Or was my client hiding something from me? Something that people were willing to break the law to get their hands on.

Delighted squeals interrupted my thoughts. Sweetie Pie launched herself into the fountain, and a cluster of young women rushed to ooh and aah over the hound and Pluto, who pretended to disdain any public display of attention seeking. I looked at the assortment of students in jeans, shorts, and skirts. The different academic pursuits of students had been a little more regimented—and easy to spot—when I went to college. Business majors had to at least wear khakis and polos and sorority girls wore summer skimmers. The theater group I hung with was all about jeans, tie-dyed shirts, cotton sarongs, and long hair. In other words, we had been throwbacks to the 1970s. Looking around me at the students enjoying the sun and the fountain, I knew without a doubt I was in a liberal arts conclave.

Sweetie Pie leaped from the fountain and shook, sending four girls screaming with horror and delight. As soon as she stopped shaking, they rushed forward to pet her.

Pluto watched them with disbelief. He had a low opinion of humans and it had just dropped another notch.

The young women, when they realized the dog was mine, had a dozen questions about Sweetie Pie, which I answered as they petted and pampered her. One quieter student with long, dark hair took a seat beside Pluto and began to stroke him. He purred and climbed onto her lap.

"Let me guess," I said to her, "you're studying literature."

Her smile was slow, thoughtful. "How can you tell? Are you a psychic?"

"Nope. You've got that bookworm vibe, and I mean that in a positive way."

"Maybe I'm into math. Math majors look a little wormy, too." She was playing with me, as evidenced by the shy smile she gave.

I studied her for a moment. "Maybe, but I don't think so." I nodded at her backpack, which she'd dropped at her feet. A copy of Faulkner's *The Sound and the Fury* peeped out from beneath a flap. "Contemporary literature, right?" This *was* my lucky day.

"Yes. My parents say it isn't practical, but I say I have to study what I love. I'll have to go on for a doctorate if I ever expect to get a decent job." She sighed. "That's a lot of time and expense for a degree that may give me a salary of fifty thousand or less a year."

"Then that would make your parents right."

She arched one eyebrow. She was a young woman with a strong sense of herself and no need to defend her choices. Rare in someone her age.

When she didn't respond, I explained. "Right in that your career choice is impractical. Not in that it isn't the right career for you." I looked around the fountain and was flooded with memories of my time at Ole Miss. "I graduated with a degree in theater."

"Wow." She laughed. "Talk about impractical. Were you ever an actress?"

"Small parts. In New York. But I didn't have what it took to stay on the big stage. I came home."

She was engaged now, and I found that I liked talking to her. "You came home to do what?"

I reached into my pocket and brought out a business card. "Private investigator."

She bit hook, line, and sinker. "And you're on a case here. At Ole Miss?" She looked around and leaned closer to me. "Is it a murder?"

"It is."

Her eyes widened. "It's that English professor, Dr. Loxley, isn't it?"

"It is."

"Everyone was so upset when it happened, but I heard some things about Dr. Loxley."

I needed facts, not gossip, but gossip would pass the time. "Yeah, I've heard some things, too, but do you know anything for a fact? Was he sexually involved and abusive to some of the students?"

My young friend eased Pluto to the border of the fountain and slowly stood up. "I shouldn't talk about this."

I was about to lose her, but Pluto came to the rescue. The cat reached out a paw and gently hooked her jeans, clearly asking her not to leave. Few people could resist Pluto when he chose to turn on his charm. She sat down and let him crawl back into her lap. She rolled her eyes at me to let me know she was fully aware of being manipulated by a feline.

"I'm trying to help my client avoid a murder charge in Sunflower County," I told her. "I'm looking for a graduate assistant to Dr. Brown named Margaret McNeese. Do you happen to know her?"

She hesitated, but finally answered. "Yes. I know Margaret."

"Do you know where she can be found?"

She bit her lip but didn't answer.

"What's your name?" I signaled Sweetie Pie over beside me.

The young woman reached over to pet my pooch. "My name is Poppy. Poppy Bright. Margaret is a friend of mine."

"She didn't show up for work today," I said, watching Poppy carefully. She looked sincerely surprised.

"She should be at work . . ." She checked her watch. "She should have just gotten off at five. Are you sure she wasn't there? Maybe she's at the library doing research for Dr. Brown."

I shook my head. "Dr. Brown said she didn't come in today or for the past two days."

"That can't be. Margaret would never shirk her studies. She's on the fast track into a doctoral program at William and Mary. She wouldn't risk getting in Dutch with Dr. Brown or the English department by failing to show up for work."

"Where would Margaret normally be at this time of day?"

I'd finally pushed too hard. Poppy put the cat aside and stood. "I have your card. I'll tell her to call you if I see her."

I wasn't going to get more than that from Poppy, who was obviously a good friend to Margaret. All I could do was wait for the phone call. And I hoped it came soon, before I headed back to Zinnia.

I checked the sun and calculated that I had at least another hour of sunlight. The days were growing shorter and shorter, but daylight savings time was still in effect. I could tarry a while longer at Oxford. And while I was waiting, I'd drop by the theater department and see what was going on there.

I was in the back of the darkened university theater watching a damn good rehearsal of *The Glass Menagerie* when my cell phone buzzed in my pocket. I exited the building with Sweetie Pie and Pluto by my side. They'd been napping, but now they were wide awake and refreshed. Sweetie Pie loped off to investigate a patch of grass. Pluto sat on the steps beside me. I didn't recognize the number of the caller but it was a local Oxford call.

When I answered, no one spoke for a few seconds, then a clipped, female voice came over the line. "This is Margaret McNeese. What do you want with me?"

"I'd like to speak with you about Dr. Alala Diakos," I said. "She's my client now, and I'm investigating the death of Dr. Loxley." I'd considered soft-shoeing my way to an interview, but I had a sense that Margaret would respond better to a full-frontal assault.

"Why can't you just let it alone?" Margaret said. "The man is dead. The department has moved on. Let it go."

"His killer was never found," I pointed out.

"Well, duh," she said. "Some mysteries are best left unsolved."

"Maybe for you, but not for Dr. Diakos. Where are you? Can we meet for fifteen minutes? I just have some basic questions about Loxley and since you were his assistant, I'm sure you can answer them."

"No, I'm busy."

"Okay, Sheriff Peters will drop by tomorrow to talk with you. You should let the school know he may have to take you back to Sunflower County." Coleman didn't really have the authority to do that, but Margaret didn't know it.

"No!"

The fact that she didn't hang up on me told me something was eating at her. She was way too guilty and easy to manipulate. "Then talk to me. It's your choice. We can do it the easy way, right now. Or you can do it the hard way with the law tomorrow."

"Dagwood Drive, 601. Yellow cottage. I'll talk to you for fifteen minutes. No more."

Well, I hoped she had an egg timer because I wasn't going to keep score. "Thanks," I said and hung up. "Let's hit it," I said to Sweetie Pie and Pluto. The truth was I wanted to clear out of the theater area. I had great memories there, working on productions while I was going to school. The theater had become my home for four years, and it was the bridge between the death of my parents and my years at Dahlia House, and the time when I struck out on my own for New York and my acting career. I didn't want to run into any of the faculty who might remember me. I'd had big dreams—Broadway. My failure on the boards still bothered me.

With the help of my phone's GPS, I found Dagwood Drive without incident. The little yellow cottage was snuggled amongst slender oak trees and had a circular drive outlined with compact plants. Someone took care of this place. It was loved.

Ferns and a beautiful dream catcher hung around the edge of an inviting front porch where Adirondack chairs and a swing offered a shady place to sit. Pluto was the one who alerted me to the woman sitting quietly in one of the chairs. She'd been so still, and her blond hair blended into the yellow of the house. I walked up and introduced myself.

"What do you want?" She made it clear she wasn't thrilled to see me.

Whatever was gnawing on Margaret McNeese had a good hold on her. There were dark circles beneath her amber eyes, and traces of old makeup were smudged there. Her curly hair blew in her face and she ignored it.

"Who killed Loxley?" I put it out there—cut to the chase.

"I don't know." She leaned forward and it was the most animation I'd seen from her.

"Did Diakos?"

She inhaled and closed her eyes. "I don't know. I don't know what happened to Loxley or what Alala might have done to him." She drilled me with a stare. "She's a woman capable of murder when she gets that Greek temper up."

"Tell me about the night Loxley was killed." Perhaps Margaret didn't know anything about Loxley's murder. Perhaps she did. But I was positive she knew a lot about what was happening in the English department at the time Loxley was killed. And I intended to weasel it out of her, even if I had to fudge the truth a lot more.

Margaret didn't offer me a seat, but I took one anyway in a chair opposite her. I could watch her closely and keep an eye on Sweetie Pie and Pluto, who were sniffing around the trees and lovely shrubbery. Margaret, to her credit, didn't seem to be bothered by my snooping pets.

"Tell me about Dr. Loxley's last day."

She started to get up but stopped herself and settled back in the chair. "Okay. I'll answer that question, and then you're gone. Alex could be the most charming man in the world, when he wanted something. At first, he was this . . . scholar. A man immersed in literature and great writing. He understood the importance of literary fiction. I was smitten. Until I agreed to be his GA. That's when I realized that he didn't care about me. Heck, he didn't even like me. He just wanted what I could do for him."

"And what things would he want?"

"Oh, papers typed, books picked up from the library, his laundry fetched from the dry cleaner's, research into one of his topics. He was always writing and publishing about *Beowulf*. He was one of the nation's leading authorities."

I smiled. "*Beowulf* was a good yarn." I knew it would drive her crazy, and I was right.

"How can you call that masterpiece a yarn?"

My plan was to get her upset enough that she blurted something out she'd meant to keep secret. I hoped I'd read her personality correctly—she was devoted to the "great works" of literature, meaning the Medieval era. Anything written after the fifteenth century would be suspect. "Great horror story, don't get me wrong. But if you want literary genius, you have to go to Tennessee Williams. He was a master of tormented relationships. He encapsulates the internal and external turmoil of each of us. Now that was a man who could tell a story."

"Piffle!" Margaret was suitably insulted.

I almost smiled but contained it. "Well, everyone's a critic." I smiled. "Look, let's get to the details of the day. I have somewhere to be." I checked my watch to give some weight to my manipulation.

"The day Loxley died, I spent most of the afternoon in the library. Alex had an ingenious idea that he could directly connect *Beowulf* to the fascination with were-wolves in popular fiction today. And skin walkers. It was sheer brilliance, and I'd found a mother lode of material to draw a direct line from *Beowulf* as the forerunner of these latter-day characters."

Another line of questioning opened up, and I jumped in. "Since Loxley is dead, are you using that research for your thesis?"

She went pale. "How did—"

"Because it makes sense, even if it may not be exactly . . . ethical."

"He's dead. I did all the research, not him. How is it not ethical?"

"But it was his idea. And now you actually benefit from his death." I didn't believe anyone would take a life over a dissertation topic, but academics could be vicious. Margaret was petite and looked rather defenseless, but a gun really did level the playing field. She could be the killer. And, I had finally hit pay dirt. Her cheeks bloomed hot pink and fire snapped in her eyes.

14

"I didn't steal his stinking idea. It was my idea. Everything worth anything that Loxley put out during the last two years was mine! My ideas, my work, my research, my insight into the original text. And he couldn't even be generous enough to credit me as his research assistant. I didn't kill him, but I'm glad someone did. He was a brute."

I'd mashed a big bruise on her ego. Loxley had been taking credit for her work since she'd first entered the graduate program. I could see why that made her hot under the collar, but had she been mad enough to shoot him in the heart? She was a credible suspect for Loxley's murder, but what about Curtis Miller? Or the Vanderbilt professor? She had no personal beef with those two men that I knew about.

"Margaret, you might look good for Loxley but I have reason to believe you didn't kill him. Work with me. I'm trying to help you." This was the turnaround where now I'd be nice, be her friend. "Just tell me about the day. That will help me provide you with an alibi, and it could help my client."

"I don't give a damn about Alala, but I'll tell you. I was at the library until five. I went back to Loxley's office with my research and he offered to take me to dinner. It was the nicest thing he'd done in weeks."

"Did you see Dr. Brown there?"

Margaret shook her head. "No."

"Were you sleeping with Loxley?"

She nodded. "It was a stupid mistake. But he could be so nice. Until he wasn't. And once I'd slept with him, that was it. He'd gotten what he wanted. He was truly a predator. He'd demand sex and then mistreat me. Physically mistreat me. But I didn't kill him. I wanted to, but I didn't."

"Who did?"

"My money is on Dr. Brown. He slept with her and then used her to leverage policies in the English department. She did everything he wanted, even cutting her colleagues off at the knees on issues that damaged their careers. A lot of the faculty still hate her. In fact, she's more despised than Loxley was."

"I heard Loxley was handy with his fists. Especially if he was confronting a smaller, less powerful woman."

"Not completely true. He seldom used his fist; he used the flat of his hand. He was a slapper, which is in some ways even more insulting. And it didn't leave so

many bruises, but if he got really angry, he'd punch."
She looked down at the gray paint of the porch floor. "I
slept with him to get even with Becky Brown. She was
so . . . superior when they first got together. Like she'd
captured the goose that laid the golden egg. The day after the first time I slept with him, I saw her in the hallway. I was so full of myself. She was scurrying by and
I stepped in front of her to rub her nose in it. She had a
busted lip and a big bruise on her zygomatic bone." She
touched her cheekbone. "He'd really worked her over.
And three weeks later, I looked in the mirror and saw
the exact same wounds."

"Couldn't you have quit your job?"

"I tried to get away from him. I tried to get transferred
to another professor, but he blocked it. And Dr. Brown
helped him block it."

"Why didn't you report him for sexual harassment?"
I knew Alala had opened the door for her to do so.

"Things don't work like that around here. I've plunked
down money for a year of school and the rental of this
house. I'm nearly a hundred thousand in debt now, with
the cost of my undergraduate degree and this master's degree. If I'd reported him, what do you think my chances
of completing my master's here would have been? No formal action would ever have been taken, but no one likes
a rat or a whiner. And keep in mind that none of my education is worth anything unless I can get my doctorate
at a prestigious school. That's my ticket to a job. Not
even a decent job, but a job."

This mess Margaret found herself in was exactly the
point of university policies against professors dating students. But this was still not the information I needed. "So
after you went to dinner, what happened then?"

"He humiliated me in the restaurant. He mocked my choice of wine, even though it was one he'd picked the week before. It was . . . mortifying. I managed to stand up and walk out. We were at the Cove, and I didn't have a vehicle, so I started walking back to town. It's about three miles. I got home about eleven. My feet were so blistered and sore from walking in dress shoes that after I soaked them I just went to bed. I'd cried myself sick on the walk home and I fell into a deep sleep. The next day when I got to campus I went straight to the library and worked there alone. It was all over campus before I heard someone had shot him. If my feet hadn't been crippled, I would have danced."

I couldn't blame her for those sentiments. I hated a bully. I felt the powerful rage that Alala, Dr. Brown, and Margaret must each have felt slowly building before Dr. Loxley was killed. But I had to tamp it down and do my job.

"Do you know where Loxley was going after you left him?"

"I don't know for certain, but there's a bar on the outskirts of town—in fact, he probably drove by me on his way there and simply chose not to give me a ride home."

"Name of the bar?"

"Homeboy Heroes. Think good ole boys in camo, out drinking whether their kids have food or not."

I knew those men—and they were essentially the same men that frequented the Red Top Bar in Sunflower County. "The men who never go to war, but think they're heroes because they have guns and kill defenseless animals?"

"That's exactly the crowd." She was pleased with my astute comprehension of the mentality.

"Why would a college professor of literature hang out in that kind of bar?" Oxford was a town that offered plenty of settings for dining and drinking, from linen tablecloths and wine lists to waxed gingham on picnic tables in barbecue joints. I would never have imagined the dead Dr. Loxley in a bar where not taking a bath everyday was a badge of honor.

"Alex had a thing for those guys. He thought they were manly." She shrugged. "He never directly admitted it, but he would say things like 'they don't let women or the government tell them what to do.'"

"And Loxley, with his degree and job teaching at a university, was welcome there?" That both Loxley and Miller had ended up in bars that cultivated anti-government, anti-women, Second Amendment kooks the very night they were murdered was more than strange.

"I never understood it. But he was friends with some of those guys. In fact, it became clear to me that he much preferred spending time with them to spending time with me or any other woman."

Most of the AR15-toting men I knew had nothing but contempt for higher education or the pointy-heads that taught. This breed of "real men" embraced their lack of formal education and valued only the skills of a blue-collar job. I never understood why they saw it as an either/or situation. You could have a great education and enjoy learning and be a plumber—the two weren't mutually exclusive.

"How often did he visit Homeboy Heroes?"

"Maybe two or three times a week. Always after dinner."

"Was he a heavy drinker? Gambler? Pool shark?"

She slowly shook her head. "No, no, and I never saw

him play pool. As far as I know, Alex thought games of physical skill were . . . a waste, but perhaps I never really knew him."

"Is it possible he insulted one of those men, said something to make an enemy?"

She shrugged. "I can't answer that."

"Did you ever see him socialize with them anywhere else?"

She frowned. "One day we were having lunch at the Frosty Mug over by the coliseum and a burly man on a motorcycle came up. He was big. Had a beard. His skin was like baked leather. I remember thinking he could have been thirty or fifty. Impossible to tell. Alex was upset that the man approached him while he was with me. He hustled him away from the table and they talked for about five minutes out of earshot."

"A friendly conversation?"

"Nope. It didn't look friendly at all. And Alex was in a terrible mood afterward. I asked him to get an iced tea to go for me when he paid the bill. When he got back into the car, he poured the tea all over me and told me he wasn't my servant."

"Where is this bar?" I asked.

"You can't go. I've never known a woman who went in there. They have a policy—no women unless they come with a member." She was wide-eyed now.

"It's okay. I'm a private investigator."

"You could get hurt, Ms. Delaney. Send the sheriff out to that bar, but don't you go. I'm serious."

"Okay." I wasn't certain what I might do, but it was pointless to worry her. "You didn't see Loxley the rest of the night once you walked out of that restaurant?"

"I didn't. I soaked my sore feet and went to bed. I was

so tired and heartsick, I didn't wake up until my alarm went off the next morning. I was late for work, and then, like I said, I went and hid at the library. I didn't even know Alex was dead until lunchtime, when another student came into the library and found me in the archives."

"I just have a few more questions. What size shoe do you wear?"

"What?" I'd thrown her off-balance.

"Just answer."

"Eight and a half, narrow, why?"

Tinkie sure knew her shoe impressions. "What were you doing in Alala's backyard?" I asked.

She lifted her chin slightly. "I don't have to answer your questions or talk to you at all."

That was true, but the other truth was that if Margaret was innocent, as she claimed, I could help her get the evidence to prove it. "I know you were at Alala's house. I have proof. Well, the sheriff has proof. I'll try to help you if you help me."

"I didn't hurt anyone. I broke into Alala's house and when Brown pulled up in the front I had no choice but to go out the back. I waited a minute, hoping Brown would knock and then go away. But she somehow got in the front door."

"Did you cut across her backyard and go through the neighbor's?"

She shook her head. "No. I slipped around the house and went back to the sidewalk. I'd parked a few blocks over. A friend had driven me over—she was visiting someone in town. Anyway, she was waiting in the car for me. We drove back to Oxford."

"Would that friend be Poppy Bright?"

"Yes, but she isn't involved in this. I didn't tell her what

I was planning to do. She just came over to Zinnia with me because she's good friends with someone who lives in your town."

"She wasn't at Alala's house with you, then?"

"No. I swear it. Please don't pull her into this."

Margaret had explained a lot, and I felt she'd been honest in her answers. Of course, a criminal would be skilled in supplying believable answers, so I didn't put a lot of weight in my opinion of her truthfulness. "Other than Brown, did you see anyone else in the house?"

She shook her head. "No, but I didn't hang around to look, either."

"What were you looking for in Alala's house?" I asked her.

"I was just going to wait for her to come—"

"Don't start lying now."

"Diakos had been spying on Alex for months. Dr. Brown let it slip that Alala likely had photographs of Alex with various women. Compromising photos." She shrugged. "I was afraid I was in some of them and I wanted them back if I could find them."

"Did it not occur to you they'd be on her phone or backed up to the cloud?" Breaking and entering for physical photos seemed so old school.

"I intended to get into her computer. That's what I thought I'd do. Find the photos and delete them. I also wanted to take a look at her book, if I could. Just to see. She got a huge contract for the book based on just an outline. I wanted to see if she'd be able to deliver."

"What happened?"

"I couldn't find her computer. I looked around, but I didn't see it. Then Brown arrived and I took off."

Now I couldn't tell if she was lying or not. There was

something slightly furtive in her face, but I couldn't pinpoint what it might be. Maybe she'd intended to delete the manuscript as well as the photos. I'd probably never know the truth, and since it didn't necessarily relate to two murdered men, I had to let it go.

"If you want to finish your master's and move on to your doctorate, you'd better go to work tomorrow. Brown is gunning for you."

She nodded. "I know. She's an unpleasant boss, and I thought my head would explode if I went back into the English department. Do you know if Dr. Diakos has . . . compromising photos?"

"I don't know." But I would dang sure ask.

"If you see anything, please take them and don't show anyone. I'm embarrassed. I was so stupid."

Not stupid, just young. If she was right about the photos, then I suddenly understood why someone might want to break into Alala's house. But why hadn't Alala been forthcoming about this?

It was time to head out. I had a big agenda to work through.

15

Darkness had fallen by the time I got back on Highway 8. I was headed toward home. Coincidentally, Homeboy Heroes was on the way to Zinnia. My plan was to check the parking lot and weigh the potential for a butt-whipping, based on what I witnessed.

The bar wasn't hard to find. Smoky blue neon lit the night as I pulled into the lot, which was chock-full of pickups fitted out with mud tires and gun racks. I knew it would be wiser to keep on driving. I was already there, though, and I wanted to see if anyone remembered Alex Loxley from the night of his murder. I'd been in plenty of bars where men drank beer, shot pool, and danced with a willing partner. I'd enjoyed those adventures, especially with a partner who could two-step. But this time I was looking for a nest of men who didn't like women, and it had my nerves jangling.

Coleman was working the Curtis Miller case, and I was eager to talk to him about what he'd found, but I figured it could wait half an hour. There was little I could do in Sunflower County, anyway. With Coleman's competent hand steering the Miller investigation, it made sense for me to focus on this Oxford killing, which was out of Coleman's jurisdiction. But I was positive the cases were tied together. Especially now that I knew both dead men had visited a roughneck bar the night of their deaths. It made sense for Curtis. It was his kind of joint. But the professor—I was having trouble connecting those dots.

The shadowy group of survivalist types—the almost exclusively white men who wanted to keep women, all minorities, and those with different sexual preferences down—that Tinkie and I had heard about at Alala's talk were at the forefront of my mind. These men could be very dangerous. The most disturbing thing was that they were organized and dotted across the nation. These bars were perfect fronts for such organizations. The men could gather and talk without drawing any suspicion. I knew too well that fear and hatred toward women and marginalized groups were real and present threats. The question was, did I want to get out of my car and possibly step right into the middle of it?

In a word, yes.

"Stay in the car. I mean it." I lectured the cat and dog knowing full well that I should heed my own advice.

Sweetie Pie gave a little huff of exasperation and Pluto only twitched his tail.

"If you get out, one of those men might skin you."

Same reaction. It was pointless to argue, and I knew

putting the ragtop on the convertible wouldn't hold them in if they decided to break free. They'd done it before and I had ended up replacing the top.

"If I'm not out in ten minutes, come looking for me."

Sweetie Pie barked as if she understood. Pluto turned slowly and presented his butt to me. Ah, a crystal-clear response.

I hoofed it over to the bar, where loud country music rang into the clear night. When I touched the door it vibrated with the volume of a tune I happened to love. I might not run into anyone dangerous, but I dang sure might lose my hearing.

When I pushed open the door, the music hit me like a wall. Subtle conversation was going to be difficult. From the look two guys at the bar cut at me, conversation might not be an option at all. This was definitely not the right place for me. Instead of retreating, I walked right in.

"Jack and water," I said to the bartender, a guy who seemed out of place, too, with long hair and a Jackson Browne T-shirt that had seen better days. The shirt made me like him.

He put my drink in front of me and leaned close. "Drink fast and leave. Unless you're here on the arm of one of these guys, you don't need to be here. This isn't a good place for a single woman."

His words felt more like a caution than a threat. I pulled up Alex Loxley's photo on my phone. "Ever see this guy in here?"

"Are you a cop?"

"Nope. Private investigator."

"Almost as bad."

"Look, I'm just making a living. Do you know this guy?"

"Loxley. Sure. College professor. He came here some. Stuck out like a sore thumb."

"Did he hang out with anyone in particular?"

The bartender refilled my drink. When I tried to pay, he shook his head. "Really, finish this drink and you should go. For your safety. Those guys over there are giving you a hard look."

I glanced over at the nearest pool table and the barkeep was correct. Four men were staring holes in me. "Those the guys Loxley hung out with?"

"Rex Bottom is the biggest one. He's their . . . leader."

"What does he lead them in doing?"

"Ask him. But if you get hurt, don't blame me."

"Thanks for the drinks and the information." I knocked the second drink back and walked to the pool table. It wasn't that I was fearless, I just didn't have another option except tucking tail and running. I didn't want to drive all the way back here tomorrow—especially if Tinkie got wind of where I was going. This was one place she surely didn't need to frequent.

"Rex Bottom?" I spoke to the biggest man. "I'd like to talk to you about Alex Loxley."

"Is that so?" He grinned. He had a nice set of choppers in contrast to his scruffy clothes and greasy hair. "Old Alex? He sure had a lot of pretty ladies following in his wake. You one of his brood?"

"I never knew Dr. Loxley, but I'd like to find out more about him." I looked around. "Was he a pool shark?"

"Never saw him pick up a cue," Rex said. The other men laughed.

"Mr. Bottom, could we sit down? I'd be happy to buy you a drink."

"I don't think so. Around here, women don't buy men drinks. You must have missed that etiquette lesson."

Now I had a line on Rex. He might dress the part of a roughneck, but the man had been raised in the tradition. His teeth were too perfect, too white, and the word *etiquette* didn't normally fall from the lips of a guy from the backwoods.

"Fine." I shrugged and signaled for another drink for me. I didn't need it or want to drink it, but I had to order it. Just to prove I could. "Can we talk?" I asked.

"I don't think I have anything to say to you. Unless you're looking for some fun. Then we might talk about your price."

He was deliberately insulting, and I wanted very much to smack him in the face, but I knew better. Instead, I smiled. "We can discuss that." I motioned him to a table in the corner while his posse whooped and hollered like high school kids.

"Show her what it means to be a real woman," one of them yelled. I smiled over my shoulder at him so I'd get a good look when I came back with Coleman to kick his ass.

"Why are you asking about Loxley?" Rex didn't waste any time getting to the point.

"We had a murder over in Sunflower County. Very similar. I'm trying to figure out if the two are related."

"At least it's not a paternity suit," he said. "You women set the trap, and when the cake is in the oven, you expect a man to foot the bills." He didn't ask a question about the second murder, which made me think he likely knew more about Curtis Miller's death than I did.

"There is no cake." I itched to punch him, hard, but I smiled again. "I never met Dr. Loxley. This is strictly an insurance case I'm investigating. You know, double indemnity." Vocabulary test! I wondered how he'd react.

"They'll pay out double for murder, right?"

"That's what I need to determine. It's all about what the police list as cause of death. If it's murder or an accident, the policy will pay out." Though I'd told the bartender I was a PI, I shaded the truth for Rex Bottom. It was safer to be an insurance investigator than a PI. "So who looks good for the murder to you? We have to be sure this wasn't some kind of suicide pact. You know, an attempt to cheat us out of the policy payout."

"How much is the policy?" Rex was suddenly very interested.

"Half a million. *If* we pay, and since no killer was ever apprehended . . ." I signaled the bartender to bring two drinks to the table. He was there in a flash with a wary look for me.

"Loxley had no reason to commit suicide," Rex said. "He had the world by its tail. The man had everything he wanted. And he wouldn't hold the gun out and shoot himself in the heart." He held his arms out as far as he could. "That would never work. It was out-and-out murder. Besides, Loxley had everything to look forward to. Man, he had exactly what he wanted."

"Like what?" I asked.

"Women falling all over him. Young women. Loads of those students would put out for a better grade." It was clear he admired Loxley. "I mean, for a *grade*! That's just gravy on top of a cathead biscuit."

"What about Loxley's wife?"

He shook his head. "Never knew he had one. If he did,

he was separated or divorced. And no children. Least ways he never talked about any. Like I said, he had the perfect life. Plenty of nookie, no hindrances."

"Anyone here at the bar have a beef with Loxley?"

Rex shook his head. "Nah. Most of the guys laughed at him behind his back. He was so . . . full of himself, with his degrees and all. He liked to talk fancy about his books and papers and faculty meetings. He was always quoting parts of some crazy monster story in a strange accent. But when it came to the important stuff, he was one of us."

"One of you?" We'd finally gotten to the place I wanted to be.

"One of the guys. He'd do the wild thing with several of those little gals who chased after him and then come tell us all about it. He was so proud of himself, talking all about how he'd had his way. How he'd showed them he was the authority and how they were meant to treat a real man."

"Did he ever talk about how he . . . controlled his women?"

He watched me closely and I knew he was looking for a chink in my armor. He wanted to find my weak spot. Yeah, the man was a lot smarter than he let on. "You mean like when a man has to take the strap to a disobedient woman."

"Not a tactic I know about."

"Then your daddy failed in his education of you. No woman is perfect. Like children, they have to be trained. That's a real problem in this day and age. Women and other folks meant to be subservient are trying to take control."

I'd heard all of this before from backwoods creeps as

well as educated men who were so afraid that a woman—
or anyone they deemed less than—would best them that
they fixed the game from the get-go. No level playing
field. They held all the cards.

"What training method did Loxley prefer?" I kept my
tone light, as if we were discussing the merits of a wine.

"Flat-handed slap. No fist. Except when he was frus-
trated. Worked, too. Loxley got a lot on the side and
no one ever turned him in to the school. They tried one
time, some student complaining, but he nipped it in the
bud."

"Surely there are women in the English department
who refused to put up with Loxley's tactics?"

"Not much chance of that. No real man's gonna take
sass off some sidepiece. When the woman earns the bigger paycheck, she can use the strap on her man, right?"
He laughed and the men, even though they were fifteen
feet away and couldn't hear a word of our conversation,
started laughing, too.

"And Loxley was a real man?"

"That's right. He could be priggish, but when the chips
were down, he was okay. Some of the men envied Loxley. No one wanted to hurt him."

"Y'all had kind of a boy's club or organization, huh?
Some place you could exchange all the secrets on training your women."

"More like a social group."

"Where did you grow up, Rex?"

He arched his eyebrows. "Why would you care about
that?"

"Just curious. You're not from Mississippi or parts
around here. There's something in your voice. Just the
hint of an accent." I nodded at his buddies. "You aren't

really one of those guys. Neither was Loxley. You're an educated man pretending not to be. I'd say you and Loxley had more in common. I just can't figure out what it is that brought either of you here to drink beer and shoot pool in this environment."

"Why's that important to you?"

"Because I'm going to figure out if Loxley was murdered or if he was into something and took his own life to avoid being blackmailed. See what I'm getting at? Now be helpful and tell me where you're from."

"Memphis, Tennessee."

"You're a single man?"

"Are you asking for yourself?"

"Sure."

"Divorced. My ex-wife, Jewel, wasn't such a gem."

He'd used that line once too often. It felt really threadbare. "Why are you here, with these guys? I'd say your career has mostly been white collar. You're educated though you're good at hiding it. You were raised with money and an eye toward an upper-middle-class life, but you have even bigger ambitions." It wasn't that I was so good at reading people, but that Rex had gotten sloppy over time. He'd let the camouflage slip from the life he was so deliberately crafting here.

I'd surprised him just enough that it showed. "So what's it to you? Unless you think I killed Loxey."

"Nope, you didn't put a bullet in the center of his heart. But now, I'm curious. Why are you here? In Oxford, Mississippi."

"Because I like it?"

I shook my head. "Wrong answer. I don't think so. There's something else going on. You're not here to hunt and fish or slap your girlfriend around."

He leaned closer to me. "Why am I here?" His eyes danced with enjoyment of this little game. He thought he had me over a barrel.

"We got a report at the office about a group of men. A political group. Organized to keep women and a few other people in their place. Maybe using force or intimidation to get what they want. If Loxley was mixed up in that, it wouldn't be good. Would definitely cancel out his insurance if he's proven to be involved in illegal activity that cost him his life." I gave it a beat. "Know anything about it?"

He stood up. "Who've you been talking to?"

I stood up, too, my untouched drink still on the table. "Oh, just people. I'll get to the bottom of all of this." I smiled. "Pleasure to meet you, Rex Bottom." I snapped a photo of him with my cell phone and headed for the door fast. I was only a little bit ahead of him when I got to my car, but Sweetie Pie was in the front seat, fangs bared, and a very serious growl coming from her throat. Pluto curled up and tucked his head in his belly. Cats.

I didn't bother with the door, but jumped in the car and took off. Rex didn't try to pursue me, even though he and his friends had rushed out the door behind me.

It was definitely time to get back to Zinnia. On the way, I called Coleman and gave him an ETA. We both had a lot to share.

16

A fire blazed in the parlor and Coleman met me at the door with a Jack on the rocks. The drive home from Oxford in the brisk night air had left me chilled. Coleman had fed the three horses, and I pulled some leftovers out of the fridge for Sweetie Pie. Pluto gave me a long, unpleasant look at the canned tuna I offered him. Both animals preferred Millie's cooking. They were spoiled rotten.

Something smelled really good in the kitchen, and when I checked the oven, I found cornbread and sweet potatoes baking. A pot of green beans was on the stove. Coleman was pretty handy in the kitchen and I was certainly glad. I was starving.

I made two plates and took one to him in the parlor,

where we snuggled on the sofa in front of the fire while we ate.

I told him about my day and did my best to brush past the dangers of going into Homeboy Heroes bar, but filled him in on Rex Bottom and the shadowy group we'd heard about. He was interested in both Becky Brown and Margaret McNeese as potential suspects, especially when I told him that both had been at Alala's house and that Brown drove a black pickup. "I think it was Becky who attacked Alala in the park. She was possibly after photos that she and McNeese believe Alala took of them with Loxley. Did you get any fingerprints off the gun Sweetie Pie and Pluto found?"

"Wiped clean. I can understand either of them wanting to set up Alala for Loxley's murder, and I can see either of them killing Loxley. But why kill Curtis?" he asked. "What could Curtis possibly mean to them?"

"That I don't know." I sighed and rubbed my eyes. "I'm exhausted."

He tilted my chin up so I had to meet his gaze. "You know we're going to have to discuss your bar-hopping tomorrow," he said. "I'm too tired tonight to get into all the reasons why what you did was not smart."

"Sure. Tomorrow. But tell me what you found today. I told you everything. Did you come up with any new leads?" My plan was to get up early in the morning and escape before he could lecture me about the dangers of bars like Homeboys.

"I did. I found out quite a bit. As you know, all three men were killed with a .38. We're getting ballistics from Nashville and Oxford. Whether this gun was used in each murder or not, your client was in all three places at the time of each killing."

"Coleman, if she murdered anyone and that is the gun, she wouldn't hide it under a bush in her backyard."

"Maybe she had to ditch the gun in a hurry."

"Isn't that a little too convenient?" I wasn't certain Alala was innocent, but it was my job to argue on her behalf. "I mean, she isn't stupid. She wouldn't leave a trail of bread crumbs that obvious."

"She might if she's a serial killer, thinking that the jurisdictions are far enough apart that no cop would ever tie them together."

"Serial killer?" That was a whole lot different than a woman who killed abusive men. That was on an FBI level.

"That's the technical definition, Sarah Booth. You know that."

"Even if she's killing out of a sense of justice?"

"Justice?" His expression was all consternation. "Justice, revenge, greed. Doesn't matter. Someone who kills multiple people—that's the correct label for them."

The thing was, I could picture my client shooting Loxley and Miller. Heck, I could see myself doing it. The men were, from all accounts and from my personal experience with Miller, awful people. Serial killer sounded so much . . . scarier than, say, "cockroach eradicator."

"Coleman, 'serial killer' just doesn't sound like Alala to me. She can't be a serial killer. She's a college professor of literature." My comment was tongue in cheek and Coleman rolled his eyes at me.

"As if educated people don't commit plenty of crimes."

"It's not that. She's just bright and passionate about her work. And she's hooked into a larger reality of lectures and books. That's her ammunition. Not bullets."

"Serial killers are passionate about their work, too."

Now he was teasing me. "I mean, they have so much passion for their work they do it again and again."

"You're a devil, Coleman Peters."

"And you're my special little imp. Let's call it a night, shall we? Tomorrow is another day."

I followed Coleman up the stairs to our bedroom, but in a dark little corner of my heart I knew he was keeping something from me. And it was likely something that would impact my client in a negative way.

I poured my black coffee into an insulated to-go cup and took off for the Roadster as soon as light cracked the eastern sky. I didn't want a lecture, and I also hadn't been able to sleep. Coleman had tied three murders together by pointing out that the same type of weapon had been used in each—also the same as the kind that had been recovered at Alala Diakos's house. It looked bad for Alala.

But what else did the murdered men have in common? That question would either tie my client in closer to the label of serial killer or help me prove she was innocent. This was the direction I had to pursue.

Sweetie Pie rode in the passenger seat, her ears flapping in the cold morning. Pluto was down on the floorboard, out of the wind that whipped through the Roadster. The cat was far smarter than the rest of us. My destination was Tansy Miller. She wasn't going to be happy to see me, but that didn't trouble me one lick.

I pulled up in front of Selena's House, wondering if Tansy would still be there. It was still really early, and I hoped to catch her at breakfast. I figured her to be a Huck Finn, meaning she'd light out for the territories once she realized there was nothing to stay for in Zinnia. With Curtis dead, nothing held her. She was a suspect in the murder of her husband, though with the deaths of Loxley and the Nashville man, it seemed less and less likely that she had shot anyone. Coleman could ask her to stay in the county, but he couldn't demand it, and Tansy was a woman who took the path of least resistance. Running would be that solution for her.

"Stay in the car," I suggested to the critters. This was a safe neighborhood, but still, I hoped to talk to Tansy and get on to other tasks. Like going to Hilltop to get Tinkie. I had to catch my partner up on all I'd discovered. It occurred to me that I hadn't heard from her last evening or this morning—though this was early for Tinkie. Breakfast at Millie's was the perfect solution to my concerns.

I was just imagining a vegetable omelet with hot peppers when I saw movement on the second floor of Selena's House. Pluto popped up in the car window, one hundred percent pure feline focus. Before I could grab him, he was out of the car and running across the lawn. Sweetie Pie was next. I had no choice but to follow, all the while snapping photos of a man climbing down a rose trellis from the second-floor window.

Someone in Selena's House had a guest, and I was willing to bet that was very much against the house rules.

The man dropped the last five feet to the ground. He wore a hoodie and I couldn't see his face. I pressed my finger into his back, like a gun barrel. "Hands in the air."

He obliged.

Darkness was already giving way to daylight, and soon the world would be up and moving. I felt I was pretty safe, especially with Sweetie Pie sitting at the man's feet growling.

"What are you doing here?" I asked.

"Uh, I was just, uh. Hey, I wasn't doing anything bad. I was invited here."

He didn't sound like a home invader or serial killer. Or an abusive spouse or boyfriend for that matter. But better safe than sorry.

"Who were you here to see?"

"I can't tell you. They'll kick her out and she needs to be here."

"I have it all on my phone. You'd better tell me the truth now." I waved my phone in front of him so he could see I meant business.

"I came to see Tansy Miller. I'm a friend of hers. And I was a friend of Curtis's."

"And you're sneaking out of the dead man's wife's room at daybreak?"

"Looks kinda bad, I know." He tried to turn around but I poked him harder with my finger. "Don't do that. I'm calling the sheriff."

"Please don't. This is really, really gonna mess up my situation if it gets out. You know those two deputies gossip like old ladies."

I took umbrage at the insult to DeWayne and Budgie. "They don't gossip." I gave it a little thought. "Much."

"Just let me go. I didn't harm anyone. In fact, I put a smile right on Tansy's face. Call up to that window and ask her. She'll tell you."

Oh, good Lord no. I wasn't going to listen to sexual testimonials from Tansy Miller about anyone. "Turn around."

He did. I knew him. "Todd Renfield." I sighed. "I thought you were living with Moody Moody?"

"She works at night." He checked his watch. "In fact, I should be getting home right now. She'll be pulling into the parking lot, wondering where I am. You have a nice day."

He started to leave but I grabbed the back of his cotton hoodie. "Hold it. How long have you been sleeping with Tansy?"

He shook his head. "Couple months. Look, she's had a tough time. Curtis was sleeping with Moody. When Tansy came to tell me, we just sort of fell into bed. Can't you just pretend you didn't see this? They will kick her out of that house. Men aren't allowed. That's a fact."

"Where were you the night Curtis Miller was shot and killed?"

"I was with Tansy early on. Then Moody."

"That's not what Tansy said." I was trying to rattle his story with a small fabrication of my own, but Moody had given him an alibi.

"Of course she didn't. She couldn't say that. You don't realize what you're playin' with. Moody will shiv me and cut out Tansy's gizzard. I picked Tansy up at the hospital after Curtis hurt her wrist. I brought her here, to Selena's House, and sat in the car with her awhile until she decided to go in. Then I left. I picked up Moody after her shift and brought her home. That old bat next door saw us."

His alibi made sense, but there were people who could check it out. I dialed the sheriff's office and when Budgie answered, I just asked him to meet me in front of Selena's House.

"I wish you hadn't done that," Todd said. "This is really going to complicate my world."

"Hate it for you," I said. I didn't believe for a second that Todd had killed anyone. He was just not that kind of guy. But in his running around all over the county helping himself to other men's wives and girlfriends, I had to wonder if maybe he'd seen something valuable. Budgie was just the right person to wiggle that information out of him.

"Todd, what do you know about that group of men who hang out at the Red Top?"

"Just a bunch of shit-kickers. Not much to 'em. They get a few bucks in their pockets and go to the Red Top for dollar-beer night to get drunk. They whoop and holler and make threatening noises, but they just go home and sleep it off."

"There's a club of some kind that meets there, right?"

Todd shrugged. He'd easily confessed to sleeping with Tansy, but this was something he really didn't want to talk about.

"Curtis was a member of this man's club. What's the name? American Values Association? Clever that the acronym is a woman's name. AVA. Kind of cool, for a club that women can't join."

Todd shook his head. "Not to me. I like women. I'd rather be around them than those men. They're . . . angry. And downright mean for no reason. And some of them need a bath."

At last, I was on the right path.

"What are they angry about?"

"They say their rights are being taken from them."

"Really. That's very interesting. What rights would those be?"

"Well, like in the past, they were always in charge. Whatever they said, their women and children had to follow. They could get all the best jobs because no one would hire a woman. Now they say women are going to be making all the decisions. They said that a woman shouldn't be working alongside men. That women are putting a man's capacity to earn a living at risk."

"But women need to make a living, too."

"Nope. That's why they should have a man. Back in the good old days, a woman could be a secretary or a bank teller or a store clerk, but she didn't make much money. She was mostly a helper. If a woman can do everything without a man, what's going to happen to the fabric of society? They can't make the same wages as a man. That would be awful. I mean why would a woman even marry? That's what they're all whinging on about."

Todd had been a little sponge at some of these meetings. I didn't see him as a joiner, just a listener. "Yeah, why would a woman marry?"

"They wouldn't," Todd said. "And who would take care of the men then? That's the bottom line. They realize they can't take care of themselves." He shrugged.

"So those big ole men are afraid of workplace competition from a woman?"

He thought a minute. "Yeah, that's about right, because it would put a lot of men in a place where they'd have to act better or get thrown out. They were pretty hot about that, saying they weren't going to change and neither was the way women are treated." He squared his shoulders. "And they didn't like Curtis much, either. He was always bossing folks around when he didn't have any reason to do so." He hesitated again. "Some of the guys felt sorry for Tansy. She can be real pitiful when she wants to and she knew a lot of them."

That was an interesting tidbit. "Do you think one of

those men could have killed Curtis because they didn't like him? Or maybe to defend Tansy?"

"Maybe, but I couldn't say who might do that."

"How about a man who was sleeping with Tansy?"

"Yeah, he might." He frowned. "Wait, I'm sleeping with Tansy. I didn't kill Curtis. I didn't like him but I didn't kill him."

"And you're sleeping with Moody Moody."

He grinned. "True. That's true. I got a lot of love and I sure enjoy spreading it around."

One thing was clear, Todd Renfield wasn't the killer. He didn't have the free time between servicing his women to kill anyone. I was surprised he had the energy to go to work.

"Todd, where do you work?"

"Tire shop. Seven to five, six days a week. Keeps me in tip-top shape to keep the ladies coming back for more."

I made an executive decision and called Budgie back and canceled my request for help. "Things are okay here," I said. "I'll call if I need you."

"Sure thing," Budgie said before he hung up.

Todd looked pretty downcast. "Don't tell the sheriff I was climbing out of Tansy's window. It could get her kicked out of Selena's House. They honestly don't allow men. It's in the rules. It won't do me any harm, but it could mess things up for her. She likes living here."

"I'm going to tell Coleman I saw you on the street, and if he wants to question you, he'll be in touch."

He brightened. "Thanks. Look, if you came to see Tansy, could you come back later? She's sound asleep. You wake her and she won't do a thing to help you. That girl takes getting her rest to heart. Let her wake up and I'll speak to her about helping you, seeing as how you're doing me a real solid. Uh, and Ms. Delaney, I have Thursday nights open, if you're interested."

"I'm booked right now, but I'll keep it in mind." Like it or not, there was something appealing about a man who was confident in his bedroom skills. Todd had found his "special talent."

17

I didn't want to go back to Dahlia House and risk running into Coleman, who would have a burn on to lecture me about going to dive bars. My reluctance came from the fact that I knew he was right to be annoyed with me. I'd known it last evening before I pulled into the parking lot of the bar. Guilt didn't make me any more inclined to verbal correction.

Instead, I drove to Hilltop to await the awakening of Queen Tinkie. She was going to be a little miffed that she missed a trip to Ole Miss, but since I was sitting in her driveway at the butt-crack of dawn, she'd be easy to beg forgiveness from.

Pluto sat on the console and watched the front porch of Hilltop. The cat was often aloof, but he had a real weakness for Chablis. The dog had begun my career as a private investigator, and I had a true fondness for the pampered little beast. I was familiar with Tinkie's routine and knew the very first thing she did in the morning was open the front door to let Chablis out to tinkle. Pluto knew this, too, and he was waiting for a glimpse of his friend.

When I saw movement on the front porch of Hilltop, I figured Tinkie was up. I sat up tall in the car seat, ready to get to work on finding Loxley's and Miller's killer. Or killers.

But instead of Tinkie coming down the drive toward me, there was a woman dressed in one of those wretchedly constraining outfits of the mid- to late-1800s. A white lawn blouse tucked into a long, navy blue skirt. Underneath was some torture device of whalebone and laces. I knew it must be Jitty, but I had no idea why she was at Hilltop or who she was pretending to be.

"I'm not in the mood," I told her when she got close to my side of the car. "Go home."

"You're ordering me around like you have a right."

Oh, no way was I ready this early in the morning for a women's libber ghost from the nineteenth century. "I'm serious, Jitty. Move along." I leaned back in the car seat and closed my eyes. When I opened them again, the woman was two feet away, her face so close I could see her individual eyelashes.

"What?" I forced myself to sit taller.

"When you love a man, you'll follow him to the ends of the earth."

Two could play this game. "If I were trailing along behind a man, I'd have to abandon Dahlia House and leave it without an heir." I had her on this one. I wasn't going to take a lesson on how to be a biddable woman. Especially not from a ghost who refused to do anything I asked. Ever.

"I followed my love all over the West." Jitty was deep into the persona of whomever she was impersonating, because I knew for a fact that she'd never left the state of Mississippi while she was alive.

"What love?" I hated to admit it but I was curious, especially when I noticed the derringer tucked into the bodice of her dress. "Who are you?"

"Mary Katherine Horony-Cummings is my name, but I go by Big Nose Kate."

"Your nose isn't that big." I hated it when people got demeaning nicknames. Except for Lottie Best, a Sunflower County High School cheerleader who was mean to me on a regular basis all through my senior year. Now, thanks to me, she went by the nickname Afternoon Fat Cankles. I'd made it a point to spread that one around the county.

"Doc Holliday liked my nose. He liked a lot of things about me. We had a real thing, you know." She looked past me to a time that was long gone. "I loved that man. We traveled the West. He'd gamble and pull some teeth when he needed a grubstake. I sold my favors to the men of the town. It was a good partnership."

I wasn't about to comment on that. I was learning that a lot of outlaw women turned tricks to get by. "What are you doing here at Tinkie's house?"

"I was born into a wealthy family. Hungarian. In my early years, I had a strict upbringing and education. My folks died when I was young and I went to a foster home. Not a place I wanted to be. Not a place any child should be. Back in those days, children weren't much valued except as farmhands. Things were awful for black women in the former slave states, but across the country, most women and children suffered. Natives were being evicted and forced on the Trail of Tears. Children were bartered and traded for the work they could do. Women were born to serve. I couldn't take it and I threw it all over for a life of adventure."

"Do you regret it?" I asked.

"No. No, I don't. I regret that Doc became a lunger. He never complained, though. Never. But when he couldn't breathe . . . that's what sent me to the laudanum." She shrugged. "No one lived long back then. And, Lord, we had some adventures. Burned fast and died quick."

If she'd partnered with Doc Holliday, she knew a lot of other outlaws. "Did you know the Earp brothers?" In my Wild West fantasies, the brothers were played by a series of very handsome A-list actors from Hugh O'Brian to James Garner to Kurt Russell. The outlaws-cum-lawmen did not lack for handsome film stand-ins.

She nodded. "I knew them all. Not men to fool around with."

"So the legend goes."

"Wyatt was the fastest man with a gun I ever saw. Deadly. He had a love of gambling, boxing, and horse racing. He could have been a millionaire nine times over, but money slipped through his fingers. Had to take a job as a lawman."

"Seems to me like an awful lot of outlaws became law-men." I wasn't thinking of my own personal lawman, Coleman Peters, who'd been a straight arrow all of his life. He was as good-looking as any Earp, but he'd never set up criminal enterprises.

"The Earp brothers weren't always on the right side

of the law, that's for sure. Wyatt involved himself in schemes. But in the end, in Tombstone, he did what he had to do to maintain law and order."

"It took a brave man to stand up to the outlaws of that day. I've read enough history to know that. But I still don't know why you're here."

She stepped back three paces. "Sometimes a woman doesn't really have a choice in life. I did. Back in my day, that was a helluva lot more than most women had." She smiled, but it was really sad. She looked as haunted as I felt. "Relish your choices, Sarah Booth. You were born into a lucky time for women. When I was young, what options were open for women? Saloon girls or wives. Domestic servants. There wasn't an in-between. I made myself another choice, and I lived it full and hard."

"Wait, why didn't you ever marry Doc?"

She shrugged. "Why bother with the legal system? What would a piece of paper have changed?"

She was right about that, and the next time Jitty started to harangue me about being unwed, I was going to bring this up. "Nothing."

"Doc was who he was. He had an eye for the ladies." She shrugged. "I had my share of men. Marriage wouldn't have prevented any of that. I made my choices."

She'd had choices, all right—to marry a farmer and work herself to death or maybe marry a merchant and lead a life of upright propriety. Or run with the outlaws and sell her body to pay her way. She was right. I'd been born into a luckier era. We still had plenty of battles to fight, but things were a far cry from what she'd experienced.

"Kate . . ." When I looked back at her, there was nothing there except some tumbleweed that just blew across the driveway and disappeared as Tinkie came out the front door.

"Oscar said you were sitting out here talking to your-self again." She was even more pregnant than the day before. She held Chablis in her arms. "What's on the agenda?" she asked.

Whatever else I might have planned, we were staying in Zinnia, and as close to the hospital as we could get. Tinkie looked . . . dangerous. "I can handle things today. Why don't you take it easy? You've got an ordeal ahead of you."

"And if I stay home, I'll do nothing but fret. I need to be busy." She dared me to say otherwise. "Let's find out who's killing men that just need killing."

I was afraid if I contradicted her, she'd get upset and deliver the baby right in the front seat of my car. That wasn't a situation I was prepared for. "Sure. Let's hit the trail." Tinkie put Chablis in the backseat with Sweetie Pie and Pluto and buckled her seat belt. Then, we were off.

The owner of the Red Top Bar was Clifford LaPlace. He was also the proprietor of a furniture sales business on the outskirts of town. Clifford had a multi-stream in-come. I drove toward LaPlace Furniture, casting sidelong glances at my partner, who was obviously uncomfort-able. What if she was having contractions?

"You okay?" I asked her.

"I have gas, if you must know. I can feel it roiling around in my gut and any minute I may explode."

"You sure it's gas and not contractions?"

"I know the difference between gas and contractions. Do you think I'm stupid?"

I bit my lip to keep from saying anything and just kept driving. Normally, Tinkie didn't talk about such things as gas or heartburn. It was Rule 892 in the Daddy's Girl Handbook. Proper ladies did not have digestive issues of any sort. Their bodies functioned perfectly at all times without any rude noises or odors. It was a tough standard to uphold.

When we got to the furniture store, I stopped at the front door.

"Aren't you going to park?" Tinkie asked.

"I was going to let you out here and then park."

"I am not an *invalid*. Stop treating me like one." Her face was red.

I turned off the car. "Tinkie, I love you and I'm concerned. That's not a crime and you need to stop treating me like it is. I hope you aren't being so snappy with Oscar."

She looked out the passenger window. Sweetie Pie leaned over the seat and licked her ear. Even Pluto got in on the action and jumped into what was left of her lap.

"I want this to be done," Tinkie said. "I hate this. I'm as wide as I am tall. I waddle. I, Tinkie Bellcase Richmond, have turned into a waddler. My feet are a size and a half bigger than normal. I cannot wear any of my favorite shoes. Everything I eat has a consequence, and I want a damn margarita. And maybe a cigarette."

My first impulse, which I squashed, was to laugh— Tinkie had never smoked in her life and was vocal in her concern about the health hazards of such bad practices. She was stressed, uncomfortable, constrained, worried, and "fit to be tied," as my aunt Loulane would describe her mood.

"Tinkie, reassure me that you aren't going into labor. Because I don't know and I can't tell and it would probably give me a heart attack if you did."

"I'm not. But I'm telling you right here and now, if I could hatch this baby in front of this store, I'd squat, grunt, and do it. But the cake isn't completely baked yet. I just have to be patient." Her jaw was clenched and her knuckles on the hand holding the door lever were white. "I can't wait to hold my little angel in my arms," she gritted out.

This time I couldn't stop the laughter. It bubbled up and over. I laughed until I was weeping. At first Tinkie looked absolutely murderous. Then she started to laugh, too.

"I really do want this baby," she said.

I nodded and laughed some more.

"I do, Sarah Booth. It's just that I've been pregnant half my life, it seems. I just want it to be over and I want my baby."

This sounded more like my partner, who'd wanted a child for years. "Okay. Then let's get some work done before your water breaks and all Hell is set free."

I pulled around to a parking spot and we both entered the store. "Clifford LaPlace, please," Tinkie told an eager saleswoman. When the woman looked askance, Tinkie grinned. "It's a personal matter. Very personal." She patted her belly, the implication being clear. The saleswoman's eyes widened and she hurried away, looking back over her shoulder several times.

"Tinkie, you know you implied that Clifford is the father of your child."

"I know." She grinned. "And it's the most fun I've had in a month."

I didn't get a chance to chastise her, because a big man, over six feet and built like a frontline tackle, came toward us like a locomotive. He didn't really walk, he swaggered. Skin-tight jeans to show off the bulk of his muscular thighs, and a T-shirt two sizes too small to highlight his pecs. He glowered as he approached. The salesclerk followed in his wake with great uncertainty on her face. When she saw me looking at him with amusement, she rolled her eyes.

"Who are you and what do you want?" He spoke loudly so whoever might be in the store could hear. There was only one other customer and at his tone, she scurried out the front door. I knew what he was up to. The man was already building a case that he didn't know us—in the event Tinkie meant to trap him in a paternity suit. He was the type of man who spent 90 percent of his time erecting defenses against the consequences of actions he knew he was guilty of.

Tinkie whipped out our business card and handed it to him. "Can you read?" she asked sweetly.

Oh Lordy, this was going to break bad. Tinkie's hormones were pinging and bonging throughout her body. Hell, she didn't suffer fools even when she wasn't hormonally jacked up. "We're investigating the death of Curtis Miller," I said, striving for a less abrasive tone.

"What do you want from me?" he asked. "I didn't kill him. I barely knew him."

"Good to know," I said. "But someone did know him and in fact someone did kill him. He was in your bar before he died. You or your patrons may have been the last people to see him alive."

"Except for the killer," he quickly pointed out.

"Yes. The killer," Tinkie said. She cocked her head. "Tell us about Curtis."

"I'm not his mama," Clifford said. "He drank beer and shot pool at the Red Top. He had a wife who was way too mouthy, always complaining about something." He shrugged. "What's to tell? That's all I know."

"That's too bad," Tinkie said, suddenly looking all forlorn and lost. She popped her bottom lip, all wet and shiny, out of her mouth. It was a maneuver that I'd seen bring a grown man to heel. "I was hoping you could help us with some information." She had his undivided attention.

I came in from the flank for the kill. "Clifford, do you know anything about a group of men called AVA?" I saw it in his eyes, the reaction that he covered very quickly, but not so fast I didn't see it.

"Don't know anything about social clubs. There's a dart team and a pool team at the bar, but I don't know anything about them. Far as I know folks are there to drink, listen to music, socialize, and have a good time. I stay out of my patrons' business. That's a rule at the Red Top."

"Now, Clifford, you know we aren't talking about that kind of club." Tinkie put her hand on his overdeveloped forearm and almost purred. "This is a secret club. You know, the kind that has political influence. It's an organization where men join up and pay dues or donate to different political campaigns to promote their political agenda. I don't know much more about it, because it's not a woman's place."

I gave Tinkie a hard stare. How did she know all that? Plus, she was piling it on mighty thick, but Clifford seemed to be eating it with a spoon. Clifford's phone rang and he turned his back on us to answer it. I drilled in on Tinkie. "Cut it out!"

"What? I'm pregnant, not brain-dead. I did some checking on my own while you were at Ole Miss. I learned a lot of interesting stuff."

Clifford put his phone away and was about to show us the door when Tinkie struck.

"AVA is a national organization with a big, fat bank account. Even the local branch here in Sunflower County has some wealthy patrons." Tinkie had moved in closer to Clifford so that she was aggressively addressing Clifford's solar plexus—he was really tall. And she was channeling Brenda from *The Closer*; I wasn't about to step in her way. She had a brain for finances, and that was often the key to solving a crime. On the drive over, I'd told her all about my adventures at Ole Miss, but I'd failed to ask her what she'd done with her time. I'd assumed she'd fallen into a pregnant woman coma. No wonder she'd been a little testy with me.

"You don't know anything about AVA," Clifford said, more wish than statement of fact.

"Oh, I wouldn't go that far," Tinkie said. "We know some, but we're going to find out a whole lot more. Us, and then there's some interest from the FBI. You know, domestic terrorism."

"You need to get your pregnant butt home to tend to your man." Clifford had had enough of both of us. "I always knew Oscar was weak-kneed. Married the rich man's spoiled daughter so he could manage the bank. That might sound good to some men, but not to a real man. If you didn't have money, no one would put up with your nasty self."

I saw what was going to happen, but I didn't know how to stop it. Tinkie was going to get hurt. Really hurt. Clifford LaPlace didn't care if she was pregnant or rich. He was going to pop her in the face. He drew his arm back for the punch.

"Sweetie Pie!" My wild cry echoed through the store and for a split second, Clifford hesitated as he tried to decipher if I was calling him an endearment or what. That was all it took. My ninety-pound red tick hound burst through the automatic door and vaulted toward Clifford. He screamed as her teeth clamped around the hand he'd drawn back to punch Tinkie. The weight of the dog pushed him over backward and took him down hard. When his head cracked on the floor, I feared he might be dead.

"He was going to hit me." Tinkie looked a little shell-shocked.

"I know. So did Sweetie Pie." Pluto and Chablis had now joined us. Chablis rushed to the body and bit Clifford's nose as hard as she could, which didn't really amount to a lot since she had such a severe underbite. Still, it left little bloody teeth marks. Seeking a more tender target, she grabbed his lower lip. When he came to, he was going to be really pissed off.

"Is he alive?" The salesclerk had joined us.

I knelt beside him. "Yeah. Strong pulse. I think he just knocked himself out."

"He's out cold?" she asked.

"Yeah, you should call an ambulance."

"Okay, in a minute." She walked closer, eyes narrowed, as she studied her boss. Before I knew what she was doing, she drew back a leg and kicked him as hard as she could in the gut. "I've been wanting to do that for a long, long time." And so she did it again, for good measure. "You have no idea what it's like to work for a misogynist like him."

I didn't have to ask why she worked for LaPlace. Sunflower County wasn't a hotbed of great jobs for anyone. Farming was the number one industry, and the local shops were mostly mom and pop, employing family members. A job selling furniture was one of the better options.

Finally, the salesperson did call an ambulance, and I leaned down to check his pulse again. It was strong and steady. I really believed he was just unconscious. Still, it would be better if Tinkie and I split before he came to. He might still have a yen to punch her lights out. I removed the business card Tinkie had given him from his hand. Just to be on the safe side, even though he'd recognized her as Oscar Richmond's wife. Still, no need to leave evidence behind. We could always pray the blow to the head would give him amnesia.

"We should go," I said to Tinkie.

"Go on," the saleswoman said. "When the ambulance gets here I'll tell them how he attempted to beat Mrs. Richmond and how the dog saved her." She smiled. "More than likely he'll just want to say he slipped and fell."

"Thanks. And you are?"

"Betty Sue Smith. Just call me Betty Sue."

"Thank you."

"Hey, I heard what you were asking Clifford. I can tell you about AVA. I keep his books for him."

Holy Christmas. We'd hit the mother lode. "When would be a good time to talk?" I asked her.

"After work. We can meet, but it has to be discreet. If Clifford finds out, he'll fire me or worse."

There were a number of juke joints and nightclubs around the Delta, but I named our favorite. "Playin' the Bones at eight?" Because the blues club drew a diverse mix of people and plenty of single women who loved the blues and dancing, it wasn't likely that Clifford or any of his AVA associates would show up there.

"See you there," she said.

Clifford moaned and Betty Sue motioned us toward the door. "Leave before he wakes up. Seriously. He's a mean, mean man. He'll try to have that dog destroyed."

Over my dead body. That would be one reason that I'd shoot a man in the heart with a .38. "Betty Sue, does Clifford have a gun here?"

She nodded. "In his desk drawer." She pulled a key from her pocket. "I hate guns. Take a look if you want. Just don't move it. He knows exactly where everything he owns is. Never met a man who kept up with his things like that. Almost like he's afraid someone's going to steal something from him."

"Tinkie, would you please get the critters into the car. We do need to beat a retreat."

She gave me a cranky glare, but she waddled toward the front door with the animals following her like a line of little ducklings. I went to the office in the back and quickly opened the desk drawer, using a paper towel so I wouldn't leave prints. In the second drawer was a pistol. A .38 caliber. I couldn't tell if it had been recently fired and I didn't touch it. But Coleman could, once he got a warrant. I had to wonder if Tinkie and I, in our search for information about AVA, might not have stumbled on Curtis Miller's killer.

18

Tinkie and I sat in a dark corner of the club. The band was onstage, rocking the old Percy Sledge song, "When a Man Loves a Woman." Kind of ironic as we waited for a woman to tell us about a bunch of men who thought beating up and controlling women were acceptable.

"I love that song," Tinkie said, shifting on her chair. She sipped a ginger ale and looked longingly at my Jack on the rocks.

"I do, too." In fact, the song made me miss Coleman, who I'd asked *not* to join us. Betty Sue had made it clear she didn't want to be involved in snitching publicly on her boss. I was doing my best to honor her feelings. Besides, Coleman was at the sheriff's office getting a search warrant for Clifford LaPlace's furniture office. LaPlace was probably smart enough not to have guns and things at the Red Top Bar, which would have been my go-to place to search first. We'd gotten a lead on the potential murder weapon, though. Now, Coleman needed to test the gun to see if the bullet that killed Curtis—or any of the men—had come from it.

The club door opened and a woman came in. "Here she is." I stood up and waved so she'd see us.

"What would you like to drink?" I asked when she made it to the table.

"Salty dog, please." She settled into a chair. "Mrs. Richmond, you look ready to give birth. I know you must be very excited that pregnancy will soon be over."

"I am," Tinkie said. "I'm counting the hours." Only I could read the frustration behind Tinkie's words. Note to self—and to Jitty—pregnancy was not necessarily the joyous hormonal state that many new mothers declared. Time would tell whether Tinkie mellowed or not, once the baby was born. We'd both been assured she'd forget all about the pain and limitations the minute she held her baby. I was paying close attention.

I left Tinkie and Betty Sue chatting while I went to the bar and got Betty Sue's drink. The song wrapped up and the band went straight into a livelier number that had folks racing to the dance floor. I took the drink back to our table.

"What can you tell us about AVA?" I asked our guest once we'd all settled into friendly conversation.

"Plenty. Clifford runs the local chapter. He was instrumental in forming it, to hear him tell it, which may or may not be factual. The man does have an issue with boasting and puffing himself up. Anyway, AVA's goal is to gather enough money to influence state lawmakers in

passing laws designed to keep women 'in their place.'"
She used air quotes. "They're working with the national
AVA organization. They've got a team of lobbyists and
legal help to write the laws that they give to state legis-
lators who've been 'gifted' with expensive things to be
sure these laws pass. It's just a payoff and a form of
bribery. The agenda is to hit the individual states first
with these laws that begin to limit women's economic,
educational, and medical choices. Once the state legis-
latures, which are so much cheaper to buy off than con-
gressmen, are on board, then they'll take the laws to the
national level."

"What, exactly, is 'a woman's place,' according to
them?" Tinkie asked.

"Busy in the kitchen or the bedroom." Betty Sue shook
her head. "That's what they think. But they aren't all
just a bunch of Cro-Magnon dummies. Some of them
are lawyers and businesspeople and they've put a lot of
money into keeping the world the way it is, at least in
Mississippi. You have to understand, holding women
and minorities back really works for them. They make
money on this, and they hold all the power. They're terrified of losing that power."

"Terrified enough to kill someone?" I asked.

"Oh, definitely."

"But why kill their own devotees?" Tinkie asked.

Betty Sue shook her head. "No idea." She held up a
finger. "You know, a few days ago Clifford got into a
shouting match at the store. He was on the phone arguing about a woman. Someone Clifford liked, but the
person he was talking to obviously thought she might be
a traitor. I kind of got the impression Clifford was sweet
on her."

"Who? Did you get a name?" I asked.

She thought a minute. "I didn't catch the name, but it was someone who knew that college professor who was killed."

"Like a girlfriend of his?"

"Yeah. That's how I read it, but like I said, I didn't hear the whole conversation. Just that Clifford said he was in charge and he felt she was on the up-and-up. I think the person on the other end of the phone was Curtis Miller."

I looked at Tinkie. It was possible they'd been arguing about Alala. Or maybe fifty other women. "Thanks, Betty Sue."

"How the hell can you even stand working for Clifford?" Tinkie asked.

"I have three kids, and my husband left me. I have a degree in art history, which is pretty useless here. But I'm a good salesperson and I get paid on commission. Women would rather buy furniture from me, because I understand their needs and concerns. I move a lot of product for Clifford. He rants and raves about his political ideology, but he knows I'm his best asset. So, he walks a line with me."

"And yet, you hate him." I remembered the two kicks she'd given him.

"Oh, I hate him plenty. But we're in this disgusting symbiotic relationship. It is what it is."

"Tell us more about AVA." Tinkie brought us back to the point. "Who belongs to the local group?"

"The membership list is very secret. Clifford won't even leave it locked up in the safe at the office, which is smart because I know the combination. He carries it with him everywhere he goes. A lot of the men are just uneducated followers who need someone to look down on. But as I said, some of them . . . they have money. Plenty of it. I don't know where it comes from, but they're well-funded."

"How well-funded?"

"They don't bank in Zinnia," Betty Sue said. "I suspect it's because they know Mr. Richmond would report them if he caught on to their agenda. They use a bank in Tupelo, where they're more anonymous. And there was more than four hundred thousand in the account the last time I had a chance to spy on it."

That would be plenty to pay off a number of local elected officials, if those officials were up for sale. Not all of them would be. But some. "And the focus of the organization is writing laws that disenfranchise women?" I asked, to be clear. Some of the guys I'd seen in the bars didn't look like writing legislation would appeal to them. They were, after all, men of "action."

"Health care—you know, birth control and things like that—is the first target. That and there's been talk of a select group who would intimidate vocal women. Silencing them if they speak out and try to raise awareness with other women. You know, weed out the troublemakers, cow them into silence." She met my gaze. "Or maybe set them up for a crime."

There it was. One of the best reasons put forth to kill Curtis and Dr. Loxley. To frame Alala.

"How many of these men are there?" Tinkie asked.

She shook her head. "I don't know. As I said previously, Clifford keeps the list with him at all times. I only know what I know because I snoop. I figure if I ever get the goods on him doing something really illegal, I'll make my move to force him out of the business and I'll buy the store."

Talk about a woman with a dream. Clifford had clutched an asp to his bosom, and he'd underestimated the venom of the snake. At the first golden opportunity, Betty Sue was going to sink her fangs in him and not let go until he was stone-cold dead. It couldn't happen to a more deserving fellow.

"Did you ever hear Clifford mention Curtis Miller?"

"Mention him? He didn't have to mention him. Curtis came into the store all the time. That wife of his, Tansy, was always lying down on the beds and wallowing around. She'd sit on the sofas, kick her shoes off, and put her feet up on the cushions. Gross. She'd bring some stinking sandwich into the store and sit at the dining tables and eat. She left a ring on a mahogany table that took me two weeks to buff out."

"Clifford never tried to show her where her place might be when they were in the store?" It was curious that he'd let Tansy damage his furniture without reprimand.

"Something was going on between Clifford and Curtis. It was like a competition. I can't put my finger on it, exactly, but there was something there you might want to look into."

"Were they friends?" It occurred to me that Clifford and Curtis might have teamed up to frame Alala. Except Curtis had no idea he was going to be the dead body that snapped the trap shut. The idea of Curtis as bait appealed to me.

"I don't know if they were working together or just two men with the same point of view about who should run the world—them. They fed off each other; no doubt about that."

"Do you know if Clifford had any more guns than the .38 in his desk?" I asked.

She nodded. "There was a rifle—the old war kind with the legs that steadied it. It was in Clifford's office, kind of like a showpiece, until a week ago. Then it suddenly disappeared. I never asked about it, because I don't want Clifford to know I snoop in his office."

Smart cookie. And I suspected that gun was sitting in Coleman Peters's office right now. Which could be another reason Curtis was dead. He'd left the rifle at Erkwell Park to be picked up by the law. "Thanks."

"That's really all I know." Betty Sue finished her drink. "Please keep my name out of this. If Clifford finds out I was talking to you . . ."

Tinkie shifted in her chair again, and I knew she was really uncomfortable. "He won't hear it from us," I said.

"Thanks for the drink." Betty Sue stood. "If I hear anything else pertinent, I'll call you. I'm sick of Clifford and all those wannabe rulers of the universe. They're all so sure they're smarter than most everyone else and always smarter than any woman."

"Oh, I think we'll show them differently," Tinkie said.

That was the best we could hope for.

When we were at the door to leave, Betty Sue turned to us. "I think those men are meeting tomorrow night. I'm not sure, but I was thinking about something I overheard this morning. Clifford was on the phone with someone and he got all hush-hush and paranoid-seeming. Makes me think something is up."

"Where would the meeting be?" Tinkie asked.

"There's a hunting lodge. It's on private property. I don't think you could get in."

"A name?" Tinkie asked.

I tried to signal Betty Sue not to say a name. Tinkie didn't need to know this or even think about it.

"The property belongs to a college professor from Ole Miss. Name of Brown, I think." Betty Sue completely missed my frantic sign language, but the name stopped me cold in my tracks.

"Dr. Becky Brown?" I was incredulous. First that she had a hunting lodge, and second that she'd loan it out to the likes of Clifford LaPlace.

Betty Sue shook her head. "Never heard the given name, but I wouldn't think it was a woman. I mean these men treat women really bad." She shook her head. "But anything is possible these days. Why would a woman professor loan her hunting lodge to a bunch of men who would take her job away from her and keep her cooking, cleaning, and having kids if they had a chance?"

"You got me," I said. Becky Brown obviously had a taste for being abused and treated as a second-class citizen.

"Some women just have to have a man. They don't feel complete without one, so they're willing to settle for the dregs in the barrel, I guess." Betty Sue sighed heavily. "They don't do the rest of us any favors. Come by the store if you need any furniture."

Betty Sue left and Tinkie and I stood at the door for a moment before we stepped into the crisp night. There was a message on my phone that Coleman had delivered Chablis back to Hilltop and would be waiting for me at Dahlia House. No doubt Coleman and Oscar had a nice chat about how they'd both like for their women to be home and not running the roads.

"What are you smiling about, Sarah Booth?" Tinkie asked. She was rubbing her belly in a way that made me believe she wasn't even aware she was doing it.

"How much easier would life be for Oscar and Coleman if they really could control us?"

She burst out in a big laugh. "Now you're in a world of really bad science fiction or fantasy. That is not about to happen in the real world."

She was right about that.

19

"Sarah Booth, I shouldn't have to tell you to stay out of places like Homeboy Heroes. It's dangerous. They have a knifing there about once a week. Sometimes bystanders get hurt in those brawls."

I reclined on the sofa with my feet in Coleman's lap. We'd opted to sit in the parlor with a fire and a drink. If I had to take a lecture, this was the way to do it. I'd resolved to let him get this off his chest so we could move past it. And it went without saying that he was right. My actions had been foolishly dangerous. "I know."

"And yet you walked right in there without even telling a single one of your friends you were headed there. You could have been hurt or, with your talent for trouble, started a fight where a lot of other people got hurt. You could have disappeared."

He wasn't kidding. "I know."

"Sometimes you do things without thinking them through."

"I know." This wasn't my first rodeo. I could recite this litany of my flaws by heart.

Coleman had slipped an ice cube from his drink and without any warning, grabbed my left ankle and pressed the cold cube to the bottom of my foot. "I *know* you *know*, but I also *know* you have no intention of listening to me."

"Hey!" The ice didn't hurt, but he was tickling the bottom of my foot. "Let go." I tried jerking my leg free without success.

"Are you going to stay out of dive bars?" He'd abandoned the ice and was down to straight-out tickling.

"Are you seriously going to tickle me into obedience?" I fought and squirmed, but he had a solid hold on me.

"Yes." The glint in his blue eyes told me that he was not kidding.

"Okay, okay. I won't go back in that Homeboy place. I swear it on a stack of Bibles." I snatched my foot free of his grip, but only because he let me.

"Not just that place, but any establishment like it. Ninety-nine percent of the guys in there are harmless, but the danger is the one percent who mean to cause trouble and rope the others into following."

"Coleman, I'm not afraid of a bunch of men who think they're all that. Most of them are just pumped up on their own testosterone. If a woman stands up to them, they back down. They're just a bunch of privileged creeps."

Coleman's forehead was a thundercloud. "Tansy Miller has a damaged arm, Sarah Booth. Some of those guys really enjoy hurting women, and just because you're from a world where a man wouldn't hit you doesn't mean they won't." He gave me the stink eye. "In your own way, you're displaying a type of privilege."

That caught me up short. Was I really acting privileged? Maybe. I chewed on it a moment longer. Because I couldn't imagine a man ever lifting a hand to me, had I had a protected—even privileged—upbringing? Maybe. Wasn't privilege the expectation that things would go a certain way without understanding how that wasn't the reality for a lot of people? The dagger of truth hit home. "Okay, Coleman, I see your point. I don't expect anyone to hit me, because my friends would likely kill them. And that is an attitude of privilege. I won't go into those places . . . unless you're right there with me."

Coleman only laughed. "And that could get us both an ass-whipping."

"Then I am at a loss what it is you want me to say or do."

"Just know the danger, Sarah Booth. I'm not asking you to give up doing anything necessary to solve a case. Just know the danger and weigh when doing something dangerous is necessary and when you could take a pass and do it more safely."

I removed my feet from his lap and sat up so that I was on my knees beside him. "That's a very reasonable request." I kissed his lips softly. "One I promise to heed."

Coleman sighed and pulled me into his arms. "Sometimes I despair, Sarah Booth. I think I've committed myself to a woman determined to drive me to drink. And then sometimes you are so . . . wonderful." He kissed me with great thoroughness.

It was a difficult thing to do, but I eased back from him. "Before we take this upstairs, which I really want to do, I have to know what you found out about Curtis Miller's murder. Did you locate the primary crime scene?"

"You want to know this right now?"

I nodded. "I need to go to Nashville to look into the third dead man, and Tinkie is about to pop. You haven't seen her. Honestly, when I'm around her it's like I hear a ticking bomb, knocking off the seconds until she goes boom! I'm not comfortable leaving town with her. Heck, I'm not comfortable leaving the hospital parking lot with her."

"And she'll never let you go without her." Coleman knew my friend very well.

"Right. So I need to know what you found out about Curtis's murder. And maybe you can make some calls to Nashville for me? Save me a trip, at least for a day or two."

"Glad to oblige, and I need to do it anyway." He got up, refreshed our drinks, and put another log on the fire. It wasn't really cold enough for a fire, but there was something so comforting about the dancing flames.

"What did you find out about Curtis?" I'd already told Coleman about my evening with Betty Sue and the gun revelation. He was getting a search warrant in the morning when the local judge was in his office. However, I had not told him about the hunting lodge. I knew he would object to my plan to go there, and I was still debating whether Sweetie Pie, Pluto, and I should sneak around and try to overhear what was going on at the AVA meeting, or if I should let Coleman arrive on the scene with the full force of the law. It wasn't an easy choice.

"You're sure Curtis belonged to AVA?" Coleman asked as he slowly paced in front of the fire.

"Yes."

"You already know he and Clifford LaPlace were mixed up in something with that group of knuckle-draggers," Coleman said. "Were you aware that Curtis had been spying on Dr. Diakos for over a week?"

This was news, with a very real implication that Curtis setting up a sniper rifle in the park was actually premeditated. "To what end was he spying on her?"

"I had a warrant for the Millers' house and De-Wayne, Budgie, and I went through it with a fine-tooth comb. We found where Curtis had been following Diakos, plotting out her daily movements. He had a whiteboard where he had it all laid out. No reason was given for the surveillance. Just notations of her movements." His eyebrows rose. "Tell your client she should vary her pattern of behavior. She's too darn predictable. If this group has plans to harm her, someone will take over what Curtis was doing. Her day-to-day actions are too easy to track."

"I'll let her know." I wasn't kidding. Curtis was dead, but evidently there were plenty of other roaches hiding under the same rock he'd come out from. "Is she in danger?"

"I don't know," Coleman said. "It's possible she's the target of AVA and might be in the crosshairs, but there's something else we have to consider. You're not going to like this."

"What?"

"It's equally possible Dr. Diakos is responsible for Curtis's murder, if not the others."

"You don't really think—"

"Oh, but I do," Coleman said. "Look at it from my point of view. She's been on the scene at every murder—that we know about. There could be more dead bodies we just haven't found. Budgie is checking into that. She's known each victim. She has a reason to want harm to come to each victim."

"We don't even know for sure she *knew* the Vanderbilt professor." I came to her defense. Coleman was jumping way ahead of the evidence, and that wasn't like him.

"All three dead men were reputed to abuse women. In fact, we can drop the word *reputed*. They were abusers and proud of it. All three were getting away with it without any real consequence. Dr. Diakos has been very vocal in her support of violence against such men, and she was in the vicinity of each murder."

"Alala wants women to defend themselves. And they should. I promise you, if someone ever hit me, they would pay. And if they cornered me, I think I could kill them."

Coleman ran his fingers through my hair. "And I would expect nothing less. And just so you know, if you didn't kill them, I'd have to. But Alala arouses passions. She's a brilliant speaker and writer, and though she is often subtle, her goal is clearly for women to stand up and strike back against any man who abuses them. She makes it clear that killing them is on the table."

"And you think that's wrong?" I would never have thought Coleman would see this issue so differently from how I did.

"No one should be judge and jury, Sarah Booth. You know I feel that way about any crime. The law investigates, the DA prosecutes, and the courts render the verdict. When one person, whether it's a woman or a man, takes all of those roles in hand, that isn't justice. It's vengeance."

He had a point. "I don't think she really incites violence." I could be stubborn, or so I'd been told.

"She does. And she'd spoken out against all three men, noting instances where they'd been abusive to women."

"You know that to be true?" Coleman must have completed some research on Dr. Loxley at Ole Miss and the dead professor in Nashville that I wasn't privy to. Yet.

"There are witnesses who say this is true, but I'll know more tomorrow. I can say for sure that there is a clear connection between Diakos and the dead men. And there were hard feelings between all three men and Diakos. That much, I've ascertained."

"Still . . ." But I honestly hadn't found another more credible suspect. There was Dr. Brown, but she seemed to have thrown in with the wife-beating group of men being murdered, allowing them to meet in her lodge. Unless she was a counterspy, infiltrating the group to expose them. I didn't see that with Brown's personality, though. It could also be Margaret McNeese. But that didn't seem likely. Margaret was pretty bland, kind of a timid mouse, and as far as I could tell had no connection to Curtis Miller or the dead man in Nashville.

Tansy had a reason to kill Curtis, but not the other two men, plus she had a sprained wrist. That injury wouldn't prevent her from shooting Curtis, but if I had to guess,

I'd say it would take both hands for her to hold a gun like a .38. She was a small, fragile woman. My other suspect, Todd Renfield, had an alibi, which was Tansy or Moody Moody, depending on what time of night he needed an alibi for. Moody was sleeping with Curtis, indicating she simply had a taste for cheating men, as demonstrated by Todd, who was sleeping with Tansy. I was going to have to build a diorama of the town and the hot sheet action to keep them straight.

I had another idea. "Maybe Clifford killed Curtis. You know, to frame Alala."

"But what about Loxley and Dr. Kevin Wilson, the Nashville professor? Why would Clifford kill them? It hasn't been established that he even knew them."

"I can't answer that question. Yet. I don't know enough about Dr. Wilson. But I think it's the Curtis and Clifford relationship that needs more exploration. Betty Sue said Curtis and Clifford were thick as thieves, but it's possible Curtis was killed with Clifford's .38."

"Or the gun we found in your client's yard," Coleman pointed out. He stopped pacing in front of the fireplace. "I'm not ruling anything out. We have three men shot with the same type of gun. We have one gun and if the gun in Clifford LaPlace's desk is involved, that's another ball game. I got a search warrant for the furniture store and Budgie and DeWayne will soon have the gun from there. If Clifford owned the sniper's rifle, we'll know that, too. Whatever the connection between Curtis Miller, Clifford LaPlace, Dr. Brown, and Dr. Diakos, we're going to find that out."

"Thanks for not writing off my theory completely. I realize it sounds far-fetched."

"I want to get to the truth, no matter how far-fetched

it turns out to be. Let's hit the bed," Coleman said, offering a hand to pull me to my feet. "It's been a very long and trying day."

I put my hand in his and went straight into his arms when he tugged me up. Now was the moment to tell him about the AVA meeting the next night. If I didn't tell him now, it would be harder to tell him tomorrow. I might not tell him at all. But I wasn't actually breaking my word to him. I'd said I wouldn't go to any dive bars. I wasn't planning on going to a bar, just a hunting club. Isolated and in the woods. With dangerous men who really didn't seem to like women very much at all.

"You're mighty quiet," Coleman said.

"Just thinking," I answered, my stomach queasy.

"That could be dangerous, Sarah Booth. If you're thinking, you're likely either hiding something or planning to do something you know you shouldn't."

"Don't be ridiculous." I eased back from his arms. I could feel a fast pulse beating under my jaw. I really hated even lies of omission to Coleman.

"You look guilty." Coleman could read me like a book sometimes. Usually the times I didn't want him to. "What are you up to?"

"Going straight to bed. I have a lot to do tomorrow. And you'll take care of checking on Dr. Wilson in Nashville? Is he another English professor?"

"Nope. Sociology and psychology." He grinned. "He was writing a book about the Southern mores of marriage. His theory is that Southern women have, in the past, been more willing to conform to the roles men prefer women to play. That Southern women, by training, climate, and or genetics were suited to the role of lady as the perfect helpmeet. And that created a kind of idyllic world where grace and charm dominated the home front."

That would really set Alala's tail feathers on fire. I could see where she'd want to hurt Wilson. "Mississippi suddenly seems to be the book destination for a lot of different subjects."

Coleman shrugged. "Wilson wasn't all that wrong, and neither is Diakos. Women in the South have always had to endure a double standard. They have to be soft and feminine while at the same time being the strength that holds a lot of families together."

He was right about that. "I will never understand how Tinkie manages to be so . . . 'diplomatic' when she's asking for something that is clearly her due."

Coleman led me toward the stairs. "She was raised that way, Sarah Booth. And you were raised to speak your mind and demand what you needed or wanted."

"Tinkie gets more done." I had to admit it, though it galled me.

Coleman shrugged and pulled me against him. "It seems your aunt Loulane had a saying that covered this situation. 'You can catch more flies with sugar than vinegar.'"

Aunt Loulane had pounded that into my head. Or tried to. "I remember." Even though I remembered also always thinking, *Who wanted to catch flies?*

"Admire Tinkie's tactics. She's very skilled and a certain type of man bends to her every single time. But never undercut your own talents."

"My talents?" I couldn't help it, I had to hear more. "Do tell."

"Well, there's your talent for getting in trouble. And

your talent for pissing off proper society ladies. And your talent for—"

"Come here, you!" I grabbed his hand and tugged him up the stairs and into the bedroom. I was a lucky woman indeed.

20

Coleman took an extra cup of coffee when he left the next morning. I got on the horn and called Tinkie immediately. "I need to do some research on Dr. Kevin Wilson, the professor who was killed at Vanderbilt. Coleman is checking on the details of his murder. I need to look into his academics. Want to join me? I'll make some French toast."

"Why don't we just run over to Nashville and interview some folks?"

Because it was a very long drive and Tinkie needed to be close to medical professionals in case she went into labor. "Nah, we're good here. I need to talk to Alala, too."

"You're afraid I'll give birth in your car."

Tinkie was nobody's fool. "That's true. Can you imagine what that would do to the upholstery?"

Despite herself, Tinkie laughed. "Very funny."

"I am quite a good comedian, I know." If Tinkie had been with me, I would have preened a little. "And I don't want to be on the side of the road bringing the next generation of Richmonds into the world. You deserve better than that."

"Okay."

I frowned at the phone. Tinkie never capitulated that easily. Something was up, but asking would yield no results. Tinkie knew how to play her cards close to her vest.

"Bring Chablis. Sweetie Pie needs some exercise."

"Will do. Sarah Booth, when I do eventually go into labor will you take Chablis and Gumbo over to your house? I don't want them to be alone."

"Sure." Tinkie could easily hire professional pet sitters, but I was flattered she'd asked me. "I'd love to do that."

"Good."

"You shouldn't be in the hospital longer than overnight. Unless you have a C-section." Suddenly, I was on red alert. Tinkie had assured all of us that she would deliver normally—no complications. I'd asked Doc if there was any reason for us to worry and he'd referred me back to Tinkie. As much as Doc loved me, he'd never talk about another patient. Not even Tinkie.

"Oh, everything is fine. No need for surgery. I'm just covering all the bases. This is a big thing for me. And Oscar. I want to totally focus on the new life we've created. I know you love Chablis like she's your own, and Gumbo will be good company for Pluto. Just to be on the safe side, I want to know they haven't been left alone for any length of time."

"I'll pick them up the minute you call." Chablis loved to visit Dahlia House, because I let her run with Sweetie Pie and torment Pluto when she felt like it. Gumbo might not feel as comfortable—cats were notoriously territorial—but I hoped that she would adjust quickly. And whatever it took to make this birth a crowning moment of glory for Tinkie, I would do it.

We hung up and I put on fresh coffee and whipped up the batter for French toast. I was glad to work around the hot stove since the morning was brisk. Tinkie arrived and I filled her in on all that Coleman had shared with me.

"Do you think Alala killed three men?" Tinkie asked, and she was serious.

"No. But it is possible. We have to remember that."

Tinkie sipped her decaf coffee, uncharacteristically subdued.

"What's wrong?"

She looked up and sighed. "I got my hair done yesterday."

"And it looks terrific!" Tinkie was seldom sensitive about her appearance, because she was always turned out like a queen. The baby made her hormonal, though. She was insecure, and I hadn't noticed her new do.

"Oh, shut up, Sarah Booth. You never notice my hair and I don't care one whit. I heard something at the beauty shop."

"Oh." I nodded. "What?"

"Alala has been talking to some of the former residents of Selena's House. She's been interviewing them and telling them to buy a gun and defend themselves. She's offered to give them shooting lessons. I heard there was a college-age woman who wanted to take her up on the lessons."

That was definitely not good. "She has to be smarter than that."

Tinkie sipped her coffee while the French toast browned in the pan. "Last week she went by to see three women who'd once lived at Selena's House. All three had moved there to escape violence. And after a couple of weeks, all three moved back with their husbands or boyfriends. Alala said she was interviewing them for her book. And handing out advice about how to liberate themselves."

"I wonder how she got their names." I knew Penny Cox would never give anyone the names of women she'd helped, even if they'd ultimately gone back into a bad situation.

"I don't know. Only Alala can answer that, and I'll bet she won't. But if the gossip at the beauty salon is accurate, Alala went to their homes when the men were gone to talk to them. She's suggesting a rebellion."

Now, at least, I had a really good reason for a member of AVA to want to hurt her. Few men would appreciate a buttinski into their marriage, especially one espousing liberation. Some men would want to hurt her. Or at least scare her.

Coleman had always told me that the most dreaded call for any law enforcement officer or first responder was a domestic violence call. The abused partners called for help and then changed their minds, sometimes attacking the officer or EMT who'd come to help them. Volatile didn't begin to describe those situations. "Was Alala pressuring the women to leave their husbands?"

"Not exactly," Tinkie said. "She was advocating that they defend themselves. With a permanent solution. Hence, the offer for shooting lessons."

Great. Alala was already considered a potential serial

killer by Coleman and now she was fomenting violent revolution that was going to get someone hurt. Most probably her. "This isn't good."

"I didn't want to tell you," Tinkie said. "That gun business makes her look good for the murders."

Tinkie was right about that.

We finished breakfast in silence and took cups of coffee to Delaney Detective Agency, which was located in the north wing of Dahlia House. The office, with a lovely glazed door with our name stenciled on it, was more of a formality than a real place to work. We did have computers, phones, cameras, files, and the necessities of any business there, but Tinkie and I worked best when we were out and about. Most of our cases involved hoofing it all over the place. Still, a certain amount of desk work came with the package.

"I'll see if I can find anything more about AVA," Tinkie said. "Are we going to the meeting tonight?"

"No." I didn't even have to think about it. Tinkie wasn't going. No matter how big a hissy fit she threw.

"We should." She was watching me.

"I know, and if you weren't incredibly pregnant, we would. But you are pregnant and we aren't."

She didn't argue, as I had anticipated. "I can't run. You're right about that."

I almost went over to feel her forehead to see if she had a fever. This was not normal Tinkie. "It won't be long before you'll be back in fighting form. Soon." I gave her a thumbs-up. "Let's see what we can find on AVA."

Two hours later, we'd found dozens of veiled references to AVA and "private clubs," often styled as "hunting clubs," with similar agendas. The official AVA website painted the group as patriots for the American way of life. It was a brilliant website—in that it lied about everything and made AVA sound like baseball and apple pie. There were photos of happy families playing horseshoes and waving American flags. There were photos of picnics and grills overflowing with steaks and burgers. Platitudes about the goodness of family life and love of country were everywhere.

In not one picture did a woman have a bruise. In a word, the website presented a "wholesome" view of AVA.

"We welcome all men of faith and love of country." Their slogan was writ large right under an American flag. "Our country belongs to men of courage. We will return to prosperity."

Pointing at the computer screen, Tinkie said, "There aren't any single women. Not one woman sitting by herself or with her children. Every woman is part of a couple. And not only are they misogynists, everyone in the photos is white."

"It's the he-man, women-hater's club. Are you surprised?"

"Only that they're so blatant about it. You would think they'd disguise it a little."

"I think that's the point. They want to return to a world where it's not only legal, but acceptable to publicly espouse the view that a woman alone is a dangerous thing, at least from their point of view. A woman alone is unpredictable, capable of self-sufficiency, which makes her a free agent. If a woman is economically capable of making it without a man—that is AVA's worse fear. If they lose the money cudgel, they won't be able to control women. I wonder how these men relate to their female children."

"I was raised to believe that men did rule." Tinkie sat down on the edge of my desk.

I had long been curious about this aspect of the Daddy's Girls but I'd never asked. After my parents' death, I was wild as a March hare. Poor Aunt Loulane had dealt with my sneaking out of the house and running through the fields. I'd been in trouble at school and everywhere else. Not serious, but enough to worry her. She'd tried to wrangle me into a dress, and make me attend social events. I took piano lessons, because Aunt Loulane urged me to, but I never practiced. Aunt Loulane signed me up for comportment classes and cotillion so I would have a shred of grace. I rebelled. But Tinkie and many of the girls my age fell right into line with the Order of Daddy's Girls. Trim, tanned, turned out to perfection, these were the girls who went to college to marry, and to marry well. "Did anyone ever explain why men should rule everything?" I asked.

I'd assumed it was economic—that the men controlled the finances, and for many generations they had. Most women had no experience with money and therefore avoided it. But, that had begun to change. Even in Mississippi.

Tinkie tilted her head. "Some of it's tradition. Mother believes in the golden, wonderful past, where the best of everything can be found. According to Mother and her contemporaries, grace and class died in 1969 with 'those dreadful hippies who stupidly gave sex away.' She says it all the time. To her way of thinking, men ruled because they were smarter. Mother grew up in the world of *Father Knows Best* and June Cleaver. Women had a prescribed role, and that was to be a helpmeet to their husbands. The husband's job was to take care of the wife and the children and provide, and provide well. Her job was to take care of him, the kids, and the house. Or in the most privileged of worlds, to manage the staff who did those chores. It was all very simple. Everyone knew their roles and, as long as they did them, life went on smoothly. As long as everyone stayed in her proper lane."

I sipped my coffee and listened as Tinkie continued.

"There was great safety in that view of the world. Nothing could go wrong if everyone just followed the rules. A woman's greatest ambition was a fine home, a healthy family, and a satisfied husband. And by satisfied, I don't mean that men didn't partake of sexual pleasures outside the marriage. That was, after all, their right."

I had questions, but I didn't want to slow Tinkie's roll.

Tinkie looked out the window, to where my horses grazed. "My father cheated on my mother more than once, and she knew it. She simply pretended that it didn't happen. She clung to the pretense that both partners were committed to their roles and never let the truth interfere."

Now I had to ask. "But your folks have weathered all of that, Tinkie. I do believe they are happy together now, don't you?"

"Happy?" She stood up and paced. "I don't know if they're happy. They're settled into those roles. Daddy handles the business and Mother shops. They travel. They dine out and drink fine wines, and when they're in town, they host lovely parties where their friends, who are all exactly in the same boat, get together. The women end up in one room and the men in another. Technically, I think they live in two very different worlds."

My memories of my parents were so different. Mama would sit on Daddy's lap as they laughed and drank with friends. They'd play cards or board games, talking and cutting up into the wee hours, men and women together. Or, they would turn on the stereo and dance, holding each other close. There'd never been a doubt that they loved me, but they loved each other just as much, and that was the role model they'd made me desire. A partner—a true partner in all regards. But, this wasn't anything I needed to share with Tinkie. Not right now.

"Maybe that is happiness for your mom." I had a sudden desire to sit and talk with Tinkie's mom. I'd spent time at the Richmond house growing up, but not a lot. And Mrs. Richmond had never warmed to me. Not really to any of the children. She was kind to us and always had wonderful birthday parties for Tinkie with specialty cakes. But I'd never ever felt she truly enjoyed my company. Or that of any child. Not even Tinkie. The truth was that the kids would always rather be at my house with my folks. And so, that's what we did. But as I'd learned as I aged, it was easy to sell someone short when you didn't understand.

"Platinum credit cards, nice cars, social status—those things make Mother happy."

"They make a lot of people happy."

She shrugged. "I'm sure they do."

I stood up and walked over to her. "That's just not you, Tinkie. Material things don't make you happy." I clearly remembered my first private investigation, when Tinkie had hired me to look into the handsome and sexy Hamilton Garrett V, who'd been accused of killing his own mother in retribution for her killing his father. The Garrett family had a tangled and tragic past. Tinkie and Oscar, married in the traditional pattern of head of household man and compliant wife, had come to a point in their marriage where they could go no further without change. Both constrained by roles that no longer fit them, it was change or divorce. I don't know how she did it, or if she even knew how, but Tinkie had moved Oscar to evolve into a man solid enough in himself to allow her to become who she needed to be. Had Oscar not changed, Tinkie would have kicked him to the curb, no matter how much it cost her financially and socially. I still counted Oscar's conversion—and Tinkie's, too, to some extent—as a miracle.

"My mother isn't happy. She's never been. Not even with me. Not even when I so desperately wanted her to be happy with me."

I wanted to lie and say that wasn't true, but Tinkie's mom never revealed her deepest feelings. Not to anyone. I had no clue what might make her content. "Most people don't know what would make them happy."

"You've always known what you wanted and needed," Tinkie said to me. If I'd worn dentures, they would have fallen on the floor.

"That's just not true. I've stumbled almost every step of the way. I came home, because I had no other choice. No other place to go. I became a PI because *you* suggested it. I finally got together with Coleman after a lot of bad relationships. I've *lucked* into the good things I have."

"Perhaps the path was accidental, but you've been smart enough to see the good things in front of you and value them."

Now *that*, I didn't want to argue with. Jitty had played a role in some of my self-awareness, but I couldn't tell Tinkie about that. "I came at this with a different expectation, Tinkie. You know that. And, for one thing, I'll never have the financial resources and security you and Oscar and this new baby will have. But I'll always make do. Madame Tomeeka told me once a long time ago that I would never go without."

"And isn't that all you need? The bargain too many women make is to have a surplus of material things and not enough of the things that really matter. Self-confidence, pride in accomplishment, independence, the space to be oneself . . ."

"Tinkie, are you a libber?" I couldn't help teasing her a little. "It might go against the laws of physics for a Daddy's Girl to turn into an independent woman."

"Then let's break some laws." She pointed at the computer screen. "Do you think that wooden building in the background of that photo is the lodge where AVA meets?"

By darn it, she was probably right. "Yeah, I think that's it. Dr. Becky Brown's lodge."

"And you know where it is?"

I did have an address, but I wasn't telling. "We are *not* going."

"I know, but we can send Budgie or DeWayne."

"We could, but why would we want to? None of those men are going to talk to deputies about illegal activities."

"We aren't certain anything they do is strictly illegal," Tinkie said. "It would be better if you and I went. We don't need a search warrant."

"Those men aren't going to open the door and invite us inside." Tinkie wasn't thinking clearly.

She shook her head. "We need to search, and you and I can search without a warrant. We aren't officers of the law. We can go *after* the meeting. Or before."

"No, we'll just be trespassers who break and enter. You can bet someone is there at all times. What we need to do is talk to our client." We had a lot of things to discuss with Alala. I put action to words and dialed her. When I got her voicemail, I told her I'd soon be headed to see her.

"We should go to the hunting lodge." Tinkie had not been sidetracked. "You're going to let a technicality stand in the way of getting the goods on those men?"

"What about if we send someone in undercover to join AVA?" Tinkie was right about one thing. AVA was the key. We needed more information.

"Remember the last time we went undercover pretending to be housemaids? That didn't go so well."

"No, but this time we have to send in a man."

"And who do you recommend?" Tinkie asked. I could see her clicking through the mental Rolodex of potential male sacrifices.

"Harold."

"Harold Erkwell?" Tinkie couldn't keep the squeak out of her voice. "Harold can't abide men who manhandle women."

"But those men don't know that, and Harold is a very good actor. He's never married. He can use that to his advantage. He can tell them he can't tolerate disobedient women, and maybe they can help him find a good one." The more I talked, the better my idea sounded.

"Harold will probably agree to do it. But what if he gets hurt?" Tinkie wasn't totally convinced my idea was the best one.

"He can take Roscoe with him. Roscoe will rip out anyone's throat if they try to bother Harold. And you know Harold is a damn good snoop." I didn't mention that I, too, would be in those woods as backup for Harold. I didn't care that Tinkie would be mad at me later—at least she wouldn't be going into labor in the middle of the woods with a bunch of men who may or may not get her to a doctor.

"Let's talk to Harold," Tinkie said. She started to stand up and just stopped, the strangest expression crossing her face.

"Are you okay?"

She nodded slowly. "It felt like the baby was turning a somersault."

"Don't they do that so they can shoot straight out the birth canal? Be careful or that baby will be nestled between your ankles."

Tinkie glared at me. "That is damn insulting, Sarah Booth. My baby will not shoot out my birth canal like it's been nicknamed Panama or Suez."

Laughter exploded between us, and I gave her my arm as we walked out of the house together; Chablis, Sweetie Pie, and Pluto right behind us.

21

Harold ushered us into his office at the bank. He was an eclectic art collector, and I was always amazed at the way he could change up the atmosphere of his office with paintings, sculptures, and interesting furniture. He kept a cushy rug near a modern sofa where all the critters stretched out for a snooze.

He asked his secretary to bring us coffee, and then settled behind his cluttered desk. "What can I do for you ladies?"

"No, it's what we're going to do for you." I'd decided on a hard sell. "We're opening the door to adventure, the excitement of risk, the art of spying. Your new nickname is Double-O Eight."

He rolled his eyes. "You want me to pretend to be

someone I'm not and spy on someone you can't." He looked at Tinkie, who nodded. Harold assessed the situation. "Tinkie can reach into the upper class, and Sarah Booth, you have reach in the boho world. I'm thinking you need access to some kind of men's club."

There were days when Harold was too smart for his own good. My face must have given away the fact he'd guessed correctly.

"I'm right!" His eyes sparkled with merriment. "I'm flattered you've come to me."

"It could be dangerous." I was always up-front with Harold. "These men are armed and if they think you're spying . . ."

"What men?"

I filled him in on AVA and their stated agenda. As I knew he would be, Harold was all in with my plotting.

"Sure, I'll see if they'll let me in the door. And if I can get any of them to talk, I'll find out what they know about Dr. Diakos and the dead men."

"You have to be really careful. You're not exactly the ideal AVA member," Tinkie pointed out. "They're liable to be suspicious of anyone new, especially someone with money, education, and class."

"Dr. Loxley, a college professor, was a member," I reminded her. "Of course that didn't necessarily give him money or class. The meeting is tonight at eight at Lake Paul." I wrote the address down on a piece of paper. "Harold, these men are mean. I'd go, but they'd never tolerate a woman, no matter how hard I tried to fit in."

"I can put on my Neanderthal act. Don't worry about me. But do tell Coleman, okay? Just in case. I'd like to be sure there's backup on the way if I need it."

It was a very reasonable request, but I didn't want to tell Coleman. "Backup will be waiting," I promised.

"Okay. Any tips?"

"Talk bad about all the smart women you know," Tinkie said. "They'll eat that with a spoon."

Leaving the bank, we stopped by Harold's house and picked up Roscoe. Due to his recent escape-artist bad behavior, he was still confined to the sunroom. Long claw marks on both solid wood doors in and out of the room let me know exactly how Roscoe felt about his loss of liberty.

"He is just plain bad," Tinkie said.

"Harold would rather get new doors if those scratches bother him too much." Roscoe and Sweetie Pie had once gone on a tear at the local high school and stolen all of the shoes and other items from the athletic department. It was a huge scandal—Roscoe and Sweetie Pie parading about the town adorned with jock straps on their heads. They had run into the street, eluding capture, and finally ended up taking a nap on the front steps of the First Baptist Church of Zinnia, adorned with the spoils of their robbery. It took Harold and me two weeks to find the buried treasure of stinky athletic shoes and return them.

If that event didn't get Roscoe in lockup, nothing would. Roscoe loved Harold to the marrow of his bones and would do anything to protect him. Harold reciprocated that love, and secretly, or not so secretly, he took joy in Roscoe's evil deeds.

When I pulled into Alala's driveway, Roscoe was the first dog out of the car. He ran to the front porch and hurled himself against the door. In a moment, he was in Alala's arms.

"Roscoe! Welcome!" She snuggled him to her. "And you don't smell like garbage. Yet." She looked over him at me. "He hasn't gotten into trouble, has he?"

"Not yet." Then I thought of the gashes in the wooden doors at Harold's. "But I'm sure trouble is coming for him."

"I told Harold I'd be glad to dog sit him."

Tinkie brightened. "A great idea. I'll be sure and remind Harold of your generous offer. And it wouldn't hurt if you and Harold got to know each other better. Harold is the most eligible catch in the Delta."

Alala laughed. "Are you a matchmaker?"

"Sometimes," Tinkie said, "when people aren't either too dumb or too stuck in their ways to listen to me." She looked right at me.

"Did you match Sarah Booth with that handsome sheriff?" Alala asked.

"Over and over again. Finally, after a broken engagement and lost months of sexual bliss, she had to admit that I was right."

I didn't exactly remember it that way, but I wasn't going to argue. "You should listen to Tinkie on this, Alala. Harold's a great catch, for sure. And he loves dogs." I didn't see Alala and Harold as the perfect couple, but Harold was plenty capable of deciding who he wanted to date or not. Alala, once she got out of lecture mode, might be a lot of fun.

"Have you made any progress in finding out who killed Curtis Miller?" Alala asked. "I'd really like to go to Vicksburg and Natchez, but I can't leave town. I must research the women who ran plantations on the Mississippi River during the Civil War while their men were off fighting. Fascinating subculture of females who managed to find ways around the laws written to hamstring them. A lot of cotton producers lived harvest to harvest and women were prohibited from obtaining bank loans, a standard practice for men. But the women along the Mississippi River were smart. They had formed a cooperative, of a sort. This is all part of the vital information I've researched for my book, but I'd like to visit the locales in person. Alas, the handsome sheriff has indicated I shouldn't leave Sunflower County right now."

"It's best to stay put," Tinkie said.

"In answer to your question, we haven't found anything solid regarding who killed Curtis. I have to be honest, finding that gun on your property wasn't good for you. I believe you wouldn't be dumb enough to plant the murder weapon in four inches of dirt in your own yard, but still. It was found there, without any prints. Now, we have some leads, but it's difficult to put someone who would kill Curtis together with a person who would have a grudge against Loxley and Wilson." I stared at her without flinching. "Except for you. You knew all three and were in the exact area when they died." I hated to point this out, but Coleman already had these facts in hand. "It's time for you to tell us about your relationship with Dr. Kevin Wilson at Vanderbilt."

Alala nodded. "It wasn't really a relationship. He was a creep, but that won't matter, will it?" She made a face. "Another dead woman abuser tied to my past. I can see why I'm a suspect."

"Yep," I said. "So, give me the details. Especially the things that could link you to Wilson's murder."

Alala fidgeted and looked out the window. "Both Wilson and Loxley could be charming when they chose to be. They were both attractive men who could be funny. Those are traits of abusers, I think. Or at least a lot of them. Kevin Wilson was one of the first faculty members to welcome me to the campus at Vanderbilt. He volunteered to show me around, and he moved fluidly among the administration. He led me to believe he was being groomed to move up the academic ladder. This was the first week I was there. Then I saw another side of him. I realized that he was showing me he had power, protection. What appears to be one thing is another. He was a trickster and beneath every interaction was a form of intimidation."

I didn't have a lot of patience for her reticence. "Alala, just tell us. We're going to find out, but you can save us time and *your* money. Spill it."

"Wilson was an awful man. But there were times I was in his office."

That wasn't exactly evidence. "Are there video clips of you doing the wild thing? Or worse?"

She closed her eyes for a few seconds, composing herself. "Wilson had a nasty habit of videotaping sessions that he had with female faculty members—legitimate meetings—and editing and manipulating the tapes or photos to imply things that weren't true. Anyone with any knowledge of film editing could tell it was fake, but how many people are going to really give it that much thought? They watch it, make a judgment, and that's how it ends."

Alala sent a look of appeal to both me and Tinkie. "I know. It sounds insane. I didn't want to bring this up, because it will only make it look worse for me. Wilson implied to me that he had such tapes he'd created of me, and that for a price, he'd give them to me."

"Funny, because Margaret McNeese said the same thing about you. That you had photos or documentation of women who'd been involved with Alex Loxley." I had intended to play this card at a later date, but now seemed to be the best opportunity.

"Oh, dear," Alala said. "I know what happened. Dr. Brown and Margaret came down for one of my lectures at Vanderbilt. I'd just arrived, so I wasn't aware yet of Wilson's true nature. Both Margaret and Becky were charmed by Wilson, because he could be extremely deceptive. He fooled even me. He was handsome, with a great laugh. All of it a façade. But now I understand why they were both searching my property. Later, when I went to work at Ole Miss and I was trying to convince them to come forward about Dr. Loxley, I implied that I'd found Wilson's stash of videos."

"He really had a stash of abuse porn?" Tinkie asked.

Alala looked down for a moment. "I lied. I said I'd taken the videos, but I said there could be others or copies. I implied that their reputations could be ruined and I said that Loxley and Wilson were working together. I thought it would discourage them from falling victim to predators if they assumed these horrible men were photographing them or documenting the sex and abuse."

"What happened to Wilson's stash?" I asked.

"I don't know. But I believe he had everything he claimed to have. Faked and real."

"No wonder this man is dead," Tinkie said.

"I never saw a video or a photo," Alala said. "But

Wilson said he'd made one of me and that he'd included some raunchy stuff, like slapping me around."

"Can someone actually do that?" Tinkie asked.

"With the technology available today, yes," I said. "A person with skill and equipment can manipulate almost any image."

"So, he essentially created abuse porn," Tinkie said. "What sickos would get off on watching that?" She rolled her eyes. "Don't answer. This is disgusting on a whole 'nother level."

"If what he claimed was true, Wilson spent hours tampering with little slices of cell phone footage," Alala said. "I'm not sorry either of those men are dead. I heard Wilson was making a ton of money blackmailing women he'd created fake tapes of. A number of women in Nashville probably wanted him dead."

Tinkie was nodding. "It's such an unfair advantage he took. Few women are willing to risk that kind of public shaming, and no matter what anyone says, the woman still carries all the blame. I don't know if I'd be brave enough to go up against a videotape showing me doing something, even if I knew I hadn't done it. People rush to judgment these days without any concern for real evidence. Once the perception of a woman being a slut or punching bag is set, it's almost impossible to undo. I have tremendous support, but I still don't know if I could face that."

"Oh, you would, Tinkie, I have no doubt." I knew my partner well. "Where do these creeps come from?"

"They're under every rock and dead log," Tinkie said, "just like grub worms."

"Alala, this is all important backstory, but who killed

Wilson? If you knew the women he was blackmailing, which one is the most likely suspect?"

"I have no idea. I only know it wasn't me, though I clapped when I heard he was dead."

"He wasn't in the Vanderbilt English department. How did you even know him?" Tinkie asked.

"About my second month there, I learned that he'd been conducting research on the development of communities that were totally patriarchal. His theory, which was total BS, was that these villages or towns were more efficiently run, more productive, more pastoral. Life was much better when a man or men were in charge. If the good little women just obeyed and followed orders, the world was right. That was his premise—that things ran better for everyone when a male authoritarian ruled."

Oh, I could see that wouldn't fly with Alala. Or me, or any of my friends. "And what did *your* research show?"

"That whenever men took over the reins of settlements, war broke out. Without exception. The male competitiveness, the masculine principle of winning by dominance and brute force have created nothing but Hell on Earth. Women and children have suffered for the egos of vain men who were never satisfied with what they had, always greedy for more. And it's time to stop this misbegotten idea that men are better leaders."

I didn't know if this was really research or personal belief. It didn't matter as long as Alala believed it—and was potentially willing to kill to defend it. That was the power of ideology and thinking oneself to be right. Ignoring facts wasn't only the province of males, though. Lots of people ignored history, science, and the truth. And all of that was aside from the reality that Alala's beliefs were terrific fodder as supporting incentives and evidence for three counts of murder.

"Do you really have evidence that men in power are more dangerous than women?" Tinkie sounded too eager.

"I have examples. History is filled with case studies. The conquest of this country itself is a perfect example of the high cost of male-dominated policy. I could make a case that it *is* evidence, but I don't know if it would stand up in court. I do believe if more women were in positions of power, the world would be more compassionate and less warlike. I'm a warrior, so to me war is not always bad. But these senseless wars over territory or religion that go on endlessly are damaging the planet. It must be stopped, and I do believe that when the most powerful countries elect female leaders, we will be closer to that goal."

"I gather Dr. Wilson believed otherwise. And he was gaining support in his department."

"He was such a fool, and so . . . obnoxious. His research was shoddy. I was in the process of proving that when he died."

"Didn't he get a big grant?" I'd done my homework.

"He did. From some very conservative group called American Values Association."

AVA. I had not seen that coming.

22

Alala returned to the room with a tray of mimosas and a big sigh. I'd asked her to tell me what she knew about AVA, and she'd agreed to do it only after we had a libation. Tinkie accepted her flute of straight-up orange juice with an evil glare. She was done with pregnancy.

"So tell us what you know about AVA," I said.

"Yes, AVA. I first heard Dr. Wilson talking about the group when I was at Vanderbilt. I thought it was some woman named Ava that he'd duped into dating him. But it was a group of unevolved men. Like those men, Wilson was completely empty of any spark of the divine. He had no soul."

She hadn't cared for Dr. Loxley at Ole Miss, but her

dislike of Dr. Wilson went far deeper. The most interesting thing to me was both men's connection to AVA.

"How did you end up at Vanderbilt?"

"I was named a writer in residence, nonfiction, on a one-year teaching contract."

"And you met Dr. Wilson when he was giving a lecture?" Tinkie asked.

"No. I met Wilson socially. He was well-spoken and handsome. I thought he was a decent guy until he showed up at one of my public lectures and called me out. He was so rude and sneering. And he used bad facts as the basis of his argument. I had to make an example of that. We had a very . . . aggressive disagreement and I shut him down. Lesson one in how to make an enemy."

"Did you threaten him?"

"I'm a warrior, Sarah Booth. I don't shy away from confrontation. I let him know I wouldn't be intimidated by a moron."

"What did you say?" Tinkie asked.

"I told him he'd die alone and begging for mercy. I said his black heart would be the thing that killed him."

"And you said this in public?"

"In an auditorium full of people a day or two before he was shot."

At least she hadn't threatened to shoot him in the heart, but Alala did have the unfortunate habit of leaving a trail of guilty-sounding commentary behind her. She'd traveled to some of the best schools in the South for brief yearly appointments. Never longer. That was a hard way to make a living, even if the pay was generous. No stability, no incentive to put down roots and make a home. Worse, she'd left three dead men in her wake.

"Why didn't you stay longer at any of the places you've worked?"

"I'm not a citizen here," she said. "I'm a Greek citizen with a visa to work in America. I don't want a permanent position."

I heard her words, but her body language confused me. She looked down and away, making me think she wasn't being completely truthful. "When you finish writing your book, what will you do?"

"I haven't decided. A lot depends on how the book is received. If it goes the way I hope it does, then I'll be invited to lecture at a series of schools. I'll go on a book tour. The door to more writing opportunities will be forced wide open. That's my true love, not teaching or speaking. I enjoy the temporary appointment to the various faculties because the university world is a fascinating place. But living in a little town like Zinnia, writing my book—that would be the best of all worlds for me."

"Will you ever go back to Greece?" Tinkie sounded wistful. "What about a home and a family? Don't you want those things?"

"Not necessarily, and I will go home, of course, but not for many years. My work and my life are here now."

The walk through Alala's psyche was fascinating, but I didn't yet have the information I needed to prevent her from being charged with murders I at least hoped she hadn't committed. An idea was bubbling in the back of my brain. "I've interviewed Dr. Brown and Margaret McNeese. They both had cause to kill Dr. Loxley at Ole Miss. Would they have a reason to want to kill Wilson in Nashville?"

Alala's dark eyebrows rose. "They both attended my lectures at Vanderbilt but perhaps they were at Vanderbilt more than I knew. I'd been in touch with Becky Brown about my contract for the coming academic year at Ole Miss. She and Margaret drove to Nashville to hear my talk on the repressive property laws regarding women. Brown and McNeese were partially the reasons I got an appointment at Ole Miss. After they heard my lecture, they both supported my bid for the post." She thought a minute. "Brown and McNeese could have become involved with Wilson. It's possible. And from what I understood, Wilson and Loxley worked together on the videos. Or that's what Loxley implied."

That was a surprising turn. "Do you have photographic evidence of this abuse?"

Again the slightly evasive turn of the face, the downward look. Alala knew something about those photos and I intended to find out what it was. "If I had any photos or evidence proving that either man was blackmailing women, I would have turned it over to the Lafayette County Sheriff's Department," she said. "I did try to get Loxley charged with assault and battery, domestic abuse, something. Without Margaret or someone stepping forward, I didn't get anywhere. If only I'd had photographs or videos."

I didn't believe her for a minute. "Then you wouldn't mind if Tinkie and I looked around your place. I mean, if you *didn't* have those photos, it's possible Brown and McNeese, one or both, were here to plant them on you. If they're framing you, it's a fine motive." I had to admit, it was a pretty far-fetched plot, but it was possible. And it was also possible that one or both of them had also planted the gun used to kill one or more of the men.

Alala's resistance was instant, though she remained cool as a cucumber. "I don't think that's necessary.

There's nothing untoward here. If any photos were here, they're gone with whoever broke in. And the sheriff has already looked around."

"Coleman made a few calls for me, and the Nashville police have no record of any complaints filed against Wilson by any students. The same is true for Loxley in Oxford," I said. "We're waiting to see if either university will supply any evidence of complaints, but so far, nothing." That was a fact. "There's no evidence Loxley was abusive toward his students or anyone in the department except for your statements and possibly those photos or videos. We really need them." One look at her face told me there might be actual evidence. "Alala, if you have this evidence, please."

"And what if it's gone? What if someone has destroyed it?" Alala asked.

"We don't have a reason to suspect anyone else of killing the two professors." Tinkie had put two and two together for Alala. "You are the prime suspect. If you have evidence of blackmail, tell us now. That would open up a world of new suspects."

"My guess is that the murderer of those two men has already found the photos and film and destroyed them." Alala didn't flinch.

"Did you have any photos or video footage?" I asked her point-blank.

"Asked and answered," she said.

"Then why would both Brown and McNeese break into your home?" I followed up.

"McNeese was a graduate assistant interested in my work. Becky, well, she was floundering. She was desperate for a big project, something that would guarantee her tenure. I wasn't a permanent member of the English department and I had the feeling she was interested in my research, something she could appropriate and turn into her own book publication. She might have been here looking for that."

Jealousy wasn't a terrible motive, but it didn't fit this situation.

"If you have physical evidence, do the right thing and give it up. It's time to stop this, before someone else ends up dead."

At last she sighed. "I know they exist but I don't have them. That's the truth."

"You had them once, didn't you?" Tinkie asked.

"I had them, but someone did steal them. Likely either Brown or McNeese, since they were here." She pinched her forehead between her thumb and forefinger. "If Margaret did kill him, she shouldn't be charged with anything. I call it self-defense."

Alala's legal opinion didn't matter a whit. "Why didn't you give those tapes to the Oxford police?" She'd tampered with a police investigation and while she might not be charged with murder, she was going to be in Dutch with the law enforcement around Ole Miss. If they chose to prosecute her for interfering in an investigation, she didn't have a leg to stand on.

"Look, I saw the tapes. Some of the women involved were married. All of them would have been humiliated. How would giving those tapes to law enforcement change anything? Loxley and Wilson were dead. I was already moving here. The kinder thing seemed to be to bury those tapes forever and that was sincerely my intention. I meant to destroy them. Without any fuss or fanfare."

"And yet you still had them. You could have burned them all when you first got here." I was annoyed.

"I should have destroyed them. As soon as they were stolen, I knew that. I made a mistake."

"Were there any other men in those tapes other than Loxley or Wilson?" Tinkie asked.

Alala tilted her head. "You know, I didn't watch all of them. I couldn't. They made me sick." She stood up and walked to the front door. Roscoe was right on her heels. If she meant to go somewhere, he was going, too. "Have you ever considered that whoever killed Loxley, Wilson, and that Miller did the world a favor?"

"It's not up to me to think that way," I said, knowing I sounded priggish.

"No, you've got that lawman to make sure justice is served for you. Not everyone is that lucky, Sarah Booth. Too often there isn't equal justice under the law. These men were brutes. They picked on women who couldn't defend themselves. Someone had to stop them. I'm glad someone did."

23

Tinkie, Sweetie Pie, Pluto, Roscoe, and I sat in my car where I'd pulled over to the curb after leaving Alala's house. Roscoe had chosen to remain with Alala, who was thrilled to have the company.

"Are we going back to search her house?" Tinkie asked, thinking I'd pulled over to watch and wait for Alala to leave.

"Do you really believe someone stole those videos and photos?" Something about this story stank to high heaven.

She shook her head. "Alala is lying."

"I agree, so yes, we're going back in to look as soon as she leaves. Coleman didn't find them when he searched. Neither did Becky Brown. But Alala has to have a computer and it has to be somewhere. She's not writing a book in longhand."

"How can you be so certain she's going to leave her house any time soon?" Tinkie asked.

"Gut." I eased the car a little farther down the street and turned into a driveway that was sheltered from Alala's house by a thick boxwood. "That and the fact that she had a grocery list on the table." I grinned. "When Alala pulls out, I want you to take the car and follow her. I'm going to sneak back into her house and find those photos."

"You are doing nothing of the kind," Tinkie said. "I won't let you do that alone."

I kept my gaze on Alala's house, but I put a hand on Tinkie's huge belly. "Tinkie, you can't run. If you stress yourself you could go into premature labor and that would be bad for the baby. Just follow Alala. See where she goes, who she meets. She's up to something, and this is really important. I'll search the house and meet you at the café."

"You don't have a car," Tinkie pointed out.

"I can hoof it." I patted my own stomach. "I need to hoof it. You're the one who's pregnant, but I'm the one eating for you and the baby." It was sadly true. I ate whenever Tinkie ate. And she had been eating often in the last few months.

She leaned over as far as she could and pulled me to her. "You're the best friend."

Out of the corner of my eye, I saw Alala's car nudge out of the driveway and head in the opposite direction. Tinkie would have to be very stealthy to follow in my Roadster, which was pretty distinctive. I would never give up my mother's old car, but maybe it was time to buy a nondescript silver or gray sedan for PI work.

I got out of the car as Tinkie came around to get behind the wheel. I gripped her shoulder. "Be careful. I couldn't stand it if something happened to you. And Oscar would kill me. And could you call Harold to pick up Roscoe from you? He'll need him for his work tonight."

"Roscoe is taken care of. And stop acting like Alala is—"

"A serial killer?" I asked.

Tinkie laughed. "I feel pretty safe with Alala. You watch out. She seems to have a lot of uninvited company. No telling who else might show up." She took off just as Alala's car turned right at the next intersection.

As I started toward the house, I realized Sweetie Pie had jumped out of the car, too. I was glad for the company. I'd just started through a neighbor's yard when my phone rang. It was a Mississippi area code, so I answered.

"Ms. Delaney?" a young female voice asked.

"Yes."

"This is Poppy Bright. Remember me?"

I did. "Sure."

"I need to talk with Margaret. Have you seen her?"

It was odd that Poppy Bright was calling me to find her friend who lived in Oxford. "No, I haven't seen her, but I'd like to talk to her again, too. Is she in Zinnia?"

"I think so. She said she had to talk to someone in Zinnia. A woman who helped women in danger."

That would be Penny Cox, in all likelihood. "I can check at the women's shelter in a bit. If she's there, I'll tell her to call you."

"Thanks. They've been looking for her at the university and I just need to let her know. I don't want her to get in trouble for missing work."

"I'll relay the message," I said. When I hung up, I looked down at Sweetie Pie, who was watching me. "Why would Margaret McNeese be in Zinnia talking to Penny Cox?"

My hound dog had no answers, and I knew I had to hustle or Tinkie would be sending out a posse to find me if I took too long.

Cutting through yards, we made our way to Alala's back door. Sweetie Pie froze and I did, too, as we listened to see if we could hear anyone in the house. Nothing except the wind sweeping through the rattling fall leaves. I tried the back door, which opened without complaint. If Alala wanted to prevent burglaries, she might consider locking her doors. In a matter of seconds, Sweetie Pie and I were in the house.

I started in the spare bedrooms, the den, the parlor, the study, the kitchen, the bathroom, and finally the bedroom Alala was using. If she had a computer—and I knew she had to have one—I couldn't find it. Where in the heck had she put it? Sweetie Pie, who was good at sniffing out stuff, had fallen asleep at the back door. If there was anything of interest in Alala's house, she wasn't sensing it.

The sound of hoofbeats outside the front door sent me running to see what was happening. Zinnia was a small town, but it had been years since anyone had ridden horses around the neighborhoods. When I glanced back at Sweetie Pie, still snoozing away, I had a clue that my personal haint was paying me a call.

I opened the door to find a stout woman, six feet or better, holding a shotgun. Her dark skin was weathered, and it was impossible to tell her age.

"What is it this time, Jitty?" I asked. "Another outlaw history lesson?"

"The proper greeting would be to invite me in for a libation."

"I'm not a proper lady and this isn't my house." I was too curious about the visitation to go back inside, though. "Who are you?"

"Mary Fields is my given name, but folks knew me better by Stagecoach Mary."

"You robbed stagecoaches?" She looked tough enough to pull that off.

"Not at all. I was a mail carrier. I delivered the mail on the stagecoach route. In 1895 I became the second female carrier in the nation. I was already in my sixties then, too."

Jitty had come to me not as an outlaw, but as a woman of color who'd also broken barriers and lived a life of independence, defying numerous odds. I did a quick calculation, concluding that Mary had been born around 1832. "Were you born into slavery?" I asked.

"I was, in Tennessee. Got my freedom at the end of the war."

"How did you end up out west?"

She smiled, and her features weren't marred by regret. "Went west to help my friend, Mother Amadeus, when she got sick. Stayed there a long while, but I don't take no guff off any man or woman. There was an incident, and I stood up for myself. The brawl turned ugly, and it was time to go. I moved on and took a job as a star route mail carrier. They nicknamed me Stagecoach Mary because I was reliable and never failed to bring the mail."

"You were never on the wrong side of the law?" So far

Jitty had only come to me as an outlaw. Now I saw that it was truly independence that was her theme, not law-breaking.

"Sometimes the law was on the wrong side of me, but I was a good citizen, once I gained my freedom. I worked hard. I moved to a little place called Cascade, the only black person who lived there." She chuckled. "When the law said no woman could go into a saloon, the mayor made an exception for me. Fact is, the town celebrated my birthday twice a year because I didn't know my birthday."

"I love this story," I told her.

"I could have stayed in the convent in Montana all of my life," she said, "but I lost that when I defended myself in a fight. I didn't want to leave my friend, but I couldn't stay. Once I got my freedom from slavery, I made up my mind I was never gonna do less than stand up for myself. There's a price for knowing who you are. Women sometimes pay a high price. Women born into slavery always paid a price." She pulled a cigar from the pocket of her dress. "Care to smoke? I've got two."

"No, thank you." She was slowly fading.

"I'm glad you ended up with a happy life."

"Part luck. Part determination." She lit her cigar and puffed. "Don't ever let anyone try to tell you who you are." She walked down the steps and along the sidewalk, a powerful woman with a long stride, until she evaporated into the fall day.

For a long moment I looked at the empty place where she'd been. The west had offered men and women independence and a chance to reinvent themselves. Options were few for women, and especially women of color, but Stagecoach Mary had managed to do the near impossible. That was a lot to think about.

I had to get busy searching the house before Alala returned. Tinkie said she would call to give me a heads-up, but I preferred to be clear of the neighborhood before she got back. I don't know what I hoped to find that three other searches hadn't turned up, but I had to look. It was part of my job—or that was my perception.

I went back in the house to find Sweetie Pie yawning back to life. "Fine watchdog you are. I was visited by the ghost of a famous female mail carrier."

She snuffled my knee and went into the bedroom that Alala used. Without further ado, she pushed at the mattress on the bed. Rolling my eyes, I lifted it up. In the middle of the bed was a thumb drive. Exactly what I'd been looking for, though I hadn't known it at the time. And it had recently been placed there—the mattress had been pushed to the floor in the burglary. Either Alala was clever at moving her hiding place, or someone was framing her.

24

I was three blocks from Alala's house and hoofing it hard when my cell phone vibrated in my pocket and almost made me jump out of my shoes. Thank heavens, Tinkie was on the horn.

"You'll never guess where Alala went," she said with eagerness in her voice.

"I was afraid she might go out of town." That had been a real concern. Tinkie would probably have followed her—a scenario I hadn't thought of when I asked her to tail the professor.

"No, she went to Clifford LaPlace's furniture store."

That was a revelation. "Is she still there?"

"I'm pretty sure she is. It's that big, wide-open parking lot with a ton of cars, so I can't see her vehicle and I can't risk getting any closer. I had to park back a ways. If she sees me, she'll recognize your car."

Yeah, it was time to buy a more stealthy vehicle for my work. Tinkie's super-duper Cadillac, the latest prototype, wasn't any better for the job. I'd ask Coleman later what the most nondescript car on the roads might be.

"Anyway, I'm parked on a side road in a subdivision in front of the furniture store. I can't be certain she's in there, but I'll call if I see her come out. And Harold has already been by and collected Roscoe."

"Thanks for handling that. Just do what you can and don't stress." Now it was time for my own revelation. "I found something."

"What?"

"A thumb drive. It was under her mattress. I don't know what's on it, but I'm walking to the *Zinnia Dispatch*. It's time to bring Cece into this. She has more computer expertise than I do and she'll be able to get the files open."

"Great plan. Once I'm done tailing Alala, maybe we can meet for drinks somewhere."

"Coffee at Millie's?" I wasn't about to encourage her in fantasies of drinking. She had nine long months of perfect baby care behind her. Now wasn't the time for falling off the wagon and having an alcoholic beverage.

"You *are* the fun police, Sarah Booth. I swear, you need a uniform and handcuffs."

"The handcuffs can be arranged."

"Don't talk to me about your kinky love life with that sheriff."

Tinkie made me laugh. I couldn't help it. "Call me when you figure it out. Maybe we can ask Betty Sue to help us again if she overhears what Alala is up to."

"Good idea. See you soon." And Tinkie was gone.

I'd made it to Main Street at the edge of the town proper and had enjoyed the walk. I had a plan of action laid out, and so I allowed my mind to wander. October was the best month on the calendar. Halloween was just around the corner, and everyone knew it was my favorite holiday. Tinkie's due date was late October, and if all went well, we could plan a Halloween bash to celebrate the new baby and Tinkie's release from "incubation quarantine." Cece, Millie, and I had already planned a baby shower. It was an old-fashioned tradition—the gathering of female friends to help a new mother get the basics she would need to start her life raising a child. Most young people had foregone the shower tradition, but I wanted to do it up right for Tinkie, complete with petit fours, mints, some kind of ice-cream-sherbet punch, polished silver serving dishes and crystal punch bowl—the whole nine yards. Tinkie could buy whatever she wanted for this baby without blinking an eye. That wasn't the point of a shower. It was the gathering of female friends to share in this rite of passage, motherhood. Tinkie was thirty-four but this baby was still a first, and all of Tinkie's money couldn't buy the good wishes and cheer of her old school chums. That was bestowed upon her because we loved her.

Party plans were spinning in my head as I legged it down the sidewalk, passing cute little boutique shops, a department store, a drugstore, and the bail bond office where Junior Evans, owner of the bail office and a long-time family friend, sat behind the scarred wooden desk. He waved at me as I continued toward the newspaper office.

Sweetie Pie, who was half a block ahead of me, stopped and turned back. At first I didn't believe what I heard—

she was growling low in her throat. Sweetie Pie was the best-tempered, most easygoing hound in the state. She never acted aggressively toward people. Something was wrong!

My body reacted before my brain and I whirled around. A black pickup truck was bearing down on me going at least forty miles faster than the speed limit. The dark-tinted windows blocked a view of the occupants in the vehicle but I distinctly saw the barrel of a gun sticking out of the driver's side window.

Sweetie Pie saw it, too, and she dashed toward the truck. She clipped me hard, making me step in the gutter and lose my balance. I fell hard on my hip, but it wasn't me I was worried about.

"Sweetie Pie!" I screamed her name as I made a dive for her, but I was too late. She leaped at the gun barrel just as the driver drew abreast of me and pulled the trigger. Sweetie Pie gave a cry of pain and the truck sped away, while my hound dog fell into the street.

The doors of businesses opened and people ran onto the sidewalk, all talking and yelling. I could only see my pup, lying motionless on the asphalt. Someone had tried to kill me and instead had shot my dog. I still couldn't grasp it.

"What the hell?" Junior was beside me as we rushed to Sweetie Pie.

"She's been shot." She was breathing shallowly and her eyes were closed. "She saved my life. They were going to shoot me but she jumped and knocked their aim. They hit her instead."

"We'll get help. Don't panic, Sarah Booth." Junior found his cell phone and called the local veterinarian. He talked hurriedly and hung up. "Lynne is on her way as quick as she can," he said as he knelt with me. "How bad is she hurt?"

"I don't know." I was terrified to look but I gently rolled Sweetie Pie over to see how badly she was wounded.

There was a long furrow down her entire side where the bullet had grazed her, parting through skin and hair, but there was no evidence of internal damage. "Oh, thank goodness," I said as I sat in the road and held my dog in my arms. "Thank goodness." When Sweetie Pie's pink tongue shot up and licked my face, I couldn't help it. I started crying. "She jumped in front of the bullet," I told Junior again.

"I saw it," he said. "That dog deserves an award. She really saved your life."

Sirens wailed toward us. The courthouse wasn't far and someone had obviously called Coleman. He parked in the middle of the street and rushed over. When he caught sight of me sitting in the road holding my dog, his face registered fear and then anger. He was beside me in a moment as he carefully examined Sweetie Pie, who moaned pitifully and rolled her big brown eyes whenever I stopped stroking her head.

"Flesh wound," Coleman said. He kissed the top of my head. "She's going to be fine. Let me pick her up and put her in the patrol car. We can drive her to the vet. Junior said he'd called Dr. Leonard, but she can do a better job at the clinic with all her equipment."

Coleman scooped Sweetie Pie into his arms and eased her into the backseat of the patrol car. I got in the front seat. Sweetie Pie was stoic; she never cried out.

"I'll call Lynne and tell her not to come here, that you're on the way," Junior said, tapping the hood of the car to send us tearing toward the veterinarian clinic.

Lynne had a table waiting for Sweetie Pie, and Coleman kept his arm around my shoulders while Lynne examined her. When she finally looked over at us, she smiled. "That's one lucky dog. She lost a little hide and hair, but the wound should heal on its own. I'll give her a round of antibiotics to be on the safe side and a shot for pain relief, as well as some pain medication for a day or two, though I doubt she needs it. She'll be as good as new. What the hell happened?"

"Sweetie Pie saved Sarah Booth's life," Coleman said, recounting the events.

An hour later, reassured that Sweetie Pie had not sustained any serious injuries, I sat in the backseat with her head in my lap as Coleman drove us to Dahlia House where Tinkie was waiting.

Chablis greeted Sweetie Pie with great tenderness and walked gingerly beside her as my hound made her way into the house and collapsed in front of the fireplace in the parlor. I suspected Sweetie Pie was hamming it up and playing the sympathy card, but I was fine with that. She wasn't seriously injured. That was all that mattered. She'd sprung into the path of an oncoming bullet meant for me. She'd been willing to give up her own life—yet again—to save me.

25

Coleman stirred up a fire while Tinkie made coffee and I consoled my brave dog. Dusk had fallen, and from my position on the floor I could look out the parlor windows to the night sky. It was "the blue hour," a time my aunt Loulane had frequently cautioned me about. This was the end of the day, when the sun yielded to Nyx. It was often the most difficult time of the day for me, because endings were always harder than beginnings.

In the dying blue light, I intensely missed the simple moments of the past, like the rattle of my mother in the kitchen, making dinner for my father, who would come in the front door any minute holding out his arms for "his girls" to give him a kiss; or my mother's mad dash in the Roadster to get home and get something cooking if she and I had been on an adventure. I could easily see her hair whipping about her face as she focused on the road but laughed with me at the joy of the wind and sunshine.

My parents belonged to the larger world. Daddy's law practice often involved life and death for his clients. My mother's work was more subversive, in groups and gatherings, in standing up for underdogs. But the moments I treasured were the times when the world was abandoned and the focus was shifted to those of us who lived inside the walls of Dahlia House.

From the kitchen, I heard the rattling of cups and flatware. Tinkie came through the swinging door into the dining room and headed for me with a big tray of steaming coffee cups. Coleman was right behind her with an armload of firewood he'd gotten from the storage shed. My friend served the coffee while Coleman stoked the fire to a crackling delight. Sweetie Pie moaned softly and rolled over to warm her belly. I looked again to be sure—and nothing had changed. Her wound was shallow and would soon be gone.

When we each had a cup of joe and Tinkie and Coleman were settled on the old horsehair sofa, I told them what had happened, from breaking into Alala's to getting shot at by someone in a black pickup on Main Street.

"Didn't you see a black pickup outside Alala's house the day she was burglarized?" Coleman asked. "And did you say Dr. Becky Brown drove such a truck?"

"I did. I think it was the same one, but I can't be certain." I remembered the call from Poppy Bright. "I also got a call that Margaret McNeese might be in town. A friend, Poppy, was looking for her. Poppy asked me to be sure and tell her the university was trying to find her."

"Why would Margaret be in town?" Coleman asked.

"Good question."

"Did you get a look at the person who shot at you?" he asked. He was being nonchalant, but I could see the muscle in his jaw twitching. That was not a good sign. He was very angry.

"I didn't. The windows were tinted too dark. To be honest, it happened so fast, I just focused on the gun barrel."

"Handgun or rifle?"

"Handgun." I knew that because it was burned into my brain. "I couldn't say what kind. One with a cylinder and not a clip."

Coleman nodded. "DeWayne and Budgie headed out the highway to see if they could overtake the truck. They searched the roads all the way to the interstate, but they never saw anything. Either it was long gone or the driver had found a place to park it away from the road. We've put out an APB to surrounding counties. There's a chance someone will spot the truck and pick up the driver."

"Thank you, Coleman." I hadn't even thought of pursuing the shooter. My entire focus had been on saving Sweetie Pie, who had now drifted into a light sleep. She shifted positions and snored softly.

"The deputies are canvasing the stores on Main Street. If anyone saw anything, they'll get the information. Junior identified the truck as a black Silverado, so at least we have a make and model."

That was better than I'd managed. "I really don't understand why anyone would shoot at me." But I had an inkling. Until today, I hadn't uncovered anything that might be of value to a killer. "I found a thumb drive at Alala's house." I pulled it from my pocket. "Damn. It's cracked. I may have damaged it when I leaped after Sweetie Pie and landed on the asphalt."

"It may still work." Tinkie tried to be upbeat, but her expression showed doubt.

"Maybe." I put it on the floor beside me.

"If Alala is to be believed, those two dead professors were up to their ears in blackmail and worse," Tinkie said.

Coleman only shook his head. "People just continue to defy my rock-bottom expectations of scum."

Before we delved into the thumb drive, Tinkie had a little adventure of her own to tell us about. "What happened at Clifford's store?"

Tinkie filled us in on her surveillance of Clifford La-Place's furniture store and Alala's unexpected visit there. No one said it, but everyone was thinking it—was it possible Alala was in league with the AVA group? It didn't make logical sense, but she was writing a book. It would be one helluva way to generate media interest in her book if she somehow infiltrated AVA. Or perhaps AVA had offered interviews or information that somehow appealed to Alala and, using that as bait, they planned to lure Alala into the woods and take her hostage. After having been shot at on Main Street of my hometown, I felt like anything was possible.

The whole thing just gave me a headache. I hated having a client I couldn't trust, but I'd learned the hard way that people had a lot of motives for doing the strange things they did.

Tinkie continued with her story. "When Alala left the store, she was in the passenger seat of his truck."

This was a bombshell. "Where did they go?" I asked.

"I tailed them to the edge of town, out toward Highway 8 like maybe they were headed to Oxford, but then I got the call about the shooting and I turned around and came back to Zinnia."

I couldn't fault Tinkie—it was exactly the same thing I would have done. "When Alala drove by you, did she look like she was . . . a captive?"

"I couldn't tell," Tinkie said. "We should call Betty Sue at the store. She may know what's going on."

"Great idea. And let's check out the thumb drive you found," Tinkie said. "Just as soon as—"

A knock at the door interrupted her.

"I'll get it." Tinkie jumped up. "I ordered delivery from Millie's."

It was hard to believe how hungry I actually was after nearly being shot. We all fell on the food like we hadn't eaten in weeks. Even Sweetie Pie, Chablis, and Pluto had special meals. When the food was gone, the critters roared out of the kitchen like Satan was on their tail.

I could hear them tearing up and down the stairs. Dr. Leonard had given Sweetie Pie a shot for pain, but as far as I could tell, she was feeling A-OK. "Sweetie Pie! Chablis! Calm down right this minute or I'll put you both in kennels."

The sound of toenails on hardwood ceased. "Let's take a look at this drive," I said, motioning Tinkie and Coleman to come with me. Pluto, leaving the dogs behind, followed us into the detective agency office.

While the computer was starting up, Tinkie called Betty Sue. Tinkie spoke with her for a moment and her face reflected disappointment. "Thanks, anyway," she said.

When she hung up, she shook her head. "She didn't

hear anything. Clifford took Alala into his office for a few minutes and then they left together. She said if they argued, they kept their voices too low for her to hear anything.

"Convenient," I said as I waved them both over. "Let's check this out."

Coleman and Tinkie leaned over my shoulder as I plugged in the thumb drive. What came up on the screen was unintelligible. I'd never seen anything like it.

"Your computer can't read it," Coleman said.

"Because the device is cracked?" I felt terrible. We'd had a big part of the puzzle in hand and I'd destroyed it.

"Not sure," Coleman said. "It could be there isn't a program to open this on your computer. If it's okay, I'll take it back to the sheriff's office and see if Budgie can work with it. He's got a lot of experience with technology."

"Sounds like a perfect plan." I hated technology and only had a cell phone because Coleman and Tinkie made me get one. And truth be told, the camera, the compass app Tinkie had installed, and the recording device had come in mighty handy. Otherwise, gizmos were not my friend.

"This is gobbledygook," Tinkie said.

"It has to be something," I noted. "People were breaking into Alala's to hunt for this."

"*If* this is what they were searching for," Coleman said. "We don't know that. This could have been in Alala's house for several years. It could be from the former occupant. We don't know anything for certain."

"Coleman—"

He removed the drive. "I will get Budgie to look at this, but please don't pin a lot of hope on it. I'm not seeing anything that gives me the sense that we'll get anything useful at all."

"Then why were people breaking into Alala's house?" Tinkie asked.

"We don't know." Coleman put a hand on her shoulder. "But we're going to find out. Right now, though, we don't have anything. We need to catch them in the act of doing something illegal. That's how we put them behind bars."

"We could catch them up to something maybe tonight. That group of pitiful men, AVA, they're meeting in a hunting lodge between here and Ole Miss." Tinkie blurted out the information.

I wanted to throttle Tinkie, but instead I looked down, hoping Coleman would not snap on my deceit. Of course, I couldn't be that lucky.

"What do you know about the AVA meeting in a hunting lodge?" Coleman asked me.

Tinkie's eyes went wide. She realized she'd put me in a bad corner, but there wasn't anything to be done about it now.

There was no point trying to dodge the truth. "Here's what I know. The lodge belongs to Dr. Becky Brown, a prime suspect in all three deaths. She, too, has connections to Loxley, Wilson, and now with the tie to the lodge, to Curtis Miller and the rest of AVA."

"That tells me about Becky Brown. What about the lodge?" Coleman asked. There was a flicker of something in his eyes. The emotion was so fleeting I couldn't read it.

"AVA is meeting at Brown's lodge. I'm going to be there." I gave Tinkie a glare. "Alone."

"Not alone. With me," Coleman said in a tone that indicated it was a closed matter.

"And me," Tinkie said. Her chin, thrust forward with determination, told the story of her muleheadedness.

"Fine, bring everyone. I'm not responsible for any accidents that happen and I'm going to be sure and tell Oscar exactly where you plan to be tonight, Tinkie." I picked up my cell phone to call her husband, but Coleman covered my hand.

"Think this through. You can't get into the lodge, Sarah Booth. Or you, either, Tinkie. They aren't going to let women in there. And especially not you two. Y'all have a reputation as private investigators in Sunflower County. Those men may not be the brightest lamps on the street, but they aren't that dumb." He checked his watch. "And we don't have a lot of time to argue."

"Well, you can't get in, either," I pointed out. "Those men are not going to believe you're some kind of closet abuser and they hate law enforcement. You're a lot more dangerous to them than I am."

"Not to worry," Coleman said, staring directly into my eyes. "Harold is going to try to get inside. He's going undercover."

"You knew about the meeting tonight?" I challenged Coleman.

"I did." He was almost smug.

Harold, that fink! He'd ratted out my plan to Coleman. That's how Coleman knew about the hunting lodge. When the first blush of frustration cleared I actually felt relieved. "I was going—"

"Don't you dare say you were going to tell me," Coleman said. "I won't believe it."

I stopped talking. I had been well and truly busted. "What did Harold tell you?"

"He said you'd guaranteed that backup would be

there. Unfortunately, he was under the impression that *I* would be the backup. Since you hadn't bothered to tell me about this big plan, I'm assuming that *you* intended to be the backup."

"She couldn't tell you," Tinkie said, probably still calculating which one of us would be more likely to let her tag along. "She knew you'd stop her. But Harold told you. She didn't count on that." Clearly, Tinkie had decided Coleman was her best bet.

"He didn't intentionally blow your plans, Sarah Booth. He called to talk about wearing a wire and setting up a safe word. He'd assumed you guys had clued me in. You do realize that if those men are backed into a corner they might not hesitate about killing Harold."

Now, I was squirming. "I didn't lie," I said. "I *was* going to be backup. I have a gun. I can shoot pretty straight."

"Do you have any idea how many guns those men likely have?" Coleman asked.

That thought had crossed my mind, but I'd forced it out. Those men made me mad, and when I was mad I was brave. "I didn't lie." I clung to my truth even knowing it was threadbare.

"A lie of omission is equally bad," Coleman said with a hint of the devil in his blue eyes. Now I could read his expression. He wasn't really mad; he was excited that he'd caught me in such a neat trap. He was *enjoying* this torment.

"I probably would have told you before tonight." I wasn't sure that wasn't a lie, but I was desperate for some cloak of deniability.

"Doubtful," Tinkie said. "Sarah Booth sure didn't let on to me she was planning on being at that lodge. She said she was sending Harold in alone, but there would be backup."

I threw up my hands. "So sue me for trying to protect you, Tinkie, and for thinking I could handle this on my own."

"And maybe you could," Coleman said, "but tonight, we're not going to test that outcome. I'll be with you."

"I'm coming," Tinkie said. "I mean it. I can come with you or I can blunder my way in on my own."

I looked at Coleman and he shrugged. "This is between you two. I don't think it's wise, Tinkie. If you tripped or fell down, you could go into labor in the middle of the woods. Do you really want me and Sarah Booth delivering your child?"

"If I tripped and fell, I would probably roll into the men at the lodge and knock them all down like a bowling ball."

And that was the end of it. Tinkie would not be swayed. Only I had one more trick up my sleeve.

26

Harold, because he had access to almost anything he needed, arrived at Dr. Becky Brown's hunting camp in a shiny red Ford pickup. Coleman and I were already in position, hidden in a thicket about fifteen yards from the lodge where we had a perfect view of the front door and the parking lot. To our disappointment, all of the windows in the front were blocked out by heavy draperies. A three-quarter moon lit the scene, creating shadows on the front porch as the sound of laughter came from inside.

Harold pulled the borrowed truck into the gravel parking lot where two dozen other vehicles were parked. Before he'd turned the motor off, the front door of the lodge opened—someone inside was obviously aware that an unfamiliar vehicle was on the property. I was so glad I'd heeded Coleman and parked a mile away so that we could walk onto the property.

I held my breath, scanning the front door and windows for any signs of a gun barrel as Harold crossed the front yard. Roscoe was a little wiry-haired shadow at his leg as he stepped onto the porch. Two men I didn't recognize came out and met him. They both had military-issue weapons held casually at their sides. I couldn't see their features clearly.

Coleman and I tensed for action. He had his gun out and ready. I'd expected a welcoming party for Harold, but not an armed one. If we'd had more time, I would have sent him to the Red Top Bar for a couple of evenings to mingle with the men, to be accepted in that scene. This cold call at the front door of an AVA meeting was risky.

The two men talked to Harold for a good five minutes before they escorted him to the door. They stopped Roscoe when he tried to enter with Harold, but I heard Harold say, "If you don't let Roscoe in, I'll have to leave. Besides, I can show you how he picks winning stocks." The men drew Harold and the dog inside. The door closed with a solid sound. Coleman had convinced Harold not to go in wired—at least not this first time. It was too dangerous, and Harold had finally agreed. Now all Coleman and I could do was wait and worry.

We tried to contain our anxiousness with small talk. Coleman relayed some of the local history of the area.

"The camp is a beautiful old rustic building, dormitory style, with a large kitchen and dining area at one end, a bathroom that accommodates several people at once in the center, and a sleeping area with a dozen cots set up on the west end." I realized Coleman was giving me the scoop in case we needed to do an emergency extraction of Harold. I was glad Coleman was there. Really glad. With each passing minute, I realized I was in over my head in this endeavor.

"How do you know the layout?" I asked, hoping to match Coleman's easy conversational tone.

His hand rested on my thigh as he pulled me closer against him for warmth. "It was the old Binkerman lodge. I came up here once with some high school buddies to spend the weekend."

"You were never a hunter." It surprised me that Coleman would even hang out with hunters for a weekend. He had strong feelings about killing animals for sport.

"No, I never took pleasure in killing any living creature. Not much of a challenge to kill something with all the fancy scopes and artillery hunters have today. I wasn't at the lodge for that. I just came up to be in the woods. The boys I was with didn't care about killing, either. We played cards, drank a little whiskey, lied about girls."

That sounded more like the high school boy I remembered. "Who were the Binkermans?"

"An old Memphis family. You might remember Gavin Wright. He was a grandson. That's who invited me up here."

I did remember Gavin. He was older than me and he always disappeared from Sunflower County during the summers. He attended high school but played no sports and developed no real ties. He was a quiet young man who seemed to be a loner. "What happened to him?"

"He was killed in a car accident going home to Memphis. He attended Sunflower County High School, because he'd been in some juvie trouble in Memphis.

Nothing serious, but enough to see him kicked out of the posh school he was supposed to attend. To get him away from the bad influence of his friends that his parents blamed for the trouble, they sent him here. One of the Binkerman relatives was on the county school board." Coleman was silent for a moment. "Gavin always went home for school vacations and holidays. He was never around for any of the fun stuff. It was a hard life for him, one foot in two very different worlds."

"I wonder how Becky Brown got her hands on the deed to this place." The lodge was rustic, but well-crafted. With the attached land, it would have cost a pretty penny.

"That's a question I'd like to ask her," Coleman said.

I snuggled up to him as we whispered. Our gazes were focused on the front of the lodge, watching for any sign of upheaval inside. Being close to Coleman made the long night tolerable. "I'll ask her when I see her." Then I had a better idea. "Or you can bring her in for questioning. That really needs to happen."

"You're sounding a little vindictive, Sarah Booth." Coleman gave me a squeeze. "Your partner could find out more about the lodge deal." Coleman knew Tinkie had a better head for business deals than I did, and it was possible any financing had gone through the Zinnia bank that Oscar ran. "I'm assuming the Binkerman family tired of the lodge, and after Gavin was killed, I don't think there was another generation interested in coming here. Selling it would make logical sense."

"Speaking of Tinkie, tell me I made the right call." Guilt still nibbled at my toes.

Tinkie was safely at home with Chablis, Sweetie Pie, Pluto, and her kitty, Gumbo. Someone had tipped Oscar off about her nocturnal plans to hide in the woods and he had firmly put his foot down. Tinkie was miffed, but in all honesty, when I'd dropped the animals off, she'd also seemed a little relieved not to be hiding in the bushes on a cold October night. I felt only a little guilty at dropping the dime on her to Oscar. But my friend's well-being was worth her being mad at me—if Oscar ever told her how he'd found out about the agenda to surveil a lodge full of horrible men.

"Was Tinkie mad?" Coleman asked.

"I don't think so. Not really. I think she was happy to stay home. I know she's very uncomfortable, and being stuck out in the woods for hours isn't easy. Unless you have a warm human pillow." I burrowed against him. "Do you think Harold's okay?"

"I do. There would be shouting or signs of an altercation if he weren't. They may not embrace him or say a damn thing of value to him, but if they were going to hurt him, they would have done it by now."

I sighed. "You're right. I could have endangered Harold. It was stupid."

"Say that again."

I craned my neck around so I could look at him, barely visible in the night and hidden in the bushes. "Why?"

"I want to record it. No one will ever believe you admitted you were wrong."

I punched him hard enough to make him grunt. "That's not funny."

"Sure it is. That's why you punched me."

He eased me away from him and I instantly missed the warmth. "I'm glad you're here with me. I mean it."

He kissed my cheek. "Me too. Stakeouts with De-Wayne aren't nearly this . . . stimulating."

"Behave."

"Okay. Then I'm going to walk around the lodge to see if any of the back windows give a view inside. I'm sure Harold is fine, but I want to know what's going on in there if I can figure out a way to spy."

"Be safe." I could have argued to go with him, but Coleman had a stealth in the woods that I couldn't copy no matter how hard I tried. I watched him go with equal measures of pride and concern. It was so strange how I could look at his retreating back and see both the broad-shouldered man he was now—a solid man who knew exactly who he was—yet also the thinner, less confident high school boy I'd always felt safe with.

He disappeared into the night and I settled back on the ground, my gaze on the front door, on the alert for any discernible movement behind the thickly draped windows. The night was growing longer and colder, and I curled up as tightly as I could, wishing Coleman would hurry and return.

27

I must have dozed off, because the rat-a-tat firing of a machine gun startled me awake. I sat bolt upright, confused about where I was. I had sense enough to duck and stay silent, as I peered through the foliage, to see an old black car from the 1930s parked in front of the lodge. Standing at the bumper of the car was a pretty woman in a tea-length black dress with a cloche hat on her head. Diminutive was the best description. The moonlight caught a shiny glint on the front of her dress, and I watched in growing horror as blood dripped from her onto the ground. She'd been shot. A number of times. That was the sound of bullets I'd awakened to.

She came toward me and though I cowered, it was useless. She'd already spotted me.

She struck a pose and began to recite. "Someday they'll go down together; and they'll bury them side by side. To few it'll be grief, to the law a relief, but it's death for Bonnie and Clyde."

"Jitty!" I knew the score. "You scared me so badly my liver turned a flip. What are you doing? You have nothing in common with Bonnie Parker."

Her smile was tinged with sadness. "No, but you do."

My heart hammered a red alert. "What?" Bonnie/Jitty was still leaking blood. Not a comforting sight at all.

"In your heart, Sarah Booth, you're an outlaw."

Now that wasn't what I'd expected. "So all of this"—I waved at her bloody body—"is so I can find my true self? You scare me half to death with machine gun fire so I can figure out my outlaw side?" I was annoyed.

"You got a law-breaking streak a mile wide and you know it."

Jitty was uncomfortably close to a truth I didn't want to admit. "Lots of folks looked at Bonnie and Clyde as heroes. Not outlaws. They had the public sympathy for a long time." While I'd been a sorry student of history, I'd paid attention to some of the more exciting moments, especially the tale of Bonnie and Clyde. Like they'd done with so many others, the criminal couple had tugged at my romanticism, my love of those who bucked authority and did so with flair.

"I touched a lot of people who had no other hope," Bonnie said.

In the brief span of her life, Bonnie Parker had been romanticized and vilified. She'd had a certain arrogance and a real love of life—and Clyde Barrow, he also had charisma. I'd read somewhere that Bonnie once wanted to be an actress, before she met Barrow and became a criminal. Barrow, who also had an artistic penchant, had favored music. The guitar and saxophone were his instruments of choice. A saxophone was found in the car at the scene of their death.

"Some folks loved us," Bonnie said, sounding pensive with a rural Texas twang. "We stood for something, an escape, a chance at something more than slow starvation and back-breaking labor."

"Bonnie and Clyde killed four innocent civilians and nine police officers." This I remembered from my studies.

"You don't know what things were like." Bonnie sat down on the ground beside me.

I had to concede that fact. "Explain it to me, but be quick. Coleman will be back soon."

"I was born in 1910. The depression wouldn't come to the rest of the country for a few years, but in dirt-poor Texas, times were already hard. My father died when I was little. All I ever wanted was for someone to love me, and I married at fifteen. My first husband beat me. He was a brute. I never divorced him, but I left before he killed me. And then I met Clyde. He wasn't like that. He wouldn't lift a hand to harm me. Fact is, he'd kill anyone who tried."

I did feel sorry for her; she'd had a hard start. But she was more than a brutalized waif. Barrow killed people and Bonnie helped him. I wasn't sure domestic abuse and true love were good enough reasons to go on a killing spree. "Violence doesn't justify violence."

She grinned. "Maybe not in your world. Don't judge until you live in mine. We killed some people, but we let most of them go. Killin' was never what we wanted. We did what we had to do to survive."

"Why? Why do it at all? The records indicate you were bright and Clyde, too. Charismatic. You could have gone in another direction. Why not follow your dream to the stage?"

"Times were bad. There wasn't work. We couldn't make money." She shrugged. "Robbin' the banks made us famous. Robbin' the grocery stores made us unpopular. Killin' that kid cop made us dead."

I remembered the historical tidbit. Clyde, Bonnie, and another member of the gang, Henry Methvin—the man who would ultimately betray them—were sleeping in the car on the side of a road when two officers found them. Methvin killed one and Barrow, feeling he had no alternative, killed the other. Barrow's logic was that no witnesses to a cop killing could be left alive. But the young officer Barrow killed was on his first day at the job and he was due to be married. The officer's fiancée wore her wedding dress to his funeral. That had been the nail in the coffin of public support for the young outlaws.

"Did you trust Henry Methvin?" I asked.

"He loved his family. Like us. Clyde thought he was honorable, but he wasn't. He talked about his mama and how much she meant to him. His pa." She made a face. "Nothing meant anything to Henry. We treated him like family, and he or someone he told sold us out so he could get a pardon himself."

"What happened?" I knew a little of it, but I wanted to hear it from her.

"Clyde and I went home to Texas whenever we could. We'd drive by the Barrow house and throw a Coke bottle with a note in it onto the porch. Inside the bottle were directions on where Clyde's folks could meet us. The plan worked like a charm. Until it didn't.

"That May, we took Henry with us so he could see his family, too. He didn't live far from the Barrows and he told Clyde he really wanted to see his folks. We were on our way to pick him up at his folks' place, after our visit, when we ran into that ambush." She put a hand on her chest. "Someone who knew our plans arranged it all—the setup, the ambush. We never even knew what was happening."

"You'd stopped to help with a broken-down car?" I asked, remembering only snatches of the story.

"Yeah, Henry's pa with his broke-down truck." Disgust thickened her voice. "We stopped to help Henry's pa." She turned away from me and her voice softened even more. "They said I was shot twenty-six times, but it was more than that. They only shot Clyde seventeen, and he was so much bigger than me. Wasn't much left of me to bury, but that undertaker we cut loose at a robbery, he did the best he could for me. He said he'd bury us, and he did."

She was a tiny little thing. She'd been twenty-four when she died. Not much of a life for a little girl who'd dreamed of being an actress.

"I wrote a poem about me and Clyde. That's what I was recitin' when I walked up. Escapin' from our lives was never much more than a dream. I knew we'd end up dead, the both of us. It was kind of the only outcome, right? Dead or prison. Clyde wasn't goin' back to prison and neither was I. At least it was quick." She took a step back. "We didn't get a lot out of life, but we didn't linger. We died quick."

I had to pull deep to summon the fortitude to sit up tall. She touched my heart, even though I fought against it. My life had been hard, but compared to Bonnie Parker, I had nothing to complain about.

"Why are you here? With me?" I asked her. "What should I learn?"

"I'm not a schoolmarm," she said with a disarming grin. "Never took to lessons I didn't want to learn. I suspect you're the same. Life is to live, not spend all your time thinking about it."

"You didn't have to die." I felt I needed to make her see that. "There were other choices."

"Not at the end. Before that, yeah, maybe. But not at the end. We'd killed a cop, a kid. Folks that used to help us turned against us. Dead was the only way out."

The sadness that enveloped me was for Bonnie, Clyde, and so many others who'd started down a wrong road and felt there was no turning back. "I'm sorry."

She shook her head and the winning smile came back into play. "Don't be. I'm not. There are worse things than death, Sarah Booth."

The sound of a band tuning up drew me to my knees for a better vantage point. The tinkling of piano ivories and then a steady beat on a drum set came out of the night, and then Georgie Fame was singing "The Ballad of Bonnie and Clyde." Bonnie did a twirl and evaporated just as the sound of an altercation came from inside the lodge.

Where was Coleman? I didn't see any sign of him. He'd told me to stay put, but what if someone was inside hurting Harold? Like a deer tensed to flee the hunters, I trembled in the underbrush, trying not to think about Jitty/Bonnie, Coleman, or Harold. What if Bonnie

Parker's message to me was that I'd taken a path with no good ending?

Panic rose in my chest. I gripped my gun and prepared to go hunting for Coleman.

28

The front door of the lodge burst open, and I was ready. I gripped the handle of the gun and forced myself to take deep breaths. If I had to shoot, I wanted to be sure I hit what I was aiming at and nothing else.

Two men roared out onto the long porch that fronted the entire building. They were hollering, cursing, snarling at each other, and stumbling, clearly drunk. In the open front door, I saw Harold standing inside. He was grinning and someone was slapping him on the back. Whatever was going on, Harold didn't seem to be in any danger.

I lowered the gun and sat down on the ground. Harold had successfully infiltrated the AVA group here in Sunflower County. The relief I felt was like a heavy weight removed from my shoulders. I watched the antics of the two men on the porch with a slight smile. They were drunkity-drunk-drunk-drunk. One stumbled into the other and they both went down, rolling across the porch. When they finally stopped and untangled their limbs, they sat up.

"Man, that hurt," one said.

"Nah. Didn't hurt me," the other said. "You just a baby."

The first one slugged the other one and they tangled up like two toddlers and rolled along the porch some more. By tomorrow morning they were going to be sore and bruised, but for right now, they were pretty good entertainment.

Some of the men, including Harold, came out onto the porch. They stood back. No one attempted to intervene. The fighting men were so drunk they probably couldn't really hurt each other. I was about to see if I could text Coleman when a woman walked out the door. For a moment she was silhouetted in the doorway, a tall, slender woman. And then she stepped forward where the light hit her face. Becky Brown shook her head at the two men on the porch who were trying to stand up but failing miserably. They'd almost make it to their feet but then would fall over.

"Come on, help me get them back inside. We can't just leave them out here," Becky said, her tone wheedling. "They might fall off the porch and hurt each other."

"So?" one of the men standing by her asked. "Not my problem. Those two get drunk and fight every single meeting. I'm tired of the distraction. We can't get a damn thing done because of these two morons." It took me a moment to recognize Clifford LaPlace's voice. So the furniture store owner was here, and so was Becky Brown. Did she know what AVA was and what it was up to? It appeared so. If Clifford was here, where the heck was Alala? The last time she'd been seen was with him.

There was much murmuring among the men on the porch, but no one made a move to pull the two fighting men apart. The drunks were mostly swinging wild and falling over. Neither was landing a blow, and when they did tie up, they only rolled around. In their padded jackets, I doubted they would suffer too much.

Suddenly, the crowd on the porch parted and fell silent. It was almost as if Moses had commanded the Red Sea to divide. Coleman stepped from the interior of the cabin into the empty space left by the spectators. My heart thudded hard as I saw him outlined in the light from the open door, and the moonlight on his face. One man, alone, against at least three dozen.

He gave a tiny nod toward the place where I hid, a signal to me that he was okay. He'd obviously found a back way into the lodge, and now he was searching for someone. "Where is Alala Diakos?" he asked the men who'd clumped together on the porch.

"She's not here!" one man answered. "And you sure as heck shouldn't be, either."

"Where is she?" Coleman asked, his voice carefully modulated to sound reasonable.

"How should we know?" the man asked.

Coleman grew silent, and I realized he was weighing options that might not be pretty for everyone involved. He couldn't arrest them all, and he likely had no cause to arrest anyone.

"Someone saw Alala come in here with Clifford LaPlace," Coleman said in his loud, take-charge voice.

"Where is she? She's not in the lodge. What have you done with her?"

I felt a knife blade of fear at my throat. What could have happened to Alala? Was Coleman bluffing or had he learned that Alala was in real danger?

From the middle of the crowd, Harold stepped forward. "Get out of here, Peters. This is private property. There's no feminist loudmouth here. We've broken no laws. You have no right or reason to be here. Now beat it, or I'll have to file charges against you."

"File all the charges you want, Erkwell," Coleman came back, his stance belligerent. "I'm searching for a missing woman, a woman who is an enemy to your precious little group of misogynists. I have reason to believe she's here on the premises. And I want her brought out to me without being harmed. If she's harmed, I'll see you all prosecuted for a hate crime. That's a federal crime and lots of time in prison comes with that kind of prosecution."

"You *want* her brought out? Want all you want." Harold sneered. "Wanting never hurt anyone. You *want* to search for your missing provocateur, then show me the search warrant."

I was riveted. I'd never seen this side of Coleman or Harold. They were both bowed up like they'd start swinging at each other at the drop of a hat. To my shock, Roscoe winded his way through the men and took a protective stance at Harold's knee. The pup started growling at Coleman as if he wanted to tear out his throat. I almost stood up to chastise the dog, but then I realized, somehow, Harold had trained him. Harold said he was the smartest dog around, and no one believed it because Roscoe was so bad. But Harold had taught that incorrigible, evil little dog to growl on command, and he was very convincing. Roscoe had a film career waiting if Harold ever wanted to pursue it. I slumped lower in the shrubs and strained to hear everything that was said.

"I never thought I'd see you involved in this kind of organization, Harold." Coleman was playing the betrayed card.

"You don't really know me, Peters. You come to my parties, you drink my liquor, you're sleeping with the woman I love, and you're too thick to even understand how much I want to make you pay."

Even though I knew they were pretending, I was still shocked. Harold sounded furious, and even though I knew it was an act, it left me feeling slightly sick to my stomach.

Coleman chuckled. "If Sarah Booth wanted to be with you, she'd be with you. Maybe she saw this side of you beneath that polished banker façade."

"If Sarah Booth had been properly raised, she would have married me when she came home. She would have done the sensible thing and let me take charge of her life. I could have made sure she'd never do without anything she wanted, and she could have given me an heir. Instead, she runs around poking her nose in everyone's business. One day she's going to get it cut off. When that happens, it's going to be on you, Peters."

"No one controls Sarah Booth." Coleman looked and sounded perfectly livid. "She makes up her own mind about who she wants to see."

"And that's a problem," Harold said. His face was distorted with anger. "Women aren't smart enough to know what's good for them. You know that in your heart of hearts. How many times has she sassed you back and you wanted to turn her over your knee and spank some respect into her?"

Coleman didn't say anything. I waited a full minute—everyone wired for a fight—and Coleman didn't say a word in my defense. Boy, he was going to pay when we finally got home. I was a little hardheaded but not that bad.

At last, Coleman spoke. "Sometimes she could use some correction. She's a little too headstrong. But I'm working on it."

That was almost more than I could take. Coleman, agreeing that I needed "correction." Oh, he had just fallen down a deep well and I wasn't in the mood to pull him out. He'd better hope his little verbal high jinks with Harold panned out, because if the mob turned on them I wasn't sure I'd be helping either one in a hurry.

Harold stepped closer to Coleman. "Look, nobody here wants to hurt a woman. But they're like children. Spare the rod and spoil the child. It says it in the Bible."

From my perspective, Harold was a little too convincing. He was spouting that crap as if he'd eaten a steady diet of it his whole life. I knew better. But where had he come up with Bible quotes?

"I don't disagree with that," Coleman said, and there was a murmur through the crowd.

"You kept arresting Curtis Miller whenever he put the law down for that wife of his," one of the men shouted out. "You're a liar."

Despite the fact that I wanted to slug Coleman myself, I didn't want anyone else to hurt him. My hand went back to the grip of my gun.

"I arrested Curtis because he wasn't smart enough to stop before he hurt Tansy so badly she had to go to the hospital." Coleman was calm. "The hospital is required by law to report those cases, and I am required to act on them. End of story. Curtis pushed it too far. You might want to keep that in mind if you decide to correct your wives. Don't leave bruises or marks and don't end up in the ER."

Coleman had covered his buttocks very neatly. I'd underestimated both men's abilities for subversive work.

Clifford LaPlace stepped forward. I recognized him in the pale moonlight. "That professor woman isn't here. There's only one female here, and the club belongs to her." He pointed at Becky Brown, who'd been amazingly silent. I hope, hope, hoped that Coleman would cuff her and arrest her. I wanted to talk to her.

"Someone saw you leaving the furniture store with her," Coleman said. He kept his tone nonaccusatory. "Where did you leave her?"

"We rode around for a few minutes while I talked to her. She made some wild accusations, and I needed to straighten her out." He put his hands on his hips. "That Betty Sue in the furniture store is the biggest snoop around. I didn't want to talk in front of her. So the professor and I rode around for fifteen minutes and then I took her back to the furniture store where her car was parked."

Coleman took out his phone. Service was spotty because we were so deep in the woods, but he seemed to have a signal. "Hello, DeWayne, Coleman here. Check with Dr. Diakos and make sure she's home and okay. Thanks." He slipped his phone in his pocket. "If she's at home, my work here is done. If she's not, I'm going to search the premises. It's not my idea of a fun evening, but it's my duty."

Coleman and the men had effectively come to a stand-off.

"Look, I took her back to her car. That's the truth." Clifford said, stepping to the forefront and effectively pushing Harold aside. I'd wondered how long he was going to let Harold act as leader of the group. Now he was asserting himself. "I can't help where that crazy woman went. She's a troublemaker and I'm smart enough to steer clear of her. She wanted to talk. I listened. Then I took her back to her car."

"Talk about what?" Coleman asked.

"She accused me of siccing Curtis on her that day in the park. I told her that was ridiculous. I'd never give Curtis a gun and send him out to do anything, except maybe kill some small varmints."

"Curtis had a gun trained on Dr. Diakos when she was speaking in the park. I have reason to believe it was your gun."

Clifford shrugged. "Maybe I loaned him a gun to kill squirrels. That has nothing to do with me. Curtis wasn't all that bright and look what happened to him. But while you're worried about Diakos, you might give a thought to what happened to Curtis, you know. Shot through the heart just like that Dr. Loxley."

"Are you saying Dr. Diakos murdered Curtis Miller and a university professor?" Coleman asked calmly.

"Well, who did you think did it?" Harold stepped in front of Clifford, taking the lead yet again.

"That's what I intend to find out."

Coleman's cell phone rang and he answered. I couldn't hear his conversation but when he put the phone back in his pocket he addressed the men. "Dr. Diakos is at home. My business here is done."

He turned on his heel and started to walk away. I backed carefully through the shrubbery without making a sound. I'd meet him on the path that led off the property and to his truck.

29

I'd never been gladder to see the backside of a place than that hunting lodge. What's more, I wasn't sure that we'd accomplished anything except for Coleman and Harold to have a whale of a good time annoying me.

When I fell into step beside Coleman, I said, "That was some show you and Harold put on."

"Wasn't it?" Coleman said. "I would never have thought that of Harold. He was terrific."

"Wait. That wasn't something you and he planned?"

Coleman gave it just long enough for me to really get worried before he said, "We had agreed to a confrontation, but we hadn't scripted it out. Harold hit the perfect narrative. Now he'll be in with them without question. I have to give him credit. He played it like a pro." He put his arm around my shoulders and drew me closer to him as we continued to walk. "And we gave you a starring role. That really aroused their sympathies for Harold, that he'd lost you to me. That was the icing on the cake in convincing those yahoos."

I didn't know whether to be flattered or to punch him on the arm. "You didn't have to go on like that in front of all those men and that weirdo Becky Brown. Seriously, it made me sound like a piece of steak two dogs were fighting over."

"Sure we did. It was perfect."

"I'll reserve judgment on that. Did you find out anything else? Anything useful?"

"A lot. There's a plan afoot for AVA to fund three Sunflower County political campaigns. One for school board, one for a supervisor post, and one for a chancery judge. These guys are meeting to discuss fundraising. The goal is to raise half a million dollars in a nationwide endeavor and to begin a campaign to elect men sympathetic to the goals of disenfranchising women and keeping them from assuming power or equality. They figure Mississippi is a great state to start in."

"Half a million dollars? That's a lot of money for this part of the world."

"It's a national outreach. Clifford and this group are grassroots, working to enlist the 'average man' to contribute small amounts. There's big money in this, though, and Harold is exactly the guy who can find out where it's coming from and who is behind all of this. Clifford LaPlace may be a great furniture salesman, but he's not the brains behind AVA."

"Who is?"

"Undetermined," Coleman said. "The people behind

this are afraid of losing power. When those who have been systematically deprived of equality finally unite, there's going to be great change in this country. A lot of powerful people don't want to see that happen."

Coleman had a point, but it didn't help me figure out who had killed Wilson, Loxley, or Curtis Miller. "And what is Becky Brown's role in all of this?"

Coleman grinned. "She's organizing the efforts. She's in this up to her eyeballs. I suspect it has more to do with money than ideology."

"Do you think Brown got involved with Loxley and let him whale away on her just to get into AVA?"

"I think it's very possible."

"Why would Brown be doing this?" I asked the question aloud, though I didn't expect Coleman to have an answer. Brown had allegedly been a victim of Dr. Loxley's abuse. Why in the world would she want to support a group of men who promoted treating women like children and disciplining them to keep them in line, fighting against equal pay and heaven knew what else? If the answer was money, it was a pitiful answer.

"Brown is an enigma. She didn't say a lot, but it's clear she carries a lot of weight with those men."

"And Alala is really at home?"

"That I don't know. DeWayne couldn't find her, but I searched the lodge and she wasn't there. I figured the smart move was to get out before violence erupted. I'd learned as much as I was going to learn. I set Harold up good and proper. When the meeting is over, Harold can fill us in on all the rest."

I was done underestimating my man. "What can I do to help?"

"I need you to search for Alala. The deputies and I are going to run down backgrounds on the men I recognized in AVA. I've known some of those guys since high school, and their membership in AVA is not a big surprise. But some of them—they weren't local. There's big money here and it's happening in my county. Can you find the professor?"

"Can do." I checked my watch. The night was still young. I could pick up Tinkie, since this wouldn't be dangerous, and begin a search for our missing client. I could only hope she was grocery shopping and that Clifford LaPlace hadn't lied when he said he'd dropped her off at her car in his parking lot.

My car was at the courthouse, and we drove there. I kissed Coleman goodbye and jumped behind the steering wheel.

"Check in every hour," Coleman said. "Please don't make me worry."

"Or what, you may spank me to teach me how to properly behave?" I still wasn't completely over his little charade.

"I doubt I have the courage for that," Coleman said. "Just do it because you love me."

"That's exactly the right motivation." Ten minutes later, I was pulling into the driveway at Hilltop. Before I could park, I heard Sweetie Pie yodeling a welcome. The dog recognized the sound of my car.

I expected Tinkie to be a little miffed, but she was all in for a search for Alala, and so were the critters as they piled in the backseat. Even Oscar, who came out to the car to see us off, was in a good mood.

"Keep an eye on her," he said to me with a wink. "She

says at least two weeks more, but I thumped her belly and she has the sound of a ripe watermelon. She's good to go any minute now."

"Oscar, you're either brave or a real fool," I said. I'd felt the baby kick—when Tinkie invited me. I'd never attempt to thump her stomach. I valued keeping my head attached to my shoulders.

"He's brave and a fool," Tinkie said as she got in the passenger seat, and Oscar closed her door. "He thinks he jollied his way past the fact that you two conspired to keep me from going to that hunting lodge tonight. But he would be wrong about that."

Uh-oh! I should have known Tinkie would figure it out. "You didn't miss a thing." I would tell her all about Harold's heroic acting when the case was over, but not right now. "The past is the past, Tinkie. Now we have to find our client. I'll tell you all the important things that happened."

I made sure the dogs and cat were loaded. Then I put the pedal to the metal and took off. For an antique, the Roadster still had a whole lot of spunk.

Alala's house was dark and empty. Sweetie Pie and I did a recon just to be sure that she wasn't inside and injured, but she simply wasn't there. Her car was gone. When I returned to the driver's seat, I called DeWayne. "Did you and Budgie have any luck determining what was on that thumb drive?"

"We're still trying. The drive was too badly damaged. I know on the TV shows there's always some really smart nerdy deputy who can get all the data back, but that's the difference between real life and TV."

"I guess you and Budgie just aren't nerdy enough," I said.

"Yeah, we'll work on that," DeWayne vowed. "We're making some progress. Have you found Alala?"

"Not yet. Would you pass that along to Coleman? She isn't home. So, we're heading to check out the Red Top. We are not going in." I said it quickly before DeWayne could protest or hand the phone over to Coleman. "We're just doing a drive-by to see if we can locate her car. I would hope she'd have sense enough not to be in that bar, but she is—"

"Exactly like you," DeWayne finished.

I didn't have the time or energy to argue with him. "If we find her, we'll check in. How's the search going for those donors?"

"Slow. We're hoping when Harold checks in that he has more solid information to go on."

"Good plan." And it was. Harold and Tinkie were the smartest people I knew when it came to money—finding it, moving it, manifesting it, or figuring out who was using it for what.

"Once we know who the big fish are, we'll be in a better position to find out what's going on," DeWayne said. "We'll be in touch."

I didn't get a chance to respond. The line was dead.

"They don't know anything new," I told Tinkie. "Let's run by the Red Top."

"We aren't stopping for a drink," Tinkie said. "If it was too dangerous to sit in the woods watching a lodge filled with drunks and wannabe big men, then it's damn sure too dangerous to go in that bar."

I grinned at her, glad to see she took the situation seriously. "No worries." I turned back toward town. At the first crossroads, I realized we were very close to Selena's House. Alala might be there. She could be interviewing someone for the book she was writing.

The same thing must have occurred to Tinkie because she said, "Take a right. Selena's House. Let's check there."

I pulled up half a block across from the two-story house, killed the headlights, and watched. I had a clear view of both floors. The lights were off downstairs, but the upstairs bedrooms had something going on, especially the one on the far corner.

The street was still, but Sweetie Pie and Chablis were anxious in the backseat. Tinkie was restless, too. But then she was fidgety wherever she was these days. And a little cross at times.

"Are you going to drive up to the door or sit back here skulking?"

"What would you prefer, Princess Tinkie?" I kept my tone light. Tinkie's hormones were all over the place. As Cece had once told me about hormonal women and little moments of stress—"That's how random murders occur." I also couldn't be certain if Tinkie was packing heat or not. Normally we didn't carry our guns unless we anticipated serious trouble, which was not the case tonight. My gun was in the trunk of the car. If Tinkie had hers, it was in that expensive leather purse she carried that was big enough to accommodate a stinger. She could have anything in that purse from a switchblade to an Uzi.

"Oh, don't patronize me," she finally said. Then she sighed. "Sorry. I'm a little cranky."

My lips were sealed tight.

And Tinkie was having none of that. "Well say something, dammit."

"Whatever I say is going to be wrong." I didn't want to argue, but Tinkie was itching for a confrontation.

"Give it a try." The hostility had evaporated from her voice. "I won't jump down your throat. I promise."

"This pregnancy will be over soon."

"Dammit, Sarah Booth, that's the stupidest thing you've ever said. Soon *to you.* Two more weeks of this and I'll weigh five hundred pounds and be totally bald from pulling my hair out. I'm already up one and a half shoe sizes. I have platypus feet. Or duck feet. And, I waddle." The last words came out on a wail.

Tinkie was normally the one who offered soothing and comfort. This wasn't my forte, but I had better learn quick. I put my arm around her shoulders and hugged her. "It's going to be so worth it when you hold that baby. You'll see. You're about to receive the thing you wanted more than anything else in life. Who gets that, Tinkie? How many people actually get that?"

"You're right." She sighed and straightened up, wiping at her tears. At last, she stretched and seemed to find a more comfortable position. "I'm sorry. I'll work on my attitude."

I snorted with laughter. "Please don't! Just be you. That's plenty fine."

I saw another flicker of movement at one of the upstairs windows—the one that had been pointed out by the philandering Todd Renfield as Tansy's. Sweetie Pie saw the dark figure, too, and gave a low whine deep in her throat. "I think something's wrong in that house." Coleman was a big believer in trusting his gut—to a point. My instincts told me something was off. I just wasn't sure in what direction. With a place like Selena's, where women went to hide from abusers, there was always the chance that a psychopathic, abusive husband might show up looking for the woman he felt belonged to him. I got out of the car and got my gun, which I handed to Tinkie. She was, after all, the better shot.

"You keep the gun in case I have to call for backup."

"You're not going in there?" Tinkie phrased it as a question, but she meant it as a statement.

"Just to check on Penny. If she's okay, I'll be right back out."

"No." She grabbed my arm. "No." She pointed to the window, where the shadow moved across again. I couldn't be certain, but it looked as if another smaller shadow shrank back from the bigger one. It looked very much like someone was bullying another person. "There's a killer on the loose, and if you go in there you could end up dead."

"That's Tansy's room. What if one of those men from AVA is up there intimidating her? I need—"

"You need to hold your horses. She's sided with her abuser in the past. And if someone wicked is there, he could be armed." Tinkie picked up her phone. "I'm calling Coleman."

"Good plan." This could so easily be something that would require legal intervention. I had none of the authority to stop a bad situation from getting worse. "Get the law here as quickly as you can."

Tinkie handed my gun back to me. "I have my own." She reached into her huge leather purse and brought it out. "I'm fine."

"I'm going to at least ring the doorbell and chat with Penny for a moment. That will give her an excuse to answer the door. If anything's wrong, she can signal me in some way. I'll be safe."

"Or you could maneuver yourself into the crosshairs." Tinkie reached for my coat sleeve, but missed.

"I won't go inside. I promise."

"Sarah Booth, don't put yourself in danger. You know I'll have to come after you and I'm not in any condition to run and dodge bullets."

That was an understatement. "I'm not going inside. I swear it. I'll just distract the person upstairs—if there is even a person up there. It could just be . . ." I didn't have a real alternative. And even as I looked, the shadow passed before the window again.

I'd thrilled myself watching too many Dracula movies with Bela Lugosi moving in on the innocent victim for a nice blood-sucking session. I had a bad feeling.

I hurried across the street and rang the doorbell before Tinkie could talk me out of it.

I looked back at her once and saw that she'd managed to slide beneath the steering wheel of the car in case we needed to make a fast getaway. That was my partner. Thinking ahead. The car door cracked and Sweetie Pie came bounding across the street with a tiny little shadow, Chablis, in hot pursuit. Pluto also had been freed and he sauntered across the street as if he had all the time in the world. I sighed. Tinkie wasn't going to let me work without backup.

I rang the doorbell three times. A serious caller, but not desperate. I gave it a full minute then rang again. Three more assertive times. I couldn't be certain, but it sounded like furniture was being moved inside the house. Another minute passed and I pressed the doorbell again. Then I used the knocker.

"Hey, Penny, it's me, Sarah Booth. I have a question. I promise it won't take long. Would you open up?" It was late, but it wasn't that late. Even if she was in bed, she should have heard the doorbell and knocker.

I'd given away who was at the door, but I hoped if someone dangerous was inside they'd think it would be easier to allow Penny to open the door and send me away. After all, as a mere woman, was I really any kind of impediment to a big, strong man? At least, I hoped that might be the thinking.

When no one answered the door, I did what I swore to Tinkie I wouldn't do. I turned the knob. The door opened smoothly. Before I could stop her, Sweetie Pie pushed into the house with Chablis right behind her. There wasn't a choice now. I looked back at Tinkie and made a motion to show I was okay and stepped into the house.

30

Inside the open front door, I stood silently in the foyer listening—trying to determine who was in the house and where they were. And whether I should venture deeper inside. Sweetie Pie and Chablis made that decision for me, though. The clicking sound of the dogs' toenails on hardwood came from somewhere on the first floor. They'd disappeared into one of the darkened rooms. I could follow them, or I could venture upstairs where I'd seen movement—what seemed like threatening behavior. I moved to the stairs.

Getting trapped upstairs by some serial abuser—or worse yet, a murderer—didn't appeal to me in the least, but there was nothing else to do. And if I didn't hurry,

Tinkie would be over here in the middle of potential danger.

Step by step I crept toward my goal, gun at the ready and flashlight in the other hand. I could hear my soft breathing as I moved to the second floor and along the hallway toward Tansy's room. There was a strange creaking sound, and someone mumbling softly. Add to that a thumping noise, some electronic static, and maybe soft laughter? It didn't make sense.

Where the heck was Penny? And what was going on in that room?

I checked my watch. Coleman and the deputies would probably be here in another five minutes, but if Tansy or anyone was in danger, I couldn't just wait around. I put my hand on the doorknob and slowly, quietly opened the door.

A man wearing an aqua-sequined thong and a full-head leather hood stood at the foot of the bed swinging a puce feathered boa in some kind of death rictus. Tansy, dressed in swirls of pink taffeta so that she looked like a human cotton candy cone, was standing on the bed, skirts lifted, in a provocative pose.

Suddenly some boom-chicka-boom music started and both of them began dancing the floss. They were moving fast with eyes only for each other, totally oblivious to the fact that I stood in the doorway, my jaw on the floor. I'd seen a lot of things in my life, but nothing that made me want to claw my eyes out nearly like this.

Sweetie Pie burst through the open door and howled like she'd seen Satan prancing down Main Street. The hooded man and Tansy froze in mid floss. They turned to me and we all three screamed, "Aaargh!"

I put the heels of my hands over my eyes and fell back

against the wall. It didn't matter. The bizarre image of the two of them was burned into the backs of my retinas.

"What the hell?" Tansy yelled. "Get out of here."

I tried to leave with my eyes shut tight, but ran into the wall with a loud smack. Sweetie Pie rushed to the rescue, baying so loudly in the small bedroom that I thought my eardrums would burst. I didn't know whether to cover my eyes or ears!

"Sarah Booth Delaney, what are you doing here?"

I recognized the voice as belonging to Todd Renfield, Tansy's lover and Moody Moody's boyfriend. Since Tansy was in the taffeta dress, it had to be Todd in the thong and hood. I closed my eyes tighter and hunkered into a ball on the bedroom floor. If I didn't look, maybe it would all disappear.

"I am going to call the cops!" Tansy declared, her voice ringing with indignation.

"Please, please call the cops." I wasn't above begging at this point. "And an ophthalmologist. I need professional help. I think my eyeballs have melted."

"Put the gun down," Todd said. "Sarah Booth, you're going to shoot yourself in the chest holding the gun that way. Put it down."

I sat up a little and let my tenuous hold on the gun go. It clanked onto the floor. I opened one eye. Todd had regained his composure and wrapped a sheet around his body and removed the hood. He sat down on the edge of the bed and sighed. "You liketa gave me a heart attack, Sarah Booth. Why are you creeping around Selena's House?"

"Yes, what in the hell are you doing here?" Tansy asked. "You can't go breaking into people's bedrooms. It's illegal. And it's sick. Are you some kind of peeper?"

"I thought you were in danger," I said. "I saw silhouettes of someone moving around in your room and . . ." Of course it was just the two of them dancing—or whatever it was they were doing. Tansy, standing on the bed, was the taller, predatory shadow. I felt like a fool, and one who had been permanently scarred by witnessing something I should never have seen.

"I'm going to press charges against you. I've had it with you and those mangy dogs you carry around," Tansy said. "You're always butting into my business. Todd and I were having a little fun."

"Fun?"

Sweetie Pie gave a soft woof as if she, too, questioned that description. I wondered if her delicate doggy psyche was damaged by what she'd seen. Luckily Chablis, who finally showed up, had been spared. "This is what you call fun?" I waved a hand at both of them.

"We're going to win a TikTok challenge. We're both excellent dancers, and with this kinky scenario, maybe we'll get some sponsors, make some money, and escape this godforsaken town. Now, you've spoiled it all. If Penny hears about this she'll boot me out of the house."

"A TikTok challenge?"

"It's a dance competition. Anyone can enter. If you get people to watch your video you can create an audience. Your dances will go viral. You can become an influencer on social media and make lots of money. Don't you know anything?"

That was the final straw. She was talking to me like *I* was the idiot. "I know you're a fool. Why would you pull something like this in a house for abused women?" I asked. "You know damn good and well that Penny docsn't allow men in this house. Satan clutching his pearls, what were you two thinking?"

"No one is here tonight. Everyone is gone, including Penny. She almost never goes anywhere. And we had everything perfectly planned, until you showed up." Tansy glared at me.

But I had an even more burning question. "Where is Penny?"

Tansy jumped off the bed to the floor and straightened the many layers of what I now recognized as a ball gown complete with hoop skirts. She had to have rented it from a costume shop. She'd been holding up the hoops to show off a pair of sexy bloomers, if pantaloons could ever be made to look sexy.

"She was here. She took off with some college chick."

"Where'd they go?" I asked.

Tansy shrugged. "Who knows. I was only glad they were gone so Todd could come over and we could play. Todd's the best at acting out roles and fantasies. And the TikTok dance was his idea."

"Good to keep in mind," I said. "When did Penny say she'd be back?"

Tansy clearly wanted me to leave. "She didn't say exactly. She only said that she had to find something at the university and that if they weren't back by midnight for me to call the sheriff and let him know." She checked her watch. "We still have time to finish this video if you'll just get out! We've rented the costumes and all and we need to get it done."

"Let the sheriff know what?" Tansy wasn't great at giving clear answers to anything.

"That Penny was missing. If she wasn't back, I was to

let the sheriff know she was missing." She gave me the "you are stupider than a box of rocks" look.

"And weren't you supposed to tell the sheriff where Penny was going so he could look for her?"

"Not yet. It's not time." Tansy grew belligerent.

"Coleman is going to be here in two minutes. He'll arrest Todd for trespassing, since you both know good and well Penny would never allow a man inside Selena's House. If you tell me what I need to know, though, maybe I'll go meet him in the yard and tell him everything is just fine. Maybe he won't have to come in. I don't think Todd would last long in prison with that fancy G-string."

"It's not a G-string. It's a thong. And you wait just a minute!" Todd blustered. "I was just wearing it for Tansy. I don't normally wear sequins for any occasion. Except maybe Mardi Gras in New Orleans."

"Tell it to the boys in orange on the cell block. Of course, Tansy can prevent all of this . . ."

Tansy shot daggers at me with her eyes, but she finally answered. "Alala came over here with some college girl to talk to Penny. Alala and the one girl left, but then another college girl was here. This one and Penny huddled up together and then they took off for Oxford to go look through some professor's office. They were looking for something. That's what I know."

"What was the college student's name?"

"I don't know. I wasn't formally introduced." Tansy flounced around in the dress and sat down on the bed. The hoop skirt shot up in the air, flew over her head, and she fell back on the bed. When she began kicking and struggling, I finally went over and pulled the skirt down and helped her back to a sitting position. She would never have passed muster for participating in a reenactment or one of the many organizations that dressed high school girls in colorful costumes depicting life in the old South. Hoop skirts were not her friend.

"What's the name of the professor whose office they were going to raid? You'd better hurry. Listen, are those sirens?"

Indeed, the long arm of the law was almost on us. It sounded like the patrol cars were only a few blocks away.

"I didn't get the professor's name or the student's name. All I know is that the student was in the literature department. She said she helped Dr. Loxley, the professor who was murdered, and another teacher. She was a quiet girl. That's what I know."

"Why was she here in the first place?"

Tansy shrugged. "Look, I'm not a busybody like you. I don't get all up in everyone's business. She was here, they were going to the university, which left the house wide open and empty for me to get my video done. That's all I needed to know. Now get outside so you can stop the sheriff from coming up here. Todd shouldn't be punished for doing something harmless and neither should I."

"Thanks." I whistled up the dogs and headed downstairs at a fast clip. If I was lucky, I could intercept Coleman or the deputies. There were some things that no one should have to see.

31

Coleman and the deputies were headed for the front door when I stepped out onto the porch. "Everything is fine inside. The only people in the house are Tansy and a friend upstairs. There's nothing going on."

"What made you rush inside without waiting for us?" Coleman asked. He was a little agitato.

"I saw some strange shadows moving around in the room and I thought Tansy was being threatened. I thought her life might be on the line, but it turned out they were just dancing."

"Dancing?" Coleman was skeptical.

"Some TikTok thing. They're trying to become social media influencers."

"Tansy? A social influencer?" DeWayne was skeptical.

"Like a Kardashian?" Budgie asked.

"Put in that framework, maybe Tansy's dream isn't that peculiar," I said.

Coleman's investigation inside Selena's House had been delayed by my version of the half-truth, but he wasn't about to buy it hook, line, and sinker. "I'm glad everything is okay, but I'll just have a word with Tansy." He started for the door.

I grabbed his sleeve. "She's fine, but I'm worried about Alala, Penny, and an Ole Miss student who I think must be Margaret McNeese. Tansy said Alala was here and left before Penny, and a female college student took off to search a professor's office at Ole Miss. It sounded like they were going to break in, and I'm thinking it may be Becky Brown's office. You know if Alala and her buddies suspect Becky Brown might be involved with abusers . . . it could go really, really wrong. Maybe we should call the local law and get them to check it out. Just to be on the safe side. It would carry a lot more weight coming from you, Coleman. Could you please ask them to send someone over to the English department? If we can stop those ladies before they commit a crime, it would be the best outcome. So many people rely on Penny to be here and run Selena's House. An arrest could impact the grants she receives. I'm sure she hasn't thought this idea through." I laid it on as thick as I could, babbling like a fool. I had given Tansy my word that I would keep Coleman from finding Todd in the house.

Coleman motioned DeWayne to make the call, and the deputy stepped back to do so. Budgie was already checking the perimeter of the house. That left Coleman alone with me.

"What's going on here, Sarah Booth?"

I tried for an innocent look, which Coleman didn't buy for a minute.

"When Tinkie called, she said someone was being murdered upstairs and you went inside even after you promised her you wouldn't." He didn't tap his foot, but his patience had worn thin.

"I had no intention of going inside, but Sweetie Pie and Chablis ran into the house. I heard something upstairs and I had to check it out. What if someone *was* being murdered? Time was of the essence." I shrugged. "Thank heavens there was nothing going on. Just the dancing. I went in, checked it out, and I was headed to the car to see if Tinkie wanted to ride over to Oxford to track down Penny. But since DeWayne has called the law over in Oxford, that will save me a trip. Now I need to get Tinkie home. She's been uncomfort—"

For the first time I turned to look at the convertible parked across the street under a poplar tree. Pluto had returned to the car and sat on the driver's headrest. Other than that, the car was empty.

"Where's Tinkie?" I said it on a rush of breath and realized that even though my lungs were empty I couldn't inhale. Fear was an iron band around my chest. Tinkie was gone. She'd vanished into the night while I'd been dithering with two wannabe kinky dance stars.

Though the Sunflower County Sheriff's Office was warm, I couldn't stop the chattering of my teeth. Coleman sat across from me and held both of my hands, rubbing them gently. I was beside myself with anxiety and guilt.

"When was the last time you saw Tinkie?" he asked.

"I was only inside the house about fifteen minutes. I

shouldn't have left her alone in the car. I left the dogs
with her, but she sent them to be with me." If I'd been
able to get up and walk to a wall, I would have banged
my head against it. My legs were too unsteady to support me.

"You didn't make a mistake, Sarah Booth. Anyone
would think the danger would be inside the house, not
on a residential street in Zinnia. DeWayne and Budgie
will turn something up. We'll find her. So when, exactly,
was the last time you saw her?"

The deputies were searching Zinnia and surrounding
areas. The state troopers and sheriffs' departments from
surrounding counties had all been contacted. Road-
blocks were up. But so far, there was no explanation
for Tinkie's disappearance. My fingers gripped my cell
phone. I had to call Oscar. I had to, but first I would answer Coleman's questions because it might help locate
my pregnant partner.

"The last time I saw her was when I went inside the
house. She'd shifted to sit behind the steering wheel in
case we needed a speedy getaway. She was fine. Miffed
that I was going inside, but fine." Was that actually the
last time? Had I glanced across the street to the car
when I came out of the house? No, I'd just assumed Tinkie would be there, in the car, where I'd left her. "I really
wasn't in the house longer than fifteen or twenty minutes." I was repeating myself, in disbelief that the facts
could have resulted in this outcome. "She was absolutely
okay. Maybe a little angry at me for going inside, but really fine." I looked Coleman dead in the eyes. "I would
never have left her outside if I'd thought—" I felt the tears
threatening so I had to shut up.

"She can't be far," Coleman said. "Who was upstairs

with Tansy? Tell me the truth. That could make a big difference if someone was watching the house."

Coleman just added another little dagger of fear. What
if some angry husband or boyfriend had abducted Tinkie? Someone who was mad at Penny or one of the women
who found refuge in Selena's House. Tinkie would have
been easy prey, sitting in a convertible. I knew I'd have
to tell Coleman the truth, but I hesitated.

"Tell me who was with Tansy, Sarah Booth. De-
Wayne and Budgie will find out, so you might as well
spill it. We can just get on with finding her faster if you
talk."

I told him the truth about Todd and Tansy. The total
truth. "They really were doing a dance competition. As
awful as it was." I rubbed my eyes, I couldn't stop myself.

"That bad?"

"Yeah, that bad."

"Did you notice anything else?"

"No, I didn't. After seeing what they were up to, I was
so intent on getting out of that room." I shuddered.

"You didn't hear anything outside? See anything ab-
normal? Other than Todd and Tansy."

"Nothing. And if you can see a way not to tell Penny
about Todd being in Tansy's room, I'd appreciate it. I told
them I wouldn't tell you. And honestly, Tansy doesn't have
very good sense, neither does Todd, but they weren't doing anything"—it was hard to find an adjective to use—
"wrong."

"If she asks, I'll have to tell her I know, but otherwise,
I see no need to rat those two out. Social media influencer would be the first honest work either of them has
done in years. I kind of admire their . . . initiative."

"You didn't see it." I had to laugh. "Let's drop this and find Tinkie." I couldn't sit in the office any longer. I had the best detecting dogs in Mississippi and I needed to put them to use—or else call Oscar and confess I'd lost Tinkie. I would rather walk on a bed of hot coals than do that.

"Load up the dogs and cat." Coleman was too smart to leave Pluto out. "When are you going to tell Oscar?"

"When I'm sure I can't find her. In other words, not until I have to."

"Maybe she went home?" Coleman suggested as we headed out the door.

"How? And she wouldn't do that and leave me worried about her. She'd never abandon Chablis."

"If she didn't call Oscar to come and get her, then my guess is she's around that neighborhood or she left with someone of her own free will, unless it was at gunpoint. She took the car keys with her, but Budgie and DeWayne went over your car as thoroughly as they could by flashlight. There's no sign of a struggle."

Gunpoint was a terrifying word. Most of the members of AVA were heavily armed men. They took the Second Amendment seriously. Such men might have an issue with the mission of Selena's House. And I'd left Tinkie sitting right outside the house.

If that wasn't enough, there was still a serial killer on the loose. But that seemed to be a person who only killed abusive men, not pregnant women. And while some angry husband or lover might have confronted Tinkie outside Selena's House, no one in their right mind would go against Oscar Richmond, who controlled the bank and 90 percent of the loans in Sunflower County. A local resident might take Tinkie, but he wouldn't keep her. Not once he knew who she was married to. That was the one thing I clung to as we headed out into the cold night.

In fifteen minutes we were parked behind my Roadster on the street where Selena's House stood, dark and silent. Apparently Tansy and Todd had finished their Tik-Tok session or taken their dancing to another location. There was no sign of life in her window. Or any window. The house looked dead and empty, giving me a chill of apprehension. To my surprise, Coleman's knock on the door was answered quickly by Tansy, who assured us Tinkie wasn't inside, nor had she seen her.

"Check if you want to." She waved Coleman inside and he lost no time bolting through the door with the dogs. If Tinkie was anywhere inside, Chablis would sniff her out.

Tansy lounged against the doorjamb. "How the hell did you lose your partner? She's enormous. Like, really, really . . . pregnant. How can you just lose a pregnant woman?" she asked.

I wanted to punch her lights out. "I didn't lose her. I know exactly where I left her. She's just not there now."

Tansy didn't bother feigning concern. "I'm sure she'll turn up. She's got no reason to leave home. She's living on the gravy train. Hey, thank you, Sarah Booth. We got the dance finished. When Todd and I are famous, we won't forget you."

"Thanks." I'd never forget them, either. Ever. It would be the stuff of my nightmares.

Coleman returned to hear the final exchange. "Tinkie's not here. Let's move on." He grabbed my elbow and aimed me toward the street. The dogs were right by him, and Coleman was quiet as he walked beside me. I didn't say a word, but I could feel my heart hammering.

Where could Tinkie have gone? Tansy was right. How did one lose a pregnant woman?

Sweetie Pie and Chablis ran to stand at the sidewalk, but the minute we turned toward them, Sweetie Pie let out the baying howl that red ticks were famous for. She was on a scent, and Chablis was right behind her. Pluto, when I finally caught sight of him, was ambling down the sidewalk half a block in the lead. The cat's spidey sense must have tingled him.

"Follow the cat," I told Coleman. "If Tinkie is around here, the critters will find her."

Coleman quickly reviewed texts from the two deputies. When he put his phone down, he shook his head. "Nothing so far, though DeWayne got confirmation that Becky Brown owns a black Chevy Silverado. Chances are good she was in the vehicle that shot at you."

"I don't care about that. I need to find Tinkie."

"The dogs and cat are our best lead."

"But why would Tinkie get out of the car and go off like this? She really is uncomfortable. Her feet are terribly swollen and it hurts her to walk at the end of the day. She warned me that she was in no condition to go after me if I entered the house."

"She must have seen something," Coleman said. "So she was sitting in the car, facing this way. She got out of the car and walked north." The dogs and cat had paused and were waiting for us. Coleman picked up the pace. "Let's say she saw something and got out to investigate."

"She did have her gun with her, and that's no longer in the car." I'd forgotten to mention that earlier, but it was important for Coleman to know.

"Well, that changes things. If someone had tried to forcibly take Tinkie and she was armed, I think she would have shot them." He put his arm around my shoulders and hugged me close. "This is more hopeful, Sarah Booth. She would have at least gotten a shot off to alert you she was in danger. We'll find her."

Sweetie Pie let out a howl that was taken up by Chablis with a yip-yip-yip. They raced past Pluto, who gave them a look of sheer contempt, and cut through the yard of a two-story brick house. Pluto followed, but at a more dignified pace.

Coleman grabbed my hand and tugged me into a run. "The animals just ran into Lee and Connie Moran's yard. Maybe Tinkie is back there. Come on! Follow the dogs!"

I still had my phone in my hand. "Should I call Budgie and DeWayne?" If so, I needed to do it while I could still talk and run simultaneously.

"No, let them continue checking the roads out of town. We can handle this."

I didn't argue. I just pushed myself harder to keep up. When we made it to the Morans' back garden, our progress hit a snag. The area was heavily landscaped with massive banks of rhododendrons, fringe trees, and other flora that impeded us. Sweetie Pie sailed over a back fence and Chablis found a way under. I knew then that Tinkie could never have made it over. Whatever the dogs were chasing, it wasn't my partner.

"Hold it." I caught Coleman's arm. "Tinkie isn't here. She couldn't run and climb through the underbrush. She's too big."

Coleman considered the situation. "I wonder what the dogs are after."

I was about to answer when I heard something. It

sounded like a cross between a laugh and a sob, and it made the hair on my arms stand on end. "What's that?"

Coleman drew his gun and stepped in front of me. "I don't know, but it sounded like it came from there." He pointed the gun toward a huge clump of bushes.

We crept forward, taking care not to make any noise, listening for the sound of something hiding in the bushes. It could be Tinkie or her abductor or an injured dog or cat. I had to be prepared for anything. What didn't make sense was the dogs clearing the back fence and taking off. They were on a trail, so what had been left here in the bushes?

Another low moan came, followed by some rustling and a sharp cry of pain.

"Is that you, Tinkie?" I called out. "Are you hurt?"

My answer was another heartrending moan. "Help me."

There was no time to waste. I tried to rush past Coleman, but he had a hold on my arm. I struggled against his grip. "Tinkie's in there!" I suddenly knew my partner was in the shrubs and that she was in danger.

"Sarah Booth!" Tinkie's voice came from somewhere in the density of garden growth. "Hey, I'm over here. I need some help."

Following her voice, Coleman and I went after her as fast as we could. We pushed back and snapped off limbs as we plowed toward a low moan followed by an outcry of pain.

"We're coming, Tinkie. Say something, so we can find you."

"Help. Please hurry."

Coleman pushed back the limbs of some lacy shrub,

and we found Tinkie curled on the ground at the base of an oak tree. She was breathing hard.

"Are you hurt? Are you shot?"

I knelt beside her and started to reach to turn her over. "Tinkie?"

"Sarah Booth!" She turned to me and grabbed my hand, clamping down with tremendous strength.

"Are you okay?" I asked.

"No. I'm not. My water broke. I'm having contractions. And when I dropped my phone, at first I couldn't find it and I couldn't walk to the house to get help."

I was still holding my phone in my free hand, and put in a call for an ambulance as Coleman beat back some more bushes. "I've made a path," he said. "I'll carry her to the street."

"I'm so glad you're here, Sarah Booth," Tinkie said as she ratcheted down on my hand. The bones were about to pulverize, and there was nothing I could do.

"We're going to get help for you," I told her, doing my best to keep my voice steady and comforting. Another contraction hit and I thought for sure my hand would be permanently mangled as she clamped down again.

"Get Doc," she said as she panted.

"You bet."

I called Doc Sawyer and told him to meet us at the hospital. Then I called Oscar. He might want to kill me later, but Tinkie needed him now. "Tinkie is in labor, Oscar. Coleman is going to carry her to the street. I've called an ambulance. If they aren't here when we get to the sidewalk, we'll drive her ourselves." I wasn't about to wait for an ambulance when I could hear my friend panting and crying out in pain. The contractions seemed to be about a minute apart. That didn't sound good. That

sounded like my worst nightmare was coming to life—
Tinkie was going to give birth without a doctor or hos
pital to help her.

"Where are you?" Oscar asked.

"Someone's backyard. Long story. We'll tell you when
we see you." I hung up and Coleman lifted Tinkie and
pushed his way toward the street. I cleared the brush
from Coleman's path as he pressed forward with Tinkie
in his arms. We hadn't gone five steps toward the street
when the lawn was flooded with lights. The home owners came out the back door, flashlights easily picking us
out of the darkness.

"What's going on out here?" a man demanded.

"Lee, it's Coleman Peters. I have a woman in labor."

"In our backyard," Connie Moran said as she came
running toward us. "What's she doing in my yard?"

"It's a long story," Coleman said. "I promise I'll explain it tomorrow, but I need to get her to the front. We've
called an ambulance."

Tinkie let out a cry like a wounded creature. She struggled in Coleman's arms. "I knew this was going to be
awful. I knew it was. *Ow!* Everyone lied and said it
wasn't so bad. Well I'm telling you, dammit, it's bad. I
feel like I'm being ripped apart."

She'd been afraid of labor and delivery, and I didn't
blame her one bit.

Connie Moran shone a flashlight onto Tinkie's face.
"That's Tinkie Bellcase Richmond."

I wanted to say something smart, like no kidding, Sher-
lock, but I didn't. I was too caught up in Tinkie's dire
situation.

"Let's get her to the front," I said. I wanted to help,
but there was nothing I could do. I didn't faint at the sight

of blood, but I had no experience in childbearing. My goal was to get her to the far better prepared location of the local Zinnia hospital.

"No, no! Put me down!" Tinkie insisted. "The baby is coming."

"Oh, no, not here," Connie said, perfectly expressing my feelings. "Not here in the grass and dirt. That's so unsanitary."

"You can't have the baby here in the grass." I agreed with Connie. "Just hold on. We'll be at the hospital in five minutes."

"I'm having it and I'm having it right now." Tinkie reached wildly and grabbed my hand. "And you are going to help me."

Tinkie's grip on my hand was her final say on the matter. "Coleman, put her down. Let her catch her breath."

He eased her slowly to the ground. Instead of standing, she went all the way down. "The baby is coming now!" Tinkie insisted.

"I'll get some towels and water and . . . peroxide," Connie said. "I'll be right back."

32

Coleman held Tinkie's head—leaving me with the business end—the one that was going to give the most trouble. I knelt beside my friend. I had no choice but to fall in line. She was again gripping my hand.

Connie and her husband returned with blankets and sheets and water and a lot of things I had no idea what to do with. Like peroxide. Was that used in childbirth? I'd watched a lot of Westerns but I never remembered peroxide being part of the birthing process. But Connie had also brought a pair of scissors and I went to work cutting off Tinkie's pants. She was wrapped in the sheet, and if the baby was coming, the pants were only clogging up the process.

When I finally took a look at her, with the aid of a

flashlight, I had to accept that Tinkie wasn't lying. "The baby's coming. Now. Call Doc and tell him to meet us here. Oscar, too. And call Cece, please."

"Why Cece?" Coleman asked.

"I need some backup." It wasn't that I didn't believe Coleman would help me, I just believed Cece might have more practical experience. "And call Millie, too. For the same reason." Millie would definitely know more about this than I did.

Coleman made the calls while cradling Tinkie's head. I grasped her hand again and talked to her. "Everything is fine, Tinkie. This is a natural process. We can do this." A strange calmness settled over me. I'd endured a kinky TikTok dance and now I was going to start the delivery of my best friend's baby. This wasn't the way I saw this day playing out, but I was ready to do whatever was necessary for Tinkie. Whatever.

Lee and Connie Moran stood at Tinkie's head with Coleman, still stunned by the sudden appearance of a pregnant woman in their backyard. Thank goodness they were smart enough not to offer advice. Tinkie, for her part, was breathing in and out in rapid puffs. The way she gripped my hand told me she was in terrible pain.

"Doc's on his way. And Oscar. They'll be here any minute." I took another peek and wanted to run screaming. I saw the baby's head. Or I thought it was the baby's head. My job, as I saw it, was to slow Tinkie down as much as I could until the professionals arrived. "Just don't push, Tinkie. Don't do anything except breathe. Be easy."

"You should have gone to childbirth classes with me," Tinkie managed.

"You had Oscar. He wanted to be with you. You

needed him to be with you to solidify the bond between the three of you. That's what all the books said, anyway." I had read a couple of books on having a baby, because I wanted to be there for my friend. As a support team member, not as a midwife.

"If you'd gone to the classes, you'd have some practical experience in doing this."

Tinkie had a point, but I wasn't about to give it to her. "Had I known you were going to deliver in a Zinnia residential area, I might have prepared a little better. Silly me, I thought you were going the 'sanitary hospital with professional help' route."

She gave in to another contraction, tightening her grip on my hand. This was happening whether I wanted it to or not.

"Breathe," I told her, easing her back into Coleman's arms. "Try to slow it down until Doc gets here, Tinkie. It would be good to have a medical professional, just to be on the safe side."

"Is something wrong down there?" she asked.

"Nope. Everything's fine. As far as I can tell. Just slow down and wait for Doc. You'll hurt his feelings if you leave him out of this."

"There's no slowing down the Orient Express and that train is shuttling home." Tinkie gasped for air. "It'll be okay, Sarah Booth. I can do this. *We* can do this." She cried out in pain as another contraction hit.

It was then that I realized my friend—the one having the baby—was trying to comfort me. Ridiculous. "You're damn straight it's going to be okay." I took a position to catch the baby. "Everything is going to be perfectly fine. Push, Tinkie, push!"

I heard the excited voices of men as Doc and Oscar

arrived together, along with the EMTs, ambulance, and Cece, who was wide-eyed and silent, with Millie in tow.

"Is Tinkie okay?" Oscar asked. "What is she doing here in the Morans' backyard?" He looked totally undone. "What's going on here?"

I didn't try to answer. I was too busy holding the baby's head in my hand as I waited for Tinkie to finish the delivery. Doc knelt beside me. I started to ease out of his way but he held me gently in place.

"My, oh, my," he said. "You're doing a great job, Sarah Booth. Tinkie, I never figured you for the outdoors kind of woman, but you've proven me wrong. This child is going to be born to the sound of hoot owls and crickets."

I started again to move, but Doc put a hand on my shoulder. "Stay there. Finish what you've started. This baby is partially yours, Sarah Booth. You encouraged Tinkie to try when no one else thought she could get pregnant. You encouraged her to believe."

I couldn't take that credit. "You'd better call the Harrington witches if you're giving out awards. I think they need this one. Whatever they did, it made Tinkie certain she could conceive. And they were right."

Doc chuckled. "Doesn't look like Tinkie needs any magic bringing this little one into the world. She's doing very well all on her own. One more push, Tinkie," Doc said.

She obliged and, before I could even say anything, I held her baby daughter in my hands, totally in awe of what my partner had accomplished. The baby began to kick and cry—the night was cold—and Doc took over, cutting the umbilical cord and wrapping the baby in warm towels that Connie handed him.

I sat back on my heels, dazed by what had just happened. I had held Tinkie's daughter in my hands the moment she was born. The little baby, with a headful of dark curls, was screaming like she was being tortured, prompting Tinkie to push up to a sitting position. She used Coleman as a back prop and then reached for her baby as Oscar took over supporting her.

I got to my feet and realized that my legs were wobbly and my knees unreliable. Coleman noticed, though, and he came to my assistance, supporting me.

"You're a little unsteady there." He inched me away from Tinkie and Oscar, giving the new parents a moment to themselves.

"I thought Tinkie might be injured or dead. Instead, she was having a baby." I felt tears threaten and I didn't know why. Everyone was perfectly fine. There was absolutely no need for tears. This was a joyous occasion. "What would have happened if we hadn't found her?" I asked.

"No point going down that trail. We did find her and you delivered the baby. I'm impressed. Don't you know your momma and Miss Bessie are peacock proud of you?"

"No doubt about that," Doc said. "I sure miss Bessie with her midwife skills, which Libby Delaney supported. Now let's get mother and child to the hospital," Doc said, motioning over to the EMTs, who'd arrived with a stretcher. In a moment, Tinkie and the baby were loaded and on the way to the ambulance. Oscar gripped the stretcher as the little family bumped across the Morans' backyard. Finally, Oscar turned back.

"Why were you here in the Morans' backyard?" he called out to me.

"Ask Tinkie." Because I didn't have the answer. In a moment they were opening the back door of the ambulance. Coleman called DeWayne and Budgie to let them know to call off the search. Tinkie had been found.

"Wait!" Tinkie said the word with such force that everyone stopped in mid-step.

"What's wrong?" I ran to my friend, afraid something was physically wrong with her.

"I have to tell you why I was here," Tinkie said. "I was following someone."

"Who?" I asked.

"Someone who was hiding in the dark outside Selena's House. I saw them moving across the lawn and I went to check. I was afraid they'd ambush you coming out."

Tinkie had put her life on the line once again to save me. "You could have been killed," I told her.

"I found the place I think Curtis Miller was murdered."

"What?" Coleman and I said together. He'd come to stand beside me. "Where?"

"Behind Selena's House. I stumbled on it chasing whoever was watching the house."

"I'll get DeWayne and Budgie right on it," Coleman said. "Are you sure?"

Tinkie shook her head. "I can't be positive, but I think it's the crime scene. Someone had started digging a grave but stopped. There was a blanket there, and it was stiff with dried blood. It looked like animals had been burrowing around it."

The memory of what Madame Tomeeka had seen came back to me. She'd seen Roscoe digging in an area surrounded by an aura of red. The scene Tinkie spoke of wasn't exactly the same, but it was close enough. And Tinkie had found something she hadn't even been looking for. The original crime scene where Curtis Miller had died.

"There's a trail back through there big enough for a car to get down," Tinkie said.

"We'll check it out," Coleman assured her. He patted her shoulder. "Good job, Tinkie. You found our crime scene and had a baby, all within the space of three hours."

"Take her on," Oscar directed the paramedics. "You two can solve this case after Doc has a chance to check out my wife and little girl. That's what comes first now."

Now and forever in the future, if I had to lay any bets.

"We're going to the hospital with Tinkie," Cece said, taking Tinkie's hand. "We'll meet you there."

"I have to find the dogs," I said. I'd drawn Cece and Millie aside and clued them in to the undercover sting operation Harold was helping us with. In front of Tinkie, though, I didn't bring up the fact that Harold was still in an enclave of abusers, pretending to be one of them. "I'll meet you at the hospital later. Don't mention anything about Harold. Tinkie has enough on her plate."

"Good plan. I'll keep it under wraps." Millie gave me a quick hug before she trotted after Cece's longer stride.

When Coleman was off the phone and Tinkie was on her way to the hospital, I sighed. "Where are those dang dogs? And Pluto? We need to find them and head to the hospital."

"You should have gone in the ambulance," Coleman said. "I've sent Budgie and DeWayne to find that crime scene, and I can find the dogs and cat."

"We made the right call. Finding the pets is critical and Oscar needed to ride with Tinkie." Tinkie and I were as close as sisters, but Oscar was her husband, the father of her baby. "I'll have plenty of time with Tinkie once we find those animals."

The long low howl of a dog came from the thicket of brush and woods. Coleman turned to the Morans. "I'll give you a call tomorrow and explain all of this—once I'm certain of the facts. Thanks for all the help. And congrats on the new Moran Birthing Center in your backyard."

Everyone laughed, breaking the grip of the tension that had held us.

Coleman continued. "We have several dogs and a cat on the loose. We need to round them up before they get in trouble or hurt."

Connie Moran pointed behind us. "There's another one."

I turned around to see Roscoe following the same trajectory that Sweetie Pie and Chablis had taken. He dove headfirst into the shrubs and thicket and in a few minutes I saw him going over the back fence. Great. Now the master criminal had joined the pack. And if Roscoe was back in town, where in the hell was Harold? I gave Coleman a panicked look and he shook his head slightly, indicating for me to keep silent.

"What's back there?" Coleman asked the Morans, pointing to the back of their property.

"It's Bluster Creek," Lee said. "If you follow the creek, it's a shortcut to County Road Twelve."

County Road 12 was a direct shot to Main Street. The road was sometimes busy, and it wasn't the best place for dogs or cats. It was time to collect the critters. Coleman and I started toward his vehicle—Tinkie still had the key to my car—when my phone rang. It was Tinkie. My heart almost stopped as I picked up the call.

"The person I was following was a young woman who ran from Selena's House when I heard the sirens approaching. I don't know who she was or what she was doing, but she acted suspicious. That's why I followed her."

"Tinkie, you could have been hurt." I couldn't help myself for fussing. I was still feeling shaky about the baby's birth and how wrong it could have gone.

"I know. But I was only going to see where she went. She went into that thicket and when I tried to follow, I felt my water break. I couldn't go any farther and I couldn't go back to the car, either. Thank goodness you found me."

"Yes, thank goodness. Who did you see?"

"I don't know. It could have been a resident of Selena's House. But she was so . . . furtive. That's what triggered me to follow her."

"Description?" I put the phone on speaker and moved closer to Coleman so he could hear.

"About five-six, slender, agile, so I'd say young. I didn't get a great look at her. She was wearing a dark hoodie, and she moved quickly. She was up and over that fence without any difficulty."

Coleman nodded. "We'll see what we can find, Tinkie. Thanks for the tip."

"How's the baby?" I asked.

"She's just fine. I fed her." Tinkie's voice cracked. "She's a miracle, Sarah Booth. She's my miracle baby. She might not be here without your help. Listen, Oscar and I have settled on Maylin for her name."

"I love it." And I did. Coleman was smiling big. "Coleman loves it, too. She is a perfect little miracle, just for you and Oscar."

"And for you, Sarah Booth. And Coleman. We want you to be the godparents. If you will."

"Sign me up," Coleman said instantly.

"And me." I slipped my arm around Coleman's waist. For all of the drama and trauma of the evening, this one moment was pure beauty.

33

Coleman and I slowly cruised County Road 12, searching the side of the road for dogs and a cat moving along the verge. Nothing.

We'd only been looking for about fifteen minutes when DeWayne called in. Coleman put his phone on speaker so I could hear.

"We found the crime scene," DeWayne said. "Just like you said. Looks like someone started to dig a grave, then decided against it. The ground here is pretty dense. Hard to dig."

"Anything else?"

"We got a terrific footprint. I'd say it's a match to the one you took a mold of at Dr. Diakos's house."

"A female print?" Coleman was surprised.

"Yep."

"Any evidence of another person at the scene?"

"Not so far, but we're still looking."

"Call me if you find anything. Especially if you see those damn dogs and cat."

"Will do," DeWayne said before he hung up.

Coleman sighed with frustration, and I felt exactly the same way. Normally the critters were helpful on a case. Not this time. They just added confusion. Coleman continued on along Highway 12 until we came to the outskirts of town. Zinnia looked completely empty. My little town had rolled up the sidewalks as it was prone to do on weeknights after six o'clock, and there was no sign of the canine felons. I tried to shake off the dread, but couldn't.

Coleman's jaw was clenched, though neither of us expressed our concerns. To say it aloud was to make it manifest. I put a hand on Coleman's leg to let him know I appreciated his worry. While the critters were said to belong to me, Tinkie, and Harold, Coleman loved them, too.

"We have to talk about Roscoe and Harold," I said. "How did Roscoe get back to Zinnia? He was at the hunting lodge. Roscoe wouldn't abandon Harold, and Harold said he'd call us once he shook free of the AVA members."

"I know." Coleman's grip on the steering wheel told me how worried he was. "I encouraged Harold to do this. If anything has gone wrong—"

"Stop it." Between the two of us we could shoulder most of the guilt in the universe if we allowed ourselves. "You have to trust Harold. Y'all did a brilliant job of convincing AVA that Harold was one of them. They bought it hook, line, and sinker, so stop taking on all that responsibility." I was giving him advice I was finding impossible to follow.

"I thought so, too. At first. But now . . . if Roscoe's in town, Harold should be, too. So why hasn't he called? I don't want to call him in case they've taken his phone."

"I don't know what's going on, but first things first: let's find the dogs. Harold is a grown man and a capable one at that. Let's solve the problem in front of us."

"Where do you think the dogs might be?" he asked, as he concluded a loop through downtown Zinnia. He pulled to a stop in front of the courthouse.

"If Dewayne and Budgie had seen them, they would have picked them up and called us."

"They haven't been hit on the road, that we could find." Coleman offered that tiny bit of logical hope.

"Do you think someone kidnapped them?" I asked, voicing one of my worst fears.

"With Roscoe in the mix, if someone did, they'll return them shortly. Does 'The Ransom of Red Chief' ring any bells?"

I knew the O. Henry short story well. And Roscoe did perfectly fit the role of Johnny Dorset, the ten-year-old terror. Any abductors would likely pay us to take Roscoe back. But Chablis was cute and so pampered that someone might think she would be easy to steal. They didn't know the little dust mop's heart. She had a fierce underbite, but she was still capable of gnawing—and I did mean gnawing—off a finger or ear if the need arose. Sweetie Pie would find her way back to me, no matter how far anyone took her. And Pluto . . . well, my guess was that Pluto was still somewhere in hiding. He was the most feline of creatures. While he'd once been the pampered pet of a very wealthy woman, he'd adapted to farm life and crime solving with great flair. He could be elusive when he chose.

"Coleman, swing by Dahlia House and let me get my spare car key, then you search for the young woman Tinkie saw. She may still be in those woods behind the Morans' place. I'll find the critters. The best use of our time is to divide up."

"No need. I'll get out here and you can take my truck. I'll get a patrol car."

That was far more expedient. I leaned over and gave Coleman a long kiss before I let him get out of the truck. I slid behind the steering wheel. "I'll call if I see them. You call if you find out who Tinkie was following."

"Deal!" he said, then turned and started to walk across the street to the courthouse.

I was about to pull away from the curb when Coleman's phone rang. He signaled me to wait as he answered. He had a very brief conversation and then came back toward me. His phone pinged and he checked the text messages. "The first call was the Oxford PD. They've picked up Penny Cox for attempting to break into the English department."

"And Alala and Margaret McNeese?"

"No sign of them. They're still looking for them. Penny isn't talking. She won't tell anyone if she was acting alone or had help. They're going to hold her for now, without charging her. The text message is from Harold and it's something you'll want to hear." His grin showed a lot of relief. "He's still with some AVA members. He said he'd call me as soon as he could." Coleman checked his watch. "If he doesn't in the next half hour, I'll send someone to check on him. I don't trust those yahoos, but I don't want to crowd Harold if he's working them."

"That's the right decision. But what about Roscoe?"

"Harold didn't mention the dog." I could tell by his tone of voice that Coleman was finding Harold's behavior a little off.

A stab of anxiety hit me. But surely if Harold had been worried about Roscoe he would have said something. "At least Harold is okay. Thanks for telling me." I blew Coleman a kiss and pulled away from the curb. I had to put my Pluto hat on to think where my animals might have gone. The dogs were smart, loyal, and courageous, but when they were off in a pack like this, I assumed Pluto was in charge. The cat simply had a way of taking the leadership role and then stepping back and letting the dogs do all the dirty work.

I came to an intersection and turned west. Penny Cox was accounted for, but both Alala and Margaret McNeese were still missing. It seemed possible they would go to Alala's house. If that were true, the critters might have gone there as well. There was only one way to find out.

I cruised down the empty streets, aware that my little town was asleep and silent. So many things about Zinnia had changed over the years, but this sense of safety was exactly the same. When I passed Cece's house, it was dark. She was probably still at the hospital with Tinkie. Where I should be. Except I had to find the critters. I pulled down the street from Alala's house, glad that I was in Coleman's nondescript truck. In a farming community, pickups of all years and models were the norm.

Before I got out of the truck, I called the hospital and spoke with Oscar, who had Tinkie's phone. The new mother was resting and Oscar was fielding her calls. "Tinkie and the baby both fell asleep after she fed her. Sarah Booth, I can't believe this wonderful thing has happened to me."

"I'm so happy for you both." I needed some details from Tinkie, but I didn't want to talk to Oscar for long. He'd have a lot of questions I didn't want to answer. Eventually the baby bliss would crack and he would remember to start grilling me. Almost as if thinking it had brought my worry to life, Oscar cleared his throat.

"Tinkie said she followed a woman into the Morans' backyard. What woman? What was she doing?"

"We agreed not to enter Selena's House." I always did my best to stick with the truth. "But I heard something and went inside. Tinkie was to wait in the car. I can't tell you what happened afterward, because Tinkie was gone from the car when I went back outside. The only thing I know is what she said before she left in the ambulance—that she saw someone and was following that person. I don't have any answers beyond that. Let's wait to ask Tinkie for the details so we get the straight facts."

"When she's feeling more like herself, we're going to have a conversation. Me, you, and Tinkie. Once she regains her strength."

"Excellent idea. Now I've got to go," I said. "Give Tinkie my love." I clicked off before I said something Tinkie might contradict. It was dicey talking to a partner's partner.

I'd left my gun in the sheriff's office so I grabbed Coleman's heavy-duty flashlight and eyed Alala's yard, making sure no one would take me by surprise before I got out of the truck. I turned off the interior light, eased out of the seat, and hurried across the street to slip behind a poplar tree. I took a moment to remember what I could about the backyard. The lot was big and the back area dense with foliage that gave the house and property lots of privacy. It was a good place for the critters to hide. And there was no time like the present to check it out.

Moving as stealthily as I could, I circled the house. There wasn't a light to be seen, which indicated Alala wasn't home. I texted her: "Call me now! Urgent." Where in the heck had she gotten off to? To be honest, I wanted to find our client, but even more than that I wanted to be at the hospital with Tinkie and little Maylin. I'd never been a baby person, but that infant, taking her first real breath while I held her in my hands, was umbilically attached to my heart. And a missing client, missing critters, and a missing Harold were all in the way of Coleman and me indulging in our godchild.

I slid the phone into my jeans pocket, because I knew there wouldn't be a response. Wherever Alala was, she wasn't answering texts or calls. I could only pray that was a voluntary decision and not because she was a prisoner . . . or dead.

Creeping around the house, glancing in windows and listening for any sounds, I was keenly aware of the absence of Sweetie Pie and Pluto. Normally they had my back—and I felt exposed and vulnerable without them. I made it all around the house. There was no sign of the critters or anyone else. If the dogs and cat weren't here, I didn't have an alternative place to check.

My cell phone vibrated in my pocket and I pulled it out, hoping Coleman or the deputies had found the errant pups, but to my surprise, it was Tansy who showed up on my caller ID.

"Sarah Booth, you have to come here quick." She was whispering and I could barely make out what she was saying.

"What's wrong?"

"Someone is trying to break into Selena's House."

"Call the sheriff's office."

"I, uh, can't."

"Why not?"

"I have some stuff up here in my room that I shouldn't have."

"Drugs?" I said that too loud.

"Not really drugs. Just some weed. But I can't call the cops. If they find it, I'll get kicked out of here."

Between her boyfriends and her illegal habits, Tansy wasn't exactly the perfect resident for Selena's House. Still, I didn't want to see her put out on the curb.

"Is Penny home?"

"No. Haven't seen hide nor hair of her since she left earlier today."

"Who's at the house with you?"

"No one. Todd didn't come back. He had to get back to the trailer before Moody got there."

"I'll be there as quickly as I can."

34

The street in front of Selena's House was empty of everything—except my car. It would just have to wait there until I had a ride to the hospital or Dahlia House to retrieve my keys. At least the sky was clear and the stars twinkling brightly. No chance of rain. The Roadster would be okay until we had time to get it. I parked Coleman's truck a block away, beneath the gently bobbing limbs of a crepe myrtle. I slipped from the truck and headed to Selena's House. First I intended to explore around the house to see if I could find the intruder that Tansy had called about. If there really was an intruder. There was no reason for Tansy to lie, but I still had difficulty believing her. She'd spent too much of her life twisting facts around to make them tolerable.

Worry about the critters nagged at me. It wasn't like them to disappear. They'd been gone for hours. And how had Roscoe found them? I wanted to text Coleman to see if he'd heard from Harold, but I decided to wait until I'd checked out the alleged intruder.

I made one circuit of the house, and when I got to the front door I stopped short. Pluto was sitting on the doorstep licking a paw. "Where did you come from?" I bent down to stroke the cat. "Where are the dogs?"

Pluto ignored me, as he normally did. I rang the doorbell and waited for Tansy to answer. When there was no response, I rang again. And again. The creepiest feeling washed over me. I'd hung up with Tansy no longer than ten minutes ago. She didn't have a car, as far as I knew. A scratching sound came from the side of the house, and the skin on my arms prickled. I swung the flashlight toward the noise and saw a dead limb from a tall shrub rubbing against the wall. I expelled the breath I'd been holding. I was letting my nerves get away from me.

I rang the bell and used the knocker, but the results remained the same. Nada. I turned the knob and the door opened into a dark house. Pluto scampered inside and I followed, ruing the fact that I didn't have a gun.

"Tansy?" I called out. If she was upstairs, stoned and with earplugs in, I was going to hit her with the flashlight. There was no answer. This was the second time I'd crept around in Selena's House and I didn't like it any better than the first. I went up the stairs to her bedroom, and pushed open the door, half-prepared to discover Tansy's corpse.

The blow came so unexpectedly that I didn't have time

to dodge or call out. There was a sharp pain on the back of my head and then only blackness.

"Hey, hey! Sarah Booth!"

I awoke to Tansy's hand firmly shaking my shoulder. It was hard to force my eyes open, until she slapped me. My eyelids flew up like cartoon window shades. "Do that again and I will hurt you."

"Then sit up. You scared me. I thought you might be dead the way you were lying there. I was about to call the morgue because you looked so dead. Then you did one of those little snort-snore things and I realized you were alive."

I sat up. "Did you hit me?"

"Hell, no. I went to the store to get some cigarettes and came back to find you here, stretched out in the foyer. I'm just glad Penny didn't come back and stumble over you. She'd demand to know . . . Why are you lying on the floor?"

"I came over here because you said someone was trying to break in. And then you were gone and you left the doors unlocked while you go buy cigarettes." I was outdone. "What is wrong with you, Tansy?"

"Not a damn thing." She bristled. "I'm just fine. And yes I went to get some cigarettes at the Sack-N-Tote, because I ran out. I've been smoking like a chimney these past few days, what with people showing up in this house without an invitation. I didn't lock the door because I don't have a key. How hard is that to comprehend?"

She directed that barb at me but I just ignored her. "Who was trying to break in?"

She shook her head. "I don't know if they were breaking in, but someone was outside roaming around. I caught a glimpse of someone in dark clothes, probably a hoodie covering their head and face. But those dogs you ride around with, they were after whoever it was poking around here."

"Sweetie Pie and Chablis were here?"

"Yeah, and that other mangy-looking mutt, too."

That had to be Roscoe. "Where did the dogs go?"

"The intruder *and* the dogs took off that way." She pointed north. "Looked to me like the dogs were chasing whoever was trying to break in. That's why I figured it was okay to go get my cigs."

Tansy's actions defied any reason at all. Pointing the obvious out to her wouldn't change a thing, though.

"Describe the person you saw."

"It was a woman, I think. Smaller and thinner than a guy, but her features were hidden—you know, the hoodie."

A person in a hoodie had struck Alala in the park. Now it sounded like that same person was here, lurking around Selena's House. Tansy might have more valuable information than even she knew.

"And you haven't heard anything from Penny?"

"Not a word. I figured she would have been back long ago." She pursed her lips. "You reckon she's okay? I swear she never goes anywhere, but this place has been like Grand Central Station all day. People coming and going. When Penny gets home you can ask her about all the visitors."

I knew she'd been arrested in Oxford, but that was Penny's story to tell. "Who was here today? No fooling around this time, Tansy. Tell me the truth."

"I don't know any of them, other than Alala. One was the girl who lived here for a while when she was a child. She was going to Ole Miss, and Penny was so proud of her. The other young woman, I think her name was Margaret. Then that beanpole with the lank blond hair showed up and talked to Penny, too."

"What was the name of the other student?"

"I'm not a damn Dictaphone. I don't remember." Tansy didn't like to be pressed.

I quickly used my phone to look up the Ole Miss website and scanned through photos of students in the English department until I located one of Margaret McNeese, sitting near the fountain. The university had a busy public relations staff that kept the website up to date and filled with photos of campus activities. "Was this the student who was with Penny?"

Tansy frowned. "That's her. That's the one who left when Penny did." She pointed to another photo. "And that's the other one."

"You're sure?" I looked more closely at the photo of Poppy Bright, Margaret McNeese's good friend and fellow graduate student.

"I'm sure. She seemed to know Penny pretty well."

"Tansy, think. Did this student say anything about why she was here?"

Tansy lifted one shoulder in a half-shrug. "She talked about her professors and how the dead one had been shagging a bunch of students. That was her word. Shagging. Like she was British or something. She said he'd gotten what he deserved."

Well Tansy was suddenly a fount of information. "Did she say Dr. Loxley?"

"Yeah, the dead one," Tansy said.

Funny, but Poppy had acted as if she wasn't really all that concerned about Loxley's behavior. It also dawned on me that she'd come up to sit by me deliberately—not by some lucky fluke, as I'd interpreted it.

Poppy had even called the other graduate student and gotten her to call me. So why was Poppy suddenly everywhere I looked?

"Did Poppy say anything else?" I asked.

"She said she loved studying literature, but that women had never really been taken seriously as writers. She said she was going to be an agent of change. I remember that because it was such a strange phrase."

The little hairs on my arms stood on end. "Like she was going to do something to change things?"

"That's kind of the impression I got," Tansy said. "Of course, sometimes those college types talk all artsy-fartsy. She was kind of antsy, like she had somewhere to be. Oh, and she said that she'd survived the worst of it and could now live the life she was destined to have."

Chills ran up my back and arms. "Did she say what the worst of it was?"

Tansy was already bored with this conversation since it wasn't about her. "I gotta go. I have some stuff to clean up before Penny gets back. She doesn't like it when I throw my stuff around and don't pick it up."

"Think hard, Tansy. Can you remember anything else about their visit?"

"I told you everything. Now either let me go or come help me pick up my room."

The thought of running across that sequined thong yet again made me hold up one hand to ward off the invitation. "No, thanks."

I started to leave when Sweetie Pie, Roscoe, and

Chablis burst into the front door. They were as wild as hoodlums.

I had plenty to do, too. I walked outside, calling the dogs and cat with me. They seemed eager to load up in Coleman's truck and head back to Dahlia House. On the way, I called Alala. She still didn't answer, and I had a niggle of real worry. If Poppy Bright was involved in the murders, chances were that she hoped to pin it on Alala. And that might be exactly what she was doing right now.

I called Coleman and got his voicemail. "We have to find Alala. I need you to call the Oxford police and ask them to let me speak to Penny on the phone. If I'm right, another student named Poppy Bright is the killer. She has a connection to Selena's House, and I think she's been snooping around here. She may have Alala. And we need to check on Harold. It's been too long. I'm worried about him, too."

I reached across the front seat and gave Roscoe's ears a good rubbing. The little dog whined, as if he were anxious. And that wasn't a Roscoe way to behave. My worry only deepened.

35

Driving through the velvety Delta night, I wanted nothing as much as to go to the hospital and be with my partner. I consoled myself with thoughts of Oscar holding his daughter, cradling his wife . . . and very importantly Oscar no longer being angry with me that Tinkie had delivered the Richmond heir in the dirt and grass because she was detecting with me. One day Oscar would forgive me. He would have to. Right now, I didn't want to get in his face. Besides, Cece and Millie were right there. Likely Madame Tomeeka, too.

But not Harold. Again, because of me.

I called Harold's cell phone and got his voicemail. The same for Alala's. I didn't leave a message. What was the point? If they could call, they would.

I called Coleman next—three for three. I wanted desperately to talk to him. I drove past the Morans' house. Things had settled down and the windows were dark. It appeared no one was up at this ungodly hour in the morning.

The one thing I could do was take the critters back to Dahlia House and lock them in where they'd be safe. I was still a little miffed that they'd taken off like that, only to reappear without explanation. And I still had no explanation as to where Roscoe had come from. The last time I saw him he was at least five miles from town. The little devil burrowed up against me, and Sweetie Pie gave me a plaintive look.

"Running away like you did—that's unacceptable. I was worried sick and so was Coleman. Sweetie Pie, you've already been shot. Do you have some kind of death wish?"

Sweetie Pie gave a low half-moan, half-yodel that was neither agreement nor disagreement. Dogs didn't have to commit to a worldview.

My phone rang and I instantly picked it up without checking the caller ID.

"Sarah Booth," Penny Cox said. "You're my one call, so please listen to me. I'm being held in the Oxford city jail on trespassing and breaking and entering charges. Could you help me out?"

I was a little aggravated with Penny. "I'm sorry to hear that."

There was a pause. "You're angry with me, and I don't blame you, but I swear I didn't know. I thought I was doing a good thing."

She sounded pitiful, and I knew in my heart that Penny only wanted to help people. Whatever had gone wrong, she wasn't part of it. "Okay, I'll find Junior at the bail bond office and he'll provide the money for you. I can get you back to Sunflower County, but you'd better get a lawyer. Tansy told me you were going to break into a professor's office."

"I am going to skin Tansy Miller and nail her hide to the front door of Selena's House."

I deduced from this that perhaps Tansy hadn't been completely accurate about what she heard. "So you weren't going to break in?"

"I was set up. Honestly. I had a visitor, someone I trusted. She said a woman was being savagely beaten but I couldn't call the police. Poppy said the woman knew me and would listen to me if I could get there and take her back to Zinnia. It was either that or she'd end up dead."

"Poppy Bright told you this?"

"She did. I rushed off without checking her story and Margaret planned to come with me for backup. I really was trying to help someone. Now I'm in a jam myself." She sighed. "Poppy had some really bad information."

I had a sneaking suspicion Penny had been sent on a wild-goose chase to get her out of Selena's House and Zinnia. Tansy had said "the beanpole" had showed up at Selena's House and then left. "Where is Dr. Brown?"

"I have no idea. She arrived just as I was leaving, asking about Alala and which women she'd been interviewing. I told her I didn't know. Even if I had known, I wouldn't have given her that information. I did reveal that someone at Ole Miss was in danger and Becky volunteered to meet me back at Oxford because she had a key to the English department. She said I could get inside legally to check for the woman. She wanted to take her own vehicle, which made sense, because she lived there in Oxford. I got there and Becky never showed up. She texted me and said she had a meeting of some sort. I was already on campus, and when I slipped into the building, the cops were waiting for me. I think she ratted me out."

Penny had hit the nail on the head, and I knew exactly what kind of meeting Becky Brown had gone to. AVA. "Dr. Brown is part of a group of men who're working to keep women in low-paying jobs and under their thumb. She's a traitor to her gender."

There was a long silence on the other end. "I don't want to believe this, but I'm afraid it's true. I fell for her pack of lies, because while I never trust a thing a man says, I'm too trusting of some women. I knew something was off with Becky. I just so wanted her to be . . . who she said she was. We need educated, articulate fighters for equality, and especially ones with family backgrounds that mean something."

"You're friends with Dr. Brown?"

"I am. It's a long story, but she's a Binkerman. I only know about it because I ended up involved in the whole sordid mess."

"The family that originally owned a lodge off Wrap-around Road?"

"Yes, a troubled family. I'd so hoped that things had turned around for them after the tragic death of that young man. Do you recall Gavin Wright?"

"Yes." Coleman had only recently refreshed my memory. "He died in a car wreck his senior year."

"What?" Penny asked. "Car wreck?"

"That's what I was told."

"Oh, yes, that was the story the family put out, but it wasn't true. Gavin got in some trouble in Memphis."

"What kind of trouble?"

"The family covered it up, but he got a young girl pregnant. I think Gavin wanted to marry her, but his family wouldn't allow it. The girl's family didn't measure up to the Binkerman standards or some such bull. I heard the Binkermans gave the girl's family a lot of money to move her somewhere Gavin couldn't find her. And Gavin was sent here, to relatives in Zinnia, but he kept going back to Memphis, looking for that girl. It was like he was obsessed with her."

"I wish I had known this." I didn't see how it fit together, but I knew this was important information.

"The family had been through so much, and I hoped that Becky could find peace."

"What does she have to do with this?" I was really lost.

"She's Gavin's sister."

Now it was my turn to be at a loss for words. "Gavin had a sister?"

"Yes, Becky Wright. She married a Brown and then divorced a few months later, but she kept his name. She's done all right for herself, coming from such a dysfunctional family."

I blew out a breath. "What really happened to Gavin?"

"The cop is giving me a dirty look, Sarah Booth. I think I've been on the phone too long."

"Just tell me about Gavin, and I need to hear it now. I'll get you bailed out."

"Okay, but I don't know how much longer they'll let me talk. Anyway, Gavin was murdered by his pregnant girlfriend's mother. Amanda Crowley was the girlfriend. Her mother was Cordelia."

"That murder didn't happen here in Sunflower County?"

"No, in Memphis." Penny sighed. "It was such a tragedy. Few people know, and those of us who heard the truth realized how damaging it would be to spread the story. Especially damaging to Becky, the only surviving sibling. I never really knew the child, but I've spoken with Becky a few times in recent years. She took an interest in abused women. She's a little twisted, I'm sorry to say."

"How did you find out what really happened?" I asked Penny.

"The Binkerman family has supported Selena's House. In fact, they sent a young woman and her child here several years after Gavin's murder. Poor woman was in a bad marriage to a husband who beat her and her little girl. It was a terrible situation."

The Binkerman family had swung a lot of weight to so successfully change the reality of what had occurred and plant a completely false story. One that even Coleman believed.

"What happened to Amanda, the pregnant girl, and her baby?"

"Amanda was implicated in the murder. She lured Gavin to the place where he was killed. The Binkermans and the Wrights didn't want Amanda to give birth to their grandchild in prison and it turned out Amanda was actually a minor, which opened another whole can of worms. What I heard through the grapevine was that part of the deal was that Amanda wouldn't be prosecuted, but Amanda and Gavin's child would be raised by guardians assigned by the Binkerman family. She wouldn't be a Binkerman or even know about them, and they would essentially control the child's upbringing behind the scenes."

"The Binkerman family let a woman get away with the murder of their son . . ." I couldn't fathom such a thing.

"They manipulated the justice system with their money. Anyway, Becky was just a small child then but she absorbed all of it. The craziness, the screaming fights with Gavin and his parents, his insistence that he would marry Amanda. He was determined that once he graduated from high school and turned eighteen, they would marry and provide for the baby. But Amanda didn't want to marry Gavin or have anything to do with the Binkerman family. She kept trying to run away. The whole thing was a mess."

"What happened to the baby?"

"That, I don't know. I assume that when Amanda gave birth, the child was taken and placed with adoptive parents, per the agreement. I only know that the whole series of events left a mark on Becky. She was never the same. Brilliant at her schoolwork. Driven, even. But her personal life was a train wreck. She was drawn to the wrong type of man."

Men like Alex Loxley or Kevin Wilson. Now I better understood her affiliation with AVA. If Amanda had been more pliant, Becky believed, more willing to follow Gavin's lead, things might have come out differently. Her brother might have prevailed—and lived. Independent women were dangerous.

"Penny, if you knew Becky was capable of killing those men, you should have told someone."

"What are you talking about?"

"You're implying that Becky killed those two professors and Curtis Miller, aren't you?"

"Why ever would she do that? The sick thing about Becky was that she was drawn to men who abused women. It's one of the things I could never fathom or change. She didn't kill those men. She supported them."

"Then who did kill them?"

"I don't know. Now come and get me out of jail. I'm not saying another word until someone pays my bond or talks to the law over here and gets me released."

"I'm on it," I said. It would be a lot quicker to get Coleman to call over to Oxford and ask them to release Penny than it would be for me to drive or even ask Junior if he'd go. I called Coleman again.

His voice crackled over a bad connection.

"Where are you?" I asked.

"The hunting lodge. Harold is gone, Sarah Booth. Completely gone."

36

On the drive back to town, Coleman made the call to Oxford and convinced the local police to release Penny so she could return home. He was concluding the call when he met me, DeWayne, Budgie, and the animals at the courthouse. I'd never seen Coleman so obviously worried. Harold's disappearance weighed on him—which made my heart skip a beat. I was more responsible than Coleman for putting our friend at such risk.

"You found the critters!" Coleman was quick to give Sweetie Pie, Chablis, Pluto, and even Roscoe affection, but his eyes were bleak when he turned to me. "I searched that lodge and there's no indication of where Harold might be. His truck is in the parking lot, the only vehicle there. I checked and the key was under the floor mat. It's clear whoever took him deliberately left the vehicle."

"I've learned a lot of things. Maybe you can see how some of what I found will help us find Harold."

"Let's go inside and put on some coffee," Coleman said. "I'm cold and tired."

It was a terrific idea. We were all silent as we listened to the coffeepot hiss and sputter. When the brew was ready, I served all four of us. I'd done it enough to know how everyone took their coffee without asking. Coleman filled the deputies in on what had occurred at the lodge and since. I told them what I'd learned from Penny. As I predicted, Coleman was stunned.

"Everyone thought Gavin died in a car accident. How the hell did the Binkermans pull this off? They were wealthy, but this would have taken considerable money."

"What are we going to do now?" I finally asked.

"Find Harold. That's the first priority. Solving Curtis Miller's murder has just taken a backseat."

We all nodded in agreement. Curtis was dead. Justice would be served, but a day later wouldn't matter to him. Harold was alive—we had to cling to that belief.

"Alala is missing, too," I reminded everyone as the deputies shifted, ready for action.

"We'll search for her," Coleman said. "I have a feeling if we find Harold, we might find her."

I had a feeling he could be right. "I should call Tinkie."

Coleman put a hand on my shoulder. "No. Don't do that. This is one of the happiest moments of her entire life. Don't spoil it with bad news about Harold." The ghost of a grin lightened his features. "Besides, if you upset her, Oscar will kill you."

He wasn't wrong about that. I nodded. "What are we going to do?"

"If we haven't found him by daylight, we'll take the dogs to the lodge and see if they can pick up a scent. How did Roscoe get back to town? He was with Harold the last time we saw him, which leads me to believe Harold is in town somewhere."

I didn't have an answer, but I realized that could be a vital piece of information. Too bad Roscoe couldn't tell us. I looked over to find all of the dogs sleeping beside the counter. Only Pluto, wise as a sphinx, watched us with unblinking eyes.

"DeWayne, Budgie, split up and take half this list." Coleman had written down the names of all the men he recognized at the lodge meeting and tore the list in half, handing part to each deputy. "Check in with these men. Get inside their homes if you can so you can check out the premises. Make it clear kidnapping and or aiding and abetting a kidnapper are federal offenses and I have no problem with the feds prosecuting them. We want Harold returned safely. That's the primary objective."

He turned to me. "You take the dogs and go back to the Morans' yard and start from there. That's where Roscoe first reappeared so it would make sense that Harold had been nearby. See if Sweetie Pie can pick up a scent or maybe Roscoe will take you to wherever he came from. Someone had to let him out, but why there? I'll go door-to-door, asking if anyone saw anything. We might get lucky." He inhaled slowly, and then released it. He retrieved a department gun and flashlight and handed them to me. "Be careful. And I'm calling in the Mississippi Bureau of Investigation, the state troopers, and the FBI. If Budgie and DeWayne don't get any cooperation, we'll start bringing those guys in on weapons charges. Some of the things I saw in that lodge violate plenty of laws. It's a place to start."

For Coleman to involve the feds, he was really worried. I put a hand on his arm. "We're going to find Harold. And Alala."

He nodded, but wouldn't look at me. He stood. "Let's get to work. I'm going to make those phone calls to the other agencies. Y'all go on and get started. Take no risks! You understand?" He eyed each of us in turn.

We all nodded, and then the deputies left. I put my arms around his waist and held him a moment. "I'll meet you on the street near Selena's House. If Penny is home, do you want me to question her about Poppy Bright?"

"Save her until tomorrow. I think you already got most of what she had to tell. She's been gone all evening, so she won't have any pertinent information about Harold."

Again, he was right. "See you there." I whistled up the dogs and we took off.

The night was overcast and cold, and I longed for daylight. And some leashes. "If you dogs run off again, I am going to cut off one leg on each of you."

The threat sounded dire, but they never paid attention to any of my menacing words. Ever.

As I cruised by, Selena's House was still dark, and I assumed Penny hadn't made it home yet. Getting released by the police was seldom a speedy affair. I parked down the street close to the Morans' house and let the dogs out. "Stay with me."

I dreaded waking the Morans again, but it was all about finding Harold. I started toward their backyard when Sweetie Pie gave a little yodel. I turned and she was waiting on the sidewalk, her tail wagging. She started

toward Selena's House, looked back at me, and stopped.
The little yodel came again. She was wheedling me to go
with her.

"What is it, girl?"

She barked, starting back to Selena's House. Roscoe
sprinted by her and down the sidewalk. Even little Chablis was in a hurry to go in that direction. Only Pluto remained beside me. It wasn't exactly the hottest lead, but
it was better than anything else I had to go on. "Come
on, Pluto." We started walking.

Selena's House seemed to lumber out of the gloom.
Every time I saw the place, I was struck anew by the size
of it. The neighborhood was upper middle class, made up
of houses of substance, but most of them had been built
during a different time. Selena's House was of newer con-
struction and accommodated the need for more bath-
rooms and other niceties that made it perfect for housing
several women and Penny.

The lot was also exceptionally big, and I already knew
that the backyard ran down a declivity to a tangle of
woods and a creek, the same one that bordered the Moran property. As the dogs cut across the yard and headed
into the back, I wasn't prepared for the dense growth. I
would have thought that Penny would have preferred a
much more wide-open backyard because of the potential
for angry men hanging around. My fingers clenched the
gun in my left hand. I didn't want to use the flashlight
unless I had to. If someone nefarious was hanging out in
the bushes, I would be a target with the light on.

Sweetie Pie came out of the brush and nudged my leg,
grabbing my jeans gently in her teeth. "Okay, lead on."

The other dogs and cat had disappeared, but I felt they
were close. Sweetie Pie was definitely on to something,

and I put my trust in her and followed. When the vegetation got so dense that I had to walk with a hand out in front of me to ward off limbs, I clicked on the flashlight. To my surprise, another building was outlined in the flashlight beam. It had been an old garage or possibly a stable for a horse—the grounds were certainly big enough for pasture if the acreage was cleared.

I tried to remember if I'd ever seen fences and a horse or pony here in my youth. I'd ridden my bicycle all over Sunflower County and as a horse-crazy kid, I would have been all over a "town" horse if I'd found one. I didn't remember a horse, but the slope of the property was steep enough that the stables and pasture could easily have been hidden from the sidewalk. Now they were covered by a forest of scrub growth and underbrush.

I moved closer to the building, and suddenly Pluto appeared, blocking my path. He didn't communicate with me telepathically, but he did remind me of my promise to Coleman. I was hardheaded, but I wasn't dense. I pulled out the phone and texted Coleman.

"I'm at the back of Selena's House. There's a building here. Come ASAP."

I was debating whether to push on the old green door that I'd discovered beneath some vines, or wait for Coleman. There didn't seem to be a big rush to walk inside. While I didn't mind confronting bad guys, rats, spiders, roaches, and snakes were another matter. Especially in the dark.

Roscoe took matters into his own hands and rushed past me before I could stop him. I hadn't noticed an open window beside the door, but he sailed through it. Inside the structure was the sound of shuffling.

"Roscoe!"

It was Harold's voice! I almost let out a squeal of delight, but remembered where I was and contained myself. If Harold was here, then it wasn't by choice. But he was alive. My heart did a little trill of triple beats and my thumb responded with a pulse of relief. The burden of guilt I'd carried slipped from my shoulders. My fervent hope was that Harold was alone, and I could get to him and effect an escape.

I crept closer to the building, going to the window beneath the Virginia creeper that clung to the structure. Pulling the vines aside, I peeped in. The enclosure was pitch-black. I couldn't see anything, and Harold was no longer making any noise.

Pluto jumped up to the window beside me, clinging to the woody vines. In a minute he hopped inside and cried softly.

There was no response from anyone inside the building.

I reluctantly turned on the light and swept the beam over what had once been an office. A desk, a chair, and bookcases were covered in dust and cobwebs. This hadn't been a stable, as I'd projected, but some kind of office building. Wherever Harold was, he wasn't in that room. I moved to the door and forced it open with the weight of my body. The vines were aggravating, but I eventually managed to climb through them. Sweetie Pie and Chablis followed.

The dogs were very quiet as I moved through the room to a door. When I turned the knob, I expected it to be locked, but it wasn't. I cracked it open but had to use the flashlight to determine that I was in a narrow hallway. At the far end of the hall, I heard what sounded like shuffling.

Then Roscoe yelped. That was all it took for Sweetie

Pie and Chablis to rush the door at the end of the hall with all they had. Sweetie Pie hit it with her full weight, and there was the sound of a commotion on the other side of the door.

I ran full speed toward the door and turned the knob as I hit it hard. The door opened and I hurtled into a dark room where I heard Harold say, "Oh, no, Sarah Booth!"

Then I heard the click of a gun as it was cocked. The cold barrel pressed into my temple.

37

"Don't move, Ms. Delaney."

I recognized the voice, because I'd heard it before. This was the young woman I'd met at Ole Miss at the fountain—the English major who'd so helpfully made arrangements for Margaret McNeese to call me. "Hello, Poppy." I tried to sound calm.

"Move over against the wall."

I shifted slightly, because the room was dark. That could work in my favor. I was still holding my gun at my side.

"Put the gun on the ground." She was almost laughing at me.

I had no choice but to do what she said. "Where's Alala Diakos?" I asked.

"Exactly where she needs to be," Poppy said. "Right where she needs to be to make my plans work out." She turned on a battery-operated lantern and I was able to see the room was empty, but there was a small door on the right.

"Where's Harold?" I asked.

She motioned toward the door with a gun. "In there. Move."

Roscoe was circling the narrow hallway, sniffing and barking. He went to the door and scratched. I opened the door. When the light spilled inside, I could see Harold sitting on the floor, his hands and feet tied up. Beside him was Becky Brown. She looked a little woozy, but unharmed.

"Sit down." Poppy motioned me toward Harold. I did as she ordered. "Tie up your feet." She kicked a length of nylon cord toward me.

"What are you going to do with us?" I asked.

"Whatever is necessary. You've been an annoyance since Alala hired you. That's why I had to slow you down earlier when I hit you in Selena's House. You should have taken the hint. You shouldn't have meddled."

"Why are you doing this?"

"Shut up."

Roscoe had settled into a corner of the room and appeared to have fallen asleep. Sweetie Pie, Chablis, and Pluto had disappeared before I was captured. I was desperate to warn Coleman about Poppy and her gun before he came charging in here, but as soon as I finished tying up my feet, Poppy told me to toss my phone to her. If I couldn't get to Coleman, he was walking straight into a trap. I thanked my higher powers that Tinkie was safely in the hospital with her daughter and Oscar.

Poppy took more cord and tied my hands tightly behind my back.

"Just let us go," I said to her. "By the time someone finds us, you can be long gone."

"I've killed three people. Scumbags who needed to die, but the law doesn't always land on the side of justice."

If I could keep her talking, maybe Coleman could sneak up on her. "I understand killing Loxley, Wilson, and Curtis Miller. But this has gone far enough. Harold and I haven't done anything to you."

"She has!" She pointed the gun at Becky. "She supports those evil men. She's as much a part of this as they were. She's given them a place to gather and plan. She has to pay."

Becky was coming to her senses and her eyes were wide with fear. Wisely, she didn't say anything.

"Why are you doing this?" I asked Poppy in a calm voice.

"Those men won't stop until they're exterminated."

That statement chilled me. "And where is Alala? You may have had a beef with those men, but what about her? She's been set up to take the fall for those murders, and she's been fighting on your side. She was exposing those men and what they stand for."

"It was never supposed to be Alala." She pointed the gun at Becky again. "It was always her. Always. She was at the scene of every murder. She knew those men and worked with them. She had a thing for Curtis Miller, which is why he's dead now. I planned it so carefully, but that sheriff and everyone else jumped to point the finger at Dr. Diakos. So, I had to step in."

"You were at Erkwell Park the day Curtis and Alala got into it?" I asked Becky.

She stubbornly refused to speak.

"And you shot at me and hit my dog."

Becky turned away and said nothing.

"Tell her the truth or I'll shoot you," Poppy said matter-of-factly.

"You'd better talk," Harold urged her.

"I was there at the park and yes I shot at you. I didn't mean to hit the dog and I wasn't going to kill you. Just scare you." Becky spoke with anger.

"Why were you at the park that day?" I asked.

"Watching. Curtis met me later at the hunting lodge but he wouldn't stay. He was determined to get to Tansy after she was released from the hospital. When he found out where she was, he texted me from Selena's House, saying he was going to break in and drag her out. By the time I got there, he was dead in the backyard. Shot through the heart, just like the others."

"How did you move him?"

"I didn't."

"Who did?"

"Clifford and some of the men loaded him up and we took him to the field behind Playin' the Bones and put him out." Becky spoke quietly. "They figured Dr. Diakos would be blamed and they were right."

"How did they find out about Curtis's body?"

"I told them," Becky said. "Curtis was supposed to come back to the lodge, and when he didn't, I went to Selena's House thinking maybe he'd been there and gotten arrested. Instead, I found him shot in the heart. I figured Alala would be blamed if the body was discovered somewhere else. Her interference was creating headaches for everyone."

Becky had filled in an important fact, but I was far

more interested in Poppy's role. "You spent some time at Selena's House, didn't you?"

"You're a little late with this revelation," Poppy said. "I was here with my mother, back fifteen years ago. I was just a kid. My adopted mother. After my adopted father beat her half to death and me, too. She came to Selena's House to hide from him and his brutality."

A lot of things clicked into place. The location, the house, Poppy's early experiences with violence. This was the foundation for her desire to kill these men. I looked at her more closely in the dim lamplight. She'd seemed like such a sweet, almost timid young woman when I'd met her at Ole Miss.

"Do you see it?" she asked, almost as if she were waiting for me to make the connection. She lifted the lantern closer to her face. I saw it then, the resemblance between her and Becky Brown. It was like a veil had been lifted. "You're Gavin Wright's daughter, aren't you? The daughter he fathered when he was in high school."

"You win the blue ribbon," she said. "Too bad you weren't smarter sooner." She turned to Becky Brown. "Hello, Aunt Becky. You might have been a little nicer to me at the college, you know, but I suppose you never expected to see me, your niece. Nope. My birth family was only too happy to forget I ever existed. But I didn't forget. I never forgot or forgave. That's why I'm going to kill all of you and arrange it so that my wonderful aunt gets the blame for all of it." She stepped closer to Becky and spoke only to her. "I'd hoped to see you prosecuted and put in prison, but it's okay if you're dead. That works, too."

A loud scratching sound came from the door, and I realized Sweetie Pie and likely Chablis and Pluto were desperate to get inside with me. Roscoe had fallen utterly into a coma. I couldn't believe it. When we really needed a hero, Roscoe was a slug. He didn't even acknowledge Harold or the serious trouble we were in.

"Those damn dogs! They've aggravated me all evening." She grasped the doorknob. "I'll be back to take care of you, but first I'm going to shoot those dogs." She went to pull the door open, but there was nothing there. No dog, no cat. "What the hell?"

"Leave them alone," I said. "They can't hurt you. Just leave them alone."

"They'll bring someone here, and I can't have that. I so much prefer that they find you several days from now, when you're starting to rot."

She had gone way, way off the deep end of the pier. "I—"

"Shut up." She retrained the gun on me.

"Poppy, let me call the dogs. You can lock them in here with us. If Sweetie Pie gets to the road, one of the deputies or Coleman will see her. They're going to be looking for me. They're already searching for Harold."

"What are you doing?" Harold asked me. "Don't tell her anything else."

"Look, just let me call them. Penny isn't home yet. She's coming back from Ole Miss."

"Shut up or I'll shut you up." This time it was Becky who objected to my talking.

I ignored her. "Poppy, listen. You can let me go. I won't tell anyone." If I could just keep her busy for another minute or two, but a noise outside the door was the final straw.

"I'll be right back." Poppy strode from the room and closed the door behind her.

Before I could say anything, Roscoe was up and beside Harold, viciously tearing at the ropes that bound his hands. Roscoe was a machine of destruction on his best days. This was a job designed for his personality and talent.

"That's it, buddy," Harold said. "Hurry."

I held my breath as Roscoe freed Harold, and then Harold freed me. I'd just turned my attention to Becky when I heard footsteps approaching. Harold jumped up and hid behind the door. I resumed my position on the floor, pretending my hands were tied behind my back. Roscoe took a position on the other side of the door.

"Poppy, you'd better get in here. Becky is getting loose." I wanted her to burst through the door. That would be our best chance.

The door flew open and Poppy stepped inside, the gun pointing where Becky sat frozen. In that split second, Roscoe was airborne. He leaped up and caught the wrist that held the gun in his strong jaws. Poppy gave a satisfying cry of pain. Harold stepped out from behind the door and let Poppy have it with a sharp right hook. The gun flew across the room to me and I picked it up as Poppy dropped like a sack of rocks.

In the distance I could hear Coleman. "Find her, Sweetie Pie. Find Sarah Booth." A few minutes later Coleman came into the room and I was in his arms.

Coleman asked me to untie Becky while he and Harold handcuffed Poppy. Before they finished, I heard the sirens. DeWayne and Budgie were on the way.

"Any idea where Alala might be?" I asked Coleman.

My client was still missing, and the near violence of the night didn't bode well for her.

"If she and that Nosey Nellie graduate assistant had gone to Ole Miss with Penny Cox, she'd be just fine. I set it up to get rid of all of them, but Alala said she had something to do and Margaret managed to put herself right in the middle of things. She went back to Alala's house to search for those stupid photos again," Becky said. "I could have saved her the trouble since I took them earlier. If that blackmail scheme got out, it would have ruined AVA. Anyway, Alala is tied up in the woods behind the lodge. With that do-nothing GA, Margaret."

"Did you hurt them?" I asked Becky.

"I detained them. Nothing more."

"Because you needed Alala alive to blame for the murders." This was a complicated mess. "Poppy was killing people to frame Dr. Brown, and Becky was manipulating evidence to frame Alala for murder. Margaret was, I suppose, collateral damage, used by all of you." I was too tired to even work up righteous anger.

"That Margaret. Loxley made a fool of her and even when Alala tried to use her for her crusade against abusers, Margaret still liked her better than me. I had no use for her."

"Where in the woods are Margaret and Alala?" Coleman asked Becky. "Be specific and be clear, because you're headed straight to a jail cell and your immediate future depends a lot on how helpful you've been."

When Becky finished talking, DeWayne and Budgie left to go find the two women. I was exhausted, but I had a couple of things I had to do. I went to Harold and hugged him, kissing his cheek. "I gather Becky abducted you?"

"My vehicle wouldn't start. Someone, I assume, messed with it. But Becky said she'd give me and Roscoe a ride back to town. I thought maybe I could pump her for more information."

"That was your first mistake." I was gently teasing him.

"And the second mistake was not checking the backseat. Poppy was there. She used something to knock Becky out and made me drive. Luckily, Roscoe was with me." He glared over at the dog. "Though he took his sweet time bringing someone to rescue me." Harold looked past me and Coleman. "Where's Tinkie? Is she okay?"

"Tinkie had her baby!" I blurted the good news. "A little girl."

"The baby is here?" Harold looked appropriately gobsmacked. "While I was tied up in a shed, Tinkie had her baby! What are we waiting for? Let's go to the hospital!" Harold put a hand on Coleman's shoulder. "Good job, Coleman."

Coleman grabbed him in a half hug. "I've been carrying a lot of guilt. I thought the AVA men had figured out you were a plant."

"No, I was fine with them. It's these women who almost killed me." He rumpled my hair. "Now we have a birth to celebrate. I need a ride to my house to pick up several bottles of chilled champagne. Tinkie has been waiting for this day for a long time. A little glass will boost her spirits."

I couldn't argue with that.

Coleman put Poppy and Becky in front of him as he ushered them out the door, through the building, and toward their waiting jail cells.

38

Dawn would be breaking before long, but I didn't care as Coleman, Harold, and I hurried through the empty corridors of the hospital. We'd left Poppy and Becky in lockup at the county jail. A quick phone call had ascertained that Penny was home safely, and Coleman promised he'd intervene on her behalf. I called ahead to the hospital to be sure it was okay to crash Tinkie's room and Cece gave us the room number.

At the door, I stopped everyone. "Let's not wake her if she's asleep."

From inside the room, Tinkie called out, "Sarah Booth, you'd better get in here and you'd better have Harold with you."

I pushed through the door and hurried to my partner

and best friend. She held the sleeping baby snuggled to her chest. Cece stood by the bed, and Oscar was sound asleep in a chair on the other side of the room.

"Madame Tomeeka and Millie just left," Cece said. "We were about to call the National Guard to search for the three of you."

"It's been a crazy night." I sank onto the bed beside her. "Really crazy."

"Doc said you did a terrific job delivering the baby. Mother and child are in excellent shape." Tinkie's eyes were bright with happiness.

I eyed the sleeping Oscar. "How mad is he?"

Tinkie laughed. "Not at all. He's relieved."

"I'm so sorry, Tinkie. You would have been at the hospital to have the baby if you hadn't gone on surveillance with me."

"And the outcome would have been the same," Tinkie said, motioning Coleman over to take the baby. "Want to hold your goddaughter?"

Coleman's grin took me back twenty years to the high school boy who could turn on the sun with a smile. "You bet I do." He took the baby with more expertise than I imagined.

"She's a beauty," he said. "Dark-haired, like Sarah Booth."

I felt a lump rise in my throat, and though I tried to swallow it back, I wasn't completely successful. "Thank goodness you're okay, Tinkie. And the baby."

"I'm fine. Just knocked out of action for a day or two." She patted my hand. "And from what I've been able to glean, the murderer of those three men is behind bars."

"She is. I have a lot to tell you about what's been happening. And I'm still waiting on Alala and Margaret to be found. The deputies are on the case."

The baby started to cry and Coleman handed her back just as Oscar woke up.

"Isn't she the most beautiful baby you've ever seen?" Oscar asked. There was no doubt he was the doting father type. That little girl was going to be spoiled rotten.

"She's magnificent," Harold said, giving Oscar a big hug.

"She's incredible," Coleman told Oscar, shaking his hand. "Let's clear out and give Tinkie a chance to feed her daughter," he said, herding us out like we were cattle. When we were all outside the door, his phone buzzed. He answered and said, "Excellent work, Budgie. Okay, put her on." He handed the phone to me.

"Sarah Booth," Alala said, "Thank you. The deputies told me you found the murderer. Good work. Can we talk tomorrow?"

"Sure thing, Alala." I was relieved she was okay.

"Tell Tinkie congratulations on the baby."

It would seem Alala was up to speed on all the news. "I sure will."

"I'm sorry I lied to you about the thumb drive. I'm sure you know by now it didn't contain photos or blackmail material. It was a list of top-dollar donors to AVA. Deputy Dattilo said it will be helpful in tracking down political contributions to the hate group."

I had a sudden stab of fear. I'd destroyed the thumb drive when I'd fallen on it. Not even Budgie could recover the information. "Alala, I—"

"I know. I had the information backed up on my computer, which was hidden in a place where no one could find it. I'll turn the list over to Sheriff Peters in the morning. I was always going to give up the list, I promise. I just needed a little more time to interview some of the men for my book."

I heaved a big sigh. "You could have told me and Tinkie about this."

"I know now I could have, but I wasn't certain I could trust you. We can talk about all of this tomorrow," Alala said before she hung up.

I returned Coleman's phone. "You aren't going to charge Alala, are you?" I asked.

"Not planning on it." He put his arm around me. "Why don't you take the critters home? They're all in my truck. I can get Budgie to meet me here and drive me out to Dahlia House later. Tomorrow, we'll sort all the different cars and who needs what."

Dahlia House sounded like the absolutely perfect conclusion to a helluva day.

I pulled up in front of the house and got out with Sweetie Pie, Chablis, and Pluto. Harold had taken Roscoe home, promising outrageous rewards for the canine rescue he'd performed. In a day or two, I'd remind Harold that Roscoe had terrorized a playground full of children at the city park. But that could wait.

I got out of the car and inhaled the sharp, clean air. The horses were peacefully grazing in the front pasture. On the way to rescue Alala, DeWayne had kindly stopped by and fed them for me. Now it was time to find a bed and collapse.

When I was finally inside Dahlia House, I debated whether I should start a fire to welcome Coleman or

merely warm the bed. The bed option won out. I didn't
have the energy to build a fire. And I had Sweetie Pie,
Chablis, and Pluto to keep me warm until he arrived.

As I turned to the stairs, I saw a woman sitting there.
She wore a long dark skirt and a white lawn blouse.
Her reddish brown hair was piled up on her head in a
style resembling a Gibson girl. It was Jitty, but in what
guise?

"I'm too tired for your shenanigans," I said, hoping to
pass by her without a long conversation.

"You delivered Tinkie's baby. You've impressed even
me."

I smiled at the memory. "I did. But Doc was right there.
It wasn't like I was alone."

"Still, that's something special. You and that little girl
will be bonded for life."

I liked the sound of that. "Who are you tonight?" I
asked. She was pretty, and sad.

"Most folks call me Etta."

I knew her then. Ethel "Etta" Place, the lover of Butch
Cassidy and the wife of the Sundance Kid. She'd been a
member of the Wild Bunch. Instead of going past her, I
sat down on the steps beside her. According to legend,
Etta was with Butch and Sundance in Bolivia when they
were killed. Then again, there were rumors that she'd survived and so had Sundance. In one story Sundance and
Etta returned to the states and he abandoned her at a hospital, escaping yet again to avoid capture. No one could
say for certain. "Did you die in Bolivia?"

"Does it matter?" she asked.

"It does to me." I'd been greatly caught up in the legend of this woman and her romance with outlaws and
danger. The movie from the 1970s had been a personal

favorite, a romanticized version of the outlaw gang famous for robbing trains, banks, and miners.

"You're drawn to the outlaw life, are you? Well, the reality was never as good as the legend. The thing is, everyone I loved died by violence. It makes for a good story, but a very hard life."

I glanced over at her, the gray eyes and pretty hair that framed her pale face. She was a looker. And she spoke more properly than I might have expected. "Why did you choose life as an outlaw?"

"I don't have an answer for that question. After Butch was killed by the Bolivian army, I gave up the outlaw life."

"So you did live! And Sundance? What happened to him?"

She shrugged. "Facts don't mean everything, Sarah Booth. Facts don't soothe the pain or change who you are."

There was a great sadness about her. "The other outlaw women, they were better known. By that, I mean their biographies were more fully fleshed out. You, you've always been a mystery. No one knew where you came from or if you died in South America. Some say you went on to live in Colorado and teach. That you even remarried. Don't you want to set the record straight?"

"No. To hell with the record. Fame only ever got us in trouble," she said. "We could have lived peacefully, but there was no getting away from the past."

"You stole a lot of money."

She smiled, and the sadness lifted. "We did. And there were times we enjoyed it."

"Stories say you truly loved Sundance, not just the life of adventure."

"I loved them both. When Butch was killed, a part of me died, too. Things were never the same." She stood up. "I have lessons to prepare."

"So you did become a schoolteacher?"

"If it pleases you to think that, be my guest."

It was clear I'd never get the truth from her, and I heard the sound of footsteps on the front porch. Coleman was home.

"Goodbye, Etta," I said, watching as she slowly faded into nothing. Like the past, Etta was gone, but she'd left me with perhaps the lesson Jitty had intended all along. We love, we lose, we continue to fight. Women could bend the future toward equality, but these battles would be hard-fought and at cost. Justice never came without blood.

The front door opened, and Coleman walked in. He was a man who believed in justice as hard as I did. And he fought for it every day, just like I did. Jitty had many lessons to teach me, but I knew one thing for certain— loving Coleman was the smartest thing I'd done in a long time.

Acknowledgments

Many thanks to the readers and supporters of Sarah Booth and the Zinnia gang. A special thanks to Hannah O'Grady and the entire team at St. Martin's who make these books so much better with their expert editing, art, and promotion. As always, thanks to my agent, Marian Young.